A Decline
in Prophets

Books by Sulari Gentill

The Rowland Sinclair Series
A Few Right Thinking Men
A Decline in Prophets
Miles off Course
Paving the New Road
Gentlemen Formerly Dressed
A Murder Unmentioned
Give the Devil His Due

The Hero Trilogy
Chasing Odysseus
Trying War
The Blood of Wolves

A Decline in Prophets

A Rowland Sinclair Mystery

Sulari Gentill

Poisoned Pen Press

Copyright © 2011, 2016 by Sulari Gentill

First North American Edition 2016

10 9 8 7 6 5 4 3 2 1

Library of Congress Catalog Card Number: 2016937068

ISBN: 9781464206818   Hardcover
      9781464206832   Trade Paperback

Poisoned Pen Press
6962 E. First Ave., Ste. 103
Scottsdale, AZ 85251
www.poisonedpenpress.com
info@poisonedpenpress.com

Printed in the United States of America

Prologue

Death wore a dinner suit.

His manners were perfect. Murder made sophisticated conversation while dancing the quickstep. He was light on his feet.

Annie Besant shuddered and closed her eyes. How clearly she saw the spreading crimson stain on the starched white dress shirt. That much was revealed…but no more. She surveyed the room. So many immaculately tailored men—all dashing, some charming. At least one was dangerous.

An old woman now, her celebrated clairvoyance was not what it once had been. The foresight was vague, useless for anything but tormenting her with a premonition of violence. The feeling was furtive, an occasional glimpse of a predatory darkness that lurked amongst the gaiety and cultured frivolity of the floating palace. A cold creeping certainty that one of the elegant gentlemen who gathered to dine, intended to kill.

Chapter One

RMS *AQUITANIA*

The RMS *Aquitania* is like an English country house. Its great rooms are perfect replicas of the fine salons and handsome apartments that one finds in the best of old English manor halls. The decorations are too restrained ever to be oppressive in their magnificence. There is no effort to create an atmosphere of feverish gaiety by means of ornate and colourful furnishings. The ship breathes an air of elegance that is very gratifying to the type of people that are her passengers.

—*The Cunard Steam Ship Company Ltd*

It was undeniably a civilised way to travel…particularly for fugitives.

Overhead, crystal chandeliers moved almost imperceptibly with the gentle sway of the ship. If the scene over which they hung had been silent, one may have noticed the faint tinkle of the hand-cut prisms as they made contact. As it was, however, the Louis XVI Restaurant was busy, ringing with polite repartee and refined laughter as the orchestra played an unobtrusive score from the upper balcony.

The tables in the dining room were round, laid with crisp white linen and a full complement of polished silverware. Each sat twelve, the parties carefully chosen from amongst the first-class passengers of the transatlantic liner. Waiters wove efficiently and subtly through the hall. Though neither as large nor as fast as the newer ships in the Cunard Line, the RMS *Aquitania* boasted a luxury and opulence that was unsurpassed. Her passengers cared less about arriving first than they did about doing so in the most elegant manner possible.

Rowland Sinclair, of Woollahra, Sydney, hooked his walking stick over the back of his chair before he sat down. He dragged a hand through his dark hair, irritated with the inordinately long time it seemed to be taking his leg to heal. It had been over seven months now since Edna had shot him. Early in the mornings the limp was negligible, but after a day contending with the constant roll of the deck, the damaged muscles in his thigh ached and he relied on the stick.

His travelling companions, who had come with him into temporary exile, were already seated.

Rowland glanced across at Edna. She sparkled, perfectly accustomed to the many admiring eyes that were upon her. Her face remained rapt in attention to the man seated beside her, the fall of her copper tresses accentuating the tilt of her head. Rowland considered the angle with an artist's eye. The creaminess of her complexion was dramatic in contrast to the chocolate skin of the man upon whose conversation she focussed.

Jiddu Krishnamurti had dined with them before, and with him his eminent—perhaps notorious—entourage. Rowland found the man intriguing; it was not often that one broke bread with an erstwhile messiah.

On the other side of Edna, leaning absurdly in an attempt to enter the intimacy between her and Krishnamurti, sat the Englishman, Orville Urquhart. A consciously sophisticated man, he had been solicitous of their company since he first encountered Edna on board. Rowland regarded the Englishman with the distance he habitually reserved for those who vied for the attentions of the beautiful sculptress. Urquhart was broad-shouldered and athletic, but so well groomed that it seemed to counteract the masculinity of his build. His hands were mani-cured, his thin moustache combed and waxed, and even from across the table, his cologne was noticeable. Despite himself, Rowland shook his head.

He turned politely as the elderly woman in the next seat addressed him. "Tell me, Mr. Sinclair, will you be staying on in New York?"

"Not for long I'm afraid, Mrs. Besant. We shall embark for Sydney within a week of our arrival."

"I take it the Americas do not interest you?"

Rowland smiled. "We have been abroad for a while," he said. "We're ready to go home."

Annie Besant, World President of the Theosophical move-ment, nodded. "I have travelled greatly through my long life," she said. "First, spreading the word of intellectual socialism, and then, when I found Theosophy, promoting brotherhood and the wisdom of the Ancients. It was always the greater calling…but I do understand the call home."

"To London?" Rowland knew that the city was where the renowned activist's work and legend had begun.

"No, my dear…I belong to India where mysticism has long been accepted."

"Indeed."

"I was in Sydney before the war, you know." She looked at Rowland critically. "You would have still been in knee pants, I suppose, so you wouldn't remember. I'm afraid I was considered somewhat controversial." She smiled faintly, a little proudly.

"And why was that?" Rowland asked, expecting that she wanted him to do so.

"Free thought, and those who espouse it are always the enemy of those who rely on obedience and tradition for power," she replied.

Rowland raised a brow.

"I gave a lecture…*Why I do not believe in God.*"

He nodded. "That would do it."

Annie Besant chuckled. She liked the young Australian. Clearly, he was a man of means, old money—well, as old as money could be in the younger colonies, but his mind was open despite a certain flippancy. His eyes were extraordinary, dark though they were blue. There was an easy boyishness to his smile and, she thought, a strength. He had often stayed talking with her when the other young people got up to dance. She put a hand on his knee—Annie Besant was eighty-five now—she could take certain liberties.

"Tell me, how did you hurt your leg, Mr. Sinclair?"

"Ed…Miss Higgins shot me." He looked towards Edna, still talking deeply with Krishnamurti.

"A lovers' tiff?"

"Not quite. She wasn't aiming at me."

"So fate misdirected the bullet?"

He grinned. "Not fate—Ed. She's a terrible shot."

"And her intended victim?"

"Oh, she missed them entirely."

"I see." Annie placed her hand over his and gazed into his eyes. "You have an interesting aura, Mr. Sinclair. I have been clairvoyant for some years, you know, but still, you would be difficult to read, I think."

Rowland was a little relieved. He was less than enamoured with the idea of being read.

Annie Besant smiled and whispered conspiratorially. "I would not be offended, Mr. Sinclair, if you were to take out that note-book of yours."

Rowland laughed. It was his tendency to draw whatever caught his interest…it was not always appropriate to do so and he regularly checked the impulse to extract the notebook from the inside pocket of his jacket. Whether or not she was clairvoy-ant, Annie Besant was perceptive.

"I should like to draw you, Mrs. Besant." He opened the leather-bound artist's journal. "Actually I'd prefer to paint you properly, but I'm afraid my equipment is in the ship's hold."

"You must call me Annie. I think we are well enough acquainted now…Besant is just the name of the man who took my children." She sighed. "Of course that was well before you were born."

Rowland was already drawing. He was aware that Annie's activism had seen her lose custody of and contact with her children. He was not really sure why he knew that—it was one of those snippets of information told in hushed tones that came one's way from time to time.

"Not that old line again, Rowly." Milton Isaacs leant in from his seat on the other side of Annie Besant. "Not every beautiful woman can be seduced with a portrait, mate."

Rowland ignored him but Annie chuckled. Milton and Annie Besant got on famously. Her past as a socialist agitator and reformist made her a hero to Milton, whose politics were definitely, and at times awkwardly, Left. She in turn was intrigued by the brash young man who called himself a poet, and made no effort to hide the letters of the word 'Red' which disfigured his forehead. Being too old to wait upon niceties, she had asked him about it on their first introduction.

"Are you particularly fond of the colour red, Mr. Isaacs?"

"It is a perfectly acceptable colour, Mrs. Besant," he had replied smoothly. "But it does not appear on my face with consent."

"Then why is it there?" she had persisted, peering at the faded but readable letters.

"I came across some men who took exception to my political persuasion and who decided that I should wear it."

It was not entirely true. Milton left out that the right-wing vigilantes who had branded him with silver nitrate had done so thinking he was Rowland Sinclair. That was several months ago now—before they'd fled Sydney.

Rowland sketched, listening vaguely as his friend gave Annie the benefit of his considerable charm. Annie Besant's face was strong, her forehead broad, and the set of her mouth determined. She wore a fashion of her own creation, a kind of anglicised form of Indian dress, in white and blue. He drew her with definite lines, concentrating on capturing both the wisdom and hope in her face, as she spoke to Milton of international brotherhood. Her eyes were farseeing, as if her focus was on something in the distance. The Theosophical movement was now in decline, but at its height it had counted powerful men amongst its number. Prime ministers, men of letters. Indeed, it was rumoured that Australia's new national capital had been designed by Burley Griffin as a monument to Theosophical symbolism. And all these men had been led by Annie Besant.

"Rowly—" Clyde caught his attention from across the table. A fellow artist, Clyde Watson Jones had, like Edna and Milton, accompanied him from Sydney on a tour that had taken them to Egypt, the Continent, and England. In London, Rowland had attended to some of his family's extensive business interests. It was of course Sinclair money that had paid all their passages and accommodated and attired them in a manner befitting. Rowland Sinclair was a wealthy man, but he chose his friends from among those who were not—not consciously, of course. It just so happened that the bohemian set of poets and artists to whom he naturally gravitated were not often from the elite and conservative circles into which he'd been born.

"Hu reckons there's a game of baccarat going in the Smoking Room tonight," Clyde said hopefully. Originally from the country, his rugged, weather-beaten face presented a little out-of-place in the dinner-suited grandeur of the restaurant.

Hubert Van Hook was the other man at their table. He had occupied himself that evening exchanging suggestive witticisms with the Hoffman sisters, who were cruising to celebrate their recently acquired status as widows. There were four Hoffmans, so their simultaneous bereavement seemed an alarming coincidence, but by all accounts it was a happy one. In his mid-thirties, Van Hook was a native of Chicago, and one of the Theosophical movement's inner circle, though he seemed to prefer his spirits in a glass. He had a fondness for cards, and consequently, was often in their company.

"I'm in," Rowland replied with a quick glance at Milton. Baccarat was a habit they had picked up on the Continent, where it was a most fashionable pastime. Milton looked towards Edna who was speaking to Jiddu Krishnamurti of her work. The sculptress liked to go dancing in the evenings. As Rowland was still unable to do so, and Clyde loathed dancing, she relied on Milton to escort her…initially, at least.

"I'm coming," he announced, deciding that Orville Urquhart could take Edna onto the dance floor if she really had to go. Otherwise she could spend the evening counting chakras with the once World Prophet.

"I demand that we be relocated, forthwith!"

Rowland's head snapped up towards the minor commotion at the next table.

A heavy-set man of the cloth was remonstrating with the harried purser who was doing his best to minimise the unfortunate scene.

"It's bad enough that his kind is allowed aboard, but I will not dine within arm's reach—it is an affront…to me and the Church!"

The purser tried valiantly in the awkward silence that followed to resolve the issue with the least amount of fuss and embarrassment. The bishop and his party were directed to an alternative table well on the other side of the dining room.

Annie Besant was the first to speak. "Ignorant buffoon!"

"Come now, Amma." Jiddu Krishnamurti urged forgiveness. "The ignorant are more in need of understanding than those whose minds are open."

Annie Besant exhaled. "You are right of course, Jiddu."

Krishnamurti took the opportunity to expand and expound on his message of tolerance and love for one's fellow man, regardless of whether it was reciprocated. Milton caught Rowland's eye and grimaced. They all liked the Indian holy man, but he did have a tendency to go on. Annie Besant noticed Rowland's fleeting smile and returned her hand to his knee.

"Jiddu is a good man," she said quietly. "In the end he was too good to fulfill his destiny."

Rowland turned towards her once again. He knew that Krishnamurti had been the Theosophical movement's anointed world leader, thought to be a reincarnation of Christ. Discovered in India as a small boy, he had been raised by Annie Besant herself. And then, just a couple of years before he was expected to take the mantle of world teacher, he had repudiated the title and left the movement, though apparently his ties to its leaders were still strong.

"Jiddu feels that the individual must come to enlightenment through his own realisation and not through the teachings of another. For this reason he walked away from the Society." Annie sighed as she reflected. "Not everyone took it well."

Rowland nodded. Few religions would take the loss of their prophet well. "It must have been disappointing."

Annie patted his knee. "We had been preparing for so long, you see. Even in your Sydney, our Mr. Leadbeater had everything ready. But perhaps that is what Jiddu had to teach us…that we must go on ourselves."

Annie's voice grew thin and faded. She gasped. The hand on Rowland's knee clutched. He stiffened in response and regarded the matriarch with concern. The colour had drained from her face.

"Are you unwell, Annie?"

She said nothing for a moment, breathless, and then, "The veil was opened again…just briefly…so briefly. I caught a glimpse of what your life holds, dear boy." She fortified herself from the wineglass before her.

Rowland's lips twitched. "Oh?"

Annie Besant composed herself now. "You must be careful, Rowland. I see trouble ahead for you."

"What kind of trouble?" he asked, smiling now.

Annie shrugged, clearly frustrated. "I don't know. There is power in your presence but it is guarded." She regarded him almost accusingly. "As I said earlier, you are difficult to read."

"Did you see any beautiful women?"

Her eyes narrowed suspiciously. "You think I am a mad old lady getting carried away by my own fancies?"

"A little," he admitted. "But I rather like mad old ladies. It's the young ones who often prove problematic."

Annie Besant followed his gaze to Edna who was explaining Cubism to Krishnamurti. "Miss Higgins is a very rare young woman, an irrepressible life force."

Rowland's right brow rose. "Repressed, she is not," he agreed.

Annie chuckled. She patted his leg again and leant in to confide, "I have no doubt that there will be beautiful women in your future, dear boy."

"That's a relief."

Milton, who had been listening, laughed. "What do you see for me, Annie?" He offered her his palm.

She slapped his hand away. "I am not some carnival Gypsy, young man!" But she wasn't offended. She beckoned Rowland closer and whispered once again, "You be careful."

Chapter Two

TERRORISM
Von Papen To Act
SPECIAL MEETING
OF CABINET

BERLIN Monday

Declaring that ruthless action was necessary, Herr von Papen called a special meeting of the Cabinet today to discuss measures to defeat political terrorism.

Nine Nazis were arrested today in connection with the bombing outrages at Schleswig-Holstein.

—The London Times

The first-class Smoking Room on the *Aquitania* had been decorated in the style of the most conservative masculine establishments. Deep red club lounges and studded Chesterfields were placed in companionable, but symmetric groups, within easy reach of smoking stands. The supporting columns were Corinthian, the high ceiling decorated with ornate recessed domes from which hung opalescent pendant fittings. Its paintings were large in scale, traditional in subject and hanging on walls of panelled wood.

The oval baccarat tables were crowded.

Rowland and Clyde had left the game for the comfort of the armchairs and after-dinner drinks. Clyde was struggling to light a pipe.

"For pity's sake, man, just roll a bloody cigarette," Rowland advised after watching him try unsuccessfully for several minutes.

"I'll get it…give me a chance…maybe it needs cleaning."

Rowland squinted. "I think you need to at least light it before it can become clogged."

Clyde cursed as he struck a few more matches in an attempt to light the tobacco. In the end he abandoned the pipe and gave his attention to a glass of scotch.

"I wonder what Ed's doing." Rowland glanced at his watch.

"Krishnamurphy's probably teaching her to talk to the dead."

Rowland smiled. "Krishna*murti*—he's not an Irishman."

Clyde seemed troubled.

Rowland tried to reassure him. "He's not a bad chap, you know—for a messiah."

"Oh, I know that," Clyde replied. "Ed's been infatuated with a lot worse…doesn't it unnerve you though, Rowly? All this black magic stuff?"

"It's pretty harmless, Clyde."

Clyde swigged from his glass and shook his head. "Don't get me wrong—I like them—I just feel like I should go to confession."

"Good Lord!" Rowland laughed. "Surely there's no need to go that far." He changed the subject, taking a copy of *The Daily Mail*, Atlantic Edition, from the occasional table by his chair and tossing it to his companion. The ship's newspaper published news received from all over the world by the ship's wireless. "It looks like it's only a matter of time before Hitler's made chancellor."

Clyde studied the article about the leader of Germany's National Socialist Workers' Party. "We were bloody lucky to get out in one piece, you know."

Rowland nodded. They had visited the country, naively, unwisely. The avant-garde had once been strong in Berlin, and so the city had attracted them, but they found that the classical tastes of Adolf Hitler had effectively shackled the Modernist School. Indeed the political turmoil in which Germany was embroiled had been unnerving. Hitler's Brownshirts roamed the streets in groups, singing Nazi songs and looking for fights. German communists obliged, and gun battles were common-place. Rowland and his friends were tourists, but Milton Isaacs was one of their number. The long-haired poet was everything that was most unpopular in Germany at the time, and he'd had the word Red tattooed across his forehead.

"It was ugly." Rowland stared at his glass. Germany disturbed him.

"Good thing you can *sprecken de Doych*—we would never have got Milt out otherwise."

Rowland winced at Clyde's dreadful rendition of German, but did not bother to correct him.

"I studied languages at Oxford," he explained. "Actually I was rather relieved it all came back so easily."

"Oh," said Clyde. "Really?"

"You're surprised?"

Clyde shrugged. "Never considered what you actually studied at University. I thought you'd just gone to play cards and meet the odd girl."

"Well, there was a lot of that," Rowland conceded. "But I did get a degree while I was there."

"Turned out to be a handy thing." Clyde scratched the emerging shadow on his chin. "Who would have the thought the King's English was not enough?" He swirled his scotch. "Kind of an odd skill for a sheep farmer, though."

Rowland's brow rose. The Sinclairs were pastoralists, but he was hardly a sheep farmer. If truth be told, he spent very little time on the Yass property where the family fortune had been founded. He preferred to reside in Sydney.

"I had to study something—it was either that or read law." He recalled that his brother, Wilfred, had been quite keen that he study law.

"You would have been a bloody dreadful solicitor."

"I wouldn't have been allowed to actually practise," Rowland replied, amused by the thought. Sinclairs did not put up shingles.

"Banco!" Milton's voice raised above the murmur in the room.

"Sounds like Milt's winning," Clyde said.

Rowland looked over. "Splendid. Hope he knows when to stop."

Clyde grinned. "Somewhat unlikely. I'll drag him away in a few minutes."

Rowland put down his glass. "I'm going to turn in." He stood, rubbing his right thigh unconsciously as he retrieved his stick.

Clyde took the pipe from his pocket once again. "I doubt we'll be long."

Rowland made his way to the upper decks where the first-class accommodations were located, gritting his teeth against the burning in his leg as he climbed the staircase with his stick over his shoulder. He did this when no one watched; each time it was easier than the last.

He shared the luxurious three-bedroom Reynolds Suite with Clyde and Milton. Edna had taken the adjoining stateroom. It was quiet in the corridors—the Depression had seen a decline in the numbers of first-class passengers and so, many of the staterooms were empty. It was in any case quite late.

Just as he was about to push open the door of his cabin, Rowland caught Edna's voice on the draught that came in from the promenade. There was something in her tone that made him stop. He walked to the doors that led out to the deck. He could hear a man's voice—an Englishman. He could vaguely make out a couple embracing on the darkened promenade.

"Come on, sweetheart," the man cajoled. "You've been calling me hither all evening. Don't be coy now."

Rowland bristled, but he hesitated. Edna would not thank him for interrupting her romantic tryst.

"Orville, stop."

The couple began to struggle. Then Edna slapped him, hard. She was not playing. Urquhart swore and grabbed her again. He handled her roughly, pressing upon her lewdly.

Rowland moved. He didn't issue a warning, simply walked up, dragged the Englishman from Edna and hit him. Urquhart tried to retaliate, but years of pulling Milton out of bar room brawls had honed the Australian's reflexes. Rowland threw a second punch, furious, skinning his knuckles with the force of the blow. Blood spurted from Urquhart's nose. He struck back, doubled over. The punch was feeble, but it caught Rowland's leg. It was enough to prompt Rowland to hit him again. By now the noise had brought others. Confused shouts and shocked screams.

It was Clyde and Milton who reached Rowland first and removed him from Urquhart.

"Steady, Rowly, I think you've made your point."

Milton grimaced as he peered at Urquhart who had collapsed against a wall. "I think you've broken his nose…we'd better get some ice—you'll want something on your hand."

Clyde inspected Rowland's bruised hand. "You'll regret this when you try to pick up a paintbrush," he murmured. "You should have used your stick."

There were a few people on the promenade now, others looking out from cabin windows. Crewmen were trying to restore order. This was not something that one would expect on the first-class deck.

Milton put his arm around Edna's shoulders as she stood looking stunned and distressed. "You all right, Ed?"

She nodded.

Urquhart began a litany of threats, demanding that Rowland be arrested for assault. His voice was somewhat affected by his injured nose and the result was rather comical—to Rowland at least.

The staff captain emerged to sort the matter out.

Urquhart complained loudly, nasally.

While the staff captain questioned Rowland, Milton and Clyde took the opportunity to have a quiet word with the bleeding Englishman. In the end, Urquhart withdrew his grievance and allowed the crewmen to take him to the *Aquitania's* infirmary. The staff captain left it at that.

"I'll have some ice sent up for your hand, sir," he said politely as he left.

The Australians retreated to the opulent sitting room of the Reynolds Suite. A crewman arrived almost immediately with a silver bucket of ice.

Edna settled herself on the upholstered arm of Rowland's chair. She gazed at him, a little sternly, and then suddenly kissed him lightly on the forehead.

"Thank you, Rowly."

"Pleasure, Ed." He plunged his hand into the ice.

"What were you doing with that bastard, anyway?" Milton pointed a reproving finger at the sculptress.

"We were talking with Jiddu," she replied quietly. "Orville insisted on walking me back to my cabin…I gave in and he seemed to think that was an invitation—"

"'Struth, Ed!" Milton unfastened his bow tie. "You can't just flirt with every man in the room. One was bound to get the wrong idea…"

"How did you chaps convince Urquhart to back off?" Rowland redirected the conversation to waylay an argument.

"Told him he was lucky that you were a gentleman." Milton grinned. "Made it clear that Clyde and I had no such pretensions."

"Mentioned he could still end up overboard," Clyde added.

"Subtle. Hope he doesn't reconsider by morning."

"How's your hand?"

Rowland flexed it. "Should be fine." He assessed the skinned knuckles. "I must have found his teeth…I swear he tried to bite me."

Edna seemed to find that funny.

"Useless pommie mongrel," Clyde muttered in disgust. "None of them know how to fight."

Rowland smiled. "That's a bit harsh, old boy."

"No, he's right." Milton was adamant. "They transported the best of themselves in the seventeen hundreds."

The conversation deteriorated thereafter as Milton waxed lyrical about colonial superiority and Clyde produced a first bottle of port.

It was not until they were ready to leave for breakfast the next morning that Rowland realised he didn't have his stick. He wasn't particularly concerned. He didn't really need it in the mornings—there'd be time to find it before his leg got too bad. It was nearly ten o'clock when they entered the first-class dining saloon. They didn't have the opportunity to sit, however.

Captain Godfrey Madding stood before Rowland Sinclair with his staff captain and two senior crewmen by his side.

Rowland was surprised. The captain was an oddly deified presence on the *Aquitania*. Only the most important of matters and passengers ever elicited his attention. He resisted a ridiculous impulse to salute.

"Mr. Sinclair, would you mind accompanying me for a moment, sir?"

"Certainly, Captain."

The seaman extended an arm towards the door through which they had just entered. He did not object when Rowland Sinclair's companions fell into step behind him. They passed Annie Besant and her fellow Theosophists in the first-class foyer.

"Isaacs!" Hubert Van Hook hailed Milton. "A gentleman would have given me a chance to even the score before turning in."

Milton spoke briefly to him and kept walking. Annie Besant frowned as she watched them go. They were on the second-class gangway before Captain Madding addressed Rowland again.

"I understand you injured your hand last night, Mr. Sinclair."

Rowland glanced at Clyde—so Urquhart had decided to pursue his complaint. "I was involved in an altercation," he said carefully.

"Can I ask what precipitated this altercation?"

"Mr. Urquhart was taking unwelcome liberties with Miss Higgins—I took offence."

"That's right, Captain." Edna skipped to keep up with the long stride of the men. "Mr. Urquhart was behaving like a cad. Mr. Sinclair's arrival was nothing but fortuitous and his intervention gallant…"

Madding smiled and nodded at the sculptress, but returned to Rowland.

"Is that how you deal with those who cause you offence, Mr. Sinclair?"

"Not always. Mr. Urquhart was just lucky."

Captain Madding motioned towards Rowland's leg as they walked. The limp was slight, but noticeable.

"You don't have your walking stick, Mr. Sinclair."

Rowland's eyes narrowed. "I don't always need it."

Madding stopped them at the end of the deck. The area, which held a number of lifeboats, was cordoned off. Crewmen were posted around it.

"What is this about, Captain Madding?" Rowland asked suspiciously.

"Perhaps I should show you, Mr. Sinclair." The captain took down the chain so they could step through. "Maybe you should stay back, Miss Higgins."

When Edna made no move to do so, Clyde grabbed her by the arm and pulled her back. Rowland followed Madding closer to a lifeboat, which had been draped with a large canvas. The officer, who stood directly in front of it, stepped back to allow them access.

"This is Dr. Yates—the *Aquitania's* medical officer," Madding introduced brusquely.

Rowland nodded. The physician seemed very young—red-haired and freckle-faced…and visibly nervous.

"All right, Yates," the captain instructed. "Proceed."

The doctor pulled back the canvas.

Rowland was aware that both Madding and Yates were watching his reaction carefully.

Urquhart was in the boat. He was dead. Still in his dinner suit, the Englishman's shirt was soaked crimson, and the bottom of the lifeboat was pooled with blood. His eyes were open, vacant. His face was bruised, but it had been attended to—his nose still bandaged. Protruding from his neck was a silver-handled walking stick.

Edna, who had come forward, stifled a scream. "Orville!"

At Madding's prompting, Yates placed a handkerchief over the handle of the stick and pulled it out. It squelched. The stick had been snapped, splintered. The jagged end had been used to impale the unfortunate Urquhart.

"Is this your walking stick, Mr. Sinclair?"

"Yes, I think it probably is."

Chapter Three

TUTANKHAMEN
Fresh Objects from the Tomb

CAIRO

Among the other objects is a beautiful wooden casket completely covered with ivory having as a lid one whole piece of ivory whereon is delicately engraved a garden scene with the King and Queen in the centre and little children picking fruit at the foot—one of the most exquisite objects found in the tomb. There are also samples of beadwork, very Victorian in appearance.

—*The Guardian*

***

Milton was the first to break the heavy silence. "You couldn't possibly think Rowly…"

"I treated Mr. Urquhart for a broken nose and other injuries just after eleven last night," Yates interrupted, still holding the remnants of Rowland's stick. "We have to deduce that he was killed sometime between then and now."

Brilliant! The doctor fancied himself a detective. Rowland shook his head.

"You understand that we are still three days from port and the authorities, Mr. Sinclair." Madding gazed at him. "I am responsible for the safety of my passengers."

"I had nothing to do with this, Captain." Rowland remained calm.

"It is your walking stick…"

"I left my stick somewhere last night." Rowland looked back at the body. "I had already dealt with Mr. Urquhart—I had no reason to kill him. I certainly would not have chosen such a barbaric way of doing so."

"How does one kill a man politely, Mr. Sinclair?"

"Dr. Yates," Rowland was beginning to feel mildly alarmed by the situation, "would you be so kind as to give the handle of my stick a sharp twist and then pull on it?"

Yates sought the captain's consent and, having got it, did so. The handle pulled off completely to reveal a six-inch blade which slid into the hollowed shaft of the stick.

"An interesting walking stick, Mr. Sinclair."

"It was a gift from a friend who finds such curiosities amusing," Rowland replied, without so much as glancing at Milton. The poet had found the stick somewhere in France, just as Rowland was discarding his crutches. "My point is, Captain, why would I run a man through with a piece of splintered wood if I knew I held a blade in my hands? Whoever killed Urquhart had no idea that he held a weapon."

"Where were you last night, Mr. Sinclair?"

"In my suite."

"Can anyone vouch for your whereabouts?"

Rowland turned towards his travelling companions.

"We were all there." Clyde stepped closer to Rowland. "We drank three bottles of port between us and, by then, we weren't really in a fit condition to go anywhere."

"There was that valet," Milton threw in. "He came up to get our suits for cleaning. We were still wearing them, so he waited. We'd had a few by then so the poor bloke was waiting a while."

Captain Madding sighed.

"So…," ventured Edna. "What do we do now?"

"Are you going to throw Rowly in the brig, or make him walk the plank?" Milton laughed.

"I don't think either will be necessary, Mr. Isaacs." Madding was curt. "And I fail to see what is amusing. A man is dead."

Milton stopped grinning.

"What about Orville?" Edna bit her lip as she allowed hers eyes to rest on the body once more. "You can't leave him here. Someone should tell Annie and Jiddu…"

"We'll see to Mr. Urquhart." Madding stared hard at Rowland.

Rowland glanced around at the open sea. "Well, I'm not going anywhere, Captain Madding."

"Considering what a louse Urquhart proved to be," Milton proffered, "I'd reckon he had other enemies on board, Captain… or at least people who knew him better than we did."

Madding said nothing for a moment, and then, "I shall let you return to your breakfast. I trust I will have the pleasure of your company at my table this evening."

Rowland looked down, smiling. "It would be an honour, Captain."

And so, the interview was concluded.

"I'm not sure I understand why the captain wants to have dinner with us?" Clyde muttered as they made their way back towards the first-class deck.

"Why not?" Milton was less circumspect. "We're charming."

"He wants to keep an eye on us…well, me anyway." Rowland tipped his hat to the crewman who followed them. "Can't blame him, really—they did find my stick in a man's neck." He put his arm around Edna. "Are you all right, Ed?"

"Of course I am," she snapped. "Why wouldn't I be?"

"Well, you had a lot more to do with him…I thought you might…"

"I didn't like him!" She sounded angry. Rowland left it.

Edna pulled idly at the fingertips of the long black gloves that clad her arms. A wide silver bracelet with Egyptian motif fell loosely around her wrist, and a scarab bead necklace hung below the low neckline of her evening gown. The latest popular revival of all things Egyptian had begun in the last decade with the excavation of Tutankhamen's tomb, but Edna had only just discovered the fashion. In her usual way, she embraced the craze with childlike zeal.

She knew Rowland was watching her, sketching. It didn't trouble or embarrass her. She was a life model who lived with artists—she had long become accustomed to scrutiny. Rowland drew her often and, she thought, rather well.

"You know, it would be rather fun to paint you against the sea…a nod to Botticelli's *Venus*…," he murmured, almost to himself.

Edna laughed, knowing well the nude painting to which he referred. "No, Rowly, it's too cold."

Clyde was struggling with his bow tie, cursing under his breath. Milton was rifling through drawers, searching for cuff links.

"Rowly," he shouted from the other room, "do you mind if I…?"

"Go ahead. Try to choose ones that match this time."

They were about to dine at the captain's table. A man had been posted discreetly in the corridor outside the Reynolds Suite and another followed them about the *Aquitania*. Officially, Orville Urquhart's death was an accident, but rumours were rife. The atmosphere on board was tense.

"You going to be all right without your stick, mate?" Clyde emerged with his bow slightly askew, but tied.

"I'll be fine." Rowland was determined that he would be so.

Clyde raised his brows sceptically, but he did not argue.

"Oh, Rowly." Edna frowned. Rowland had already set back his recuperation more than once by refusing to give his injury time to heal.

"I'm perfectly fine," Rowland repeated without looking up.

Appropriately turned out, they proceeded to the dining room where they were ushered to Madding's table. The captain stood to greet them, gazing appreciatively at the young sculptress.

"Miss Higgins," he said as she sat down. "You are without doubt a shining ornament to the *Aquitania*."

Edna accepted the tribute with the practised grace of one who often received such compliments. She even managed to blush a little.

Madding introduced the other guests at his table. They were dining with an American couple, the Hickmans, whose well-coiffed, obviously unmarried daughters seemed excessively pleased to see them. Also present was the clergyman who had taken such offence at Jiddu Krishnamurti the previous evening. Bishop Hanrahan was accompanied by two lesser-ranked men of the church. The taller was a fair-haired, bespectacled priest, introduced as Father Murphy. The second, clean-cut and square-jawed, was Father Bryan.

Rowland sighed as he regarded the trio of black-cassocked men standing by their chairs like rigid sentinels of virtue—the company promised to be awkward.

Bishop Hanrahan glared at them. Milton already looked belligerent, and Clyde nervous.

Edna was ushered to the chair between the bishop's young frocked offsiders. She smiled devastatingly at each, ignoring their holy status and treating them as men. Rowland couldn't help but be amused as he observed the effect.

Milton and Clyde were each seated with a Miss Hickman to their left, and Rowland was directed to the chair on Milton's right, beside the captain. He assumed it was so that Madding could just reach out and grab him should he try to kill anyone.

"Will I say grace then, Captain Madding?" Hanrahan asked with no question in his voice.

Madding was clearly startled. Grace was usually the captain's prerogative.

Hanrahan began before he could reply, launching into prayer in a booming Irish accent.

"Bless, O Lord, this food we are about to eat; and we pray thee, O God, that it may be good for body and soul; and if there be any poor creature, hungry or thirsty, walking along the road, direct them to walk into us…"

"We're on a boat," Milton muttered for Rowland's ear. "They'd drown."

"…that we can share the food with them as thee share thy gifts with all of us."

Rowland straightened, happy to move on…but Hanrahan was not finished.

"Bring thy righteous fury down upon those among us who have strayed from thy word and commit blasphemy in the name of evil doctrines and false prophets, who consort with the devil and summon the spirits of the dead."

Again, Rowland raised his head, only to have to lower his eyes once more.

"Remind the sinful, the unchaste and immoral of the power of thy wrath, O Lord, instill in them a fear of eternity and bring them to thy divine justice. Through Christ our Lord. Amen."

Rowland looked up, carefully, unsure whether Hanrahan had finally concluded. It seemed he had. The clergymen were busy crossing themselves. The extraordinary grace left the table in a stunned silence. Under his breath, Rowland thanked his Protestant God that it was over.

"Bishop Hanrahan and his colleagues are on their way to Sydney," Madding said in an attempt to initiate conversation as the first course was served.

"How wonderful!" Edna directed her enthusiasm at Father Bryan. "Sydney is the most delightful city—you'll have a fabulous time."

"No doubt, it will have its share of souls to be saved from eternal damnation," cut in Bishop Hanrahan.

Edna blinked. "Oh—yes…I'm sure you'll find one or two at Government House."

Milton laughed. Clyde gazed at the ceiling in disbelief. The bishop glowered, moving his eyes from the sculptress to Milton Isaacs. He squinted at the poet, trying to make out the shadow of the word Red, in the subdued light of the dining room. His upper lip curled with distaste.

"What, in God's name, would you be having on your forehead, son?"

"My principles," Milton replied coldly.

"Oh, God," Clyde groaned.

Hanrahan inhaled. He reddened. "Mannix warned me I'd be finding your kind in the colony!" he said, none too quietly. "Captain, it seems it is not sufficient that you allow black heathens aboard, but now you'll be seating men of the true Church with Lenin's godless spawn and a Jezebel..."

The Hickman girls twittered at the last.

"Now, Your Grace...," began Madding.

"I will not be breaking bread in such company!" The bishop stood, sending his chair clattering behind him. He glared at Milton, who winked in return.

"You, sir," Hanrahan's finger shook with rage as he pointed at the long-haired poet, "are an abomination, an affront!"

He stalked out of the dining room. Father Murphy got up reluctantly, muttered a hasty apology, and followed. They all turned expectantly to Father Bryan. He cleared his throat and continued to eat his soup.

"Well, that went well." Rowland too returned to his meal. Captain Madding grunted. It took several minutes for the muted shock in the dining room to dissipate.

They dealt with the remaining awkwardness by ignoring it. Indeed the first course was not yet finished before Milton was thrilling the Hickman girls with tales of the savage Australian outback. He paraphrased shamelessly from the work of Paterson, passing off verse as his personal experience. Of course, the Hickmans were American and oblivious to the Australian balladeer. To them, Milton Isaacs cut a rugged, romantic figure.

Clyde snorted occasionally, but otherwise did nothing to shatter the illusion. Edna was busy bewitching Father Bryan. Rowland found himself talking with Captain Madding. Initially, neither mentioned Orville Urquhart, though at times it almost seemed he was sitting between them.

Unexpectedly, considering the circumstances, both found the other good company. Rowland suspected that Godfrey Madding was interrogating him, but he did not particularly object. He had nothing to hide, and he was curious as to how his walking stick finished up in Urquhart's neck.

"So, you are not a Theosophist?" Madding asked.

"No."

"But you don't object to them?"

"We Protestants don't get quite so worked up as the good bishop."

Madding stroked his short naval beard. "Yes, His Grace is rather direct."

"Eloquent, though."

"You knew Urquhart?" Madding asked, lowering his voice.

"Not well. He had been pursuing Miss Higgins since we came on board."

"And did that offend you?"

Rowland glanced up at Edna who was laughing—an unrestrained bubbling giggle, completely inelegant, entirely uninhibited. "Not at all," he said. "You'd have to be dead not to pursue Miss Higgins." He stopped, realising what he'd just said. He winced. "That was probably unfortunately put."

Madding nodded. "Quite."

"What I meant to say," Rowland explained, "is that Miss Higgins has many admirers. My issue with Mr. Urquhart is that he chose to press his admiration without consent. If she welcomed his attentions, he and I would have had no quarrel."

"You broke his nose, Mr. Sinclair."

"And settled the matter."

Madding sighed. "I am inclined to take you at your word, sir, but no other candidate presents and this is my ship."

Rowland nodded. He could see Madding's dilemma. "I shall speak to Mrs. Besant, if you like," he offered. "She may know more of Urquhart's background…"

"I would rather you didn't tell her that Urquhart was murdered," Madding said, frowning. "The last thing we need is for the passengers to panic."

Rowland smiled. "Mrs. Besant is clairvoyant. Urquhart's probably having dinner with her now."

"You believe that infernal nonsense?"

"I believe Mrs. Besant is rather astute and extremely perceptive. I doubt, very much, that she'll accept that Urquhart slipped and hit his head."

Madding thought for a moment. "Very well," he said finally. "It may help to know more about Urquhart. I've radioed New York and London—there are all manner of jurisdictional problems on top of everything else."

"Do you know where he went after he left the infirmary?" Rowland asked.

The captain shook his head. "According to Yates, he was feeling rather sorry for himself."

"I've been thinking about my stick—where I left it." Rowland frowned thoughtfully. "I had it as I went out onto the promenade…Clyde—Mr. Watson Jones— mentioned it at one point. I'd say that may have been where I left it."

"I know," replied Madding.

Rowland was surprised.

"My staff captain remembers that you didn't have it when you left the promenade. He recalls you using the wall to steady yourself."

"Oh." Rowland hadn't realised he had done so. "So I'm no longer a suspect?"

Madding leaned back. "Well, you may have returned to find your stick, but it does indicate that other men also had the opportunity to get hold of it." Stern grey eyes met dark blue. "As I said, I'm inclined to believe you had nothing to do with it, but, you understand, I have to be cautious. Either way, there is a murderer somewhere on board the *Aquitania*."

Hubert Van Hook appeared at the table as the final course was concluded. He spoke to Milton and Clyde of the American jazz band that would be entertaining in the ballroom that night and suggested that Prudence and Felicity Hickman join them all after dinner.

"Rowly," he added, in his loud Chicago accent, "Annie wonders whether you'd care to have coffee with her."

"I'd be delighted," Rowland replied as he stood. He was not, in any case, going dancing. He glanced towards Edna who was still talking with the clergyman and wondered fleetingly if Father Bryan was allowed to dance.

Taking his leave of Captain Madding, Rowland wished the others goodnight.

Annie Besant waited for him at her table. She watched him approach.

"Why, Rowland dear," she said, standing. "You've given up your stick…are you sure it's not too early?"

"Probably overdue," Rowland replied leaning on the back of a dining chair. "I'm afraid I'm getting a bit soft."

"If you don't mind, I thought we might take coffee in my suite." She smiled wickedly. "I must warn you, we'll be unchaperoned."

Rowland laughed. "Well, if you're willing to jeopardise your reputation Annie, I'm sure I can risk mine." He offered her his arm.

"I'm afraid I walk rather slowly—it's unbecoming for a woman my age to trot." She linked one arm in his and took her own walking stick in the other. They strolled up to the first-class deck and to Annie Besant's suite. Coffee arrived shortly afterwards on trays delivered from the dining room. Rowland noticed the crewman posted outside the door. Captain Madding remained vigilant.

Rowland sat thankfully while Annie poured coffee.

"Well, young man." She handed him a steaming china cup. "Suppose you tell me exactly what you got up to last night."

For a moment Rowland felt like a child caught out. "Has someone been telling tales, Annie?"

Annie Besant's face clouded. "Actually, Orville came to see me."

"When?"

"After he left Dr. Yates."

"Oh."

"I must say, I wouldn't have believed you capable of such brutality, Rowland."

"Afraid I am. What did he tell you, Annie?"

"That you attacked him in a jealous rage. Is that true, Rowland?"

"It wasn't quite a jealous rage," he said quietly.

She eyes were sharp, assessing. "This was to do with Miss Higgins?"

"Yes. I found Mr. Urquhart's manners wanting."

Annie Besant sighed. "I see. I was afraid that might have been the case."

Rowland's interest was piqued. "Why?"

"Orville's always been spoiled, even as a child. He was a particular favourite of Charles', and I am afraid he was indulged somewhat."

"Charles?"

"Charles Leadbeater. He leads the Australian chapter of the movement...you may have come across him."

Rowland hadn't, but he had heard of Leadbeater. Rather a bizarre figure, by all accounts.

Annie Besant shook her head sadly. "Charles will be heart-broken."

"I'm sorry for your loss, Annie," Rowland hoped that he didn't sound insincere. He had after all, broken the man's nose.

"Poor Orville." She regarded Rowland sharply. "Am I correct in assuming someone killed him?"

"Yes."

She gasped. "I was afraid of this...if only..."

"You knew he was in danger?"

"I knew there was danger...I felt the presence of some kind of malice...sensed something...I just didn't know who..."

"What do you know about Urquhart, Annie? Who would do this?" Rowland pressed gently.

"I've known Orville on and off since he was a small boy. His parents were great friends of Theosophy and he grew up in the movement. Essentially, he was a nice young man." She finished hesitantly.

"But…?" Rowland sensed a qualification.

"But," said Annie Besant carefully, "he was not always a gentleman. He has got himself into trouble before." Rowland noticed her fist clench. "I had hoped he'd learned his lesson, but the moment he came to me complaining of you, I suspected…"

"Who?"

She wiped away a stray tear. Her distress was genuine. "There were a few girls over the years—it upset Jiddu immensely. I sometimes wonder if that helped him decide to leave us."

"And no one did anything?" Rowland scowled. This was monstrous.

"Nothing so direct as you," Annie replied, patting him on the knee. "There were complaints; we all spoke to Orville…each time he was contrite, but…" She shook her head. "We should have done more." She looked up at him, the voice weary. "You tell Miss Higgins how sorry I am."

"Is there anyone on board who has reason to wish Urquhart ill?"

"Oh, Rowland, we were all frustrated with Orville. If nothing else he was damaging the movement with his behaviour, but Theosophy is about brotherhood and love…"

"Well, what happened to him wasn't terribly loving…" Rowland put down his cup and saucer. "I should say goodnight," he said as he moved to stand.

Annie Besant grasped his hand tightly. "You be careful in the hallway."

"Did you have a premonition?" he asked, curiously. Was the spirit of Urquhart walking the corridors of the *Aquitania*?

Her face was solemn. "The light near the stairs isn't working."

"Oh, I see."

Chapter Four

THE CORONATION OATH

LONDON

The Dublin Corporation has recommended a modification of the oath to be used at King George's coronation, by which the description of the Roman Catholic Mass as 'blasphemous' will be omitted.

—*The Observer*

Rowland Sinclair spent the remainder of the evening with the literature that Annie Besant had pressed upon him, including a book that she herself had penned. He fell asleep in his armchair, immersed in brotherhood and mysticism. It was in this state that his friends found him on their return to the Reynolds Suite.

Edna shook him awake softly. "Rowly, darling, wake up."

He opened his eyes groggily. "What time is it?"

"Late." Clyde, removed his jacket. "Or early. What are you reading?"

Edna picked up the book. "*Isis Unveiled.*"

"Sounds risqué." Milton fell into the couch. "You're a bit of a dark horse, Rowly…"

Rowland laughed. "I wish. No, it's a sort of Theosophy bible, I think."

Clyde regarded the book as if it might suddenly burst into flame, and crossed himself.

Edna giggled, whispering, "Clyde's worried you'll go to Hell."

Rowland rubbed a hand through his hair as he grinned at Clyde. "Between Lenin's godless spawn and Jezebel here—we're all going to Hell, mate."

Clyde smiled. "Sorry, old habits."

"Did you enjoy the jazz band?" Rowland stretched.

"A fine time was had by all," Milton replied breezily. "Prudence Hickman even persuaded Clyde to dance. It seems American girls are quite happy to endanger their toes."

Clyde sat down without bothering to defend himself. His dancing was that bad...there was little point in denying it.

"So did Annie summon Urquhart for you?" Milton undid his tie.

"Afraid not...but she did tell me a bit about him." Rowland related what he had learned about Orville Urquhart's less than impeccable character.

Edna perched on the arm of Rowland's chair and grabbed his hand fondly. "I'm glad you arrived when you did, Rowly. Still, it was horrible what happened to Orville. Jiddu must be so distraught."

Milton snorted. "Jiddu Krishnamurti and Father Bryan—you're flitting between theological extremes here, Ed."

"Don't be ridiculous, Milt—Jiddu is a holy man!"

"And Father Bryan?"

"Matthew is a deacon." Edna beamed. "He hasn't actually taken orders yet."

"Matthew?...God...No!" Clyde put his head in his hands. "You can't be serious."

Milton fell back laughing. "The bishop will explode...Good for you, Ed...save Matthew from the church—make a man of him!"

"This is not funny," Clyde raised his head. "You can't..."

"Ed, stop tormenting Clyde." Rowland poked her, hoping that was all she was doing.

Edna sighed and leaned over to pat Clyde's knee. "Very well, I'm not serious…not really. It is a tragic waste, though. He's very handsome."

Clyde smiled thankfully. "So who do you think killed Urquhart?" He was clearly glad to change the subject to something a lot less frightening.

Rowland shrugged. "Sounds like he may have had a few enemies."

"I wonder why the killer put him in a lifeboat?" Milton mused.

"To hide the body, I suppose," Clyde offered.

"I don't think so." Milton shook his head slowly. "It would have been a lot easier just to toss the blighter overboard than to lift him into a lifeboat. He was a hefty chap remember."

"He was killed in the lifeboat," Rowland pictured the scene of Urquhart's demise. "There was no blood on the deck around the boat. There would have been if he'd been dragged or carried into it."

Clyde nodded. "By George, you're right, Rowly. There was a good two inches of blood in the bottom of the boat but nothing outside."

"So what the blazes was Urquhart doing in a lifeboat on the second-class deck?" Rowland gazed absently at the blue glass beads which hung around Edna's neck and caught the light.

Milton looked a little sheepish. "Perhaps some kind of lovers' tryst?"

"Why wouldn't he just use his stateroom?" Edna asked the obvious. "A lifeboat…" She shuddered.

"Perhaps his young lady did not want to risk being seen— maybe he was concerned that the other Theosophists were watching him…maybe he's got some odd preferences." Milton shrugged. "It explains why he'd be sitting in a lifeboat."

Rowland nodded. "It's possible…"

"You don't think a girl could have killed him?" Clyde interrupted. "It would take a fair bit of strength to impale someone like that."

"Maybe this girl had her own Rowly, following her around like an avenging angel…"

"I wasn't following Ed around," Rowland protested, embarrassed by the suggestion.

"You know what I mean." Milton glanced at him apologetically. The torch Rowland carried for Edna was not a secret, but they didn't talk of it in her presence. It was an understanding between gentlemen.

"How's your leg holding up, Rowly?" Clyde deftly redirected the conversation.

"Aches like the blazes, actually." Rowland shifted his leg gingerly.

"Maybe we should find you another stick," Edna said, touching his arm in concern. She was normally dismissive of the occasional ailments and complaints of the men she lived with, but this was a little different—*she* had shot Rowland.

"We're not going to get one on board unless I rob some old lady." Rowland rubbed his thigh. "I'll pick up one in New York if I need to."

Milton brought the conversation back. "So tomorrow, we try to find out if Orville Urquhart had some kind of assignation on the second-class deck."

Rowland smiled. "Perhaps I better talk to the captain before we unleash Sherlock here upon the *Aquitania*.

"I hate to be the voice of reason," Clyde said tersely, "but it's really not our responsibility to find out who killed Urquhart. It's nothing to do with us."

"I don't know," Rowland replied. "I must say I was rather fond of that walking stick."

Godfrey Madding listened as Rowland told him of his conversation with Annie Besant. They sat opposite one another at the large mahogany desk in the privacy of the captain's quarters. The shelves behind Madding's leather chair were filled with naval memorabilia, and the odd item that Rowland recognised as a trophy of the Great War.

"So it's possible that Mr. Urquhart had many enemies." Madding, idly tapped the bottled model ship on his desk. "Indeed the Theosophists themselves had reason to wish Mr. Urquhart gone."

"The Theosophists?"

"Well, it sounds like he was a source of constant embarrassment to the movement."

"Yes," Rowland agreed hesitantly. "But murder seems to be rather against their doctrines."

Madding snorted. "I don't know that doctrines hold much sway with those moved to kill, Mr. Sinclair."

Rowland held his own counsel on that point and raised the question of the lack of blood outside the lifeboat.

Madding nodded. "You're quite right, Mr. Sinclair, but what would Mr. Urquhart be doing in a lifeboat?"

Rowland recounted Milton's theory.

Madding's brow rose. "I see." He stroked his beard. "I'll speak to my staff captain—see if the crew noticed anything. The question still remains as to how such a person got hold of your stick."

"One has to assume he picked it up on the promenade after my run-in with Urquhart."

"How many people were on the promenade that night?"

"Not many before I hit Urquhart, quite a few after."

"The Theosophists have the staterooms that look out on that side of the promenade," Madding commented. "As well as Bishop Hanrahan and a number of American couples."

"The bishop?" Rowland smiled.

Madding laughed. "Of course," he continued soberly, "there is always the possibility that Urquhart himself took your stick and had it with him when he was attacked. The killer then just used it as a weapon of opportunity."

"Well," Rowland shook his head, "it seems we've managed to narrow it down to anybody on board the *Aquitania*."

Madding's lips pursed. "Yes, a sterling piece of deduction."

"May I enquire, Captain, as to what will happen if no killer has emerged by the time we make port?"

Madding took out his pipe and stuffed it. "I'm afraid the murder of Orville Urquhart will become a maritime mystery," he said. "Both Scotland Yard and the New York Police Department are at pains to declare it outside their jurisdiction." He patted his pockets for a lighter. "The best we can hope for is that the blaggard disembarks in New York and doesn't join us for the leg to Sydney."

"Yes, far better that a murderer runs loose in the streets of New York."

"It's not ideal, Mr. Sinclair, but it really can't be helped. Let's just hope that it was only Mr. Urquhart against whom the killer had a grievance."

They talked for a while longer, allies now; and then Rowland made his way back to the first-class deck where he found his companions huddled in blankets upon wooden deck chairs. It was mid-autumn in this part of the world. The day was grey and sea breeze cold.

Rowland turned up the collar of his coat before he took the deck chair they'd saved for him. Edna handed him a blanket.

"Tell me again," he muttered, as he unfolded it, "what the blazes are we doing out here?"

Edna pointed to the long lines of deck chairs, bearing wrapped passengers peering out at the dark sea in the bracing wind. "Seems to be the done thing, Rowly."

"We are experiencing the majesty and glory of Neptune's realm." Milton motioned dramatically towards the water. "Defying the unknown oceans whilst Britannia still rules the waves, even though the sea is flecked with bars of grey, the dull dead wind is out of tune…"

"That second part is Oscar Wilde, the first part is nonsense, and it's flaming cold," Rowland grumbled, entirely uninspired.

"Someone will bring tea shortly," Milton said, returning to his book.

Rowland looked across at Clyde who was leaning forward, gazing towards the horizon.

"Seascape?" Rowland recognised the expression on the other's face. Clyde pointed to a shaft of light breaking through the grey of the clouds—seabirds seemed to be flying towards it, upwards to the source of the beam.

Rowland nodded. "Yes, that could be worth painting," he murmured.

Clyde smiled. "You could put a naked woman in the foreground." Rowland Sinclair d' not paint landscapes.

"Ed's already said it's too cold," Rowland replied. "No work ethic, I'm afraid."

"Edna! What a pleasant surprise." Father Bryan stood before them. "Gentlemen, how are you this morning?"

"Matthew, how lovely to see you." Edna craned her neck along the line of deck chairs. None was empty. She drew her legs up and made room at the foot of her own. "Why don't you join us?"

"Don't mind if I do." The clergyman sat. "It's a fine morning."

The Australians did not contradict him. They had grown accustomed to what Englishmen seemed to think was a fine morning. It called for compassion.

"Are you hiding from the bishop?" Edna asked pleasantly.

"Ed!" Clyde choked.

"It's all right." Matthew Bryan laughed. "I am in fact trying to stay out of his way. His Grace is in a fearsome temper."

"Oh? What particular abomination is troubling the good bishop today?" Milton asked.

"Gout." Bryan pointed at his foot. "And of course this matter with Isobel."

"Who's Isobel? I don't believe we've had the pleasure."

"His Grace's niece. Isobel is travelling with her uncle to Sydney."

"Taking her to a nunnery, is he?" Milton ignored Clyde's glare.

"Not yet, but he just might," Matthew Bryan shook his head. "A bit of a wild creature, is Isobel."

"Really?" Milton winked at Rowland. "Why didn't she join us at dinner last night?"

"She was a bit distraught—this Urquhart thing you know... wouldn't come out of her cabin."

Now Rowland was interested.

"She knew Orville Urquhart?"

"Apparently so. His Grace was quite beside himself about it."

"Yes, we noticed he was excitable."

"His Grace is a passionate man, one of the Good Lord's most loyal soldiers." Bryan defended his superior. "He was a boxer in his day," he added, "before he joined the seminary. Why, I'm sure the Holy Father himself is terrified of him!"

They were interrupted at that moment by the service of tea.

Father Bryan did not stay. He rose regretfully. "I must go and prepare the chapel. His Grace is celebrating Mass in an hour or so. I'm just mustering a congregation."

He regarded them hopefully.

Rowland shrugged apologetically. "Protestant," he said.

"Lenin's godless spawn," Milton volunteered before the clergyman could even look at him. "But Clyde will go—won't you, Clyde?"

Clyde sputtered. He didn't often take his Catholicism that far—he turned to Rowland for help.

Rowland considered it. "I think you should go. Pray for us."

If Father Bryan hadn't still been standing there, Clyde might have sworn at him. As it was he had little choice but to promise his attendance.

"And I'll see you there, Edna." Matthew Bryan beamed at the sculptress who smiled back at him with wide-eyed innocence.

"Of course."

It must have been that the friendly deacon had eyes only for Edna, because he did not notice the looks of shock on the faces of the gentlemen around her. They waited till he had gone before they challenged her.

"You told him you were Catholic, didn't you?" Milton accused.

"No…I just didn't tell him I wasn't…he simply assumed…"

Clyde groaned and slumped back in his deck chair.

"Ed, you've just agreed to go to a Catholic Mass," Rowland informed her.

"Oh yes, I believe I did."

Clyde groaned a little louder.

"It's a bit different from an ordinary Anglican service."

"I suppose it is."

"Have you ever been to Mass before?" Rowland asked.

"Of course not, I'm not Catholic."

"That was my original point, I think."

"Don't be so dramatic, Rowly." Edna was unconcerned. "I'll just go along and do exactly what Clyde does."

Milton laughed. "Assuming Clyde knows what to do."

"We'll be fine, won't we, Clyde? We'll stay at the back."

"I haven't been to Mass in a while," Clyde admitted grimly. "Thanks for your help, Rowly." He kicked at Rowland's deck chair in disgust.

"Sorry about that, old mate." Rowland was sincere. "I thought going to Mass might be a good chance to meet Isobel."

"Why do I want to meet Isobel?"

"To find out if she was meeting Urquhart in a lifeboat."

Milton sat up. "God, Rowly, you're right. It could have been her—and what's more I wouldn't put it past the bishop to deal out a little divine justice of his own."

Rowland's lips twitched upwards. "Apparently, the Pope's afraid of him."

Clyde looked slowly from Milton to Rowland. "Just so we're clear…you think His Grace is some kind of murderous lunatic who impaled a man for dallying with his niece, and you want me to go into *his* Mass, with Jezebel on my arm, and accuse that same niece of meeting Urquhart in a lifeboat for immoral purposes?"

"I didn't plan on Ed," Rowland confessed. "Who would have thought that she was masquerading as a Catholic?"

Clyde sighed. "My mother's right—I'm moving with a bad crowd."

"Did you notice that Bryan is somewhat indiscreet for a priest?" Milton said suddenly. "A nice change, I'll admit, but unusual."

"I told you, Matthew is a deacon," Edna corrected. "He hasn't actually been ordained yet."

"The other one—Murphy—he's much more priest-like," Milton continued. "You don't find him inviting pretty girls to Mass."

Clyde grunted. "Maybe he's canvassing the second-class deck."

Chapter Five

KRISHNAMURTI—
A New Philosophy
'Star of the East' Disbanded

LONDON

Krishnamurti, the young Indian who some years ago was hailed by the Theosophists as "The New Messiah," has reappeared in London with a new philosophy.

He said that he had disbanded the Order of the Star of the East because he declined the revenues and possessions heaped upon him. Krishnamurti's creed now is—"Free yourselves from the fear of all convention, social moralities, and organised religions, and discover the truth within you, guided thereby not by anything taught or told."

—The London Times

Rowland sketched the party of high-haired women who sipped from tall frosted glasses at the table opposite. They were typical of the matrons who inhabited the first-class decks: greying hair, coiffed in upward-sweeping styles, fox stoles draped like wreaths about their shoulders. Rowland grimaced unconsciously as he drew in the sad glass-eyed faces of the garments. He looked up briefly in search of Milton. The poet had struck a conversation with a becoming young lady in tennis attire. It appeared she had come into the Long Gallery to ask the purser about replacing a lost ball. Milton was assisting her with her enquiries. The poet was nothing if not gallant. Rowland returned to his notebook.

In time, Milton returned and then Hubert Van Hook joined them both. It seemed he had been wandering the ship in search of some distraction, and so he approached them most warmly. Van Hook took a cigarette from a slim silver case and fumbled for a light, chatting without pause as he did so. It was he who raised the subject of Orville Urquhart.

"This malarkey about an accident…" he started.

"Don't ask, Hu," Milton warned.

Hubert stared at them. "Old Ahab gagged you guys, did he?"

"Ahab?…Oh, you mean Madding…" Milton laughed and dealt him in. "In a word, yes—so don't ask. Rowly is particular about these things."

"Okay." Van Hook grinned broadly, affably. "I'll shut my trap."

"Had you known Urquhart for long?" Rowland asked.

"Since we were kids," Van Hook's expression hardened. "He used to make the crossing often enough—his parents were loaded—big shots in the movement."

"What did you make of him?"

Van Hook shrugged. "Couldn't trust him. Real wiseguy… looked out for number one, if you know what I mean."

"So, he had enemies?"

"I suppose so. He could turn on the honey when he wanted to. The babes seemed to like him and he had old Annie snowed."

"I think Annie may have worked him out." Rowland recalled their conversation the previous evening.

"Baloney!" Van Hook returned. "His manners may have made her burn up occasionally, but she thought he was the cat's pyjamas! Spoke up for him every time." He grinned at Rowland.

"Heard you boffed him in the kisser for messing with Edna... Don't blame you...she's a doll."

There was a pause, partly because it took Rowland a second to work out exactly what Van Hook was saying, and partly because, once he had, he wasn't sure how to respond.

"Yes..."

"Attaboy! Don't feel bad about it. He had it coming." Hubert Van Hook tossed down his hand. "You fellas going to sit around beating your gums, or are we playing here?"

"We're playing." Rowland glanced at his hand.

It took the Australians about an hour to bring the game to a profitable conclusion.

"Well, fellas, it's been a real gasser." Van Hook stood. "But I'm going to scram. You boys have cleaned me out—haven't got jack."

Rowland and Milton watched him go.

"Seems wrong to take his money," Milton said quietly. "Poor chap can't even speak English."

Rowland nodded. "We have a week's stopover in New York. We could be in trouble if they all talk like that."

"Is a gasser a good or bad thing, do you think?"

"It's hard to tell...could be either."

Edna and Clyde came into view. The sculptress was dressed in a becoming floral, with a chaste Peter Pan collar. Her hat was stylish, but conservatively so, as were the kid gloves she wore.

"Well?" Milton asked as they sat down.

Rowland turned to Clyde. "Did Ed manage to pass as—?"

"She took communion."

Milton laughed. "Don't you have to be admitted to some kind of holy order for that?"

"It is traditional to be confirmed in the Catholic Church before one partakes of the Eucharist," Clyde said tightly.

Edna pulled off her gloves. "Stop fussing, Clyde." She patted his arm. "It's not all that different from our communions... except there was no wine. Did you know they didn't share the wine, Rowly? I daresay Bishop Hanrahan likes to keep it all for himself."

Rowland tried not to laugh for Clyde's sake. Milton had no such inhibitions. He called over a waiter and ordered drinks for them all in an attempt to compensate the deprivation.

"So how was the service?" Rowland asked once the drinks arrived.

"Hanrahan's certainly heavy on the brimstone," Clyde shook his head. "Scared the hell out of me."

Milton raised his glass. "Don't worry, mate, we'll put it back."

"Did you see Isobel?"

"Yes—pretty girl. Cried a lot and spent the rest of the time glaring at Hanrahan. Ed spoke to her."

"Only for a little while. Poor thing seemed in need of a friend." Edna added reflectively, "She's taking tea with me at four o'clock."

"Well, if she's pretty, we might all join you," Milton suggested.

"Oh yes, do." Edna welcomed the idea. "She might even find you amusing."

"How about we try our hands at deck tennis in the meantime?" Milton ventured, stretching. "Provided Rowly's delicate constitution can cope with the outside air."

Rowland looked sharply at the poet, mindful of the young lady who'd lost her ball.

Milton smiled innocently.

Rowland sighed. "Yes, why not."

They made their way onto the appropriate deck and found a purser, who equipped them with racquets and erected a net. The deck court was so small that Rowland found he could play a reasonable game standing still and relying on his reach. The mild exercise of the game mitigated the cold a little. Milton, on the other hand, carried on as if he was centre court at Wimbledon, turning regularly to acknowledge an audience of young ladies who'd abandoned their own games to watch.

Despite the bleak day there were several people out playing shuffleboard or simply taking a turn about the ship. Rowland noticed Annie Besant walking, arm in arm, with Jiddu Krishnamurti. Hubert walked with them.

Some time later they noticed voices rising above the back-ground of passengers at play.

Rowland caught the tennis ball in his hand and turned towards the argument. Hubert stood near the rail, facing Bishop Hanrahan. The wind carried most of their words away, but they were clearly heated. Hanrahan was shouting something about blasphemy; Hubert was returning with derision. Jiddu Krish-namurti appeared to be trying to soothe the situation whilst Annie seemed both shocked and amused.

Suddenly Hubert poked the bishop in the chest. Hanrahan reacted explosively, punching the young man in the jaw. Hubert reeled, falling back heavily against Annie who was leaning against the rail. The passengers on deck seemed to react as one, arms outstretched, as the old woman was pushed hard against the balustrade and for a moment, seemed about to plunge over. Jiddu Krishnamurti's hand flew out. He caught Annie about the waist and dragged her away from the railing. A collective sigh of relief. And then spontaneous applause. Crewmen appeared to ensure that no one had been hurt, and to reassure the shocked passengers.

"Maybe he can walk on water," Clyde said quietly as the crowd burst once again into ovation for Krishnamurti, the hero of the moment.

For his part, Bishop Hanrahan was anything but contrite. He finished with a few further words to Hubert and stalked off the deck, with his deacons in tow.

"That was too close!" Edna folded her arms indignantly.

"His Grace can pack a punch," Clyde muttered. "Hubert's no lightweight and he sent him flying a fair way."

Milton agreed. "No wonder the Holy Father's scared."

Chapter Six
RMS *Aquitania*

Menu

Oysters – Marennes
Grape Fruit Cocktails
Epicurean Ham   Anchovy Salad
Radishes   Salted Almonds
Olives
Œufs Mayonnaise   Celeri
Canape Suedoise

———————

Pot au Feu   Potage St. Hubert

———————

Supreme de Britt – Sauce Normande
Fried Fillets of Whiting – Ravigote

———————

Mousse a l'Ecarlate
Cotelettes d' Agneau – Reforme

———————

Prime Sirloins and Ribs of Beef – Horseradish Sauce
Haunch of Venison – Oporto
Roast Turkey – Cranberry Sauce
Baked York Ham – Nouilles

———————

Brussels Sprouts　　　Rice　　　Fried Egg Plant
Boiled, Roast, Puree, and Rissolés Potatoes

— — — — — — —

Sorbet à l'Orange

— — — — — — —

Roast Pheasant – Saragota Potatoes
Salade de Saison

— — — — — — —

Plum Pudding – Anglaise　　　Bavarois Suchard
Friandises　　　Glace Vanille
Coupes Tutti Frutti
Dessert　　　Café

High tea was being served in the Garden Lounge on the *Aquitania*. There was no actual garden of which to speak. But the lounge was not unlike a conservatory. Large picture windows allowed passengers to take in the vista of the ocean whilst sitting at wicker settings with their teapots and cucumber sandwiches. A string quartet provided a refined musical background. Isobel Hanrahan sat at a table towards the back, looking furtively about her from time to time.

"You weren't lying, Clyde." Rowland observed the classic Irish beauty. The bishop's niece had long dark hair and large, heavily lashed eyes. Her figure was very slim, girlish, but there was something seductive about her nonetheless.

Isobel stood as they approached, evidently alarmed by the arrival of so many.

Edna grabbed her hand warmly. "Hello, Isobel. I brought some friends—I hope you don't mind." She introduced her gentlemen.

Isobel appeared a little flustered, but she took the seat that Milton pulled out for her. A waiter arrived with a trolley of cakes and petite sandwiches from which Clyde and Edna chose a generous selection with all the excitement of children. Silver teapots were placed at the table's centre and fine china, which bore the crest of the *Aquitania*, at each setting. For a short while, Isobel Hanrahan was lost in a friendly flurry of pouring and pastry-passing whilst Clyde and Milton argued over who had actually won the game of deck tennis which had been interrupted by Annie Besant's near accident.

Rowland poured tea into Isobel's cup. "Do you take milk or lemon, Miss Hanrahan?"

"Milk, definitely milk, Mr. Sinclair," she replied shyly. Her accent was as broad as her uncle's, but the lilt was not unpleasant. "It would be all I can take with this wretched seasickness."

Milton passed her a plate of bread and butter. "I trust you are otherwise enjoying life at sea, Miss Hanrahan," he said as she declined.

Immediately, her eyes welled and she began to weep.

Clyde kicked Milton under the table. "What did you say?"

Rowland looked helplessly at Edna, who rolled her eyes, took the young woman's hand and patted it consolingly. Rowland handed Edna a handkerchief and the sculptress passed it on. In a few moments Isobel had composed herself.

"Forgive me," she gulped. "I miss Orville so dreadfully."

"Oh, dear." Edna encouraged Isobel to sip her tea. "It was a terrible accident."

"Did you know Mr. Urquhart well?" Rowland asked carefully.

Isobel nodded. She pulled a silver locket from under her collar—an unusual piece, engraved and set with seed pearls.

Edna gasped softly. Rowland tensed.

"He gave me this grand jewel, just the morning before…"

Milton met Rowland's eye. "Did Mr. Urquhart put his picture in it?" the poet asked evenly.

They all recognised the locket. Rowland had given it to Edna years before. Ever since, it had held a picture of her late mother.

Isobel shook her head and released the clasp—it was empty. "Orville promised he'd have a portrait taken for me."

Rowland glanced at Edna uncertainly. The sculptress' face held more pity than anger. Silently, he marvelled at her compassion.

Milton spoke gently, holding Isobel with his dark gaze. "Here, take my picture; though I bid farewell, thine in my heart, where my soul dwells, shall dwell."

Isobel's sighed, her eyes dewy. "Why, Mr. Isaacs, that is so very beautiful. It gives me such comfort."

"Words are all I have to offer in your moment of loss, Miss Hanrahan."

"John Donne's words," Rowland murmured.

Milton ignored him. He'd always considered Rowland's obsession with who wrote what entirely unwarranted.

"It was an engagement gift." Isobel disintegrated again. "I am sorry…what must you think of me…? We are barely acquainted."

"How long had you known Mr. Urquhart?" Rowland stirred his tea, feeling intrusive in the face of her grief.

"We found each other the moment we came aboard," she replied with lip atremble.

"Pardon me, if I am too familiar, Miss Hanrahan," Milton ventured, "but has your engagement been announced?"

"It has not…not yet…"

"And your uncle?"

"Sweet Lord, no!" She coloured. "Uncle Shaun would never allow…I suppose it matters little now…I would meet with Orville in secret." Isobel raised Rowland's handkerchief to her face and wept into it once more.

The Australians waited patiently. They had been subjected to the disapproval of Bishop Hanrahan. They could feel nothing but sorry for the young woman.

"On the night Mr. Urquhart died…" Rowland began.

Isobel nodded. "I was meeting Orville around midnight…we had a place where we could be alone." She turned her face away and blushed a little. "Uncle Shaun is usually in his bed by ten."

"Usually?"

"Father Murphy came to my stateroom around half past ten…Uncle Shaun had sent him to hear my confession—apparently he insisted."

Edna hugged her impulsively. "Oh, you poor old thing. How simply frightful…What ever did you do?"

"I confessed to having terrible, uncharitable thoughts about my uncle."

Rowland and Milton laughed, and even Clyde was unable to repress a chuckle.

"Father Murphy stayed and stayed. I confessed and confessed." Isobel's shoulders slumped wearily. "'Twas nearly midnight before he left…by then, I was sure Orville would be angry." Her cheeks flushed red once more. "He is not…was not…a patient man."

"So you went to meet him?" Edna asked quickly as she noticed Isobel's eyes well again.

"I would certainly have done, but Uncle Shaun arrived to say the rosary with me."

"In the middle of the night?" Rowland put down his teacup.

"Uncle Shaun is often moved by the Holy Spirit at unusual times," Isobel informed him sadly.

Milton looked at Clyde. "This rosary thing…does it take long?"

"If you do it properly."

"One supposes a bishop would do it properly," Rowland noted.

Isobel nodded emphatically.

Rowland Sinclair watched the bishop's niece thoughtfully. Her distress at Urquhart's demise seemed thoroughly genuine, though she had known him only a few days. He was somewhat relieved that Isobel appeared utterly unaware of his altercation with Urquhart. She would probably not have looked well on him for that.

"What part of Ireland are you from, Miss Hanrahan?" he asked, deciding to take her focus from Urquhart and his unfortunate end.

"Dublin, Mr. Sinclair." She smiled as she thought of home. For several minutes she told them of the Irish capital, of her family. She spoke wistfully of her parents' edict that she accompany her uncle to Sydney. She did not elaborate on why and they did not press her. Eventually, she stood to leave, concerned her uncle would soon notice her absence.

"You cannot be walking me back," she protested, when the men stood and Rowland moved to walk her to her room. "Thank you kindly, Mr. Sinclair, but Uncle Shaun will be furious if he saw me with the likes of you. He is more than sufficiently cross with me. I'll not risk angering him further."

"I'll accompany you, Miss Hanrahan," Clyde volunteered. "I'm a lot less objectionable than Rowly, and I did sit through Mass."

That decided, Rowland and Milton returned with Edna to the Reynolds Suite, whilst Clyde saw Isobel Hanrahan to her door.

Rowland dropped into the couch, rubbing his leg. It was holding up well, he thought. He hadn't won the deck tennis, but he had played.

"Do you want a drink, Rowly?" Milton was already pouring.

Rowland nodded. "Thanks."

"Ed?"

The sculptress declined and sat down beside Rowland. She was quiet.

He put his arm around her. "I'm sorry about your locket, Ed," he said softly. "Do you want me to talk to her?"

She shook her head and then leant against him, curling her legs up next to her. "You can't tell the poor thing that he gave her a stolen locket. It would break her heart all over again."

"You're a good sport, Ed," he murmured, hearing the sadness in her voice. He could smell the familiar rose of her perfume as she left her head on his shoulder.

"Rowly…"

"Hmmm?"

"What do you think he did with the picture of Mama?"

Rowland tightened his grasp upon her. He suspected that Edna didn't have another photograph of her late mother. "I don't know, Ed. I'll talk to Madding—we'll have Urquhart's stateroom searched."

Milton proffered a glass to Rowland. "Get off the man's drinking arm, Ed."

"Rowly's ambidextrous," she replied staying exactly as she was.

"Since when?"

"I started out with a preference for my left." Rowland took the glass with the hand in question.

"I've never noticed you using…"

"I don't generally. Was persuaded to use my right hand when I started school."

"Persuaded?"

"They have ways."

"Rowly paints with his left hand sometimes," Edna said. "I can't believe you haven't noticed."

Milton remained surprised.

"I don't paint with my left often," Rowland qualified. "Just when the work isn't going well—sometimes it helps."

"Well, as long as you can still drink." Milton took to the armchair with his own glass. "I wonder how that mongrel got hold of Ed's locket."

"I was wearing it the day before he died." Absently, Edna touched the hollow of her throat where the locket had nestled. "I hadn't even noticed it was missing."

"You know, Rowly…" Milton sat back and contemplated his Scotch. "I'm inclined not to care that Urquhart's dead. Perhaps we should just raise our glasses and wish the killer the best of British—he may have done us all a favour."

The door opened and Clyde walked in.

"You took your time," said Milton.

"The bishop was waiting for Isobel." Clyde rubbed his forehead wearily. "Poor girl might have an easier time in a nunnery." He cast his eyes to the ceiling. "God forgive me—His Grace is a bloody nutter."

"What if it was the bishop who killed Urquhart?" Rowland turned to Milton. "Should we still wish him luck?"

The poet hesitated. "Well…there's Isobel."

"And the next bloke who wins her heart."

"Do you think really he could have killed Orville and then returned to say rosary with Isobel?" Edna was sceptical.

Milton shrugged. "Maybe it was the bishop who needed to ask for forgiveness...or whatever it is that you do with the rosary."

Clyde poured himself a drink. "We make port tomorrow."

"Bishop Hanrahan and his entourage will board again for the leg to Sydney." Rowland grimaced. "We'll have the dubious pleasure of another few weeks in His Grace's company."

Clyde sat down and pulled a deck of cards from his pocket. "He can move in and call me 'darling', but I'm not going to Mass again." He proceeded to deal. "Ed, get off Rowly—you'll be able to see his cards from there."

———————————————————————

Their final dinner aboard the *Aquitania* before she reached New York Harbour, was a celebration of particular grandeur. Only Jiddu Krishnamurti and the clergymen weren't in white tie and tails, remaining in the attire of their respective religious affiliations. The ladies glittered in their most lavish gems, both true and paste. Edna's claret gown had been purchased for her in Paris. She wore no jewellery this night. She was startling.

"What the hell are we going to do with these outfits when we get home?" Clyde tried to sit without catching the tails of his coat.

"We'll be the best-dressed blokes at Trades Hall." Milton grinned. "Even Rowly might have trouble finding a fancy enough do for these get-ups."

They were seated again with Theosophists. In Orville Urquhart's place was Richard Waterman, a middle-aged surgeon, whose accent only just betrayed him as Australian. His wife was an American, severe eyes, lips drawn tight like the neck of a drawstring bag. The only time she stopped looking disapproving was when she spoke to Krishnamurti, whom she seemingly held in high regard. Also at the table were the Colonel and Mrs. Benson, an elderly couple who started in the movement with Annie Besant. They were on their way to Sydney to stay with Charles Leadbeater at *The Manor*, which served as the Theosophical Society's southern headquarters.

Annie spoke with Rowland who had clearly become a favourite of hers. In this conversation she extolled the virtues of Co-masonry over its more traditional prototype, Freemasonry. The new Lodge had adopted much of the ritual and regalia of the original, but its membership was not restricted. Unaware that the Sinclairs had been Freemasons for generations, she did not curb her criticisms of the exclusively male society.

"Freemasonry has much to commend it," Annie declared. Her hand once again found Rowland's knee, where, it seemed, she preferred to keep it. "But it is a patriarchal anachronism—determined to exclude women."

Rowland smiled. "I would not have thought you so keen to wear an apron, Annie."

His membership of the secret society was a family tradition more than a personal choice, though his brother, Wilfred, took the Lodge quite seriously. Indeed, Rowland only attended meetings under sufferance when Wilfred insisted. He honestly couldn't imagine why women would want to join.

"I will write to Charles." Annie Besant was undeterred. "You must go and see him when you return to Sydney. I am sure you will get as much from Co-masonry as I have over the years. You must take your companions too."

He tried to dissuade her without admitting to being a Freemason—it was, after all, supposed to be a secret society. Annie Besant would not be moved, and so, it seemed he would be compelled to call on Charles Leadbeater with a letter of introduction.

Father Bryan came by their table to admire Edna, as did many young men. She dealt with it graciously, as she always did.

Milton nudged Rowland and pointed out Isobel, who sat at a table on the other side of the hall beside her uncle. Her gown was white, extremely modest with girlish flounces at the shoulders; her face was mutinous.

The ship's orchestra struck up a waltz and Captain Madding led his partner onto the parquetry floor. Many couples followed. Edna grabbed Rowland's hand.

"Come on, Rowly, let's test your leg."

He regarded her dubiously.

"Oh, don't be such a coward," she said pulling him up. "It's a waltz—just grit your teeth and dance. Excuse us, Annie."

The result of Rowland's first dance since the bullet had done its damage was not altogether successful, but neither was it a disaster. Edna chatted blithely in her usual manner, ignoring the fact that her partner was concentrating on forcing his leg to take the weight required of it.

"Sorry," he mumbled as he stumbled slightly on a turn.

She smiled at him. "Just don't fall—everybody's watching."

Rowland glanced up...the eyes of several young men were indeed following their every move.

"They're waiting for a chance to cut in." He winced as they cut into another turn. "They're probably hoping I'll fall."

Edna giggled. "You're not going to—you used to quite like dancing—what happened to you?"

"You shot me, I believe."

"Are you still going on about that?" She laughed. "I thought you'd forgiven me."

"Nothing to forgive, Ed."

She gazed at him openly, intensely, and he looked away in case his knees buckled again.

"We've had fun, haven't we, Rowly?" she said. "I never imagined the world to be so marvellous."

Rowland nodded. "It's been smashing. Are you sorry to be going home?"

"We have a while before we see Sydney," the sculptress replied. "And we'll see the world again." She rested her face against his lapel. "We have yet to conquer it, Rowly."

"I rather think you already have," he said, though he knew she was talking of their work. Edna had always been more ambitious than he—for both of them.

"As I thought." Rowland caught sight of Hubert Van Hook weaving towards them.

He relinquished Edna to the arms of Van Hook and returned to the table. Milton and Clyde were on the dance floor, so he sat again with Annie Besant.

"You did very well out there, Rowland," the old lady commended as they watched Edna reign over the ballroom. "Your stick will be a distant memory soon."

"I certainly hope so." He leant in towards her. "Tell me Annie, did you know about Urquhart's association with Miss Hanrahan?"

She nodded gravely. "I'm afraid he was quite cocky about it. I begged him not to treat her badly...such a sweet, innocent thing." She fumbled for a handkerchief and dabbed her eyes.

"I'm sorry, Annie, I didn't mean to upset you."

"Quite all right, my dear boy...this has been such a tragic affair in every way. Miss Hanrahan is not a worldly creature... I've never seen Jiddu so angry. He, Orville, and Hubert all grew up in the movement...but only Jiddu truly understood the teachings of the Society...and Orville grew to be the furthest removed from them."

She smiled knowingly at him, her aged hand finding his strong one. "I'm eighty-five, Rowland. I had rather wished I could die leaving the ideals I have worked for in good hands. I had hoped to convince Jiddu to return but there is little chance of that now."

"Perhaps there will be someone else...."

She shook her head. "I cannot help feeling we have run out of time. Not so long ago the world was ready to hear of hope and tolerance, of brotherhood and love."

"And now?"

She sighed. "I have just come from Europe, Rowland. Mad, evil men are coming to power...men with closed minds and dark hearts...and before you ask, it is not clairvoyance but common sense that leads me to that belief." Her eyes were soft and bright with sadness. "I worry about young men like you, like Mr. Isaacs, who wears his ideals so outrageously, loyal Mr. Jones with his quiet decency...You must promise me that you will not let yourselves be changed—that you will keep your minds open."

Rowland pressed her hand warmly. He admired her, believed her, though he was not entirely sure what she was saying. "Annie, would you care to dance? I would consider it an honour and a kindness if you would."

Annie Besant laughed. "I should be delighted, Rowland. I am not yet too old to raise the occasional eyebrow, I think."

And so Rowland Sinclair danced with the great liberationist. Their steps were careful, without flair or showmanship, but their conversation was that of sincere friendship and mutual regard, and in that respect there was no misstep.

Chapter Seven

THEOSOPHISTS IN CHICAGO

CHICAGO

Mrs. Annie Besant was cheered when she expressed
hope of a reunion with the faction of Theosophists in
this country in her address at the annual convention
of the American Section of the Theosophical Society
held to-day at the rooms of the Chicago branch, in
the Athenaeum Building. An additional interest was
imparted to the occasion by the presence of the Countess
Wachtmeister and Miss Wilson.

—*The New York Times*

It was the first hours of the day. The party of Australians had
discarded their coattails, and sat in their waistcoats with their
shirtsleeves rolled as they dealt with the serious business of
cards. They played in the comfort of Godfrey Madding's private
suite in the company of both the captain and Yates, the ship's
ginger-haired doctor. Edna still wore the dark crimson gown in
which she had captivated everyone the previous evening, but she
was focussed now on the cards she held. A reasonable sum had
already changed hands in the course of the game.

Madding poured whisky generously for all except Rowland, who never drank the malted liquor voluntarily. It was a lively informal gathering, neither unduly raucous nor overly refined.

"I am afraid we were unable to find the photo of Miss Higgins' mother," Madding told Rowland quietly. "I'd say Urquhart disposed of it."

Rowland nodded. He had suspected as much. He would tell Edna later. For now, let her play cards.

"My staff captain confirms that Urquhart had been liaising with Miss Hanrahan since we left England. The crew had noticed them," Madding murmured. He shook his head.

"Do you think His Grace was aware of it?"

Madding shrugged. "I hope not, for the girl's sake."

Milton had just upped the ante in a show of bravado when the game was interrupted by an urgent knocking. Clyde answered the door to admit a crewman who sought Dr. Yates and the captain.

"There's been an accident on the first-class deck, sir," the sailor reported. "Dr. Yates is required to attend."

Yates rose immediately. He had been losing anyway.

"Spit it out, man," Madding demanded impatiently. "What happened?"

"Excuse me, sir. Mrs. Besant has fallen down the stairs."

The Australians now discarded their cards and stood.

Madding raised his hand. "You'd all best stay here," he said. "I realise Mrs. Besant is a friend of yours…I'll let you know as soon as possible…"

Madding and Yates left forthwith. Milton finished his drink and poured another as they waited.

"She'll be all right," he said, a little too loudly. "Annie's a tough old bird."

Madding was as good as his word and a crewman arrived within thirty minutes to inform them that Annie Besant had sustained a nasty knock to the head but was otherwise unhurt. Yates was keeping her in the infirmary until they made port in New York. The evening thus dramatically and abruptly concluded, they returned to their own suites to retire.

When Rowland Sinclair and his friends visited, Annie Besant was looking quite well despite the large bandage that swathed her forehead. She was sitting upright, sipping a cup of tea. Jiddu Krishnamurti was reading in the easy chair beside her bed. There were no other patients in the *Aquitania's* infirmary and so the nursing staff were most solicitous of her every comfort.

"Drunk again?" Milton suggested grinning.

"Don't be impertinent, young man!"

"How are you, Annie?"

"Thoroughly embarrassed, if you must know!" She smiled at the several young people who had entered the infirmary. "Everybody has been most kind, which only leaves me feeling sillier for my clumsiness."

Rowland Sinclair, Milton Isaacs, and Clyde Watson Jones lined up at the foot of her bed, all leaning against the rail as they asked about her health. Annie Besant regarded them fondly. It was a particularly Australian habit, she observed—to lean. Australian men seem to lean whenever possible—against walls, posts, chairs. Her late husband would have considered it offensive, slovenly, but Annie found it somehow charming…Australians had the ability to relax in any company or circumstance—they would face Armageddon itself leaning casually on a fence. It put her at ease in their presence.

"We're lucky you weren't more seriously hurt." Edna refilled her cup from a silver jug on the bedside table. "Whatever were you doing?"

Annie Besant chuckled. "I can't remember anything, Edna, my dear, but I'm sure I was not sliding down the banisters."

"What a superb idea." Milton laughed.

Krishnamurti shook his head making a clicking sound. "I had only just closed the door to my rooms when I heard the commotion," he said. "I ran out and found Amma had fallen."

"What's the last thing you remember, Annie?" Rowland asked.

"Why, I was dancing with you, dear boy."

Rowland smiled. "Well, that's not something you should forget."

"After that, things are a little confused, I'm afraid...I remember turning the key...but nothing else."

"We'll be in New York Harbour in a few hours." Clyde's weathered face furrowed. "Will you be strong enough to disembark, Mrs. Besant?"

"Dr. Yates seems to think so," she replied. "Don't you be concerned, Clyde dear—I will be well tended by our friends in New York. They've installed me at the Plaza—you must come and see me if you have time."

"We'll find time," Rowland assured her.

They stayed talking until Hubert Van Hook arrived with the Watermans and the Bensons, at which point they wished the Theosophists well and made their way to the observation decks. The vast majority of passengers had gathered for the *Aquitania's* entry into New York Harbour.

Rowland had visited America before, but his friends beheld the Lady of Liberty for the first time as the ship passed between Governors and Ellis islands. He stood back from them a little with his notebook, drawing their figures in the shadow of the colossal statue, capturing their awe and excitement in the forward lean of their bodies, the crane of their necks. He worked quickly, making individual studies of their faces, widened eyes, unconscious smiles, the backdrop of the great city itself.

"Bloody oath! Look at the size of those buildings!" Clyde gazed out at the arresting skyline. "They'd have to be thirty stories high."

"Seventy-seven, actually." Rowland spotted the decorative peak of the Chrysler Building.

"Americans!" Milton grunted. "Overcompensating."

"For what, exactly, Milt darling?" Edna's eyes glinted mischievously.

"The fact that we've got a better bridge," Clyde replied before Milton could.

The process of berthing and disembarking was a long and tedious exercise. They were detained only briefly to speak to the New York Police. As Madding had suspected, jurisdiction over Urquhart's murder was neither clear-cut nor coveted and the investigation seemed only cursory. Consequently, they were free to go only a short while later.

It was the end of October and winter had come early—the cold was damp and clawed at their lungs from within, the wind bit at the exposed skin of their faces. The port seemed to hold more people than lived in Sydney, all in great coats, their faces obscured by scarves.

Dispirited crowds of men huddled around lit drums and loitered near the shipping offices. Tattered women spruiked chestnuts and apples for pennies and underdressed children perched on ledges.

"Things are hard here, Rowly," muttered Clyde, who always noticed such things.

Rowland nodded. Just as the buildings and crowds in New York were bigger, so too did the economic hardship seem amplified. Perhaps it was the cold. Poverty would be particularly bitter in the New York winter.

"Oh, here's trouble," Milton warned, as he noticed Edna distributing the contents of her purse amongst a group of ragged children. Within moments she was swamped in a jostling crowd of juvenile beggars. Milton grabbed her hand, pulling her out and bundling her into one of the Cadillacs which were being loaded with their trunks. "Good thing your old chum sent cars for us," Milton said as he climbed in next to the chauffeur, "what with Ed trying to start a riot."

Rowland agreed. He looked a little troubled. "Perhaps I should explain about Daniel."

"Come on, Rowly, get in—you'll catch your death," Edna called from the backseat of the first car.

Clyde pushed Rowland in next to her, and then climbed in himself. "Where does this friend of yours live, Rowly?"

"The Warwick—he has the thirty-first floor, I believe."

"Thirty-first! You're kidding."

"I really should explain about Daniel…"

"You met him while you were at Oxford, didn't you?" said Edna. "I didn't know Americans went to Oxford."

"What line of business is he in?" Milton, turned back towards them from the front seat.

"Inheritance. His family is in railways. He likes to paint."

Clyde seemed to brighten a little. "So he's an American version of you?"

Rowland shifted uncomfortably. "I suppose so."

"He'll be all right, then."

"Danny's an excellent fellow, but…"

"He doesn't talk like Hubert, does he? That could be confusing."

"No, Danny's rather embraced European custom…or an interpretation of it anyway."

"You look nervous Rowly," Milton grinned. "Are you afraid he'll tell us what you got up to at Oxford?"

"Look Rowly, that must be Central Park!" Edna leaned over him until her face was pressed against the window.

They continued through the streets of midtown Manhattan, finally turning into West 54th Street at Sixth Avenue. The Cadillacs lined up outside the elegant entrance of the Warwick Hotel.

"Mr. Cartwright is expecting you, sir," the driver informed Rowland as they piled out. "I'll see that your trunks are sent up."

They did not linger out in the frozen day, and hurried into the foyer of the grand renaissance-revival building. The lobby itself was small and private but every detail spoke of quality and quiet opulence. A uniformed doorman directed them across floors of polished marble to brass-doored elevators.

"Mr. Cartwright's apartments, please."

The operator nodded. "Certainly, sir. Mr. Cartwright told me to expect you."

They watched the dial as the elevator climbed to the thirty-first floor. Rowland paid the operator—this was not his first visit to New York and he understood the American tradition of tipping. They stepped out into a small foyer, facing a large oak door nestled into a decorative arch.

Rowland hesitated before he knocked. He turned and spoke quietly. "I should probably warn you…"

"Rowly, old man!" The door flew open, making them all jump. "What the dickens are you doing out here?"

Daniel Cartwright stood in the open doorway, beaming. He was a rounded young man, with a full head of curly blond hair. His upper lip bore a thin, waxed moustache which gave him a distinctly European air. The gold brocade of his waistcoat stretched over the generous curve of his torso, and contrasted with the burgundy velvet of his smoking jacket. He grabbed Rowland Sinclair by the shoulders and kissed him on each cheek all the time exclaiming in unintelligible French.

"Bloody hell," Clyde murmured.

Rowland stepped back and shook Cartwright's hand. "It's good to see you, Danny."

"Ah Rowly, *mon ami*…it has been too long, far too long… how long has it been?"

"About five years, I should think. You haven't changed, Danny."

"You're too kind, Rowly my friend, too kind." Daniel Cartwright's accent was painstakingly British, even when he was speaking French. It was unusual for an American.

"May I introduce Miss Edna Higgins…?"

Daniel Cartwright exploded into a string of what sounded a little like French, as he clasped Edna's hands and kissed them. Rowland flinched at the appalling pronunciation and Edna, whose mother had been French, giggled. Rowland finished the introductions. Their host greeted Milton in the same ostensibly Continental style that he had Rowland. Clyde thrust out his hand, more an act of defence than greeting, and kept a wary distance.

Rowland laughed.

"You can't kiss Australian men, Danny boy—I thought I'd told you that."

Daniel Cartwright smiled. "I'd hoped that civilised custom had made its way to the outpost colonies by now."

"We may need a few more years," Clyde said brusquely.

"I say, why are you all standing on my doorstep like hopeful carpetbaggers? Come in, for heaven's sake…I'll have my man organise refreshments."

He left the door open for them and turned into the apartment, calling, "Bradford…Bradford…where the devil have you got to?"

The sitting room they entered was lavish—the wood panelling had been painted white as had the stately columns and arched architraves. The walls were deep red and ornately framed works of art hung at regular intervals. The furnishings were more extravagant than masculine or even fashionable.

A stern-faced man in black tie and tails came into the room. "You called, sir?"

"Oh, there you are." Cartwright beamed. "May I introduce my man, Bradford," he said. "Bradford, these are the guests I've been expecting—my old chum, Rowland Sinclair, and his dear friends, Miss Higgins, Messrs Isaacs and Watson Jones."

Bradford inclined his head in acknowledgement. "Shall I serve tea, Mr. Cartwright?"

"I suppose you could…I was rather hoping you'd serve something a good deal stronger."

"Certainly, sir."

The butler retreated to fulfill the request.

"I thought America was still dry," Milton said, with reference to the prohibition enforced since the early twenties.

"Just a formality," Cartwright assured him. "This is New York City—there's a speakeasy on every corner and Bradford is a member of the best dozen."

Cartwright demanded that they make themselves at home and inform him of their every whim. He took them into the large space he used as a studio. It was furnished with several massive easels, shelves laden with equipment and materials, and immense drying cupboards. Upon the far wall were hung three magnificent mirrors, each at least ten feet high and framed in gilt.

The familiar smell of oils and turpentine reminded Rowland of how much he missed working. He and Clyde had set up a makeshift studio in France where they had stopped for some weeks, but since then he had been able to do nothing but capture ideas and images in his notebook. It wasn't the same as painting.

Cartwright stood before a work in progress, explaining his choice of palette to Edna. The painting was a self-portrait; its scale larger than life. Rowland studied it from a distance. Cartwright's work had improved, refined in the past years.

Milton and Clyde had been taking in the paintings on the other easels, as well as the gallery of canvases that lined the unmirrored walls. They came to stand on either side of Rowland, their arms crossed as they watched Cartwright discuss the finer details of classical composition with Edna.

"Rowly," Clyde's voice was low and touched with disbelief. "These paintings...they're all of him...Cartwright...all self-portraits."

Rowland nodded. "Yes, Danny only paints himself."

"What? Always?" Milton whispered, incredulous.

"Never known him to paint anything else. I must say," Rowland motioned towards the latest portrait, "he's getting quite good at it."

"Does it not strike you as odd?" Milton persisted.

"It's bloody odd," Rowland confirmed. "You should see his nudes."

Bradford appeared suddenly to inform them that refreshments had been served in the dining room.

"Marvellous! I'm perfectly famished. Thank you, Bradford." Cartwright offered his arm to Edna and led the way.

"I say, Rowly," he said as they entered the Baroque-styled dining room. "You're limping..."

"Old injury, long story, Danny." A twelve-foot table had been laid with white linen and set with silver cutlery. It appeared Bradford's idea of refreshments was a banquet for at least a dozen people. The butler stood by a silver trolley mixing cocktails. Another large portrait of, and by, Daniel Cartwright dominated the internal wall. The external wall boasted large windows overlooking Sixth Avenue.

Edna ran to the windows delighted by the view and the autumn glory of the street trees.

"This is simply breathtaking, Mr. Cartwright."

"Danny," Cartwright corrected. "Yes, it is rather a pleasing view. Of course Marion's is better—she has the penthouse—but you'll see that this evening."

"This evening?"

"Marion?"

"Miss Marion Davies—you may have seen one of her pictures—she's having one of her little supper soirées this evening—positively fabulous in every way."

"And we are invited?" Edna stammered. Miss Davies' films had screened in Sydney. Her fame was more than trifling.

"Why, of course," Cartwright replied. "She's a peach, dear Marion, and takes an inordinate delight in fellow artists. I've taken the impertinent liberty of accepting for you, so it's settled."

Bradford served the cocktails he had just mixed and they sat before the elaborate luncheon. Edna asked excitedly about Marion Davies, and Cartwright was only too happy to oblige with tales of his illustrious neighbour.

"They are here infrequently," he explained. "Marion has many houses in which she and Randolph entertain…"

Rowland was only half listening, having been presented by Bradford with a silver tray on which lay a letter from home. He was not surprised by the correspondence. His brother, Wilfred, seemed to be keeping a careful eye on their itinerary. Letters met him at most of their stops, containing matters of business, instructions and cautions, and the occasional line of personal discourse. For the most part, Rowland complied with whatever errand Wilfred devised, without question. The protection and expansion of the Sinclair fortune had always been his brother's prerogative and talent. Rowland had instead secured the role of prodigal son, and he found it suited him.

"From Wilfred?" Clyde asked, as Rowland cast his eyes over the neat, precise hand.

Rowland nodded. "Apparently Lenin's been chasing sheep…" he murmured, smiling. "Wil's threatening to have him shot." Lenin was Rowland's dog—a particularly ugly one-eared greyhound of dubious bloodline, who had been in Wilfred's care since they left Sydney.

"Poor Lenin." Milton sipped Bradford's excellent vodka martini. "It's probably his destiny to be shot by the ruling class."

"Wil's just being Wil. He's more likely to shoot me than the dog." Rowland read on and laughed aloud. "Apparently Len's been having his wicked way with the working dogs."

"So, you're not the only one upsetting the Sinclair breeding plan," Milton sighed.

"Fair go." Clyde grinned. "Rowly could still find a nice girl from a good family and make a quite suitable marriage."

"I say." Cartwright dragged himself from his conversation with Edna, having overheard the last. "I could introduce you to some splendid young ladies tonight…not exactly suitable in the strict sense…but quite charming in an inappropriate sort of way."

"Marvellous idea, Danny," Rowland replied. "Thoroughly decent of you."

They spent the remainder of the afternoon in casual uninhibited conversation. Daniel Cartwright proved an easy host, whose past association with Rowland Sinclair gave rise to reminiscences and stories—some of which Rowland refused to confirm, others which he flatly denied. Bradford and other domestic staff appeared every now and then, to see to the table, refill glasses and unobtrusively ensure the comfort of Daniel Cartwright's Australian guests.

Chapter Eight

Movie Review
Blondie of the Follies –
A back-stage comedy

The assumption in "Blondie of the Follies", which was jamming the auditorium of the Capitol yesterday, is that there is still something to record about the life of a Follies girl.

Marion Davies and Robert Montgomery are completely satisfactory in the leads. Both as light comedians and as seriously disturbed and frustrated lovers, the two players are admirable.

—The New York Times

The penthouse was crowded, the party in full swing. A jazz band played in the main hall and uniformed staff moved amongst the guests with elaborately laden platters. Daniel Cartwright announced their arrival with a cacophony of very bad French, kissing the cheeks of everyone within reach.

Rowland tried not to look embarrassed.

The New Yorkers, however, seemed not to find his behaviour odd.

Cartwright led them through the shuffling forest of people to meet their hostess. Marion Davies was elegantly ensconced on a chaise, the pleated folds of her white chiffon gown draped over the gentle rise and fall of her famous figure. Her hair was platinum, almost dazzling, and swept into carefully ordered curls on the top of her head.

"Danny, darling," she crooned as Cartwright kissed her hand and greeted her with more of his appalling French. He introduced his guests.

To the men, Marion Davies was gracious; to Edna she said, "Why, my dear, you're exquisite! Are you in the business?"

Edna responded enthusiastically that she had played a member of the crowd in the Australian production of *On My Selection*.

Milton and Clyde laughed. Even Rowland smiled. They had never taken Edna's forays into the cinematic world seriously.

"Oh, never mind them." Marion Davies moved so that Edna could sit beside her. "We all started as extras."

Milton sighed. "We'll never hear the end of this," he grumbled under his breath.

With Edna having found the favour of their hostess, Cartwright introduced his male houseguests to a succession of party-goers. Soon, they had all been armed with drinks and separated, as they were snatched into different circles of conversation.

It was some time later that Rowland broke away from one of the young ladies to whom Cartwright had introduced him. She was a little enthusiastic, for his taste. Beautiful, though. He wasn't sure when he'd become quite so particular. Perhaps he would not be so easily deterred after a few more drinks.

He found one of the small army of waiters, and procured another glass of gin. He cast his eyes back towards Edna who was still sitting on the chaise. Miss Davies' place was now occupied by a man. It was not surprising. Edna's companion was tall, clean-cut, no more than thirty. Rowland started as a flash went off beside him.

"That's Leach—or was Leach...he may have a new name now."

Rowland turned to look at the photographer, a wiry young man in a brown suit, with precisely parted and heavily slicked hair. The photographer smiled a crooked smile and stuck out the hand that was not holding a camera.

"J.C. Henry—my friends call me J.C.," he said, changing the bulb on his flash with one hand as he spoke.

"Rowland Sinclair."

"You're English—a friend of Leach's then?" Henry asked, continuing to snap pictures.

"Australian, actually," Rowland corrected. "Never heard of Leach. Is he English?"

Henry nodded. "They have a way with the ladies—Englishmen." He grinned as Leach took Edna's hand. "Of course Leach is an actor—that'd help, I guess." He looked Rowland up and down suddenly. "Say, you're not in the business are you?" He lifted his camera.

"God, no! Put that thing down."

Henry grinned sheepishly. "Sorry, professional habit…Newspaper business, you know."

"You're a newspaper photographer?"

The American nodded. "Marion sells papers." He winked and aimed his camera back into the crowd. "Being Mr. Hearst's girl makes her very photogenic."

Rowland glanced towards the newspaper magnate. He stood in the shadow of his glamorous mistress, but his manner was confident. A man aware of his own power and certain of Davies. Cartwright had briefed his guests on the unconventional relationship between Randolph Hearst and Marion Davies to ensure there would be no accidental gaffes.

"So what line of work are you in, Sinclair?"

"I'm an artist."

"Living the dream then? Marion's parties are full of dreamers."

"I suppose so," Rowland replied, not entirely sure what he was admitting to.

"Here, hold this." Henry handed him the camera, and taking a comb from his pocket, proceeded to groom his immaculate hair. He winked at Rowland. "Have you ever seen so many dolls, Sinclair?"

"Miss Davies certainly keeps some attractive company."

Henry retrieved his camera and turned the lens towards a pair of statuesque women.

"So," he said, "do you think the world is ready for another Austrian artist?"

"Australian," Rowland said patiently, but firmly. He had become accustomed to the apparent obscurity of his country. "There's quite a difference."

Henry laughed. "No kidding—get us some drinks, Sinclair, and you can tell me about the dames in your part of the world."

Rowland signalled a waiter and relieved him of two vodka martinis. J.C. Henry continued to talk, juggling the camera, flashbulbs and cocktail with extraordinary dexterity. The newspaperman was a personable, forthcoming sort of chap. He seemed to be well versed in what he termed "scuttlebutt," and shared this insight quite generously.

"I say, who's that?" Rowland pointed out a large woman in a shapeless gown of flowing purple. She wore a turban rather than a hat, and was talking earnestly to Milton.

"That's Madame Milatsky—she's a medium, quite celebrated, I'm told. She was very big in the Theosophical movement once, but she broke ties with them when all the scandal broke."

"What scandal?"

"Years ago now—I was just a kid." Henry changed his flashbulb yet again. "Nearly destroyed the Society, I'm told."

"Go on."

Henry shrugged. "Some kid—supposed to be a prophet of some sort—accused that Leadbeater character of indecency."

"Good Lord! Was it true?"

Henry shrugged again. "Leadbeater was supposed to be a bit queer, but he was cleared. Misunderstanding, apparently. The Society backed him, in any case."

Rowland stared at his glass. Charles Leadbeater, of whom Annie Besant spoke so highly.

J.C. Henry pointed his lens at the parquetry dance floor where Edna was now dancing with Leach. He let out a low whistle. "She's a new one—Leach does well, but she's outstanding." The flash exploded again.

Daniel Cartwright threw a paper onto a table laden with platters of bacon, eggs cooked in every conceivable manner, and a vast array of pastries. His house guests were at breakfast.

"Edna, my dear," he exclaimed. "Barely a day in New York, and already you grace the society pages."

"Really?" Edna opened the paper without bothering to mask her excitement.

Cartwright helped her find the appropriate page, which was dominated by a picture of the sculptress dancing with Leach. The caption declared the actor to be in love with the mystery woman in his arms.

Milton laughed. "Notice he's looking at the camera rather than at Ed."

"Archie's so handsome," Edna gazed at the photograph. "He's in films, you know—he's going to be a star."

Rowland raised his brow as he sipped his coffee, Clyde sighed audibly and Milton rolled his eyes. Edna's loves were hardly rare.

"Flash in the pan, Ed." Milton dismissed Leach as he reached for a croissant. "In a year or two no one will have heard of Archie Leach—he's giving you a line."

"He's invited me to dine with him tonight." Edna smiled, ignoring Milton, as was her habit.

They finished breakfast and embarked into the streets of New York, again staggered by the towering size of the city. Cartwright headed the expedition, drawing somewhat far-fetched comparisons between the modern commercial structures and the classical buildings of European antiquity. They listened with amused indulgence, though Milton laughed out loud when he referred to the Chrysler Building as the "Parthenon of the New World."

They took the elevator from the marble-lined foyer of the Empire State Building, to the observatory on the 102nd floor. From there, Cartwright pointed out the landmarks of Manhattan.

When they descended again to street level, Milton dragged them all into a cinema, on sight of the playbill. *All Quiet On the Western Front* was still showing, although it was now a few years since its original release. The film had been banned in Australia despite critical acclaim, making Milton all the more determined to see it. Very quickly Rowland became thankful for the darkness of the theatre. He had lost a brother to the war, images of which were now flickering on screen. Unconsciously, he leant forward, drawn into the film.

Aubrey Sinclair had fallen in France when Rowland was just eleven. He and William Dowd had been summoned by the headmaster together that day. They had both lost brothers. They had never spoken to each other again.

Rowland still did not know how exactly Aubrey died—children didn't ask such things. Instead he had fashioned an image of a quick and painless death, a single bullet, body and dignity intact. A heroic boyhood fancy he had come to believe in.

The film contradicted that notion with unflinching, graphic realism. Soldiers died screaming in no-man's-land, caught on barbed wire, drowning in mud and blood, in terror. He was unprepared for how much it hurt him to watch it.

He felt Edna grab his hand. Clyde pressed his shoulder briefly. Apparently, the darkness had not afforded him as much privacy as he thought.

Milton leaned into him as they left the cinema. "I'm sorry, mate, I didn't think."

Rowland shook off the apology. "It was a good film, Milt— bloody stupid to ban it."

Daniel Cartwright insisted they take luncheon at the Waldorf-Astoria. The hotel's chef was, according to their host, one of the city's greatest attractions.

"Where to now?" Edna asked, as she played with what she considered a bizarre combination of walnuts and apples, presented as a salad. She had ordered it on Cartwright's recommendation, but she remained unsure.

"I thought we might go see Annie," Rowland replied, also approaching the Waldorf's namesake dish with caution. J.C. Henry's revelations played on his mind. He wondered about Jiddu Krishnamurti and Charles Leadbeater.

"Capital idea!" Milton agreed.

Both Clyde and Edna were more than willing, and Cartwright intrigued to meet the renowned Annie Besant, so they finished the meal and climbed back into two of their host's white Cadillacs for the short drive to the Plaza.

Jiddu Krishnamurti and Mrs. Waterman, whom they had met on the *Aquitania*, were also visiting Annie Besant.

"Oh, how delightful." Annie was pleased to see them. "Jiddu dear, send the boy for more tea."

"How are you, Annie?" Rowland asked after the customary introductions and greetings.

"Much better, thank you, Rowland." She patted the place beside her for him to sit. "I see you are too," she added quietly, as she rubbed his knee. "You're barely limping at all."

"Solid ground quite suits me, I think." Rowland smiled.

Mrs. Waterman glared at the scandalous placement of Annie Besant's hand, her lips pulled into a tight line. Rowland had become quite used to the old lady's fondness for his leg. It was unusual, but then, so was Annie.

He tried to break the tension with a pleasant enquiry.

"Will you be staying long in New York, Mrs. Waterman?"

Mrs. Waterman sniffed. "Not long, we'll be taking the *Aquitania* back to Sydney when she sails."

"Then we will be fellow passengers again," said Edna warmly from where she sat beside Krishnamurti. "I'm just sorry Jiddu and Annie won't be coming too."

Mrs. Waterman looked at her coldly. "Yes, quite."

Edna shrank back.

Jiddu Krishnamurti put an arm protectively around the sculptress. "Yes, we will miss our new Australian friends—what do you say, Amma?"

"I more than you, Jiddu," Annie replied. "You at least are young enough to hope you may cross paths with our friends again. At my age, every farewell has a permanent ring."

Rowland watched carefully as Mrs. Waterman sniffed again. She was clearly disgruntled. He observed her closely for the first time—she had never really caught his attention on board. She was a tall, broad-shouldered woman, her size and posture quite manly. She hunched as she sat, as if self-conscious of her solid frame. Her face was long, her teeth large and her skin appeared as though it might once have been freckled. His painter's eye looked for her point of beauty—the feature he would bring out if he were painting her. There was perhaps a regal arch to her brow… but not much more. He wondered where her husband was.

The conversation moved to the crime spree currently pre-occupying the American media. Clyde Barrow and Bonnie Parker had been shooting their way to notoriety for the past several months. Milton countered with stories of bushrangers in a patriotic claim that Australian criminals were…well, more criminal. Daniel Cartwright offered the misdeeds of the American underworld in response and good-natured argument ensued. Jiddu Krishnamurti stood to make a telephone call. Rowland saw his chance to speak with him alone while the others were distracted. Excusing himself, he followed the disavowed prophet to the next room. He was surprised to find Krishnamurti sitting behind the room's large desk, waiting for him. He motioned for Rowland to close the door.

"Were you wanting to speak with me, Rowly?" he asked. "I got the impression that there was something on your mind."

Rowland nodded.

"Is it a question of faith?" the holy man enquired encouragingly. "You know, if you open your mind it is not necessary to reject your old beliefs in order to entertain new ideas."

"Oh…sorry…it's not that I'm afraid…" Rowland ran his hand through his hair as he regarded Krishnamurti awkwardly. "I wanted to ask you about Charles Leadbeater."

Krishnamurti's smile vanished. His dark eyes shifted nervously.

"Why do you ask?"

Rowland dishevelled his hair again. This was difficult.

"Annie's given me a letter of introduction. She thinks highly of him…"

"Amma's judgement is usually impeccable."

"In this case?"

"She is not infallible."

"Look Jiddu, you've known Leadbeater for many years. Tell me, man to man—do I want to know him?"

Krishnamurti shrugged, and then he said very slowly, "I think Charles Leadbeater is evil. If I were you I would destroy Amma's letter of introduction." He studied Rowland. "Amma genuinely believes he is innocent, you know."

For a moment Rowland held his gaze and then lowered his eyes, regretting that he had intruded into something so appalling, so personal. His enquiries seemed so trivial now. "I know. I'm sorry."

Jiddu Krishnamurti shrugged again. "It was a long time ago. We have all moved forward."

Chapter Nine

SPEECH BY HOUDINI, THE GREAT MYSTIFIER:

Can the Dead Speak to the Living?

"The first step towards the lunatic asylum is the Ouija board. Anyone who claims to be able to talk with the dead is either a self-deluded person or a cheat. Can the dead speak to the living? I say they do not. I am particularly well qualified to discuss this subject, as I have always been interested in spiritualistic and psychic phenomena. I have personally known most of the leading spiritualists of the last quarter of a century and it is a strange fact that they have been intensely interested in me."

Rowland stepped back from the canvas to survey his work. Daniel Cartwright was singing some dreadful French ballad from behind his own easel. The American was, of course, both artist and model.

Both Clyde and Rowland were happy for the opportunity to paint. Clyde had set out early that morning for Central Park, inspired by the colour of the American Fall. Milton had gone with him.

Rowland didn't even try to paint landscapes anymore, and he was not fond of working outdoors in any case. Instead, he had elected to use Cartwright's studio. Edna had stepped out with Archibald Leach once again, and consequently Rowland was forced to use his host as a model. And so it was that both men spent the day painting Daniel Cartwright.

"Danny, turn this way, will you?" he requested as he highlighted the points of light in Cartwright's eyes and on the tip of his nose.

"I say, Rowly, this is rather like the old days at Oxford," Cartwright said happily. "Two chums, *Les Frères d'Art*…"

Rowland really wished his friend would stop trying to speak French. Still, he'd enjoyed painting Cartwright. The American stood in a wine-red smoking jacket and beret, between a canvas and a mirror, once again in pursuit of the perfect self-image. Rowland's depiction caught Cartwright as he peered intently at his own reflection, paintbrush and palette in hand. He captured the slight curious smile that showed a man both pleased and fascinated by what he saw in the glass.

"So what did you make of Annie Besant?" Rowland asked in an attempt to bring an end to the French folk songs.

"A perfectly charming lady." Cartwright glanced from his canvas to the mirror to check that he had done himself justice. "The epitome of cultured hospitality. I found her delightful. Quite the gracious contrast to that Waterman woman, but I suppose that's to be expected."

Rowland looked up. "Expected? Why?"

"By George—don't you know? I thought being from Sydney you would have heard."

"No. What?"

"Richard Waterman—he's rather big in sugar, I gather, aside from his surgical practice—made a small fortune before the crash…I suppose you might not know him—new money, really."

Rowland waited for Cartwright to get to the point.

"He married an American girl—now Mrs. Waterman—she introduced him to the Theosophical Society—she was quite devoted to that chap, Krishnamurti."

"He's not really with the Theosophical movement anymore," Rowland pointed out.

"Precisely," Cartwright replied. "The Watermans worked with Leadbeater for years preparing to bring the World Prophet to Sydney—built some kind of Roman amphitheatre for Krishnamurti's arrival."

Rowland knew the amphitheatre on Balmoral Beach. He had always believed it just another folly built on the excesses of the twenties. "And then Krishnamurti abdicated."

Cartwright nodded. "Waterman had ploughed a king's ransom into building the amphitheatre, and of course the embarrassment of it all affected confidence in his other business affairs. It was a complete financial cock-up."

"So how do you know about all this?"

Cartwright shook his head. "Richard Waterman is in New York trying to borrow money to keep his other Sydney interests afloat. This sort of story has a way of getting round."

"Embarrassing."

"Rather."

Rowland put down his brush and wiped his hands absently on his waistcoat, smearing it in the same alizarin red he'd been using to capture Cartwright's smoking jacket. He could hear Bradford's formal courtesy in the other room. Apparently Clyde and Milton had returned.

They came into the studio a bit wind-blown but in good spirits. The venture into Central Park had seen Clyde produce several dramatic studies of seasonal colour as well as a few darker sketches of the dissolute, ragged men who now slept there. The bedraggled figures were stark in contrast to the landscaped beauty around them, but they had become as much a fixture as the benches upon which they huddled.

Clyde studied Rowland's finished portrait of Cartwright. He laughed. "This has worked, Rowly." He noted Rowland's paint-stained waistcoat and streaks of lighter pigment which showed up in his dark hair. "You're a mess as usual—I'd swear you were finger painting."

Rowland smiled and ran his hand through his hair again. He'd always been somewhat exuberant in the way he applied paint—it could be a little messy.

"Good Lord, Rowly, this is magnificent!" Cartwright looked at the painting for the first time. "I just cannot allow it to leave these premises…"

"It's still wet, Danny," Rowland replied, amused. "I couldn't take it even if I wished to do so." He considered his portrait of Daniel Cartwright, among the many others which adorned the various walls. "You're right—it belongs here…where it will be in good company."

"Quite so, quite so…I have just the place for it." Cartwright grabbed the still wet painting and headed into the main sitting room. His guests followed.

"I'll have it framed of course," Cartwright announced, "but you'll see that this is the perfect position…"

He gave Rowland's painting to Clyde and dragged over a chair so that he could remove the work that already hung over the mantelpiece. He tossed that painting carelessly to Rowland and retrieving his portrait from Clyde, hung it on the former's hook.

"See…perfect."

Rowland examined the painting in his hands, and glanced at Clyde and Milton.

"Danny, this is a Picasso."

"Yes, I believe it is. Was never really happy with it. Would you like it?…I have nowhere to hang it now…"

"Danny, this is a Picasso," Rowland repeated with slightly more emphasis, finding it hard to believe Cartwright had virtually flung the work at him.

Cartwright sighed. "Yes, I know, he's very fashionable now. He just always picks such dreary subjects…" He waved his hand dismissively at the painting and gazed appreciatively, almost lovingly, at the one he'd just hung on the wall. Clearly, he was satisfied with the exchange.

They dined that night without Edna, whose time was being monopolised once again by Archibald Leach. The sculptress seemed quite taken with the English actor.

When the meal was complete, they saw the evening out with brandy and cards. Daniel Cartwright insisted they play bridge. The Australians indulged their host's choice as they were just four. Cartwright explained trumps and tricks, bids and rubbers and they did their best to make a good fist of it, though they thought it a silly, overcomplicated game. They were quite pleased when Edna returned—with a fifth player they would have to play poker.

With this in mind, they showed a great deal more interest than they might have otherwise in the events of her day with Leach. Edna sat down and pulled off her gloves. Rowland dealt her in.

"Oh no, Rowly, I just want to sleep...it's been the most delightfully exhausting day." Her eyes glistened dreamily.

"But we want to hear all about it." Milton looked sideways at Cartwright in case the American sought to resurrect the game of bridge. "Stay and tell us everything...while you play a hand."

Edna regarded him suspiciously, but then overcome by an enthusiasm for the as yet unopened Broadway musical, to which Leach had taken her, she picked up her cards. "They were rehearsing some of the big dance numbers...I've never seen anything like it. Archie introduced me to the lovely man who played the lead—losing his hair he's but the most extraordinary dancer."

"So what's this show with the balding lead called, Ed?" Rowland took up his own hand.

"*Gay Divorce* I believe. It was completely wonderful."

"They're expecting it to be a hit," Cartwright agreed.

Edna continued to chat happily about her day discovering New York and, of course, Leach.

"Oh, you poor dear girl!" Cartwright's round face was a picture of empathy and concern, as he refilled a large silver trimmed pipe. "You mustn't let Archie break your heart."

Rowland smiled, Milton and Clyde laughed.

Cartwright seemed aghast that they could be so callous.

Edna was clearly touched. "Don't worry, Danny—Archie's very sweet...I think he'll be quite sorry when I go. We'll always be dear friends."

Milton rolled his eyes and Clyde muttered, "Poor bastard." Rowland dealt again.

"So will you be joining us tomorrow evening?" Milton asked. "Or are you forsaking us again for that...actor?"

"What do you have planned tomorrow?" Edna re-ordered her cards.

"We're going to a séance," Milton said casually.

"Did Annie...?"

"No," Rowland replied. "It was that Milatsky woman from the party. She was quite taken with Milton, apparently."

"Very perceptive, these clairvoyants," Milton added.

"So she wants to introduce him to the dead?"

"You might say that." Rowland pondered over a card.

"Tomorrow's the thirty-first," Milton informed the sculptress. "Halloween."

"I know." Edna tried to catch a glimpse of Clyde's hand. "It's nice that we'll see an American festival before we head home."

"It's also the anniversary of Harry Houdini's death," Milton explained patiently.

"The magician?"

"The world's greatest magician," Cartwright corrected. "I saw one of his shows when I was a boy—amazing...quite thrilling."

"It seems that the anniversary of his death gives rise to séances to summon the man himself," Milton went on.

"But why?" Edna was still a little perplexed.

"Could be something to do with the ten thousand dollars his widow has offered to the medium who manages to contact her late husband," Clyde said gruffly. Apparently, he was not altogether happy with the proposition.

"I thought Houdini didn't believe in spiritualism?" Edna yawned.

Milton shrugged. "So his ghost will be embarrassed." He laughed, pleased with the image of a red-faced apparition.

Edna rubbed her nose. "So you're hoping to see Houdini's ghost?"

"Of course not—it's nonsense. Rowly wants to talk to Madame Milatsky."

Edna turned to Rowland. "Why?"

Rowland picked up a card. "Madame Milatsky used to be a Theosophist. Thought she might know something about who'd be trying to kill them off."

"Oh, Orville," Edna said quietly. She shuddered involuntarily. "What do you mean *kill them off?* It was only Orville…"

"I'm not so sure about that…there's Annie."

"She fell—it was an accident."

Rowland put down his cards. "I'm starting to have my doubts. I figured out what was bothering me about that accident, when I was painting today." Painting had always focussed his mind— even about unrelated events.

"Annie's room was at the bottom of those stairs, not the top. Why would she have climbed them? It was Krishnamurti's room at the top of the stairs. I don't know many gentlemen who allow ladies to walk them to their door."

"Jiddu saw her fall."

"No, he heard a commotion and assumed she had fallen when he found her at the bottom of the stairs. Maybe she was attacked at her door."

"Couldn't she have gone back up the stairs to talk to Jiddu for some reason?" Edna persisted.

"She'd have had to be very close on his heels…he'd only just closed the door himself when he heard her "fall"…why wouldn't she have just called him back?"

"So you think this all has something to do with the Theosophists more than Orville personally?" Edna was thoughtful.

Rowland shrugged. "Maybe."

"And you think that Madame Milatsky might know who would want to kill the Theosophists?"

"I think they probably have their skeletons…nothing like a disenfranchised member for that kind of information."

"Bit of a long shot, Rowly." Edna looked at him sceptically.

He smiled and widened his eyes. "You're right—I just want to see a ghost."

"Now you're being silly—I'd better come with you." She helped herself to Milton's drink, beaming suddenly. "Mr. Houdini was very handsome, you know."

"Good Lord, Ed," Clyde muttered. "Surely you draw the line at ghosts."

Rowland glanced at Edna as she giggled over Milton's brandy. If anything could bring a man back from the dead…

Chapter Ten

Houdini's Death

It has become known that Houdini the "handcuff king," who died recently in New York, addressed a class of students in Canada on spiritualistic tricks. He commented in his address on the phenomenal strength of his abdominal muscles and their ability to withstand hard blows without injury. Without warning one of the students struck him twice over the appendix. He suffered no distress at the time, but in the train complained of pain. His doctor at Detroit advised an immediate operation. Houdini however, refused to disappoint his admirers, and gave his usual show at the Garrick Theatre, though as it subsequently appeared, the student's blow had ruptured his appendix. Peritonitis developed after the operation.

—*The New York Times*

Madame Anna Milatsky's rooms were in a less than salubrious part of the city. The buildings were noticeably dilapidated and the streets dotted with glowing drums around which huddled men who may or may not have had somewhere to sleep. Daniel Cartwright's white Cadillac was parked on the curb outside the

Manhattan Arms. The driver sat behind the wheel, smoking, watchful.

The foyer of the Manhattan Arms was old and worn but it was clean. Madame Milatsky lived on the eleventh floor. The elevator was out of order and so they climbed.

"Are you all right, Rowly?" Edna whispered, noticing the strength of his grip on the banister as they passed the ninth floor.

He nodded, though he was very aware of his leg. Still, it had been just over a week since he'd lost his stick. He motioned towards Cartwright, who was wheezing loudly, his round face red with exertion. "Better watch Danny, though."

The clairvoyant's door boasted her name on a polished brass plate above a heavy knocker fashioned to resemble a sphinx.

Several people were already within—it seemed Madame Milatsky had invited a sizeable audience for her communion with Houdini.

The lady herself came out to greet them, dressed again in a shapeless diaphanous gown of indigo, and an elaborate feathered turban. Though Rowland had gathered from his conversation with J.C. Henry, that she was a good deal older, Madame Milatsky appeared to be in her late forties. She held both of Milton's hands, closed her eyes and swayed a little as she seemed to sing, "Welcome my kindred brother, welcome."

Clyde glanced at Rowland. "Doesn't anyone just shake hands anymore?" he muttered as he hung back.

Milton introduced his companions and though she voiced welcome in the same melodious style, she did not clutch or sway again. Rowland smiled and gave Clyde a reassuring nudge.

A shrivelled man shuffled amongst them with a large tray of sliced sausage and cheese. Anna Milatsky insisted they take glasses of what she called ambrosia and which tasted to Rowland like black-currant wine.

Clyde sipped cautiously. "A couple of glasses of this and we'll all be seeing Houdini."

"Better keep an eye on Milt," Rowland warned. The poet

was already on his second glass. "If anyone's going to offend the dead…"

They milled sociably for a time, mingling with the eclectic gathering. Clyde studied the artworks that cluttered the papered walls. Strange representations of occult subjects, portraits of bearded men in robes and medallions, and then several saccharine oils of kittens with balls of wool. Observably, the artist in Clyde was more affronted than the Catholic, and it was these last paintings that caused him to recoil with horror.

"Who are you?" A stocky man with nervous downcast eyes approached Rowland.

"Rowland Sinclair." Rowland proffered his hand, which the other shook briefly.

"Is your mind open? This will only work if our minds are open." The man sounded very much on edge, and gulped the so-called ambrosia in gasping swigs.

"I don't believe I caught your name?"

"Whitehead." The answer was mumbled. The man would not look him in the eye.

"Gordy, darling!"

Whitehead jumped as Anna Milatsky approached and draped her substantial form around him.

"You must not be worrying, my liebchen," she crooned. "Mr. Houdini will only see welcome and open hearts here—his reception will be warm and loving and perhaps you will have the opportunity your conscience seeks." She pulled Whitehead's face into her ample bosom and, embedding it there, she stroked his hair soothingly.

Rowland shifted awkwardly and stared at his glass as the embrace prolonged. He wondered if Whitehead was suffocating. Eventually she released the man.

"Come!" The medium clapped her hands sharply. "We will begin!"

The room fell into a bustle of activity. A large round table was carried into the centre of the room, draped with a number of dark silk squares and surrounded by chairs. Curtains were drawn, candles were lit in their dozens, and incense burned. As the electric lighting was switched off, Anna Milatsky asked them all to sit around the table.

Rowland found a seat between Clyde and Edna. Milton sat to the right of their hostess, Whitehead to her left. There were more than a dozen people in the circle. Rowland observed with interest the faces cast in the warm gentle light of the candles. Shadows accentuated as well as softened features, eyes widened and sparkled in the dim, flickering light. He usually painted only in natural light but he was suddenly intrigued by the possibilities afforded by the naked flame.

Anna Milatsky sat imperiously and asked that they all join hands. She began to intone something that was halfway between a prayer and an incantation. She called on all present to emanate love from their very beings, to cast it outwards from their mortal bodies.

"Children of God," she commanded, "let your brothers and sisters feel your goodwill. As your heart beats, pulse the rhythm of your love through your hands." The medium began to squeeze the hands she held.

Rowland's brow rose just slightly. Edna's hand pulsed in his and trembled with suppressed laughter between each squeeze. Across the table, Milton was participating enthusiastically, squeezing with such vigour that Rowland could see the bespectacled man to the poet's right wince in rhythm. Clyde, in contrast, was not pulsing in either direction. The woman who held Clyde's other hand was becoming visibly frustrated that her squeezes of brotherly love were not being returned. Rowland noticed that Clyde's lips were moving silently in recitation. He was pretty sure it was the Lord's Prayer.

Madame Milatsky began to chant, imploring Houdini to make his presence known. The smoke of the incense wafted around the table creating a perfumed fog. Rowland noticed a draught—someone must have opened a window. Suddenly, the medium stopped speaking and collapsed onto the table still holding the hands of Milton and Whitehead. Rowland glanced at Clyde, wondering whether they should do something to assist the apparently stricken woman, but the unconsciousness was short-lived. Abruptly she was bolt upright, her limbs stiff, her eyes open and glazed. Garbled noises and a bubbling foam erupted from her mouth. Rowland blanched—was she having a seizure? Nobody else seemed concerned. And then Madame Milatsky began to speak in a strange harsh voice.

"I am here. Who calls me?"

For a moment nobody seemed willing to admit to having summoned Houdini from the beyond. Then Whitehead spoke.

"Mr. Houdini?"

"Call me Harry."

"Harry, Mr. Houdini—it's me, Gordon Whitehead."

"Why have you called me?" The medium's voice still rasped and spittle continued to froth at the edges of her mouth.

"I'm sorry, Mr. Houdini. I just wanted to tell you I was sorry." Whitehead's voice was thick, choked with tears.

Rowland watched him carefully. Whitehead was a young man, no older than he; his accent had faint French overtones—Canadian perhaps. His eyes were grey and haunted.

Whitehead sobbed quietly as he repeated his declarations of remorse.

Finally the medium spoke again.

"It is done, Gordon. We have all made mistakes—I have made my own."

Whitehead broke down completely.

Madame Milatsky collapsed again; the circle startled as her head hit the table with an alarming thud. As before, it was short-lived and the medium lifted her face and wiped the foam from her mouth in just a few moments. She seemed a little confused.

"He has gone," she said wearily, as someone turned the lights back on. Hands were hastily released. Edna's eyes were merry, Clyde's still uneasy. Madame Milatsky took Whitehead's face into her bosom once again and consoled him as he wept.

"What is that all about?" Rowland asked Milton quietly as glasses and drinks were once more offered.

The poet shrugged. "Poor chap seems to think he killed Houdini."

"Oh. One would expect him to be in prison then?"

"He's probably mad," Clyde muttered. "Everybody else here is bloody barmy."

Milton laughed and grabbed Clyde's shoulder. "Open your mind, mate—we obviously didn't pulse enough brotherly love into you…"

"Don't touch me."

The party started to disperse. Anna Milatsky farewelled each of her guests with extravagant endearments. Whitehead too departed, but not before his face was pressed yet again into the comfort of the medium's bosom. Soon there were only the Australians and Daniel Cartwright left.

"Come, sit." Their hostess invited them into a small sitting room and called to the wizened man who had carried the tray of sausage. "Victor, bring some more ambrosia."

The medium directed Rowland to the chair by hers. "There are things you wish to know?"

"Yes."

She reached into a sewing basket by her feet and extracted a pack of cards. "Your aura is difficult to read," she sighed. "I will require the help of the tarot."

Rowland was startled. "No, I'm afraid that's not the kind of information I need."

Anna Milatsky's chest puffed haughtily. "Perhaps you don't want it, liebchen, but it remains to be seen what you need."

Rowland smiled. The old man brought in several goblets of the blackberry wine and handed round the glasses with ancient, shaking hands.

"I had hoped you might tell me a little about the Theosophical Society—I understand that you were once celebrated among them." Rowland chose his words carefully.

"Why?" Anna Milatsky regarded him suspiciously but Rowland's gaze remained steady.

"I have a letter of introduction to Charles Leadbeater," he said evenly. "And the sincere wish of a good friend that I begin an association with the gentleman."

The medium shrugged. "There was some ugliness years ago."

"And that's why you left the movement?"

"There were many reasons."

"Come on, Anna," Milton cajoled. "Rowly's all right. Can't you see how pink his aura is?"

The clairvoyant stared at Rowland, apparently assessing Milton's claim. "You are difficult to read," she said. "But there is yellow…"

"Yellow?" Rowland exclaimed, mildly affronted as he made the usual association with cowardice.

"Yellow signifies intellect," Milatsky explained.

"Must be the light," Clyde muttered.

Rowland tried to keep the doubt from his face.

"There is also blue," the medium mused. "It indicates devotion."

"That's got to be wrong," Clyde exclaimed. "Rowly's a Protestant."

Milatsky fixed Clyde with a chilling glare and he retreated. "Sorry…go ahead…"

She turned back to Rowland. "There is also a darkness. Your interest is to do with death." Anna Milatsky sat back smugly.

Rowland said nothing, waiting for her to go on.

"Orville…poor Orville," she said. "Perhaps, liebchen, you would like me to call his spirit."

Rowland shook his head. "Afraid I didn't take much to him when he was alive."

"And yet it is his death that brings you to me—I see the disturbance in your aura."

"Did you know Orville, Madame Milatsky?" Edna decided Rowland had been subjected to quite enough scrutiny.

The old clairvoyant sighed and drank deeply from her glass of ambrosia. "Yes, I knew him as a boy. I knew them all."

"All? The Theosophists?"

"Yes, the Theosophists, too. But I meant his family, liebchen. His mama and papa and the other one…Arthur."

"Arthur?" Milton asked.

"The Urquharts had two boys—as different as night and day. Arthur never accepted the wisdom of the Mahatmas…I suspect Orville didn't either, but he was by nature compliant." Madame Milatsky drained her glass. "Arthur left to live with relatives when he was still a child—broke his mother's heart. She took many boys into her care after that, mothering them to close the hole left by the loss." The old woman shrugged sadly. "Orville found that difficult of course…he did not like sharing his mother. Still, she always hoped Arthur would return—it is why they arranged their affairs as they did." The clairvoyant paused as the aged gentleman refreshed her drink. The dark liqueur seemed to be overcoming her initial reluctance to speak of the Theosophists.

"Just how did they arrange their affairs?" Milton was the first to ask.

"Ahhh, liebchen." Anna Milatsky sipped again. "The Urquharts were immensely wealthy, you know…but those poor boys were orphaned about a year after Arthur went away. Their fortune was held in some special account—administered and controlled by people even now, I believe."

"People?" Cartwright broke his polite, somewhat flabbergasted silence. "Do you mean trustees?"

"Yes, yes, liebchen, that's it."

"Do you know who the trustees of the Urquhart estate are?" Rowland asked hopefully.

"Of course…it is not a secret," the medium replied. "Annie Besant, naturally." Her voice took on a caustic tone. "Madame President got involved in everything. Then there is Charles Leadbeater—the Urquharts never believed the allegations…indeed, Orville spoke for him…" Anna Milatsky's voice was thick with the ambrosia and her eyes had become a little glazed and heavy.

Edna reached over and nudged Rowland. "We should say goodnight I think, Rowly."

"Yes, of course."

They stood and thanked the medium for her hospitality. Rowland pressed a roll of bills into her hand as he said goodbye. She slipped the payment into her significant cleavage and then gripped his arm. Her eyes were suddenly clear. "You be careful," she said.

Chapter Eleven

CRIME IN NEW YORK

According to Mr. Flynn, chief of the Secret Service of New York, the American metropolis beats Paris and every other city for organised gangs of criminals, and London by comparison is the most virtuous city in the world.

—The Argus

Rowland adjusted his tie as he stood before the gilded mirror of the dresser. He ran his hand through his hair as he turned away, making redundant the short time he'd just spent combing it into place. It was their last morning as guests of Daniel Cartwright.

The gentlemen were waiting for him in Cartwright's studio— Edna was spending a final few hours with Archibald Leach. Rowland found Cartwright discussing washes with Clyde whilst Milton perused the paper.

"Tell you what, Rowly," Clyde looked wistfully at the piece he was working on. "It's going to be hard to stop working now that we've started again."

"I've sorted that," Rowland replied casually. "I've taken another suite on the *Aquitania* so we can use it as a studio. It's a few weeks to Sydney."

"Capital idea, Rowly old boy," Cartwright approved. He always took multiple staterooms himself.

"They can do that?"

"Apparently half the first-class accommodations are empty these days—Cunard is more than happy to have me take the suite."

Cartwright departed to let Bradford know they were ready for breakfast. Milton followed him to make sure that the American pancakes of which he had become fond would be on the menu.

Rowland hung back because he noticed Clyde seemed troubled. "Problem?"

Clyde shifted, embarrassed. "I dunno, Rowly…this trip is already costing you a fortune…another suite…?"

Rowland laughed. "Oh, that. Don't worry about it, Clyde."

Clyde shook his head. "I hate to sound like your bank manager, mate, but we're in the middle of a financial Depression. Wool prices are down…surely even the Sinclairs…?"

Rowland smiled. He rarely talked about money. He was touched and a little amused by Clyde's concern. He leant back against an empty easel.

"The current Sinclairs are benefitting from the law of diminishing heirs," he said solemnly. "I believe I'm technically worth more now than I was before the crash…though you'll have to ask Wil if you want actual figures…" He grinned at the implausibility of Clyde doing any such thing.

"Diminishing heirs?" Clyde was clearly dubious.

"Really—it's an established economic theory. Trust me, I was at Oxford."

Clyde snorted. "Exactly how are you diminishing?"

"Sinclairs seem to have a habit of dying without producing heirs," Rowland replied sagely. He was not speaking entirely in jest. "It means wealth gets consolidated rather than divided with each generation…the more wayward sons live lives of indulgence and scandal, but in the end do their bit by leaving no acknowledged issue to dilute the family fortune." He laughed. "I believe that's why we're tolerated."

"No acknowledged issue?" Clyde's brow lifted askance.

"Well, we're not monks."

Clyde laughed now. "No, I guess not…"

Having reassured Clyde that his fortune could withstand his present rate of squandering, they joined Milton and Cartwright for breakfast. The conversation lingered for a while on the previous evening's séance. Milton now claimed an ability to see auras. Clyde called him an idiot. Rowland was inclined to concur.

"If you chaps don't mind," Rowland checked his wristwatch, "I'd quite like to call on Annie before we board."

"We'll have to get moving then, Rowly." Milton devoured his pancakes with more haste. "We board at midday."

"You go—take one of the Caddies," Cartwright directed. "I'll see that your trunks are loaded, pick up Edna, and meet you at the boat…don't you worry."

"Good show, Danny…you're a gentleman."

"I'll make sure they've organised the second suite whilst I'm at it," Cartwright continued affably as he fussed with the edges of his moustache.

"Are we just saying goodbye?" Clyde poured syrup over his own stack of pancakes.

"Not entirely. I thought I should warn Annie."

"Really? You're that sure someone's trying to kill off the Theosophists?"

"No. I'm not sure at all," Rowland admitted. "But I thought I should say something—just in case."

"She's going to think you're mad," Clyde warned.

"Annie talks to dead people, Clyde," Rowland reminded him as he glanced through the paper. Edna and Archibald Leach graced the society pages once again. "I hope Ed remembers we're sailing today."

Once breakfast had been adequately dispatched, they set out to call on Annie Besant. The Plaza was only a short walk from the Warwick and so they refused Cartwright's offer of a motorcar. The day was sunny, but the brightness held no warmth. Their breath misted before their faces and the sidewalks were glazed with ice. Still the walk was not unpleasant. The vertical magnitude of the city was imposing, unsteadying, with a sort of reverse vertigo.

Clyde took off his hat and gazed straight up.

"What are you doing?" Milton demanded as they waited for him to start walking again.

"Just checking that the sky's still there."

They announced their arrival at the Plaza's elegant reception and were taken straight up to Annie Besant's rooms. Rowland noticed the several voices as he knocked—apparently they were not the first to visit. Jiddu Krishnamurti admitted them warmly.

Annie was holding court in the sitting room with Hubert Van Hook, two uniformed police officers, and a man in an ill-fitting, dark brown suit.

The holy man introduced the Australians to the detective and his colleagues, who were in the process of taking their leave.

"Okay Annie, what have you done?" Milton asked once they had gone.

Annie smiled at the long-haired poet. "You really are the most impertinent young man...they were just here about the shooting."

"Shooting? Who was shot?"

"Nobody, thank goodness. Some ruffian shot at Jiddu and me in the street yesterday..."

"Good Lord," Clyde exclaimed. "Are you all right? Did they catch him?"

"We're both quite unharmed, Clyde dear, and no, they didn't catch him."

"Did you see him?" Rowland asked, frowning.

"I'm afraid not, Rowland...but you mustn't worry. It was probably some poor desperate vagrant...."

Rowland said nothing as he leant pensively on the back of an armchair.

"New York's a dangerous town," Van Hook said from where he sat beside Annie. "There's always some bum trying to bump off big shots for a few clams."

Milton looked blankly at the American. "I beg your pardon?"

"I'm just saying some sap may have figured Annie and Jiddu

for high hats with deep pockets and tried to jump on the gravy train, if you know what I mean."

"Actually, I have no idea,' Milton replied calmly.

"It may not have been random, Annie," Rowland interrupted.

Annie Besant's old eyes narrowed. "Why would you say such a thing?"

"Because I am afraid you may be in real danger." He regarded the old woman with undisguised concern. "I think someone may be trying to kill the Theosophists—or at least the eminent ones." He told them of his suspicions—that Urquhart had been killed because of his connection with the movement, and that Annie's "fall" on the *Aquitania* was not what it seemed. "And now this latest attempt on your life."

Annie Besant reached out and caught his hand. "My dear boy, you are so sweet to worry about me…but I am not new to such threats…I was, you know, a suffragette…"

"Perhaps you should listen to Rowland, Amma." Jiddu Krishnamurti's countenance was serious.

She sighed. "I have decided to go home to India," she said quietly. "I will accompany Jiddu when he sails next week." She laughed ruefully. "There is after all no place safer than home."

"Perhaps I should tag along," Hubert Van Hook suggested. "To India, I mean—be your goon so to speak…just to make sure everything's copacetic."

"No, Hubert dear, that won't be necessary." Annie Besant seemed to have no trouble understanding Van Hook's peculiar turn of phrase, but then, she was clairvoyant. "I will have Jiddu, and Charles is expecting you in Sydney. I will look forward to seeing you in Lahore, in March. We will have plenty of time to organise things then."

Van Hook protested and they argued back and forth for a time. Krishnamurti spoke quietly to Rowland.

"I will arrange for security. I will take Amma home safely."

Rowland nodded. "I may be wrong," he said. "I hope I am— but I'd rather be cautious."

Annie finally prevailed.

"If you say so, Ma." Van Hook scowled. "I wouldn't want to disappoint old Charlie."

To Rowland, it appeared a fleeting discomfort crossed Annie Besant's face, but he couldn't be sure.

He noted the time. "We'd better get moving or we'll be left on the docks," he said. "Are you coming with us, Hu?"

Van Hook nodded.

They shook Krishnamurti's hand and wished him a safe journey. The holy man responded with a short dissertation on friendship and understanding. Annie Besant farewelled them tearfully once more and seemed certain that she would not see them again. Her conviction may have been clairvoyant, or simply because she was eighty-five.

The Plaza's concierge arranged a motorcab, ensuring Van Hook's trunks were loaded, and they proceeded to the docks where the *Aquitania* had been berthed since she had delivered them from London. They disembarked into an excited press of boarding passengers.

Van Hook left them to find a porter for his luggage, and they made their way towards the gangway.

"Rowly, I say, Rowly! Over here!" Daniel Cartwright's voice rang over the noise of the crowd.

They spotted Cartwright and Edna standing in a pack of men. As they approached, Rowland recognised J.C. Henry, who responded to his salutation by taking a picture. It seemed to set off the others and Rowland blanched as they were greeted by a barrage of exploding camera bulbs. Then, the reason behind the fuss became clear. Archibald Leach had come to see Edna off.

Leach offered him the hand which was not entwined with Edna's. Rowland shook it. "Leach. Good to see you again."

Cameras flashed. Rowland wondered momentarily what caption would accompany that particular picture.

The actor was charming, joking with the photographers and journalists with the air of one entirely at ease in the spotlight. He spoke movingly, tragically, of the impending parting. Edna said very little, playing absently with the string of pearls Leach had presented her as a parting gift. The cameramen were insatiable, taking photograph after photograph.

Eventually they turned to make their way onto the gangway, beyond which only passengers were permitted to pass. Leach caught Edna in a dramatic farewell embrace and kissed her passionately. The cameras clicked into action once more.

"I say, that's a bit forward," Cartwright blustered as they watched from the background.

"Actors!" Milton muttered in disgust.

Rowland ignored Edna and Leach, and shook Cartwright's hand warmly. "Thank you, Danny boy."

"A pleasure, *mon ami*," Cartwright returned. Inevitably he felt the need to express the depth of his amity in French. Rowland tried not to flinch as the language was desecrated by his old friend. Typically, the American finished by kissing the Australian on each cheek in a way that was vaguely European.

Clyde and Milton, too, thanked their erstwhile host, though they threatened to harm him should he try to kiss them. Cartwright laughed and called them colonial philistines. Edna finally dragged herself away from Leach, to embrace Cartwright and farewell him in the French he so adored, but had never mastered.

J.C. Henry caught up to them.

"You're off then, Sinclair." He dropped the flashbulb he held into his pocket and shook Rowland's hand. "Bon voyage, pal." Rummaging inside his jacket, he produced a card. "Let me know if you want copies of those pictures. They say Leach could be big someday."

Rowland smiled. He doubted it. "Good luck J.C. Look me up if you're ever in Sydney."

"I'll do that, Sinclair. You keep living the dream."

Brass bands were in full swing now, a colourful paper rain of streamers fell around them; the atmosphere was festive.

"Living the what?" Clyde asked once Henry had disappeared into the crowd.

"The dream, apparently," Rowland replied.

Milton shook his head. "Americans!"

Chapter Twelve

RMS *Aquitania*

And to complete her likeness to a splendid home in which the passenger is a distinguished guest, the *Aquitania* offers service that is perfect. Much of the attendance on the wants of the traveller is so skillfully accomplished that one is unconscious of the means by which his wishes are fulfilled.

—*The Cunard Steam Ship Company Ltd*

Rowland and Clyde inspected the Gainsborough Suite which had been set up as a studio. Most of the furniture had been removed, save a couple of armchairs and a chaise lounge. Daniel Cartwright had done an admirable job in seeing it was well-stocked, and in anticipating those painting supplies that were not contained in the trunks brought up from the *Aquitania*'s hold. He'd even had one of his signature self-portraits hung in the main room for their viewing pleasure.

Clyde smiled as he studied the painting. "He's a good bloke, your Danny."

"Outstanding," Rowland agreed. "Once you get used to him."

Having established that the rooms had been adequately equipped they returned to the Reynolds Suite to dress for dinner.

"I'll be glad when we're home and not expected to change clothes three times a day." Clyde struggled with his bow tie.

"It gives the upper classes something to do," Milton replied, looking every inch the gentleman himself. "Otherwise they'd be wandering the streets in search of a purpose."

"We have a purpose," Rowland looked up briefly from his book. "We just like to serve it in dinner suits."

"Drink, Rowly?" Milton poured himself a glass of scotch.

"No, I'm fine." Rowland glanced at Clyde who was swearing at the strip of material with which he had been wrestling. "For pity's sake, help Clyde out before he hangs himself."

Shortly thereafter they set out for the restaurant, picking Edna up on the way out. As the sculptress was not yet ready they waited in the narrow hallway. A few minutes later Bishop Hanrahan and his party approached from the other direction. The bishop forced his squat form through them with a grunt. Father Murphy followed, in a mumbled exchange of "excuse me" and "I beg your pardon." Isobel squeezed past next. She paused as she brushed against Rowland and smiled. Since the bishop's niece had been in tears through most of their acquaintance, he was surprised by how lovely the smile made her face.

"Miss Hanrahan," he said cordially, and for some reason she blushed deeply.

Finally, Father Bryan sidled through behind Isobel. He greeted them affably as was his fashion. He asked hopefully after Edna and promised to catch up with them all later.

Milton knocked loudly on Edna's door as they watched the bishop's party descend the stairs.

"Hurry up, Ed!"

Eventually she emerged resplendent in a gown that plunged daringly at the back. Her sunset hair was caught loosely into a knot at the nape of her neck.

"What took so flaming long?" Milton complained.

"You look pretty, Ed," Rowland said quietly.

She put her arm through his, and once again he was the beneficiary of an enchanting smile. "Really? My back's a bit cold."

He looked at her from behind. "Yes, I can see how that would be an issue."

They were seated that night with the Theosophists who were continuing to Sydney. Among them were the Watermans, Colonel and Mrs. Benson, and Hubert Van Hook.

The numbers were evened by Mrs. Amelia Sommerville and her daughters, Alice and Margaret. Australians, they had just completed a tour of Europe and were returning home, having absorbed a great deal of culture and purchased several excellent hats. Amelia Sommerville was keen to get back to Sydney society, which she assured them, would have sorely missed her daughters.

"Sinclair?" she said when Rowland found a pause in her conversation long enough to introduce himself. "You must be one of the Woollahra Sinclairs?"

"Actually, I believe I'm the only Woollahra Sinclair these days," Rowland replied, a little uncomfortable with the elation of the society matron's voice.

"Why of course!" she gushed. "Girls, this gentleman is the son of Mrs. Henry Sinclair. Young man, your mother and I were great friends when she lived in Sydney. Indeed, my late husband and I dined often at Woodlands House. How is your dear mother—I haven't had word from her for some years now."

"I have every reason to believe she is well, Mrs. Sommerville," Rowland said politely.

"Oh dear," Amelia Sommerville lamented. "The war spoiled everything. If not for the war, I daresay your mother would not have left Sydney and you young people would have already been well-acquainted." She gestured expansively towards her daughters. Margaret smiled primly and Alice giggled. They were not unbecoming—coiffed, aging debutantes.

Rowland wasn't quite sure how to respond. His mother had left Sydney after Aubrey was killed serving in France. She had taken the loss of her middle son very hard—in fact, she still did. It was a little disturbing to have it reduced to a social inconvenience.

He decided to introduce his travelling companions. Amelia Sommerville's enthusiasm seemed to wane a little. Rowland had no doubt she was now remembering the scandalous rumours which surrounded Woodlands House in the last few years: stories of vice and immorality, Bolshevism and nakedness, hedonistic disrespect for propriety. Exaggerated, of course, but not altogether unfounded.

Nevertheless, Amelia Sommerville seemed delighted to find him seated between her daughters.

On the other side of the table, Edna tried valiantly to engage Mrs. Waterman in conversation but the Theosophist remained cold and curt. Despite the competing chatter of the Sommervilles, Rowland could hear the cutting responses to Edna's friendly enquiries. He could see the hurt and embarrassment on her face and he bristled. He was not the only one to notice. Hubert Van Hook intervened to engage Edna whilst Clyde spoke to Mrs. Waterman, who seemed less hostile with him. Rowland relaxed and returned some of his attention to his own conversation.

The Watermans retired first and the mood at the table improved markedly with their absence. It was Edna who noticed the wrap that Mrs. Waterman had left behind.

Rowland stood. "Shall I take it back up to her now?" he volunteered, glad to have some reason to escape the zealous attention of the Sommerville women. He winked at Edna. "Wouldn't want the old crone to come back looking for it."

Clyde tossed him the wrap.

"Good show—most thoughtful of you, son," Colonel Benson approved. "I believe their stateroom is number thirty-nine...the first-class deck, of course."

Rowland thanked him. The Bensons were a little stuffy but much easier company than the Watermans. He left the dining room and walked out onto the deck as he headed towards the first-class accommodations.

It was a mild night, the moon full and immense above the dark Atlantic. He stopped at the rail, taking in the black velvet sea beneath the encompassing sky. Glorious, but unpaintable.

There were some things that could not, should not, be captured in oil and canvas.

"Mr. Sinclair. It is a grand night, is it not?"

Rowland turned, startled by the unexpected voice. Isobel Hanrahan stood close behind him.

"Miss Hanrahan." He half expected a clergyman to emerge from the shadows. "Are you alone?"

"I am. I saw you leave, Mr. Sinclair. My uncle thinks I am visiting the powder room." She laughed softly. "He won't be following me there at least."

"But you're not there."

She gazed at him plainly. She was certainly beautiful. Even in the colourless cast of the moon, her skin seemed warm.

"I came after you." She stepped closer.

"Really? Why?"

Isobel smiled, conspiratorially, seductively.

"I was hoping you might like to kiss me, Mr. Sinclair."

Rowland was startled. He was perfectly accustomed to women who had come of age in the heady liberated twenties. Indeed, he found it entirely agreeable—but Isobel Hanrahan was a bishop's niece. It was hard to reconcile that she intended to be so forward.

"I would never presume…"

She leant into him. "I wish you would presume."

Common sense told Rowland that such a course of action was ill-advised, and yet he had no desire to offend the lady. Surely it would be discourteous to refuse such a forthright invitation. Isobel Hanrahan put her hand gently on his arm. In the end, civility prevailed over sanity and he bent down and let his lips find hers.

Again, he was surprised by the intensity of her kiss…there was little about it that was shy or chaste. It was ardent and lingering, and most definitely, pleasant.

Finally, she allowed him to pull away.

"I had better be getting back, Mr. Sinclair." The bishop's niece was decidedly breathless. "It's been grand—I shall look for you again."

Rowland studied her, somewhat bemused by Isobel Hanrahan's unexpected favour. "I think you had better call me Rowly."

She kissed him again, briefly this time, and walked back towards the dining hall. For a moment Rowland couldn't remember what he was doing standing out on the deck and then he glanced down at the wrap in his hand. Oh, yes. Mrs. Waterman—stateroom thirty-nine.

It was in this slightly preoccupied frame of mind that he approached the door of the Watermans' stateroom. The corridors were empty as most passengers were still at dinner. The door was ajar. Raised voices from within made Rowland hesitate.

"It's bad enough to have you simpering after Krishnamurti, but must you be so abominably rude to everybody else?" The surgeon's voice was furious.

His wife's strident American twang was quick and sarcastic in response. "Gallantly to the aid of the pretty young thing, Richard," she spat. "I can't make small talk with these insufferable people when there is so much to be done."

"For the last time, Frannie, we are *not* following Krishnamurti to India!"

"But don't you see, Richard? Annie is eighty-five. When she's gone, Jiddu will need a confidante—someone to help him with his work. This is my calling."

"Krishnamurti seems to prefer the pretty young things himself," Richard Waterman said cruelly. "Anyway he has resigned from the movement." The surgeon's voice was tightly controlled. "For Chrissake, woman, you have all but ruined us with your obsession with that man. I wish to God we had never got entangled with Theosophy. What use will your brotherly love be when we are bankrupted?"

"Let us be bankrupted then!" Francesca Waterman screamed in reply. There was a crash as something was flung against the wall. "I will go to India, Richard. You cannot stop me!"

There was silence in the wake of her declaration. Rowland saw his chance and knocked.

Richard Waterman answered the door, his face still red from the heated exchange that Rowland had overheard.

"Sinclair! What are you doing here?"

Rowland held out the wrap. "Mrs. Waterman left this behind."

The surgeon took the garment, clearly flustered. "I say, that's frightfully good of you. Frannie would forget her head…"

"No trouble at all," Rowland assured him. There was a brief moment of awkward silence.

"I might say goodnight, then." Rowland checked his watch. "I should return before I'm missed."

"Yes, of course," Waterman babbled. "I wouldn't be leaving that Miss Higgins alone for too long either." He grinned clumsily.

Mrs. Waterman's sniff was audible. She said nothing else but once more something was thrown against the wall. It sounded like glass.

The surgeon had Rowland's sympathy. The poor man appeared to have married a shrew.

"Well good night, Sinclair," Waterman blanched as his wife proceeded to hurl items about the stateroom.

Rowland's eyes were compassionate. "Good luck, sir."

Chapter Thirteen

GIANT AIRSHIPS

Large commercial airships will in the future be common
vehicles for long distance travel, especially for trans-
oceanic trips according to Mr. W. D. Shilts secretary of
the Goodyear Tyre and Rubber Company at Akron,
Ohio, USA, who recently spent several weeks in Australia on company business.

—*The Canberra Times*

Edna pegged another print to the line above her head, inspecting the result in the red safe-light. They had converted the
smallest room of the Gainsborough Suite into a dark room so
that she could develop the film shot on their travels. She had
originally left Sydney with her father's Box Brownie, determined
to chronicle their exile. Amused by her sudden enthusiasm for
photography, Rowland bought her a Vollenda in Germany—the
latest in photographic ingenuity. The camera was compact and
less cumbersome than the Brownie and importantly, it took
roll film. Over the past months Edna had become increasingly
fascinated with the medium, using it as an outlet for the creative
energy she would have otherwise expended in sculpture.

They had, since leaving New York, been on board more or less continuously for nearly a month now. The *Aquitania* had docked briefly in Ceylon, and they had spent a couple of days on the tropical island. They had stayed with some old friend of Rowland's father—an exotic sojourn of heat and spices, imperial luxury under mosquito nets. Other than that, the trip had been unbroken. They found themselves retreating to the improvised studio of the Gainsborough Suite more often as the days seemed to become increasingly similar. Pleasant, indulgent, but repetitive all the same.

When not occupied in the studio, they still spent many hours playing cards, dining, dancing, or being otherwise entertained. It was not a difficult existence. Hubert Van Hook joined them regularly, and Isobel Hanrahan sought refuge in their company whenever she could escape the notice of her uncle.

Edna ran her eyes over the series of prints she'd just pegged up. She'd taken them in Ypres where they'd stayed for some weeks. The haunting rows of white military headstones were sadly stark in the dim crimson light, the images poignant: Rowland, still on crutches, before the stone that bore his brother's name; Clyde gazing out at the reality of the war that they had been too young to join; Milton at the Menin Gate, reading the names of those whose remains were not recovered. She sighed, guiltily glad that the men she loved most had escaped the war.

She shuffled through the pile of prints from Germany. Was it because she'd just been looking at photographs of war graves? The pictures from Berlin seemed ominous. Milton larked for the camera as he always did, but in the background the onlookers appeared hostile, contemptuous. Photographs on the Zeppelin. Rowland had insisted they go—she'd been terrified of the vast and silent airship. Her new camera was the only thing that kept her mind from the fact that they were half a mile in the air, hanging beneath a bag of gas. There were several photographs taken in the Zeppelin's elegant passenger lounge. Even in these, there were brown-shirted officers seated behind them—they had been everywhere, watchful and arrogant.

She put the sheaf of prints down, thumbing through a selection she'd developed the previous evening—taken on board the *Aquitania* before they'd reached New York. There was a picture of Rowland and Annie Besant, deep in discussion. Orville Urquhart smiled at the camera from a chair beside the old lady.

Edna remembered that Isobel Hanrahan had wanted a portrait of the Englishman for the locket he had stolen. She thought sadly of her locket. Rowland had given it to her—though she couldn't remember why. Men of Rowland's means did not need occasions. He had dropped it casually into her hands and returned to drawing her. Perhaps he had just wanted to sketch her delight. She had never before owned anything so fine. Still, Orville was dead and none of this was Isobel's fault. She took the photo and slipped out of the blackened room.

Rowland and Clyde were both painting in the large parlour of the Gainsborough Suite. Milton sat in an armchair immersed in some supposedly celebrated book he'd picked up in New York, which he claimed was about "a bloke who didn't go to his own parties."

Rowland was working on a portrait of Annie Besant. Edna had offered him numerous photographs of Theosophy's World President, but he preferred to rely on his notebook and memory. For a time, Edna watched him work.

"What do you think?" he asked noticing her gaze.

"You didn't need my photographs," Edna murmured. "Annie's just magnificent, isn't she? Fierce and compassionate at the same time."

"I thought so."

Edna sighed. "I hope I matter like that one day."

"Matter?"

"Like Annie. She's changed the world, Rowly…imagine changing the world."

Rowland rather liked the world the way it was, but he wasn't going to risk starting a debate on equity and social justice. He was a Sinclair. It was not an argument he could win.

"What are you going to do with the background?" Edna touched the bare canvas around Annie Besant's likeness.

Rowland shrugged. "I'm not really sure."

"Paint her aura," Milton said, without looking up from his book.

Rowland laughed. "I'd consider it, but I can't say I've ever seen an aura."

"You need to be really drunk."

"What have you got, Ed?" Clyde emerged from behind his easel.

"Oh, this." Edna handed Clyde a photograph. "I developed it this morning. That's Orville standing by Annie…I thought Isobel might like to have it."

Milton laughed. Rowland returned to his painting.

Clyde grinned as he handed the photograph back. "I think you'll find Isobel's no longer grieving for Orville."

"Oh. Are you sure?"

Clyde looked at Rowland. Rowland kept painting.

"Isobel Hanrahan seems to have set her cap for our Rowly," Milton informed the sculptress. "All that Art can add to love, yet still I love thee without Art."

"Wilmot," Rowland said, "and a trifle melodramatic."

Edna dropped into the chaise lounge. "Really?" She smiled delightedly at Rowland. "How lovely."

"Yes, quite." He did not object to Isobel's interest. She was a beautiful woman, charming and inexplicably eager. Rowland Sinclair was not an insecure man, but he found the young woman's sudden passion a little unusual. He couldn't help but wonder if there was more to it.

Milton and Edna were now gossiping about Isobel's infatuation as if he were not in the room. In truth he was a little irritated that the sculptress was so personally indifferent to the overtures of the bishop's niece. He hadn't really expected her to be jealous—he just wished she was not so enthusiastic. He ignored them and continued to work.

The scream took them all unawares. A cry of pure terror, repeated. Rowland dropped his brush and stepped without delay into the hallway. He could see a door open a few rooms down—the epicentre of the shrieking. He knew that room. He walked towards it, Clyde at his shoulder and Milton and Edna just behind. Other doors were opening along the corridor. Rowland grabbed the handle and pushed the door wide.

All they saw at first was the maid's back, hunched and clenched. She was facing into the room, screaming hysterically, fresh towels dropped at her feet. Rowland sidestepped past the woman and he saw what caused her panic. Francesca Waterman was hanging by her neck from the baggage shelf. Her eyes were open, bulging from their sockets, her mouth twisted in agony, her tongue swollen and protruding from blue lips. Her hands were stiff and clawed. She swung on the end of a rope, her feet just a few inches from the plush piled carpet, swaying with the gentle rock of the ship.

"Ed, don't…," Rowland started, but too late. She stood in the room, staring, her eyes large.

"Ed…"

Edna pulled her gaze from Francesca Waterman and turned instead to the maid who was still a siren of distress. She put her arm around the distraught woman. "Come on, let's get you out of here, shall we? Are you all right?"

The maid began to sob.

"Let's find you a cup of tea, shall we? Rowly will take care of Mrs. Waterman." Soothingly, she coaxed the woman from the room.

More people were gathering around the door. Rowland wondered where Richard Waterman was.

"Rowly," Milton whispered, "shouldn't we cut her down?"

"I don't know—it's too late to save her…where the hell is Madding?"

Even as he spoke, the captain walked in. Yates, the ship's doctor, was in tow. Madding gave directions immediately to disperse the passengers outside the stateroom and to close the door.

He looked silently at the corpse suspended from the baggage rail. "Cut her down."

The Australians stood back as the crewmen severed the rope and placed Francesca Waterman on the bed.

"What happened, Sinclair?" Madding turned to them.

Rowland shook his head. "No idea. We heard the maid screaming and found this."

"Where is the maid?"

"Ed—Miss Higgins—took her out. She was understandably distressed."

"We'd better find Richard Waterman." Madding sent a man to do so.

"Do you think she could have topped herself, Doctor?" Milton asked of Yates.

The poet's bluntness made him cringe, but Rowland had been wondering the same.

Yates glanced at Madding and then shook his head. "It seems unlikely," he said gravely. "There's no chair." He went over to the baggage shelf. "See these grooves in the paint—looks like the rope was placed around her neck and then she was hoisted up—she seems to have struggled a fair bit. Not a particularly nice way to go."

Madding exhaled. "Is it too much to ask for one trip without the passengers killing each other…?" He gave instructions for Mrs. Waterman's body.

"We must find Mr. Waterman," he said looking impatiently for the men he sent to find the surgeon. "We're still a week from Sydney—we'll have to deal with this matter carefully."

Rowland nodded. He wondered whether Madding wanted to offer Waterman his condolences or arrest him.

"I have an idea where he is," Clyde volunteered

Madding turned to Clyde. "The sooner we find him the better."

"It's Sunday and there is one place he would go without his wife."

"I can think of several places a man would go without a wife," Milton interrupted.

"I think Mr. Waterman may be at Mass." Clyde ignored Milton. "I noticed him that day Rowly made me go—he was on his own."

"Waterman's Catholic?" Madding was surprised. "I thought they were Theosophists?"

"Mrs. Waterman brought him into the movement." Rowland recalled his conversation with Cartwright. "He might have left the Catholic Church for her."

"One never leaves the Catholic Church," Clyde observed. "It has a way of clawing you back."

Chapter Fourteen

WOMEN WANT "SPICY" FILMS
Morality Organiser's Fears

LONDON

That women picturegoers were responsible for the showing of objectionable films, was suggested by the organising secretary of the Public Morality Council (The Hon. Eleanor Plumer), addressing the Mothers' Union. She said that an exhibitor had told her that unless programmes included something spicy, women stayed away.

"People want entertainment in cinemas, not education nor uplift," she added. "The majority of films have a pagan outlook, with hardly any suggestion of a Christian approach to problems. This is their most serious weakness."

—*The Guardian*

Clyde scrutinised Rowland Sinclair carefully. He was reasonably sure his friend was bluffing, but it was hard to be certain. It was not that Rowland didn't have any tells, but that he was aware of them. It made it hard to trust the momentary twitch of his brow or the way he ran his hand through his hair. Clyde cursed under his breath—Rowland was a bloody fine poker player—it was a good thing he never collected his winnings.

Edna wasn't playing on this occasion, curled instead on the sofa, eating Belgian chocolate.

"I thought those were gifts for your father," Milton reminded her, as he waited impatiently for Clyde to make his play.

"Papa will understand," Edna continued to soothe herself with the dark sweetness.

"Are you all right, Ed?" Clyde glancing up at her. She always fed distress.

"That poor woman," the sculptress said pulling her knees up towards her chest. "What do you think the captain is telling Mr. Waterman?" She shuddered. "At least he didn't have to see her hanging there…"

"Presuming he didn't kill her," Milton pointed out.

Clyde finally called.

Rowland grinned—he hadn't been bluffing. Clyde groaned.

"Do you really think he killed her?" Edna's voice was shocked.

"He may have, Ed." Rowland dealt again. "I told you about their argument—maybe he'd had enough."

"But to kill her…he's a surgeon."

"And a Catholic," Clyde added.

Milton snorted. "Hardly a defence."

"Say, Rowly," Clyde said thoughtfully, "you don't suppose your Theosophist killer got back on board?"

"It's possible, I guess." Rowland shrugged. "Mrs. Waterman may have been killed for her Theosophical connections… but then again it may have just been because she was jolly unpleasant."

"Well, at least we're safe." Edna sighed.

"Maybe," Rowland replied. "I could be entirely wrong about the Theosophist link…and Mrs. Waterman's murder mightn't even be connected to Urquhart's death, or for that matter, Annie's fall."

"How long before we're home?" Edna broke off another piece of chocolate.

"Apparently we're not stopping in Fremantle—so about ten days," Clyde said. "I wonder where they're going to stow the body."

"Have to be in one of the cool rooms," Milton grimaced. It had been getting progressively warmer as they crossed the Indian Ocean. They would disembark in a little over a week into the height of the Australian summer.

A knock at the door announced Captain Madding. "I daresay I should let you all know how this matter is being handled." The seaman sounded quite weary.

They waited expectantly. Milton poured the man a drink.

"Mr. Waterman was not unexpectedly very upset. He is adamant that Mrs. Waterman was alive and well when he left for Mass this morning. This is all very unfortunate."

"So, what do you plan to do with Waterman?" Clyde asked.

"Oh, we'll give him another stateroom."

"You don't think he might be dangerous?"

"We have no evidence that he was involved in Mrs. Waterman's unfortunate end," Madding said carefully.

"What if Waterman killed his wife?" Milton went bluntly to the point.

Madding chewed his lower lip. "There is that," he said. "I'm having him watched, as I did you, Sinclair…I'm hoping the decision turns out as well."

"What are you planning to tell the passengers?" Rowland asked.

"Nothing—I'm hoping any passengers who were in earshot this morning will assume Mrs. Waterman took her own life."

Clyde shook his head. "Waterman won't like that—he's Catholic."

"Unless he killed her," Milton persisted. "Mortal sin would be quite a handy explanation in that case."

Madding stood. "I'd best be getting back."

"Yes, shouldn't you be steering this thing?" Milton topped up his glass. "Or at least watching for icebergs?"

Clyde kicked the poet under the table.

Madding said nothing for a moment, and then he laughed. "If only it were that simple."

The news of Francesca Waterman's death spread quickly through the *Aquitania*, and was discussed at length over both cocktails and tea. The notion of such misadventure aboard ship made the luxury liner's passengers more cognisant of the great isolating body of water that surrounded them. However unfortunate, the news did relieve the length of the trip with a little trepidation, titillating the conversation at opulent dinners with speculation and scandal.

Rowland Sinclair and his party did their level best to avoid being drawn into such conversations. Their presence at the scene of the crime felt intrusive enough. Instead they carried on enjoying the superlative hospitality of the *Aquitania* as they passed the time at cards and shipboard games. As the weather warmed they frequented the ship's massive swimming bath and spent more time on the now sun-drenched decks.

Isobel Hanrahan appeared to become bolder in her solicitation of the company of Rowland Sinclair, stealing him away to accompany her to the *Aquitania*'s theatre, or concert hall, on a regular basis. She no longer seemed to fear the impropriety of him walking her back to her stateroom. Rowland did wonder about it. Perhaps the rumours around Mrs. Waterman's death had made her more cautious about walking the halls alone. Whatever her reasons, Rowland found himself thinking increasingly of the bishop's incorrigible niece, whether or not she was in his company. Isobel Hanrahan had a way about her.

It was on one such occasion when he had walked her to her room following an afternoon at the cinema, that the bishop's niece did not leave him at the door, but dragged him inside her cabin and secured the lock. Isobel pulled his face down towards hers and made her intentions clear.

There was a fleeting moment, during which Rowland wondered what on earth he was doing, but then she kissed him again and the moment passed, as his mind was occupied with the task at hand.

Still, he was now alone with a lady in her stateroom, uncomfortably aware of the fact that the bishop had the next apartment; how exactly he came to be there, a combination of Isobel's contrivance and his own acquiescence. He was not unwilling, just surprised, as he had been when Isobel had first decided to secure his affections. It was his experience that women of her social class rarely addressed the mechanics of a tryst so directly. He had expected to do a little of the work himself.

And yet, it was Isobel Hanrahan who now pressed her body against his and pushed the jacket from his shoulders. It was she who whispered for him to make love to her, not shyly but urgently. If he'd had time, he might have been perplexed.

Isobel pushed him back into an armchair and proceeded to loosen his tie, her lips soft and moist on his neck. This done, she pulled away, standing before him. Giggling, she released her hair from the coif into which her dark tresses were twisted. Expertly, with seductive progression, she unbuttoned her dress, and let it drop, as she did the slip beneath it.

Rowland inhaled sharply. There was nothing so perfect as the female body.

Isobel's creamy skin was suffused with a blush of rose as she displayed herself to him. His eyes lingered on her breasts, full and round despite her diminutive frame. She smiled, almost posing as he took her in. He would paint her like this, he thought—a brash, impudent nymph of classical allusion. His eyes drifted down her slim body and then in a cold splash of realisation, he saw that which explained everything.

Briefly there was panic…What did a gentleman do in this situation? Exactly how did he walk out now? His mind returned to painting her…perhaps it would buy him time to figure out what to do next.

"Don't move," he said reaching for his jacket. "You're just lovely in this light, inspiring—I have to draw you just like that." He couldn't believe what he was saying—it sounded ludicrous even to him. Still, he could think of nothing else.

Rowland extracted the artist's notebook from the pocket of his jacket and opened to a clean page.

At first, Isobel appeared bewildered. This was clearly not what she had expected or planned. "But I thought...don't you want to...?"

Rowland hesitated, stung by the hurt in her voice, surprised by his own disappointment. "You are beautiful, Isobel," he said quietly.

Isobel relaxed a little. She smiled, reassured. "You can draw me first, then." And so she posed for him, and when Rowland repositioned her and drew her again, Isobel did not object. She chose the third position herself.

The knock at the door startled Rowland out of his concentration. Despite the situation he had lost himself in his work.

"Isobel?"

The voice was Bishop Hanrahan's.

Rowland froze.

"Yes, Uncle."

"You're not still lying abed, are you girl?" the bishop called through the door. "Are you poorly?"

"A wee bit of seasickness is all, Uncle Shaun."

"Well, get yourself up," Hanrahan ordered. "Supper is at seven and I'll be expecting you to join me for the rosary beforehand."

"I'm coming, Uncle. I won't be but a moment."

Rowland started to breathe again as the bishop moved away from the door. He was doubly relieved—now he had a reason to leave.

Isobel Hanrahan gazed at him, frustrated. "I'll see you tomorrow," she sighed.

Rowland stood and reached for his jacket.

"Would you give me one of these?" Isobel whispered, looking at the notebook.

"Of course. Any one you like."

She tore out a page and handed the notebook back to him.

"Will you make me into a painting one day?" she asked. "Paint me like this."

Again, Rowland was surprised. "Yes, if you'll allow me."

Isobel Hanrahan giggled, and pulled on her slip. "Uncle Shaun will faint dead away," she said, obviously delighted with the idea. "We'll hang it over the mantel in our grand home for the world to see, and our babies will know their mother was beautiful."

Rowland stiffened. This was going to be complicated.

"Isobel, we're not…," he started.

"You had better be getting away," she interrupted him. "Uncle Shaun will be wondering where I am."

"I think…"

She kissed him into silence. "Quickly now, or Uncle Shaun may come back." Quietly she checked the hallway, and hurried him out of the door.

Rowland tried to readjust his tie as he walked down the narrow corridor towards his own rooms. He turned briefly as he heard a door open behind him. Bishop Hanrahan emerged from his stateroom and knocked again on Isobel's door. The clergyman's eyes narrowed. Rowland nodded politely and kept walking.

Milton and Clyde were playing cards when he walked into the Reynolds Suite. Edna perched on the sofa fiddling with her camera. Rowland threw his jacket over the back of the armchair and sat down. Edna glanced up.

"Are you all right, Rowly?" she asked, concerned. "You look like you've been in a fight."

"I have," Rowland groaned as he clenched his fists in his hair.

Milton and Clyde looked up, suddenly interested.

"I thought you were with Isobel?" Clyde put down his hand and abandoned the card table to sit with Edna.

"I was in her stateroom."

Milton grinned approvingly.

"Don't," Rowland muttered. "I can't believe I got myself into this."

Edna moved to sit on the arm of his chair and nudged him playfully. "Don't be melodramatic, Rowly—did you quarrel?"

"Well, no, but I rather think we are about to."

"She thought you were taking liberties?" Edna asked a little incredulously.

"She didn't think I was taking enough." He winced. "She was quite insistent about it."

"You're not saying that offended you?" Again Edna seemed sceptical.

"Well, no." Rowland saw no point in pretending to be particularly virtuous. He took his notebook out of his jacket and handed it to Clyde. "I've just finally realised why she's so keen to replace Orville Urquhart."

Clyde flicked through the book, and stopped at the drawings of Isobel. He let out a low whistle.

"Bloody hell, Rowly—you didn't…"

"No, I noticed as soon as she took her clothes off…"

"Noticed what?" Milton grabbed the notebook from Clyde.

"Isobel's expecting," Rowland said flatly.

Milton squinted. "Are you sure…maybe she's just putting on weight?"

Rowland shook his head. "That's not the way women put on weight…Clyde and I have painted enough girls to know…"

"So Isobel Hanrahan's trying to find a father for her baby?"

Rowland shrugged. "Well, if you didn't know she was already…well you'd do the right thing, wouldn't you?"

"Oh, Rowly." Edna rubbed his shoulder. "It doesn't always work that way."

"It would with me," Rowland said almost to himself.

"Perhaps Isobel realised that," she replied softly. "Obviously the man who got Isobel into trouble didn't feel the need to do the right thing."

"That's fraud!" Milton was outraged.

"Some men are…" Edna started.

"No, I mean Isobel. She's entirely immoral!"

"Not immoral," the sculptress corrected. "Desperate. In a couple of months she won't be able to hide it and the scandal will ruin her. I'm sure it's been done before."

"I suppose Urquhart is the cuckoo?" Milton remained disgusted.

Edna shook her head. "Not if you can tell she's expecting—she met him less than eight weeks ago. I'm pretty sure it doesn't happen that quickly."

"If she knew she was in trouble, that might explain why she was so keen to marry Urquhart in the first place," Clyde agreed.

Rowland rubbed his brow. "Father Bryan did say she was wild—maybe that's why they sent her to live with the bishop." He pushed the hair out of his face. "God, what was I thinking?"

Clyde regarded him sympathetically. "Look, Rowly, it was a close call, but in the end…"

Rowland flinched. "Isobel doesn't realise I know. She seems to think I'm going to save her…this is flaming awkward."

"You're not angry?" Milton was surprised.

"More embarrassed than angry," Rowland admitted. "I feel bloody sorry for her."

"How sorry?" Milton sounded alarmed.

Rowland smiled. "Not enough to marry her…but her life's going to go to hell in a hand basket, when the bishop finds out." He loosened his tie, angry at the situation, at what he was going to have to do, and aware of how much he didn't want to. "Dammit!"

"So what are you going to do?" Clyde asked.

"I'll have to make something up…tell her I've lost interest."

"You're not going to tell her why?"

Rowland shook his head. "I'll feel like a cad but what's the point of humiliating her? It would just make everything worse." He groaned again.

Milton stood. "I think you'd better have a drink, Rowly."

Chapter Fifteen

PARENTS TO BLAME

For "Unmarried Mother"
Scandal

All the twisting and closing of eyes cannot get away from the fact that the average girl, be she educated or otherwise, has not much of a chance when she is forced to go out into the world, and fight her own way. Many of the reports and letters published in the press during the past few months show how easy it is for the unsophisticated girl to be led astray by the promises of the jackals who infest every city.

—*The New York Times*

Quite predictably, Rowland Sinclair's meeting with Isobel Hanrahan did not go well.

At first she refused to understand what he was saying.

"Come with me," she whispered, taking his arm. "I know a place where Uncle Shaun won't find us—even if he were walking right by."

The lifeboats. Could she possibly mean the lifeboats?

"Isobel, no..."

Rowland spoke to her gently, trying to be kind, a gentleman, despite the impossibility of it in the circumstances. He did want to help her, just not in the way she planned. He didn't mention the "condition" he was now certain she was in.

The bishop's niece cried and then raged—accusing him of deception and false promises. She hit him, several times. It was a fortunate thing that she was such a small, light woman, for there was really nothing he could do. Rowland was as unprepared for the ferocity of her reproach as he had been for the intensity of her favour. For the most part he said nothing as she shouted at him, cringingly aware of the other passengers on the deck where he spoke with her. He watched her run away, sobbing brokenly, leaving him to the disapproving scrutiny of those who had witnessed what appeared to be the cold jilting of the young Irishwoman by the wealthy playboy from Australia.

Rowland did not stand alone for very long.

Edna slipped her arm through his. "I'll go speak to her in a minute," she assured him quietly. "She'll understand in time."

Rowland didn't respond.

The sculptress squeezed his hand. Rowland had never been careless with the feelings of others—unaware occasionally, but never careless. It was obvious the bishop's niece had meant much more to him than he cared to admit or even realised, and he was more than a little winded by his own sense of loss.

"I have such a talent with women." He shook his head.

Milton laughed and nudged him. "You do all right, mate."

"Come on," Clyde glanced uncomfortably at the other passengers. The atmosphere on the *Aquitania* had been noticeably tense since word of Mrs. Waterman's death had spread. "Let's go in."

"I'll be along in a minute," Rowland leant against the rail and gazed out to sea.

Edna released of his hand. "We can make sure she's all right, Rowly," she said softly. "She needn't be alone in this."

They left him to deal with his own thoughts. Rowland tried to forget the collapse of Isobel Hanrahan's face when he told her that there couldn't be anything between them, the complete panic in her eyes. He grimaced as he remembered how she had pleaded with him, begging him to tell her why he did not care for her anymore. Perhaps it would have been less cruel to confess he knew her secret. He hadn't created her situation, he knew that, but he felt appalling nonetheless—responsible at least for her immediate disappointment. He wondered if she'd allow him to help her, he wondered how he could. Unmarried mothers were not unheard of, just not spoken of…at least in the company Isobel was used to keeping.

The crack was heard clear across the ship. Rowland felt the bullet whistle past his head. Instinctively he fell to the deck. Another shot splintered the boards a couple of feet short of him…and then nothing. The shocked silence was short-lived and followed by screams and shouts of terror.

His friends reached him first, for they had not gone far.

He had already risen to his knees. Edna put her hands around his face, hers a picture of relief.

"God, Rowly, are you hurt?"

Rowland stood, dusting off his jacket. "No, I'm fine. What the hell was that?"

Clyde handed him his hat.

Madding and several of his officers were there by then.

"Are you all right, Mr. Sinclair?"

"Perfectly well, Captain. What happened?"

"It appears someone tried to shoot you."

"Me? Are you sure?"

"Both shots were in your direction." Madding looked down at the damaged deck.

Rowland watched as a crewman retrieved the bullet embedded in the boards with a penknife. "Damn! Did anyone see the lunatic?"

"Afraid not. We'll have to talk to the other passengers…but at this point we only know that the shots seemed to come from the stairs." Madding's brow furrowed. "You haven't fallen out with anyone in particular, have you, Sinclair?"

Rowland responded calmly. "I can't say I'm aware of anyone wanting to shoot me, Captain Madding."

The seaman studied him carefully. "Can I ask you to stay in your stateroom whilst I look into this?"

Rowland sighed. "I was going to work today anyway," he said. "Will you let me know what you discover, Captain?"

Madding nodded. "I'll come and see you this evening." The captain motioned a couple of crewmen to escort Rowland Sinclair to his rooms.

Rowland threw his jacket over the top of his easel and fell into one of the Gainsborough Suite's armchairs. "I think I'm a bit fed up with cruising."

Milton shook his head. "The high seas seem to be getting more treacherous by the minute."

Clyde sat down, and fixed Rowland with his gaze. "Rowly, mate, why didn't you mention Isobel to the captain?"

"She didn't try to shoot me," Rowland replied. "Where would she get a gun?"

"Who else would want to shoot you?"

Rowland glanced at Edna and smiled. "The last person who shot me didn't really want to…at least I hope she didn't."

Edna shoved him. "How can you joke about this, Rowly? You could have been killed."

"Isobel didn't shoot at me, Ed."

"Women have done crazier things for love," Milton muttered as he poured drinks. "They can be quite vindictive—" He swigged his scotch. "Even dangerous."

Clyde scoffed. "You're thinking about that blonde from Glebe, aren't you? She wasn't in love with you—she just liked knives."

"No," Milton said sadly. "I think I broke her heart."

"We were talking about who is trying to kill Rowly," Edna said pointedly.

"How about we wait to see what Madding finds out?" Rowland opened the book Milton had left on the settee and stared at the page, refusing to participate further in the conversation.

Edna watched him, chewing her lower lip thoughtfully. She stood and pulled her gloves back on.

"Where are you going?" Milton asked.

"To find Isobel."

"Now? Why?"

Edna leaned over and closed the book Rowland was pretending to read. "Because Rowly's still worried about her. He's not going to pay attention to who's trying to kill him till he knows she's all right—he's daft like that. She's probably in her stateroom."

"Ed, I don't know if..." Rowland began. The sculptress was not wrong, but he wasn't sure he wanted her wandering the ship with a gunman on the loose.

She regarded him sternly. "I'm going to check on Isobel and then we are going to talk about who could be trying to shoot you." She headed towards the door.

"Madding said to stay here," Clyde reminded her.

"The captain said Rowly should stay here. Nobody shot at me."

"Still, Ed..." Rowland protested again.

"I won't be long," She ducked out of the door.

"Ask if she owns a gun," Milton called after her.

Chapter Sixteen

FOR THE BRIDE

For that greatest day in her life, the bride should be a picture of happiness and beauty which her husband, her family, and her friends can carry the memory of, all their days. And any girl, even without beauty of features, can be lovely on her wedding day—provided she plans wisely.

—*The Daily Mail*

Edna knocked on Isobel Hanrahan's door.

"Isobel darling, it's just Edna. May I come in?"

There was no answer, just sobbing, broken and desperate. Edna tried the door—it was unlocked. Isobel was on the bed, her body racked with gulping misery.

Edna sat down beside her and held the young woman until she had calmed.

"Isobel, Rowly is really sorry if he hurt you. He didn't mean to."

"Did he not?" Isobel replied bitterly. "He was supposed to marry me—he took liberties."

"What liberties exactly?" Edna asked. Isobel had her compassion, but instinctively she wanted to defend Rowland.

Isobel regarded the sculptress, her tone became accusing. "Is it yourself you want him for, then?"

Edna smiled wistfully. "No. Rowly's not meant for someone like me. I know you're disappointed, but you must try not to be angry with him. He'll be a good friend—he'll always help you if he can."

Isobel was spiteful now. "Like he helps you? What exactly do you do for him in return?"

Edna reacted calmly. It was not the first time that her lifestyle had been questioned. The bishop's niece was distressed, caught in what must have seemed like a hopeless situation. Edna refused to be offended. She was determined to be understanding. Still, her voice carried warning.

"I am trying to be nice to you. You could at least be civil."

Isobel began to sob again, and Edna regretted the sharpness of her words. Repentant, she held Isobel's hand and endeavoured to say nothing more whilst the unhappy Irishwoman raged about Rowland Sinclair, and wished him all sorts of ill. Inevitably, however, Edna's compassion was exhausted. Surely they could not continue with this charade? They would resolve nothing by simply not mentioning it.

"For pity's sake, Isobel, you can't blame poor Rowly for everything! This is not his fault."

The bishop's niece seemed wounded at first, and then defiant. She pulled her hand away.

Edna was angry too now and ready to give the young woman a piece of her mind.

The impulse was halted by a knock on door.

"Isobel! What's the matter with you, girl? Are you poorly again?"

"I'm fine, Uncle Shaun."

The door burst open and the bishop strode in. "Well, what are you...?" He stopped short when he saw Edna. He glared openly at the sculptress.

"Good afternoon, Your Grace," She stood hastily.

The bishop said nothing.

"I guess I should be running along…" Edna manoeuvred past the clergyman's substantial girth on her way to the door. "I hope you're feeling better soon, Isobel."

She jumped as the door was slammed behind her. Clyde stood in the hallway just outside.

"What are you doing?" she asked.

"Just looking out for you," he said as they walked back to the Gainsborough Suite. "With people being murdered left, right and centre, we're all getting a bit nervous."

"I thought Rowly was sure Isobel had nothing to do with the shots?"

"He is. I believe it's the bishop who worries him."

Edna laughed. "Oh, he's harmless. He's just rather loud."

Rowland looked up from his book when they came in. Edna did not wait for him to ask. She settled on the arm of his chair. "Isobel will be all right, I think, Rowly—she's more angry than heartbroken…and scared, of course."

"Did she tell you?"

Edna shook her head. "No." She thought guiltily of what she had been about to say to Isobel Hanrahan. She was glad now that the bishop had interrupted them.

"More to the point," Milton interrupted, "did she try to kill Rowly?"

Edna hesitated. Isobel Hanrahan had been very angry. "I didn't see a gun, but…"

Rowland went back to his book. "Thank God, we're nearly home. You're all starting to lose your minds."

As the afternoon slipped into evening, Captain Madding called in, as he had promised. He took a seat and spoke of the grim events.

"We haven't been able to find the gun, and I'm afraid we are no wiser than we were this morning."

"So what are we going to do?" Edna asked uneasily. "Someone's trying to kill Rowly."

"Someone may have tried," Rowland corrected. "There's nothing to say they'll keep trying."

"So you're relying on this assassin throwing in the towel because he missed the first time," Milton shook his head in exasperation.

"Milt's right," Clyde said firmly. "The *Aquitania* doesn't seem the safest of places these days."

"I can assure you, Mr. Jones," Madding stiffened, affronted, "Every precaution will be taken to ensure there is no repeat of this unfortunate incident."

Edna leaned forward and touched Madding's arm. "Please don't be offended, Captain. It's just that we are all rather fond of Rowly."

Madding relaxed a little. "Indeed, Miss Higgins. I have no intention of losing another passenger either—the death toll's getting embarrassing, if nothing else." He turned to Rowland. "Mr. Sinclair, I'm afraid I'm going to have to ask you to stay in your suite until we reach Sydney."

Rowland groaned.

"I understand this is inconvenient, Sinclair, but there are well over two thousand souls on board—we cannot keep an eye on all of them. You're safest here."

"We'll be home in three days," Edna reminded Rowland as he resisted. She was scared for him. "Please, Rowly."

Reluctantly, for her sake, Rowland conceded. "You'll let me know if your investigations reveal anything?"

Madding stood. "Of course."

It was the early hours of the morning. Rowland Sinclair pulled on his jacket. After two days, the tastefully papered walls of his suite were beginning to close in on him. Though it had not been an inordinate length of time, the knowledge that he could not step out was testing him.

"Where are you going, Rowly?" It was Clyde.

"Just onto the deck," Rowland replied guiltily. "There'll be no one out and I'm really getting cabin fever."

Clyde did not try to argue with him. It was three in the morning, and he'd watched Rowland become progressively more restless. "Give me a minute to get some clothes on, and I'll come with you."

A short time later they left the Reynolds Suite and headed out onto the first-class deck. It was a pleasant night, warm. The breeze was gentle and, for a moment, Rowland fancied he could smell eucalyptus on the balmy movement of air. He laughed at himself, at the improbability of the notion. Perhaps he was more homesick than he thought.

He and Clyde stood out on the deck, talking quietly of home under the broad southern sky. The state government had changed whilst they were away, and the conservative forces were again in control of New South Wales. That was more important for Clyde and Milton who were Communists, than for Rowland who managed to remain entirely indifferent to politics. Still, when they left Sydney the country had seemed on the verge of civil war. It was only the threat of criminal prosecution that had convinced them to walk away from the fight which had appeared imminent, but never eventuated.

The twisted end of Clyde's rolled cigarette glowed red in the darkness.

Rowland leant against the balustrade looking out over the lower decks of the ship. There was still a little movement; primarily the crew ensuring all was well while the passengers of the *Aquitania* slept. He wasn't nervous but he did wonder who had tried to shoot him, and why.

"Sinclair. So the snake finally leaves its hole!"

Rowland recognised the broad Irish lilt before he turned. Bishop Hanrahan stood on the deck, fists clenched, already trembling with rage.

Clyde sighed loudly.

"Your Grace," Rowland said evenly.

"Defiler, despoiler. Would you ruin an innocent girl with your carnal desires?"

"I assure you…"

The bishop stepped forward and staggered Rowland with a punch to the jaw.

Clyde moved to aid his friend, but hesitated. Years of childhood Mass, of doctrinal fear, intervened to render him useless. Rowland too was unsure of how to respond.

"You can be married before we get off this infernal boat!" Hanrahan grabbed Rowland by the collar. "You will not be leaving her with a bastard!"

Now Clyde found the courage to lay hands on the bishop, but Hanrahan twisted and sent Clyde reeling with the closed fist of his free hand.

"I'm not…I didn't…" Rowland gasped.

"You would deny your own child? Abandon an innocent girl? Shameless, predatory fornicator. Isobel told me how you took advantage of her." The bishop hit him again. "God shall judge thee, but the child shall not bear the stain of your sin."

Shocked by the accusation, Rowland wrested himself free of the bishop's grip. What the hell had Isobel told her uncle?

"I am not responsible for Isobel's predicament," he said tersely, wiping the blood from the corner of his mouth. "I will not be marrying your niece."

"You, sir, are a liar and I shall beat God's truth into thee!" Hanrahan launched himself at Rowland again and proceeded to do just that. Clyde had now stumbled to his feet and tried in vain to pull the incensed clergyman off. The noise was attracting attention. Hanrahan was trying to force Rowland over the balustrade of the deck.

Milton reached them in shirtsleeves and braces, having dressed in haste. Godless spawn of Lenin that he was, he had no compunction about hitting the Catholic bishop. He grabbed Hanrahan by the shoulder and pulled him around, stunning the Irishman with a quick blow to the nose. Clyde dragged Rowland away from the deck's edge.

It was only then that Bishop Hanrahan pulled the revolver from his cassock. Rowland froze. So, too, did the crewmen who had finally emerged to sort out the disturbance on the first-class deck. Lights came on.

"Isobel! Isobel! Get over here, girl!" Hanrahan bellowed with the gun trained on Rowland.

Isobel approached, tear-stained and disgraced. Even now, Rowland felt sorry for her.

"Now, Sinclair, will you be setting things to right?"

Rowland stared at the gun and then at Isobel. There was no going back, whatever he did.

Voices of support murmured from the crowd that had now gathered.

"Do the right thing, you cad!"

"Marry the girl—take responsibility—what's wrong with you?"

"Scandalous…just scandalous!"

Rowland glanced at Isobel. She wouldn't look at him. This was ridiculous. He now had to defend himself to all and sundry.

Edna pushed her way to the front of the crowd.

"Make your decision, Sinclair!" The bishop cocked the gun.

Chapter Seventeen

REGISTERING A CHILD

Dispute Concerning Fatherhood

An important judgment of the Full Court today defined the duty of the registrar-general in regard to birth registrations. The case was an application for a writ of mandamus to compel the registrar-general to amend an entry respecting the birth of a child, of which the applicant denied being the father, by deleting his name from the register.

Mr. Justice Draper, in concurring in the judgment, said that the registrar had refused to amend the register because he thought that he would illegitimatise the child, but the registrar's reason and conclusion were both unfounded.

—*The Argus*

Rowland Sinclair glared at the revolver that supported the bishop's proposal of marriage.

"No…" he replied, before he had fully considered the advisability of such a response.

"Isobel!" Edna stepped towards the bishop's fallen niece and shook her furiously. "For pity's sake, Isobel—that's a gun...you must put a stop to this...tell your uncle the truth!"

Isobel turned from her uncle to Rowland. Her eyes full and tremulous; a creature trapped.

"He's speaking the truth, Uncle. Mr. Sinclair has been naught but a gentleman."

Bishop Hanrahan may have paled—the light was too poor to tell. His righteous fury certainly took a visible blow. "But..."

"I lied to you, Uncle Shaun. I wanted it to be him."

The clergyman destroyed Isobel with his gaze; she seemed to crumple under it.

"You, my girl, are dead to me." He dropped his hand.

Now Madding's men surged to arrest the bishop. Isobel ran weeping from the scene. The curious disapproving spectators were dispersed. Rowland watched on, a little stunned. Clyde stood grimly by him. "That couldn't possibly have been worse... though I suppose he didn't shoot you."

Milton joined them. "What the hell were you two doing? He's an old man and he had the both of you on the ropes."

Clyde glanced sideways at Rowland. "He's a man of God."

Milton snorted, disgusted.

Edna was speaking with Father Bryan. The deacon looked grave and a little lost. Rowland moved towards the pair and put his arm gratefully around the sculptress.

"Arrived in the nick of time, Ed."

She shoved him. "What are you doing out here? He might have killed you!" She softened as she studied his face. "Oh, Rowly, that's going to bruise."

Rowland scanned the deck, frowning. Madding was having words with Bishop Hanrahan. "Look Ed...Isobel...could you...? she looked so..."

"I'll go after Isobel," Father Bryan volunteered. "She may need more than a friend, given the circumstances." He turned to Rowland and offered his hand. "Mr. Sinclair, please accept my apologies. His Grace can be rash."

Rowland took the handshake. He picked his words carefully, now gun-shy of seeming too interested in Isobel Hanrahan. "You'll let me know if there's anything I can do for Isobel?"

Bryan nodded and set off in search of the bishop's wayward niece.

Madding walked over to them whilst his staff captain and a couple of officers escorted the clergyman away. Father Murphy followed unobtrusively, as it seemed he always did.

"Mr. Sinclair, what were you doing out here?"

"My rooms were becoming a tad claustrophobic, Captain. I didn't think there would be anyone about at this time…of course I was mistaken."

Captain Madding walked them back to the Reynolds Suite. He sent down to the kitchens for ice despite Rowland's assurances that it was unnecessary.

Milton poured generous balloons of brandy. "What are you going to do with Hanrahan?" He handed a glass to the *Aquitania's* captain.

"We're holding him in the brig. He denies that he had anything to do with the shots fired at you, Sinclair. Also denies that he intended to shoot you on the deck just now…claims he was just trying to make you do the right thing by Isobel."

Rowland twirled the brandy slowly in the balloon.

Madding addressed him directly. "What do you think? It was you he pointed the gun at…would he have used it?"

"He might have," Rowland replied thoughtfully. "But I don't know that he planned to. I think he was really trying to…Actually I'm not sure what he was trying to do, but I don't think killing me would have helped."

"The bullets, Captain," Edna asked, "the one that ended up in the deck…did they come from the bishop's pistol?"

"They were small calibre bullets—fired from a similar gun—but the Webley was standard issue during the last war. Every man on board who saw service probably has one—I have one."

Rowland smiled at the irony of it—it was a Webley with which Edna had shot him earlier that year. It had been his brother's service revolver and it was in fact now packed in one of his trunks. Wilfred had arranged a licence and insisted he take the weapon as a precaution. "To be honest," he conceded, "I really don't think Bishop Hanrahan would shoot a man in the back."

"You're right," Milton agreed. "He's much more likely to empty the barrel into your face."

"How did His Grace know we were on the deck tonight?" Clyde applied a cloth of ice gingerly to his blackened eye.

"It seems he came upon you by chance on his way to the infirmary."

"Was he unwell, then?"

Madding shook his head. "No, it was Mrs. Atkinson—she's a bit of a hypochondriac, I'm afraid—there's one every trip. She seems to have taken up residence in the infirmary."

"I'm not sure I follow."

The sea captain explained. "Convinced that the end was near, Mrs. Atkinson called for last rites. We sent for Father Bryan initially, but he is apparently unable to administer last rites. He had us send for the bishop instead. As His Grace was coming across, it seems he found you and Mr. Sinclair."

"Was he planning to finish the old bird off?" Milton asked. "Can't imagine why else he'd have a gun?"

Clyde laughed.

Madding coughed, poorly disguising a chuckle. "You do have a point, Mr. Isaacs. I'm afraid that didn't occur to me...but I'll be sure to ask the bishop."

"How is Mrs. Atkinson?" Clyde asked, obviously feeling a little ashamed of having found mirth in a dying woman's last moments.

Madding was solemn. "Well, as His Grace did not arrive, I'm afraid she had to put off dying for the moment."

Chapter Eighteen

Sydney Welomes the RMS *Aquitania*

Sydney

Dwarfing the six tugs which manoeuvred her to her berth and the scores of small craft which moved about her in a welcoming procession, the RMS *Aquitania* arrived at Sydney on Saturday. Every vantage point was lined with sightseers for the huge liner, regarded as the most luxurious ship afloat.

—*The Sydney Morning Herald*

Rowland was shaving when Clyde called out to him.

"Get a move on, Rowly—we'll be coming into the harbour soon."

He didn't reply, concentrating on shaving over the bruises on his jaw without sustaining any further damage. Under normal circumstances, he would have used the barbershop on the *Aquitania*, but after the previous evening's encounter he was happy to keep a low profile. Rowland wiped his face with a towel, inspecting the results in the mirror. He didn't look as rough as Clyde, and at least now he was clean-shaven.

He joined his companions in the sitting room. They would be home soon. The *Aquitania* would sail into Darling Harbour that morning.

Rowland sat down beside Edna. "I wonder if Bryan found Isobel."

Edna poured him a cup of tea.

"You're still worried about her—after what she did?" Milton shook his head. "Hanrahan might have shot you before she got there to tell him she lied."

Rowland took his tea. "She's pretty much alone, Milt. Hanrahan's disowned her—she doesn't have anyone here. Maybe we could…"

"Cripes, Rowly, you weren't actually in love with her, were you?"

Rowland pictured the bishop's niece on the night she had first kissed him on the moonlit deck—beautiful and unexpected. He preferred to think of what she'd done afterwards as an act of desperation rather than malice. He watched as Edna spooned a ludicrous amount of sugar into her tea. That was a different thing—a futile comparison.

"No—I wasn't," he said finally. "But, given time, I could have been."

"Probably for the best, mate." Clyde was reflective. "Can't imagine what Wilfred would have said if you'd brought a Catholic home."

"Honestly, Clyde," Edna huffed. "You make her sound like a puppy."

Rowland smiled. "Isobel isn't your traditional Catholic."

"That's what they all say," Milton drained the teapot, "until after you've married them."

"I'm sure I'll probably end up disappointing Wilfred one way or another," Rowland murmured.

"One can only hope," the poet agreed.

Edna relinquished her teacup and gathered her camera. "Shall we go?" She did not attempt to mask her eagerness. "It feels like we've been away forever."

"Had enough of travelling, Ed?" Rowland asked, amused. It was Edna, more than any of them, who had relished the grand adventure of their travels.

"There's someone trying to kill you, Rowly."

"Oh, yes." He stood. "Shall we?"

As it had been when they entered New York, the deck was crowded with both returning and visiting passengers. The *Aquitania*'s brass band struck up "Waltzing Matilda" as the great liner passed through the harbour's famous headlands. The crowd cheered periodically, the atmosphere on board becoming progressively more festive and excited.

Edna took pictures. The rejoicing passengers waving at nothing in particular. Sydney emerging on the horizon. Rowland, Clyde, and Milton together against the unadulterated blue of the sky. Her photographs would not capture the colour but they would preserve the easy happiness, the relaxed friendship of the moment.

Hubert Van Hook found them. Rowland gave the Theosophist his card and an open invitation to Woodlands House.

"Swell! That's a scorching idea. I'll level with you, Rowly— Old Charlie makes me a bit hot under the collar!"

"Oh!" Edna exclaimed, disappointed as she tried to snap Van Hook. "The roll's run out."

"Do you have another?" Rowland asked.

"Yes, but I left it in your suite—I put it down when we were having tea."

"I'll go get it," he volunteered. "I won't be a moment."

"Oh no, Rowly, don't bother…" Edna began, but he was gone.

Hubert Van Hook grasped her about the waist and kissed her on the cheek. "Well, I'll be seeing you doll!" he said grinning.

"You keep those fellas honest and we might cut the rug in Sydney sometime. I'll give you a bell at Sinclair's joint."

Edna returned his embrace. "Yes, do keep in touch, Hu."

The American waved and disappeared into the throng. Edna moved to stand between Clyde and Milton at the rail. A swarm of smaller boats, tugs, fishing vessels, and private yachts were surging out to meet the ocean-liner. The air was crowded with music and laughter and the noise of the harbour.

And yet, Edna heard the scream over it all. It was just a single desperate cry. More chilling in the midst of the homecoming festivity. In the confused silence that followed, she cast her eyes around, searching erratically for an explanation. Then she saw the passengers who were looking over the side.

"My God, someone's jumped!"

The crowd pitched towards the portside, pressing against the rail and shouting uselessly. Edna gasped as she was crushed against Milton by passengers desperate to view tragedy. Clyde leaned over the guardrail; pale, unable to take his eyes from the water below. He had seen the body hit.

Rowland reached them several minutes later. By then the crew was calming and reassuring the distressed passengers. Smaller boats had gathered in the *Aquitania*'s wake where the body had sunk beneath the foaming water. The atmosphere was subdued; the more delicate ladies wept politely. Already the horror of the incident was dissipating—the thought of someone jumping to her death was not as shocking as it may once have been. The Depression had seen to that.

"What happened?" Rowland asked, bewildered. He had missed the incident entirely.

"I think someone jumped," Milton replied.

"Bloody hell."

Clyde grabbed his arm. He looked sick. "Rowly, I think it was Isobel."

Chapter Nineteen

PASSING NOTES

By Mercurius

I have written a long letter of sympathy to Superintendent McKay, of the New South Wales Police Force, expressing my regret that the sword of De Groot frightened him so badly. For in his evidence the Superintendant said: "De Groot might have slashed at me with his sword. I do not like a man waving a sword at me." Of course not; who does like it? It is a terrible thing, and suggests danger. I have infinite pity for Superintendent McKay just as I have for James I of England, who used to turn pale at the sight of a sword, or even a dagger.

—*The Mercury*

Rowland Sinclair gazed vaguely at a scale model of the *Aquitania* as he sat in the captain's office on the ship itself. He was alone. The ocean liner had now made port at Darling Harbour and the process of disembarking over two thousand passengers begun. Isobel Hanrahan's body had been recovered. Detectives from Sydney Police Headquarters had boarded to take charge of the investigation. He'd been waiting for a couple of hours now, with nothing but his own brooding thoughts.

Rowland rubbed the bridge of his nose as he pictured Isobel; beautiful, seductive Isobel, who had fallen from grace and to her death. Could he have helped her? Could he have somehow treated her more kindly and protected her from despair? The thought tormented him.

Madding had said the police wished to speak with him. He had expected as much. Guilt and regret haunted him. Perhaps if he had never left his suite that night, she would not have been forced to reveal her secret. He wished he'd at least gone after her himself. It needn't have been as hopeless as she saw it.

There was a brief knock on the door and Detective Constable Delaney walked into the room. Rowland stood.

"Sinclair." Delaney extended his hand. "Welcome home. Didn't think I'd be seeing you again so soon—on an official basis, at least."

Rowland shook the man's hand. "It's a hell of a thing, Col."

The detective took Madding's chair and motioned Rowland to sit. "Leg seems to have healed up, Rowly." He glanced down. "You were on crutches when I saw you last."

Rowland nodded.

Delaney sighed, perhaps sympathetically. "Suppose you tell me about this woman, Rowly. The one in the harbour."

Rowland shrugged. "Miss Hanrahan—formerly of Dublin. Travelling with her uncle, a Bishop Hanrahan."

"A bishop?" Delaney was stopped short by the implications. "Afraid so."

"And you were involved with her?"

"Depends what you call involved?"

"She claimed to be expecting your child."

Rowland shook his head. "Not possible."

"Are you sure?"

Rowland glared at the detective. "Yes, I'm sure. She admitted it herself—I think she might have known she was in trouble before she ever met me."

"She admitted it?"

"Last night, when the bishop was trying to shoot me." Rowland rubbed his face. "If I'd known she was going to jump, I—"

"Jump?" Delaney interrupted him. "Rowly, this is a murder investigation. Isobel Hanrahan was thrown from the deck."

Rowland started. "How do you know?"

"By all accounts, there was a delay between the time the scream was heard, and when the young lady's body hit the water. It's unusual for a jumper to scream at all, but if they do, it's usually when they're actually falling. Rarely is there an intervening period of silence before they hit the water."

Unsure whether he really wished to know the mechanics of such a thing, Rowland struggled to accept what Delaney was saying. Isobel had been murdered.

"Are you sure?"

"One can never be sure—but it seems likely. There were some injuries to her face, her dress was torn. It looks like there may have been a struggle."

"Lord, poor Isobel. What kind of monster...?"

"Well, that's what we're here to find out." Delaney studied him. "Where exactly were you when Miss Hanrahan hit the water?"

Rowland's thoughts were on Isobel's last moments. Stricken by the violent, desperate images, he did not think to be concerned by the question. "On the deck...no, wait—I believe I went back to the suite, to get a roll of film for Edna."

"Do you remember seeing anyone? Did you talk to anyone?"

"No—everybody was on deck, I guess." Rowland looked up, startled. "You don't think I had anything to do with...?"

The detective sighed. "Here's the problem, Rowly: you had every reason to be very angry with Isobel Hanrahan and, unfortunately, you are also implicated in the deaths of the other two victims." Delaney shuffled through the reports in front of him. "You discovered the body of Francesca Waterman and had some kind of altercation with Orville Urquhart."

Rowland groaned. Put like that…"Have you spoken to Madding?"

"Yes—he doesn't believe you had anything to do with any of the deaths. How did he put it?" Delaney smiled. "'I'm afraid, Sinclair just has a habit of being in the wrong place every possible time. I would think twice about standing next to him.'"

"Oh, smashing," Rowland muttered. "What can I tell you, Col?"

Delaney took out a marbled pen and his notebook. "Everything. Let's start with Urquhart."

They spent the next hour and a half in this way. Rowland told Delaney everything he remembered and answered the detective's questions as best he could. Delaney prompted, and took notes. He was particularly interested in the attacks on Annie Besant and the possibility of some sort of connection with the Theosophical movement.

"Neither the murder of Isobel Hanrahan nor the attempt on your life fits that theory, however…" Delaney leaned forward towards Rowland. "What's your take on Bishop Hanrahan?"

"Your traditional fire and brimstone, scarier than Hell itself, Irish Catholic priest," Rowland replied. "But he's been in the brig since last night."

"Apparently not," Delaney said, flicking through his reports. "It seems you managed to convince Madding that the bishop had nothing to do with the first attempt on your life and that the second was just a misunderstanding."

"Oh." Rowland could remember thinking and saying something to that effect, but now Isobel was dead.

The door flung open and two men walked in. The first in uniform, a tall broad man with a pugnacious jaw on a boyish face. Bill MacKay, Superintendent of the Criminal Investigation Bureau. Not a man to be trifled with. He and Rowland Sinclair had already had dealings.

Close behind MacKay, a man in his early forties—impeccably, but conservatively attired. A silver fob chain hung from his waistcoat pocket, and a traditional bowler sat straight on his head. His deep blue eyes regarded Rowland sternly over bifocals.

Rowland stood. "Wil, what are you doing here?"

Wilfred Sinclair shook his brother's hand, gripping Rowland's shoulder briefly with his other. It was an unusual display of warmth, which surprised Rowland a little, but then, they had not seen each other in several months. Wilfred's eyes lingered on the bruises which had now darkened on his brother's face but he let it pass without comment. "I was in Sydney, so I came to meet your boat," he said. "That long-haired buffoon told me you'd been arrested."

Rowland smiled faintly. Milton. Wilfred had never approved of his friends—particularly Milton.

"I have already assured your brother, Mr. Sinclair, that you are simply assisting us with enquiries at this stage," Bill MacKay said brusquely.

Rowland glanced at Delaney. "Glad to hear it, Superintendent."

"Well, I think we're finished here," Delaney closed his notebook with a snap. He nodded at Rowland. "I'll be in touch, Sinclair."

MacKay signalled for Delaney to follow him out of the room, leaving the Sinclair brothers alone in the captain's office.

Wilfred stood silently for a moment.

"God forbid you should return without some sort of scandal," he said finally.

Rowland didn't respond.

"I shall ensure that none of this reaches the papers. But inevitably there'll be rumours." Wilfred removed his spectacles and polished them with his handkerchief. "What could you possibly have been thinking, Rowly?"

Rowland assumed his brother was talking about his involvement with Isobel Hanrahan. Wilfred couldn't believe he killed anyone.

"I wasn't thinking anything, Wil."

"That much is clear," Wilfred replied curtly. "You seem determined to make the most inappropriate, improper associations possible."

"She's dead, Wil." Rowland's voice caught. He looked at Wilfred searchingly. "Do the police know who killed her? Did MacKay say anything?"

Wilfred's face became a little less severe. "They're looking into it, Rowly, but at the moment they don't know. I guess it's fortunate that everybody of interest will be in Sydney for the next while."

Rowland thought of Urquhart, whose death had been lost, unavenged, in a jurisdictional abyss. He would not allow that to happen to Isobel Hanrahan. He grabbed his hat from the desk. "Shall we go, then?"

Wilfred nodded. "I've sent your friends back to the house—the police finished with them a couple of hours ago."

Rowland's mouth flickered upwards. Wilfred always managed to say "your friends" as if he were talking of some feral plague. He hadn't seen his brother in a while, so it amused, more than annoyed him.

Godfrey Madding caught them as they were about to head down the gangway. Rowland introduced Wilfred.

"I'm afraid this has been an unfortunate way to end a cruise," the captain said apologetically. "But then this particular trip seems to have been fraught with unfortunate incidents."

"I appreciate the way you've handled things, Captain," Rowland replied.

The captain pulled him aside. "Look, Sinclair, we're just packing up Isobel Hanrahan's stateroom. I presume the bishop will have her things sent back to Dublin." He pulled an envelope from his inside pocket. "I remembered that this belonged to Miss Higgins—you might like to return it to her."

Rowland opened the envelope and inspected its contents. Edna's locket. He couldn't recall Isobel wearing it since they had re-boarded in New York.

"Thank you. I'll see that she gets it."

"Good man. You can also tell Mr. Isaacs that His Grace is in the habit of carrying a gun. Apparently the Lord's army is equipped with more than just the Good Book. He has a licence for the weapon."

"I see."

Madding smiled congenially. "I do hope this unpleasantness doesn't put you off sailing with us again."

Chapter Twenty

A Gay and Festive Christmas

Decorating the home in a festive garb for the Christmas jollities is just as old a tradition as turkey and plum pudding is for the Christmas feast. It is delightful to plan out a scheme for gaily adorning the entrance hall and living rooms with paper festoons, lanterns, garlands, balloons, streamers, and holly; and the dining-table with masses of crackers. Then there is the Christmas-tree with its dozens of sparkling novelties, and tiny candles, which give it such an exciting appearance.

—*The Sydney Morning Herald*

Wilfred did not take his brother back to Woodlands House, but to the Masonic Club in the city centre. Now, in the lead-up to Christmas, the traditional wood-panelled décor was tastefully accented with wreaths and the odd sign of appropriately understated festivity.

It was not until they were seated in the leather club chairs with drinks that the conversation left the events on *Aquitania*.

Wilfred raised his glass. "Well, for what it's worth, Rowly, welcome home."

Rowland put down the glass of scotch his brother had given him. For some reason, Wilfred seemed unable to accept that he loathed all forms of whisky. It had become something of a ritual for his brother to pour him a drink that he would leave untouched.

"I trust Kate and the boys are well." Rowland noticed the warmth that invaded his brother's eyes on mention of his family. It had always been so. "When can I meet this new nephew of mine?" Wilfred's younger son had been born whilst Rowland was abroad.

Wilfred smiled proudly. "You're coming home for Christmas, of course. You can meet Ewan Dougal Baird Sinclair then."

"Ewan Dougal Baird?" Rowland grinned. "I say, didn't know you were having one for Scotland."

Wilfred sighed. "Kate's family," he muttered by way of explanation. "It's a flaming miracle they didn't insist on McDuff McTavish."

Rowland laughed. Wilfred had written that the name of his new son had become something of a family battle. Obviously he had lost. Wilfred didn't lose often.

"There's another matter I should discuss with you. We're having Ewan christened on the sixth of next month."

"Yes, of course." Rowland knew well what a Sinclair christening would entail. All Sinclairs were baptised at St. Mark's in Darling Point. The family would be rallied to Sydney for the occasion. They would need to be accommodated.

"I thought we'd put up Kate's people in Roburvale," Wilfred informed him. Roburvale, once the home of their late uncle, was the Sinclairs' other Sydney residence: a mansion nearly equal to Woodlands House in size and magnificence. "I would rather not risk having any of them at Woodlands in its current state."

Rowland ignored the implied reproach. The Sinclair family home had, under his stewardship, become somewhat unconventional. It suited him.

"Which means," Wilfred continued, "our people will have to stay at Woodlands."

"Oh, I see." Rowland tried to look unconcerned.

Wilfred checked his pocket watch. "I have already spoken to Mary Brown. I've instructed her to retain some extra staff for the next month at least. I expect the family will start to arrive just after the New Year—you shall have to do something about the state of Woodlands before then. Mary understands what I expect."

"What exactly do you want me to do?" Rowland asked, realising that Wilfred envisaged more than a general polish. Mary Brown had been the housekeeper at Woodlands since before the war. She never forgot her place, but Rowland was aware she was unhappy with the way he ran his house. He had no doubt that what Wilfred expected met with her approval.

"Try and recall what the place looked like when you first took up residence, Rowly—before you turned it into a refuge for all manner of unemployed, subversive ne'er-do-wells!"

"You want me to throw my friends out?" Rowland's tone carried a warning that he would countenance no such thing.

"Just make them less visible, for pity's sake," Wilfred said irritably. "Instruct them how to behave in polite company—tell Miss Higgins to keep her jolly clothes on and, for God's sake, direct them to keep their Leninist principles to themselves."

Rowland's eyes flashed. Wilfred could really be insufferable. "Look Wil," he said tightly, "let's not quarrel already. We can all put on whatever airs and graces you require."

Wilfred let it go, but reluctantly. "You'll have to take down your paintings," he said finally. "There'll be women and children in the house."

At this, Rowland smiled. "Of course. I'm not planning on corrupting my nephews, let alone the Sinclair women."

"Your plans are not what worry me."

Rowland changed the subject. "I see you were successful in seeing Lang off." He knew Wilfred would consider the sacking, and consequent electoral defeat, of the left-wing premier, a triumph for the forces of good. Now that New South Wales was in the control of the conservatives, perhaps Wilfred's obsession with defending against a Communist revolution had abated.

Apparently not.

Wilfred spent the next hour apprising his brother of the political manoeuvrings which had ensured a "retreat from Moscow."

"Bertie Stevens is a good man." Wilfred tapped his fingers on the arm of his chair. "He'll certainly make a better fist of the Premiership than Red Jack. Many of our own chaps have taken seats—but vigilance is the key, Rowly...uncompromising, eternal vigilance."

Rowland wondered about his brother's part in the change of government. The "chaps" who'd taken seats were obviously Wilfred's compatriots from the Old Guard, the secret army, which less than a year ago had been poised for a coup. And now they sat in parliament, exerting their own brand of insanity on the government of the land. It was Rowland's theory that the conservative forces operated within degrees of madness. But he knew better than to ask for particulars. Wilfred did not completely trust his allegiances.

Rowland was, in any case, more vested in the fate of Eric Campbell and his New Guard. He had made an enemy of the fascist movement earlier that year. It had ended badly. Though Wilfred had managed to keep him out of gaol, he had sent Rowland abroad to keep him from the New Guard's vengeance.

"The New Guard's day is over," Wilfred said dismissively.

"Why?"

"Campbell's security guard—some chap called Poynton—turned informant. Confessed to Delaney actually...just walked in and told him everything...no one could really fathom why." Wilfred maintained a sharp and intent eye on his brother as he spoke.

The smile was in Rowland's eyes. Good old Poynton—a man to be relied on.

"Campbell and the New Guard never quite recovered from the public outrage." Wilfred stopped short, suspiciously. "Rowly, you didn't have anything to do with...? I thought I told you—"

Rowland shrugged innocently. "Good heavens, Wil, I was abroad."

Wilfred glared at him. "Quite."

It was evening when Rowland returned to Woodlands House; still light, but only because the midsummer sun did not set till nearly eight. Externally, the Woollahra mansion was unchanged since the days when his parents had run the house. Perhaps the ivy was a little thicker on its sandstone walls. The garden was dotted with some of Edna's more experimental works, but to Rowland's eye they ornamented the clipped formal layout of the grounds.

He let himself out of the Rolls-Royce as soon as it paused in the circular drive, leaving the chauffeur to take the car round to the stables.

"Johnston," he said, pausing as he climbed out, "the family will be coming up in January. We might need another driver, and another car. Would you see to it, please?"

"Very good, sir."

Johnston had been at Woodlands House since before Rowland was born. He understood the difference between the expectations of Wilfred and Rowland Sinclair.

Rowland entered his house for the first time in several months. Edna opened the door before he reached it. It appeared his friends had begun to worry that he may, in fact, have been arrested.

"Rowly, where have you been? We were just about to go back for you."

"Sorry." Rowland loosened his tie with the hand that was not holding his jacket. "Did you get everything back all right?"

He followed the sculptress into the main drawing room, which had also served as his studio. His easels still stood by the large windows. The canvases stacked against the walls seemed to have been neatened somewhat, but essentially the room was as he had left it. Rowland smiled, sure that Mary Brown had managed to dust and polish around the jars crammed with paintbrushes and palette knives, the bottles of mineral turpentine, and the half-finished works in which he had lost interest. He was sure that she did so whilst sighing repeatedly. Plaintive exhalations were the housekeeper's anthem, a kind of requiem to Woodlands under his father's rule.

Rowland threw his jacket over one of the wing-backed armchairs and descended into its seat. He liked the drawing room the way it was, but no doubt Wilfred considered the parlour ill-used. Rowland glanced at the life-sized portrait of his late father, which glared down at him from the wall. Henry Sinclair, he supposed, would have agreed with the eldest of his sons.

Milton poured him a glass of sherry. "Come on, Rowly, what happened?"

"Nothing really, Delaney just needed to ask some questions." Rowland told them about the interview and the revelation that Isobel Hanrahan had been murdered.

"Oh, Rowly." Edna grabbed his hand in both of hers. "I don't know which is worse."

Clyde shook his head. "Who'd want to kill the poor girl?"

"Well, the bishop wasn't too happy with her," Milton said grimly. "And perhaps the bloke who really got her into trouble was a bit worried when she admitted it wasn't Rowly…or maybe he was jealous." He frowned. "Bloody awful what happened to Isobel—but she was playing with fire."

"Excuse me, sir." Mary Brown stood by the door. "Are you ready for supper?"

Rowland stood and put his jacket back on. "Thank you, Mary. I'm famished."

He offered Edna his arm and though she giggled and told him he was pretentious, she took it. They proceeded into the dining room.

The current residents of Woodlands House did not usually dine so formally, but Mary Brown had obviously decided that this was an occasion on which they should. The table was covered with crisp white linen and each place set with enough cutlery for at least five courses. A pair of grand Victorian candelabra graced the centre of the long oak table and three service maids stood in line against the papered wall, waiting discreetly until they were required. Rowland assumed Mary Brown was practising for Wilfred's arrival. His brother liked things done properly.

Milton pulled a chair out for Edna, bowing ridiculously. "So with a world, thy gentle ways, thy grace, thy more than beauty…"

"I think you'll find that's Poe," Rowland said as he took a seat.

Clyde looked at the table, and then surreptitiously back at the maids, who were now busy at the sideboard. "I feel like we should have dressed for dinner." He might have been inclined to whisper, but the length of the table and the consequent distance between the four places necessitated a reasonable volume.

"Yes, about that." Rowland grimaced. "I'm afraid that we are about to face an inundation of Sinclairs."

"A what?"

"The family's coming up to Sydney for a christening—Wilfred's younger boy—I'm afraid they're all staying here."

There was a short silence as the words were absorbed.

"Of course they're staying here," Clyde said finally. "This is their house. When are they coming?"

"Not till after the New Year." Rowland started his soup. He looked apologetically at Clyde and Milton. "We may need to bunk together for a while."

Clyde laughed. "I'm from a family of twelve, Rowly. There was always at least three to a bed—sharing a room with you two is still an opulent use of space by Jones standards."

"Don't sound too enthusiastic," Milton murmured. "People will talk."

"I'm afraid we're going to have to move our easels and gear somewhere," Rowland went on as Clyde shot Milton a withering glare. "Wil wants Woodlands to look like a mausoleum again."

Edna smiled. "It might be fun pretending to be a lady."

"I have never thought you were anything else, Ed," Rowland replied calmly. He squinted at Milton down the candlelit table. The letters emblazoned by silver nitrate had faded considerably, but they were still just discernible. "Maybe we should do something about Milt's forehead…"

Edna studied the poet's face. "I could cover that up with a bit of rouge and powder."

Clyde chuckled.

Milton put down his spoon and stared at the sculptress. "I rather think the Sinclairs might find a man in rouge and powder as alarming as one labelled *Red*."

"I'm afraid he's right," Rowland agreed. "Let's just not mention it, and hope for the best."

Mary Brown came into the dining room with a platter bearing the second course. Those seated at the table shared their plans for Christmas as the maids served roast potatoes, steamed carrots, and snap peas to accompany the individual beef and kidney pies. Rowland and his house guests usually scattered to their own families for the holiday. Edna's father and Milton's grandmother both lived in Burwood. Clyde's large family still lived in the Snowy Mountains, west of Canberra.

"When are you heading home, Rowly?" Clyde asked as he cut into the golden pastry of his pie.

"The day after tomorrow."

"We'll catch the train together, then," Clyde suggested. He would have to travel through Yass Junction in any case.

Rowland nodded. "I'll be glad of the company. I'm just making a lightning visit—have to get back and organise things here—but you needn't. I can pack up your studio if you like."

Clyde shook his head. "Mum goes to town with the fancy food whenever I come home. They can't afford for me to stay more than a couple of days."

Rowland didn't pursue the matter. Clyde was from very humble circumstances, but they were proud people. Though he had never met them, he had a vague suspicion that the Jones family did not quite approve of their eldest son's association with Rowland Sinclair.

"It's settled then," Milton waved his fork at them. "We'll see

1933 in, in style, and then we'll try not to disgrace Rowly for the rest of January."

"Just January, then?" Rowland asked, amused.

"Yes, January is more than enough."

Rowland reached inside his pocket, remembering suddenly, the envelope that Madding had given him. He tossed it to Edna, with enough height to clear the candles. Mary Brown sighed audibly.

Edna caught the envelope and opened it.

"My locket! Rowly, how...?"

"Captain Madding—they were packing up Isobel's things to send back to Dublin. He thought you might like your locket back."

"Oh the dear, dear man..." she hesitated. "Rowly, do you think it's wrong to...?"

"I don't think either Urquhart or the locket had a lasting place in Isobel's affections," he said firmly. There was nothing to be gained by Edna looking at the jewel with sadness or guilt. "Besides," he added as he watched her hold it, "I gave it to you long before Isobel ever saw it. It was always meant to be yours."

The sculptress smiled, slipping the chain over her head and pressing the locket to her breast.

Rowland watched her thoughtfully. "Ed, you don't know where Father Bryan is living in Sydney, do you?"

"Staying, not living," Edna replied. "Matthew's just here for three months, and then he's going to India as a missionary of some sort."

"So, where is he staying, then?"

"I believe he and Father Murphy will be at the seminary."

"Why do you care, Rowly?" Clyde asked.

"I thought I'd call on him."

Edna's eyes softened. "You're thinking about Isobel."

"I just wondered if he found her, after she ran off," Rowland replied. "And if he did, where?" He put down his knife and fork. It occurred to him that Isobel Hanrahan had been alive that morning. The murderous act, which had taken her life, was only a few hours old.

"Bryan might also be able to tell us what the bishop did, once he'd been released from the brig," Milton added darkly. "Frankly, mate, I think you've been far too trusting of both the Hanrahans."

Rowland did not respond. Milton was probably right. But still.

"You're taking a direct interest in this investigation then, Rowly?" Clyde asked.

"Yes, I daresay I am."

"Getting to be a bit of a habit."

Rowland grinned. Clyde could be an old woman sometimes. "Just asking a couple of questions…don't worry, Bryan's a priest."

"A Catholic priest, mate," Clyde reminded him. "Abstinence makes a man bad-tempered. You'll find they're more formidable than your poncy Proddie ministers."

Chapter Twenty-one

CHURCH COLLEGE
Not Liable For Rates
SUCCESSFUL APPEAL

SYDNEY

Six Justices of the High Court were unanimous today in allowing the appeal of the Roman Catholic Archbishop against the judgment of the Chief Judge in Equity, declaring that the Archbishop "was liable for rates on land occupied directly in connection with the building known as St. Patrick's College Manly."

The question at issue was whether the college was used solely for religious uses. The Judges said they could not agree with the Chief Judge in Equity that the college building was used as a sort of estate.

—*The Canberra Times*

St. Patrick's Seminary was a building from an era past. A truly massive Gothic structure, its stone facades were raised high upon the rugged hills behind Manly Beach. The six stories of its central belltower loomed like the mast of some vast flagship of faith.

Rowland wondered whether his Protestantism was visible. It felt uncomfortably so. He had known Catholics before, but generally they had been fallen, or at the very least, lapsed. The residents of St. Patrick's were a different thing altogether. Edna, on the other hand, seemed perfectly at home in this enclave of men. But that was her particular talent—she was entirely at ease in her own skin, and in any other place, really.

Matthew Bryan was waiting by the majestic staircase in the reception. He greeted them warmly, informally.

"Edna, Rowland, how delightful to see you so soon. I was so glad to get your call."

"Matthew, this is charming." Edna's eyes glinted impishly. "It might even be bigger than Rowly's place."

Bryan laughed. "It is rather grand. I must say I'm jolly glad I'm here in the summer, though."

Rowland looked up to the twenty-foot ceilings. "I daresay it would be hard to heat."

"This time of year, however," Bryan led them up the staircase, "you can stand on the parapets, cooled by the ocean breeze, and taste the salt on your lips. You can look out upon the glorious, uncontainable, unknowable sea and understand the nature of God."

"Or you might see a whale," Edna added helpfully.

Rowland smiled. The sculptress had a way of blithely finding the ridiculous in the most earnest of situations.

Matthew Bryan showed them around the seminary, or at least those parts to which they were allowed access. They were in the belltower taking in the vista of beach and ocean when Rowland finally broached the subject of Isobel Hanrahan.

"I wanted to ask you, Father," he said quietly, "did you find Isobel, that night on the boat?"

Matthew Bryan bit his lip and paused to gather himself before he replied. "Yes. I found the poor girl in the chapel."

"Oh." Rowland wasn't sure what he had hoped to hear. This told him nothing. "Did she...?"

"I heard Isobel's last confession," Bryan grasped Rowland's shoulder in a show of sympathy. "The confessional is sacred confidence, but I can say that the public humiliation to which she had just been subjected was more than Isobel could bear."

"Yes, of course." Rowland looked towards the waves.

Edna slipped her hand into his. "It was Bishop Hanrahan who chose to make a scene, Rowly," she reminded him gently. "You would never have done that to her."

"I'm afraid Isobel felt very abandoned and ill-used," the clergyman continued with an audible note of reproach.

Edna stepped between Rowland and Matthew Bryan. She turned her back on the deacon and did not release Rowland's hand.

"In the end," Bryan went on, "she ran out of the chapel. If I'd known what she intended, I'd have never let her go."

Rowland tensed. Matthew Bryan still thought Isobel had taken her own life.

"Someone killed Isobel, Father."

The clergyman was clearly startled. "But I thought…"

"The police are sure. Some evil mongrel threw her from the deck."

Bryan leant back against the wall and crossed himself. "Well, this changes things somewhat."

"Why?"

Matthew Bryan was flustered, distressed. "Well, she did not die by her own hand—the bishop will want to know. For that, at least, her soul will not be damned."

Rowland bristled, but he said nothing. The belltower of St. Patrick's Seminary was not the place to challenge Bryan on theological dogma.

Bryan sighed heavily. "I'm sorry—I'm being insensitive." He glanced at Edna's hand in Rowland's, and his voice hardened again. "I can see that Isobel meant a great deal to you."

"Did you see Isobel again after she left the chapel?" Rowland ignored the censure in Bryan's scrutiny. "Did you go after her?"

"No," Bryan replied, perhaps regretfully. "I thought she wanted time alone. I hoped that she had gone to make peace with His Grace."

"Bishop Hanrahan? She went to see her uncle?"

"I don't know what made me think she might have," Bryan said carefully. "Perhaps it was just hope." He checked his wrist-watch. "I'm afraid I must be getting back."

Rowland shook the clergyman's hand. "Thank you."

"It was lovely to catch up with you, Matthew," said Edna. "You must come out and see us sometime."

"I should be delighted." Bryan's eyes lingered on the locket, which hung over the neckline of her blouse.

Edna closed her hand over the pendant uneasily.

Again Rowland was irritated. No doubt Bryan had recognised the locket as the one Isobel had worn, but however it looked, Rowland would not tolerate anyone judging Edna.

Bryan turned back to Rowland. "You will let me know if the police make any progress?"

Rowland nodded.

"I must write to Isobel's parents…" Bryan shook his head. "She came from a righteous, God-fearing home—how could she have strayed so far?"

Rowland did not respond. There was no point.

They let Bryan return to whatever it was that required his attendance and walked the steep road away from St. Patrick's.

"Come on, Rowly." Edna dragged on his hand. "Shall we take a walk on the beach before we go home? Papa wants some cuttlebone for his pigeons."

It was clear any resistance to Edna's decision to collect cuttle-bone would be futile, so Rowland removed his jacket, rolled up his sleeves and allowed the sculptress to lead him down to the sand. The shoreline was full of holiday-makers, locals and those who had caught the ferry across to enjoy the white sand and sheltered beaches of Manly. Children dug in the sand and played with balls whilst their parents indulged the current passion for lying in the sun on deck chairs. Young men paddled out into the foaming surf on long boards under the watchful eye of the surf rescue volunteers.

Rowland watched as Edna scoured the wet sand collecting cuttlebone, the breeze whipping her copper tresses in all directions. She returned to him with the hair of a madwoman, her hands full. She smiled triumphantly, as if she had gathered gems.

"I'll just put these in your pockets, Rowly," she said, slipping the salt-encrusted shells into the pockets of the jacket he carried over his shoulder. "They'll make my handbag smelly."

Even if Rowland Sinclair had been capable of denying the sculptress anything, it was too late to protest.

They stopped by the kiosk to take tea. Edna tried to smooth her windblown hair whilst Rowland poured. She beamed happily at him. "It's rather nice to be home, isn't it, Rowly?"

He nodded, pushing the sugar basin towards her. "It's rather nice we made it home, the way things were going."

Edna stirred her tea pensively. "Where do you think Isobel went after she left the chapel?"

"The poor wretch could have gone anywhere, Ed."

Edna heaped strawberry jam and cream on a scone and passed it to him. "Do you think she might have gone to see Bishop Hanrahan?"

"We could ask him, I suppose." Rowland grimaced at the very thought.

Edna shook her head. "We'll ask Father Murphy instead. I've not seen him more than two feet from His Grace."

"You have got a point." Rowland glanced back up the hill toward the alma mater of the Catholic priesthood. The bells were calling the seminarians to prayer, or perhaps lunch. It was probably a busy time of year for priests in training. "We'll get Christmas over with," he said as he bit into a scone, "and then we'll go see him."

Clyde thumbed through his well-worn volume on the life and work of Max Meldrum, whose theory of art as a science had been controversial for over a decade. Unlike Rowland, Clyde was not formally trained—the Ashton School had always been beyond his financial reach. He learned his craft by reading and through other artists. Nowadays, Rowland dragged him along to workshops and classes, but he still found inspiration in the books he'd acquired when his life was hard.

Rowland sat across from him in the first-class compartment, behind the *Sydney Morning Herald*.

"Apparently Bradman will be right for the next Test," Rowland murmured. "Might turn things around."

The touring English cricket team had won the first match of the series, whilst they'd been abroad. They had returned to find Sydney in the grip of outrage over the tactics employed by the visitors.

"Do you think they'll continue with this bodyline thing?" Clyde had never played cricket—he wasn't sure about the rights and wrongs of the English strategy.

Rowland shrugged. "Why wouldn't they? It appears to be working. The English seem more interested in winning than playing cricket."

"Bradman better learn to duck, then."

"That's exactly what we don't want." Rowland checked his watch. "We'll be in Yass soon."

Clyde closed his book. "Better get ready to rejoin the proletariat."

Rowland shook his head. Clyde insisted on travelling in the second-class carriages from Yass, adamant that he couldn't be seen alighting from the front of the train. To Rowland it was mad.

Clyde closed his eyes. "You have no idea of the grief my old mum will give me if she thinks I'm getting above myself." His voice rose in an imitation of his mother's. "The Joneses are working people and working people's carriages is good enough for us."

Rowland laughed. He'd noticed that Clyde had put on his oldest suit for the trip home. "You'll have to introduce me to your mother one day."

Clyde chuckled. "Oh, mate, you know not what you ask."

The train pulled into Yass Junction. Rowland wished his friend a Happy Christmas and stepped out onto the platform. Midday in Yass, at this time of year, was stifling. Sydney summers were alleviated by sea breezes, but Yass was a long way inland.

Wilfred's chauffeur found him and had his trunk loaded into the gleaming black Rolls-Royce. The driver opened the rear door.

"Wil!" Rowland was surprised. It was not Wilfred's practice to meet him at the station.

"Get in the car, Rowly. We haven't got much time."

Rowland climbed in. "Time for what exactly?"

"Polo match. We seem to be a man short. You can change at the field."

"I can what?"

"I've had ponies taken to the field for you." Wilfred either missed or ignored the horror in Rowland's voice.

"You want me to play? Have you lost your mind?"

"As I said, we're a man short. If I could get someone else, I would."

"Wil, be reasonable. I haven't played polo in years. I haven't been on a bloody horse in…"

"I'm sure you haven't forgotten how to ride," Wilfred dismissed his protest. "Come on, Rowly. I don't want to cancel the match—people have come from all round the district."

"I was shot," Rowland said feebly.

"You're barely limping…it'll be the horse that's running, not you."

"It's the middle of summer—why are you playing now?" Rowland persisted.

"It's a friendly exhibition match," Wilfred replied, as the Rolls started to move.

"Who's playing?" Rowland asked wearily. It appeared he was going to play, regardless of what he said.

"English team." Wilfred sat back. "Some chaps who came out to watch the cricket…thought they'd play a spot of polo between Tests."

"So couldn't you have just called in the Ashtons?"

The Ashton brothers were indisputably the elite of Australian polo. Their victorious tour of Britain had already become smug legend in polo circles.

"The Englishmen are staying at Markdale," Wilfred said naming the Ashton property near Crookwell. "Using Ashton ponies, in fact. Philip thought some of the other fellows would enjoy playing them."

"Jolly decent of him," Rowland said irritably. Bloody Philip Ashton and his great ideas.

Wilfred smiled. "Chin up, Rowly. It's only four chukkas. Kate tells me that every young lady in the district is coming out to watch."

Rowland laughed despite himself. Wilfred never missed an opportunity to throw suitable young women in his path. "I really don't think I'm going to impress anyone playing polo, Wil. Have you forgotten?"

Wilfred ignored his trepidation. "Just stay on your horse and you'll be fine—it's a goodwill match."

Rowland looked at his brother unconvinced. Goodwill or not, Wilfred was competitive.

"Wil, almost anyone can play better than I can—couldn't you have found someone else?"

"No time—Penfold only pulled out about an hour ago."

Rowland knew Skippy Penfold—he was as polo mad as Wilfred. "Why did Penfold pull out?"

"He's not conscious yet."

"What?"

"A mishap at practice."

"What kind of mishap?"

"Got hit in the head with a mallet."

Chapter Twenty-two
POLO

Molonglo Club

The Molonglo Polo Club had a practice last Saturday,
on the grounds near Duntroon, and will have another
practice next Saturday, when it is hoped to have a full
muster of players. This club had a most successful
season, and, in view of the number of clever young players, the prospects for next season are equally as bright.
—*The Canberra Times*

Rowland emerged from the players' marquee in the knit jersey
shirt, jodhpurs, and high boots that Wilfred had brought in for
him. He carried a pith helmet under his arm and appeared for
all the world like a man who could play polo.

The field was on the McWilliamson property. Its boarded
perimeter was crowded with spectators in their race-day best.
The broad-brimmed sunhats of the district's ladies surrounded
the playing field like milling beds of flowers. Union Jacks and
Australian flags were both waved in politely even numbers.
Rowland muttered under his breath. He was about to be publicly humiliated.

He had played polo before, but he had never been very good at it, even when he'd played regularly. Now, it was a couple of years since he'd picked up a mallet.

"Rowly!" Wilfred called him over to where the ponies were being readied, and introduced their teammates. Rowland shook hands with Bradley Wainwright and Jeffery Kynaston, both men of Wilfred's ilk.

"Jolly relieved to see you, Rowly." Wainwright smiled broadly. He winked at Wilfred. "This should even up the handicap—the English chaps are a seventeen-goal team."

Rowland glared at his brother. So that was it. Polo teams played with handicaps that were an aggregate of each player's. Having a lower handicap than the opposing team could be a distinct advantage. Wilfred was a six-goal player. Presumably Wainwright and Kynaston were similar. Rowland's handicap was one.

Wilfred handed him a mallet. "Mount and get your eye in, Rowly," he suggested. "You'll play at number one—we have about fifteen minutes."

Rowland glanced at the English team who were already on the field warming up, mallets swinging in wide strong arcs. Wilfred was going to get him killed…with spectators.

He mounted, trying to get used to the saddle after a considerable absence. Wilfred had selected the horse. An excellently sized and proportioned animal, obviously well-trained. But then, Wilfred knew how to select horses…it was his choice of players that Rowland found dubious.

The tournament opened with "God Save the King," the anthem of both nations. Rowland patted the side of his pony's neck nervously. Hopefully, the horse knew what it was doing.

The teams lined up, the ball was tossed midfield and the match was underway. The first seven-minute chukka was, to Rowland, a blur. The game was played at a gallop, the ponies churning the three-hundred-yard field at speed. He concentrated on following Wilfred in attack, avoiding the mallets and staying on his horse.

Wilfred shouted instructions.

"Tail it!"

"Take the man, Rowly!"

"Turn it now!"

"Rowly, what are you doing?"

All the other members of Rowland's team stepped in to play his position from time to time.

Rowland Sinclair had been struck by the bamboo ball twice and by mallets often, by the time the first change of horses was called. He'd committed one foul and collided with an umpire.

"We're two goals behind," Wilfred told him as they mounted fresh ponies.

"Oh. That's not good." Rowland had lost track of the score as he tried desperately not to be noticeably incompetent.

Wilfred did not seem worried. He looked towards the English four. They were sweating profusely, their faces bright red beneath the white helmets.

"The heat will knock them up by the next chukka," Wilfred advised.

Rowland nodded. "Heatstroke. Good strategy."

"We're going to have to work on your swing, old boy," Wilfred ignored both the comment and his brother's simmering rebellion. "I'd swear you were playing tennis out there."

Rowland was about to do some swearing of his own, when they were called back onto the field. True to Wilfred's prediction, the English team started to flag.

The score was tied by half-time. The spectators surged onto the field for the traditional treading in of the turf dug out by the horses' hooves.

"I say, Sinclair, your brother's digging more divots with his mallet than all the ponies combined," Wainwright noted.

Wilfred found this extremely funny, Rowland less so.

By the third chukka, the Australians were three goals ahead, despite having to compensate for Rowland, who was being reminded that polo was a contact sport.

As they changed horses for the final chukka, Wilfred spoke quietly of strategy. "They've realised Rowly's out of his depth."

"I must say, it's bloody obvious," Kynaston agreed, taking Wilfred's lead on tact. "I thought you said the lad had played before."

"What say we leave Rowly with defensive plays," Wilfred said quickly, as he saw his brother rile. "We can keep up the offence between the three of us. Rowly, you just make yourself a nuisance to the English—particularly their number one—but leave the ball alone."

"Let's just get this over with," Rowland mumbled.

They rode out for the last chukka. In this final seven minutes, the English team seemed to find a second wind. Suddenly the game was tied again. As instructed, Rowland did not attempt to take control of the ball and confined his play to riding off the opposing players or hooking their mallets to prevent a stroke.

At some point, one of the English players retaliated. Rowland wasn't really sure which, or how. All he knew was that he came off his horse. The crowd gasped dramatically making him feel like even more of a fool. A foul was declared and a penalty awarded against the English team. There were now only a few seconds of play left. Rowland had remounted and found himself the beneficiary of a free hit for goal when the match was tied.

Wilfred was clearly worried. Rowland couldn't blame him. The shot wasn't impossible, but it wasn't entirely straightforward. He'd have to hit the ball fairly hard to make the distance, and the goal was defended. It was the kind of shot one practised time and again in the hitting pit…but then, he hadn't been near a hitting pit for at least three years. Still, here was an opportunity to redeem a little dignity.

Wilfred leant over to him. "Straighten up your back swing and follow through properly."

Rowland lined up the goal. His head was still spinning a little from the fall. He swung—Wilfred's advice remembered only midshot. He listened for the crack of bamboo against bamboo. The sound was more of a thud. He'd missed—not entirely, but almost. The ball deflected with enough momentum to roll only a few yards. Annoyingly, the crowd gasped again. The English team took a second to realise that the ball was going nowhere near the goal and turned to charge towards it. Wilfred galloped up behind his brother and swung. The ball fired into the now undefended goal like a shot. The crowd cheered: male voices and the enthusiastic clapping of ladies, too genteel to shout. The whistle blew shrill and the match was theirs.

Wilfred rode back to Rowland and slapped him on the back.

"Brilliant feint, Rowly," he said loudly. "Cleared the goal completely."

Wainwright reined in his horse beside Wilfred. "Got to admit," he said to Rowland, grinning, "I thought you'd really cocked it up for a moment. Should have known you Sinclairs were cooking something up."

Rowland was just glad it was over and that he had finished the match astride his horse.

The victory was applauded appropriately with speeches from the back of a truck festooned with bunting and flags. The Sinclair brothers received particular approbation from the spectators. Rowland accepted the congratulations in Wilfred's shadow, wondering if anybody had actually watched the match. He was well aware that he hadn't done much of use.

The McWilliamsons were hosting a garden party to follow the match and soon he was being plied with champagne and canapés.

"Uncle Rowly!"

Rowland turned as a five-year-old boy tore through to him.

"Ernie!" Rowland dropped to one knee and ruffled the child's wet-combed hair. "Good Lord, you've grown."

Ernest put out his hand.

Rowland shook it solemnly.

"Welcome home, Uncle Rowly. I trust you enjoyed your time on the broad."

Rowland smiled. "Abroad, Ernie. Yes, I had a jolly nice time abroad. Where's your mother?"

"Kate's back at Oaklea with the baby." Wilfred came to stand behind his son. "You know what new mothers are like."

Rowland had no idea, but decided to take Wilfred's word

for it. "Shall we go then?" he suggested. "I'm keen to meet this new nephew of mine."

"Mrs. McWilliamson insists I introduce you to a few people first," Wilfred said firmly. "Ernie, go and play for a while. I'll come and find you when your uncle and I are done."

Ernest nodded obediently.

"There's a good boy."

Rowland turned to his brother suspiciously. "Mrs. McWilliamson? I barely know the woman—who could she possibly want me to meet?"

"I couldn't say, Rowly, but she's our hostess. It would be most impolite to refuse."

Wilfred took Rowland up to the main house, a grand federation homestead with wide, tiled verandahs.

Mrs. McWilliamson was on the verandah having tea with a perfumed, pastel congregation of young women.

"Oh, for God's sake!" Rowland exploded under his breath as he turned to leave.

Wilfred grabbed his arm and hailed their hostess.

"Why Mr. Sinclair, how lovely to see you back in Yass," Mrs. McWilliamson effused. "Won't you sit down and tell us about the match. I must say I haven't watched a game so thrilling in years."

"I'm sure Rowly would love to stay and chat with you ladies," Wilfred said pleasantly. "I must speak to Harold for a moment—he's in the house, is he? I'll leave you to it shall I, Rowly? Righto, then."

Rowland smiled courteously and took the seat Mrs. McWilliamson offered him, silently plotting the murder of Wilfred Sinclair.

It was at least an hour before Wilfred returned. By then Rowland had made the acquaintance of several suitable young women who had bombarded him with competing charm and light repartee. They had twittered and giggled over his every word, being careful to appear neither aloof nor forward. It was probably a good thing that their hostess was serving tea to this cloistered gathering, as Rowland might otherwise have resorted to drinking.

When Wilfred appeared, Rowland got to his feet so quickly that the wicker chair on which he had been sitting overturned. He apologised and righted it without taking his eyes off Wilfred, in case his brother decided to disappear again.

"I'm afraid I'm going to have to drag you away, Rowly," Wilfred said, perfectly aware that no dragging would be necessary. "Kate and Mother will be anxious to see you again." To the refined gaggle of young women, he said, "I trust we will be seeing you ladies at Oaklea on Boxing Day."

The Sinclairs had hosted a Boxing Day garden party in aid of the Red Cross since the War. It was quite the social event of the region.

Rowland made his farewells politely, graciously, for he was a gentleman of impeccable breeding.

"Charming girls, don't you think?" Wilfred said as they set out to find Ernest. "You wouldn't believe the number of couples Alice McWilliamson has introduced at polo matches—she's got quite a knack."

Rowland glanced at his brother. "You're bloody lucky I haven't got a mallet."

Chapter Twenty-three

SOUTHERN CROSS

Damaged in Night Landing

Air-Commodore Kingsford Smith after returning from participating in the display of illuminations at the Harbour Bridge on Saturday night, suffered a mishap at Mascot in which the plane *Southern Cross* was damaged.
—*The Sydney Morning Herald*

Oaklea had changed a little since Rowland Sinclair had last been home. His sister-in-law had been renovating the original building for a number of years now, adding modern features to the massive Victorian mansion. The Art Deco additions were probably not in keeping with the Romanesque features of the original structure, but Rowland didn't mind them. He rather liked the eclectic quirks that Kate had introduced, probably quite unintentionally, to the traditional magnificence of the Sinclair residence.

Kate met them at the foot of the entrance stairway. A quietly lovely young woman, she was a couple of years younger than Rowland and sixteen years her husband's junior.

"Welcome home, Rowly," she said with genuine warmth as he kissed her cheek. She noted at the polo uniform he still wore. "You played! Oh, I'm so sorry I missed it. Did you win?"

Rowland smiled ruefully. "Yes, but that had little to do with me. Wil was the hero of the hour."

Kate gazed adoringly at her husband. "Of course he was, but I'm sure you're just being modest, Rowly."

Wilfred laughed. "No, he isn't."

"Well, come inside and meet Ewan." Kate took Ernest's hand. "Your mother is resting at the moment but she'll be so glad to see you."

Rowland was introduced to Ewan Dougal Baird Sinclair, a pudding-shaped infant who gazed passively at him with the dark blue eyes that distinguished all the Sinclair men.

Kate told Rowland proudly of how the child had grown, how well he ate, and how much he adored young Ernest.

"He looks just like Wil, don't you think?" she said as she kissed the chubby cheek.

Rowland looked from the drooling six-month-old in her arms, to his brother, with no clue as to the similarity of which she spoke. "Spitting image."

"I'm going to shower and change before Mother gets up." He nodded towards young Ewan. "You've done well, Kate."

Wilfred smiled at his wife as he swung Ernest up under his arm. "She has rather."

Rowland went to his room to wash off the perspiration and dirt of the polo field. His trunks had already been taken up and unpacked.

He was just buttoning a fresh shirt when there was knock at his door.

"Uncle Rowly?"

"Come in, Ernie."

The boy opened the door and came in, dragging an ugly one-eared greyhound behind him.

"Lenin! How are you, mate?" Rowland bent to greet the ill-bred hound Milton had rescued from the track.

The dog recognised him. Its excessive tail wagged so hard that its entire body writhed like a snake and its paws slipped and skittered on the polished hardwood floors.

Rowland picked the creature up and dropped it onto the bed. Lenin rolled onto his back, continuing to twist with excitement.

"Daddy won't let us call him Lenin." Ernest watched his uncle romp with the dog.

Rowland tickled Lenin's single ear. "What are you calling him, then?"

"Daddy calls him 'Rowly's bloody dog.'"

Rowland laughed. "Thank you for bringing him up to me, Ernie."

"Don't tell Mummy—I'm not 'sposed to."

"I'll cover for you."

"What are you two plotting?" Wilfred walked in unexpectedly. He glanced at Lenin who was now circling into the bedclothes. "Oh, I see."

Rowland dug into the pocket of his trousers. "I have something for you, Ernie."

In truth, he had an entire trunk of gifts for his nephews—he and his friends had reverted to childhood and become somewhat carried away in the magnificent toy stores of London and New York. But the trunk could wait until Christmas. He handed a flattened spool to the boy.

"Thank you very much, Uncle Rowly." Ernest inspected the gift perplexed.

Rowland took the toy back from him and demonstrated. "It's called a yo-yo, I believe. All the rage in New York. Here, you try."

They watched Ernest struggle with the yo-yo for a few minutes.

"Why don't you go outside and practise, Ernie?" Wilfred grimaced as the wooden spool crashed against the floorboards yet again. "I'll take your uncle to visit with your grandmother for a while…oh, and take Rowly's bloody dog with you."

Ernest did as he was told, studiously throwing the yo-yo onto the floor and trying to jerk it back as he walked out.

"How's Mother?" Rowland asked, as he knotted his tie. He gathered that was what Wilfred had come to speak to him about.

"She's no better."

"I hadn't really hoped for that, Wil," Rowland assured him quietly.

"Still, Rowly…"

"It's all right, Wil. I know what to expect by now. I didn't imagine Mother had suddenly recovered whilst I was abroad."

"I suppose not."

Rowland finished with his tie. Somehow he found his mother's particular malady easier to accept than Wilfred.

"Is Mother coming up to Sydney?" he asked as he buttoned his waistcoat. Elisabeth Sinclair hadn't returned to Woodlands House since Aubrey had been listed amongst the fallen of Ypres.

"Of course," Wilfred said, a little grimly. "The war's been over for fourteen years. Mrs. Kendall will come along to attend to her."

Rowland pulled on his jacket and followed his brother to their mother's rooms.

A handsome woman, Elisabeth Sinclair belied her sixty-seven years. She still dressed fashionably, and meticulously, her snowy hair coiffed elegantly. It was only her eyes that hinted the toll taken by years and loss. For Rowland, there was a bittersweet gratification in the way those eyes grew elated when he walked in. It was not really him that she was so glad to see, but still, it made her happy.

"Aubrey, you've come home at last. Where on earth have you been?"

It was many years since his mother had recognised Rowland as anyone other than Aubrey Sinclair. It had been easier to forget that her youngest son ever existed than to accept the death of his brother. Perhaps it was also easier for Rowland to be Aubrey than to accept her disappointment that he was not.

Rowland sat with his mother for a while. He did not ask or expect that she recognise him. So Elisabeth Sinclair spoke to him of music and polo, and all those things that Aubrey had loved. Rowland didn't say a great deal. It was just his presence, his countenance, with its startling resemblance to Aubrey's that the old woman needed.

In time, he escorted her down to dinner.

Rowland seated his mother and took his own place at the formally set table. He winced. His muscles were starting to stiffen, his body protesting the punishment of the polo field. The ache had returned to his wounded leg. Aside from having been battered by ball and mallet, and knocked from his horse, he was unused to riding. Reacquainting himself with the saddle at a gallop had probably not been the best idea, but then, it had not been his idea.

Wilfred invited him to say grace.

"No—you go ahead. Just make it short."

Ernest's jaw dropped.

Wilfred glanced at Kate. "Are you sure you want him to be Ewan's godfather?"

Kate smiled. "I'm sure Rowly will do a wonderful job."

"Of course, I will," Rowland replied. "My godfather taught me to play poker. A fine tradition."

Kate assumed he was joking and laughed. Wilfred appeared less sure. In her fashion, Elisabeth Sinclair ignored any conversation inconsistent with the belief that she was sitting beside Aubrey.

Wilfred said grace, and they broke bread over talk of the approaching christening. An unfaltering hostess, Kate asked Rowland of his time abroad. He told her of London and Paris, of Berlin and Cairo, consciously avoiding mention of his troubled journey home. Neither did he speak of Ypres in his mother's presence.

Young Ernest talked gravely of the impending arrival of Father Christmas in Yass' main department store, and Wilfred discussed the sorry state of wool prices.

Once the ladies and Ernest had retired, Wilfred casually informed his brother that he had purchased a neighbouring farm. The proprietors had apparently been less able to weather the decline in wool prices than the Sinclairs.

"You can come out with me tomorrow to have a look at it."

"And the owners?" Rowland was uncomfortable with the notion. These people were their neighbours.

"Left the property some time ago, Rowly. Poor Jefferies hanged himself in June."

Rowland flinched, aware that his brother had known Stanley Jefferies well.

Wilfred lit his pipe frowning. "He'd been very exposed in the stock market—lost almost everything." Wilfred puffed as the tobacco took. "Clarice tried to keep things afloat for a couple of months—but it got too much for her. Selling to us allowed her to walk away with a little dignity. Enough money for a house in the city and a small income. It wouldn't have been so if the bank had foreclosed."

"What about James?" Rowland had been at school with James Jefferies.

"He's a solicitor now—been living in Sydney for some time…not happy about losing the property, but that's hardly our fault." He looked at Rowland over the top of his bifocals. "This is business, Rowly. We helped them while we could but they were not viable."

Rowland nodded, resigned. "You know what you're doing, Wil."

The following morning they set out for what had been the Jefferies' property, whilst Kate and the nanny took the youngest Sinclairs into town to see the Christmas pantomime.

The Jefferies homestead was an overbearing federation building with an excess of leadlight and unnecessary finials. It had been extended several times. An elaborately engraved shingle swung from a post at the entrance declaring the property name as Emoh Ruo. Wilfred was indifferent to the house—it would probably end up as a manager's residence.

They followed the road which divided the property, surveying paddocks and assessing fence lines. Wilfred pointed out the water sources, the large spring-fed dams and bores marked by iron windmills. Rowland gathered that it was the water that interested his brother. The countryside had suffered a couple of dry summers. Reliable water could mean a significant difference to yield.

"Half the property is under crop," Wilfred motioned towards the western paddocks. "Wheat and barley mainly...of course there's still not much point in growing wheat but we're putting in more silos."

"Uh huh."

"We've picked up some properties in Gundagai and I've purchased a snow lease for next season...it'll probably be a good idea to put in a few hundred acres of oats."

Rowland nodded vaguely. Wilfred was just updating him, not asking his opinion. Apparently the Sinclairs were expanding.

The Rolls-Royce pulled up outside a collection of machinery sheds. The chauffeur opened the door for Wilfred. Rowland let himself out.

"What's in here?" Rowland asked.

"Possibly the reason why poor Jefferies went under in the end." Wilfred took out a key and unlocked the padlocks that secured the largest shed. "Stanley had to have the latest tractors and headers. Always buying new equipment and then trading the moment something bigger came onto the market." He pulled open the doors. Rowland followed him inside.

"He bought this about two years ago—it's barely been out of the shed. I'll have to put the word out and find a buyer."

Rowland gazed up at the Gipsy Moth. The silver wings extended from a two-tone fuselage in British racing green and white. The name *Rule Britannia* was emblazoned near the tail-plane. She was magnificent.

"No, don't do that," he said.

"Why?"

"We should keep her."

"Whatever for? What could you possibly want with a plane?"

"I'll learn to fly her."

"Why?"

"I might crash her otherwise."

"Don't be smart, Rowly," Wilfred said curtly. "Why do you want to fly a plane?"

"Do I have to have a reason, Wil?" Rowland climbed onto the lower wing and into the cockpit. He inspected the instrument panel. She was beautiful.

"God forbid you fail to indulge every passing whim," Wilfred muttered.

"Don't sell the plane," Rowland said again.

Wilfred studied him disapprovingly. "For pity's sake, Rowly, you're nearly twenty-eight—isn't it about time you started acting responsibly...found some direction...?"

Rowland refused to be drawn. He tapped the dash. "As luck would have it, she has a compass, Wil."

"One good reason, Rowly," Wilfred demanded. "Just give me one good reason why we need a plane."

Rowland had now climbed onto the fuselage to examine the fuel tank housed in the bulging airfoil that formed the centre section of the upper wing.

"We don't want to be the last people to get one, Wil," he said smiling. "How would it look?"

He climbed down and stood next to his brother. "She could make the trip to Sydney in an hour. That's got to be useful."

Wilfred regarded *Rule Britannia* distastefully. "You'll get yourself killed."

"Believe me, I'm much more likely to die in a polo match," Rowland replied.

Wilfred seemed to give up. "Fine," he said shaking his head. "God knows, once you get some cockeyed notion into your head..."

"Capital!"

Wilfred removed his spectacles. "Sadly, Stanley Jefferies' passing has left another vacancy, Rowly."

"Oh yes?" Rowland was preoccupied with the aircraft. "God-awful name..." He wondered if it would be bad luck to change it.

"His position on the board of Dangar's hasn't been filled as yet."

Rowland nodded absently. Dangar, Gedye and Company was some kind of wool-broking firm, in which the Sinclairs had a significant shareholding.

"I want you to take his place on the board."

Rowland stopped. Of course—he should have known—this was a transaction then. "Wil, what would I know about sheep?"

"About time you learned—the company's moving further into mechanisation—tractors, generators, even refrigeration. You might find it interesting."

"I doubt it."

"It's just a quarterly meeting." Wilfred began to polish his spectacles. "It'll do you good to have some form of responsibility."

Rowland regarded his brother coldly. "I don't need a job, Wil."

Wilfred smiled faintly. "You know, Kingsford Smith is setting up some sort of flying school later this year." He returned the spectacles to his nose. "Oversubscribed, as you'd expect, but I could have a word…"

Rowland swore.

Wilfred ignored him.

Rowland thought momentarily about telling his brother what he could do with Dangar, Gedye and Company, and then he looked again at the Gipsy Moth. She really was a glorious machine. He laughed. Maybe Wilfred knew him better than he thought. He didn't have a chance of getting into the Kingsford Smith School without his brother's influence.

"Fine then, I'll sit on your board until they realise the bloody tea lady knows more about running companies than I do."

"I knew you'd come round, Rowly."

Rowland wasn't listening. He was back in the cockpit, convinced that he had just agreed to pay dearly for the *Rule Britannia*. It was not something he could help, however.

Chapter Twenty-four

CRITICAL WOOL POSITION
Effect on National Income
Matter for Grave Anxiety

By TJA Fitzpatrick of Warre Warral

"The time has come" the growers said
"To talk of many things;
Of wool—and prices—and interest rates,
Of wages, cost—and rings,
And why the market has gone to pot,
And whether sheep have wings."
—*Wagga Daily Advertiser*

The next days at Oaklea passed in a congenial blur, fuelled by eggnog and goodwill. Unashamedly besotted, Rowland took Kate and Ernest to visit his plane, extracting from them the excitement and admiration he so felt the aircraft deserved. He relegated to the back of his mind the promise Wilfred had extorted in return for the indulgence. He knew full well that his brother had manipulated him—but then, it was just a quarterly meeting. Wilfred probably had the right to expect that much from him.

His good humour survived even the onslaught of suitable young things, to which his well-meaning sister-in-law subjected him. By Boxing Day he had been introduced or re-introduced to every young debutante in the district.

"You know, Rowly, my dear friend Lucy is still very taken with you," Kate confided, as the family shared breakfast.

Wilfred snorted as he ate his eggs. It was unclear whether it was in response to Lucy or the fact that she was taken with Rowland.

"Lucy Bennett?" Rowland stirred his coffee. "Hasn't someone married the poor girl yet?"

"I believe she rather hoped *you* would," Kate said pointedly.

Rowland laughed. Lucy Bennett and her well-rehearsed charm. He couldn't remember giving her any reason to assume her interest was reciprocated. In fact, he was sure he'd offended her—unintentionally of course, but fortuitously.

"Good Lord—she won't do. I couldn't let Wil have the prettier wife." He winked at Ernest who noted everything.

"You may just have to get used to it," Wilfred muttered without looking up from his plate.

Kate blushed and glanced shyly at Wilfred. She stood, flustered. "Excuse me…I should check on Ewan."

Wilfred didn't appear to notice.

Rowland smiled. Kate had always seemed unable to remain in the same room as a compliment from her husband. It was a good thing that Wilfred Sinclair was not an effusive man or they would never see her.

After breakfast, Rowland rang through to Delaney in Sydney. He spoke quietly, not wanting his interest in Isobel Hanrahan's murder to be overheard. He was unsure how much of the affair Wilfred had told Kate.

Delaney informed him that he was looking into the background of several of the passengers who had sailed on the *Aquitania*, but to date had discovered little.

"I don't know, Sinclair," the detective admitted. "One would expect there to be a connection between so many murders in such proximity, but there doesn't seem to be anything consistent. Urquhart and Waterman were Theosophists, but Isobel Hanrahan was a Catholic…and then someone shot at you. As unlikely as it seems, perhaps the incidents are unrelated."

Rowland told Delaney of his conversation with Matthew Bryan, and his plans to speak to Murphy about whether Isobel found her uncle the morning she died.

"Good," Delaney agreed. "You do that. I have to be careful going after Hanrahan in an official capacity. Archbishop Mannix is already alleging religious persecution…and Mannix has enough connections in the Force to threaten more than just damnation. You let me know what you find out."

Next, Rowland called St. Patrick's Seminary. After going through a succession of intervening clergy, he spoke with Father Murphy. The young deacon seemed nervous, but agreed to meet with him on the twenty-ninth of the month.

Satisfied, Rowland returned to being gracious as guests began to arrive for Oaklea's annual garden party. The marquees had been festooned in red and white bunting, the arbours and walkways more naturally decorated with wisteria in full bloom. The gardeners had dressed the fountain with plantings of primrose and violas, nurtured to be at their best on this day. Wilfred's beloved roses were resplendent.

Once again, Rowland was introduced to an inordinate number of young women. He bore it stoically, guessing that his entanglement with Isobel Hanrahan must have intensified Wilfred's determination to see him settled with an appropriately well-bred Protestant.

Wainwright and Kynaston also arrived, apparently intent on reminding him of his dismal performance on the polo field.

"Of course, Wilfred told us you were a one-goal player," said Kynaston. "We thought it must have been an aberration. You're a Sinclair, after all."

Wainwright took over. "Imagine our surprise, old man, when we realised that one goal was in fact optimistic."

"Yes, imagine," Rowland replied.

"I daresay your stroke needs work," Kynaston informed him, "but some solid days in the hitting pit might sort that out."

"Your main problem is that you're a tad skittish," Wainwright looked Rowland up and down, perplexed. "I was sure Wilfred said you boxed at Oxford."

"The point of boxing is to avoid getting hit," Rowland said flatly. He had tried his hand at boxing, quite successfully in fact…because he knew how to move out of the way.

Wainwright was not convinced. "You can't flinch every time the ball comes near you. Five times out of ten it won't hit you."

"And the other five?" Rowland asked curtly.

Kynaston's expression was quite frankly surprised. "Well, you have a helmet, old boy. You didn't see service did you? That would have sorted you out."

Rowland had never before considered war as preparation for polo. Images of Wainwright and Kynaston in the trenches with their mallets and pith helmets came too easily to mind. Between the sycophantic admiration of the unmarried minions and the brutal honesty of Kynaston and Wainwright, he was drinking rather a lot.

At some point Wilfred took him aside. He seemed a little amused.

"You're looking a trifle beleaguered, Rowly. Come on—we'll have Mrs. Kendall make us some coffee." He inclined his head at the party now in full swing amongst the marquees. "I think they might cope without us for a while."

Rowland followed his brother into the library. Mrs. Kendall, who had served at Oaklea since well before the war, brought in a tray of coffee and another of the shortbread he had loved as a child. The housekeeper beamed, gratified by the enthusiasm with which he helped himself to a handful of the dainty biscuits.

"It's so lovely to have you home, Mr. Rowland," she said warmly. "You always did like a nice biscuit—I'll have a tin packed into your trunk…now don't you eat too quickly…" She looked at him, clucking like he was one of her chicks. Wilfred cleared his throat, and finally she left them to it.

"It's astounding she doesn't still cut your meat," Wilfred grumbled.

Rowland sank back into an armchair and brushed the crumbs from his tie. Alice Kendall had started excessively mothering him when Aubrey had been killed, and his own mother had become distant. He had been a bewildered child then, but even now he found her fussing rather sweet and comforting in its way. He was, in any case, very fond of his brother's housekeeper.

It was nearly nine o'clock. His train would leave from Yass Junction in the early hours of the morning. He had hoped to get a couple of hours' sleep first.

Wilfred pulled a number of volumes from a shelf and placed them onto the table beside Rowland.

"Here, you'd better read these."

"What are they?" Rowland was too busy eating shortbread to actually open the books.

"Reports—they'll give you a bit of background to Dangar's company affairs."

"Oh." So it was time to start paying for the Gipsy Moth.

"I reminded Mrs. Kendall to make sure your regalia was packed."

"My regalia! Whatever for?"

As Rowland only attended Lodge when Wilfred dragged him to a local meeting, he had never taken his Masonic regalia back to Sydney. There was no need.

"Rowly, you are about to join the board of Dangar's. You'll need to go to Lodge occasionally—how else do you expect to do business?"

Rowland groaned.

Wilfred ignored him.

"You can come with me to Lodge Victoria at the Masonic Centre in January…it'll be a good opportunity to introduce you to the rest of the board…I'll make the arrangements and have you affiliated there. You might be wise to brush up on your charges."

Rowland, whose resistance had been mitigated with an afternoon of champagne, was feeling a bit under siege. He decided to retire before Wilfred told him that marrying Lucy Bennett was included in his agreement to become a director of Dangar, Gedye and Company.

"I've ordered you a kilt," Wilfred added as his brother stood to leave. "I'll have it delivered to Woodlands."

"A kilt! Have you lost your mind?"

"The Sinclair tartan," Wilfred said calmly. "You know what Kate's people are like."

"Yes. They're mad. There's no reason we should be too."

"It would be a nice gesture…" Wilfred did not dispute that his in-laws were mad. "They want some sort of formal dinner in Ewan's honour, before the christening."

"Kilts?"

"It would make Kate happy."

Rowland groaned again. He was very fond of his sister-in-law, but she wasn't his wife. Surely that had to count for something. "I'm going to bed."

When Clyde came up to the first-class compartments, Rowland was seated somewhat uncomfortably, with part of Lenin in his lap. The remainder of the rather large dog was stretched out on the leather seat.

The dog launched himself at Clyde, pushing off against Rowland's ribs and winding him in the process. Clyde laughed. He was sure that animals, particularly those as ugly as Lenin, were not permitted in the carriages. Of course, such rules did not seem to apply to the Sinclairs or their dogs.

"Hello, Clyde." Rowland shook his hand warmly once he could breathe properly again. "How was your Christmas?"

Clyde sat down and stretched. "We fixed the roof," he said contentedly. "The yo-yos were a big hit with the kids. Mum thought the other stuff was too extravagant—but she'll get over it. Oh…she wants me to get married."

"To whom?"

"No one in particular—as long as she's Catholic. She's afraid you're introducing me to loose-moralled Proddie girls."

"Well, she's not entirely wrong there."

"And I'm not entirely ungrateful." Clyde shook his head. "You look tired, mate," he said studying his friend critically in the dim light. "What have you been doing?"

"Of course, I'm tired." Rowland yawned. "It's three o'clock in the morning." He proceeded to tell Clyde of his time at Oaklea: the polo match, *Rule Britannia,* and what he found himself promising in return for her.

Clyde laughed at him. "Wilfred will have you in parliament next. I hope it was worth it, Rowly."

"You should see her, Clyde." Rowland smiled at the very thought of his Gipsy Moth. "I'll organise hangar space at Mascot."

"Careful…" Clyde grinned. "The Mercedes won't be happy about sharing your attentions."

Rowland's supercharged, S-class tourer had to date been his great passion. The spoils of a poker victory, he had brought the extravagant Mercedes back from Oxford, and despite the post-war antagonism towards German motorcars, he had been loyal to her.

Rowland rubbed his brow thoughtfully, almost guiltily. "I'm sure the three of us can come to some arrangement."

It was still early when the train pulled into Central Station. Johnston had their trunks loaded into the waiting Rolls-Royce. Lenin climbed into the front with the chauffeur, his misshapen, one-eared head lolling happily from the window.

They arrived at Woodlands to find that Mary Brown had already begun the process of returning the Sinclair mansion to the propriety it had once enjoyed. The series of large urns modelled on the naked female torso, were gone. They had just recently lined the driveway, like earthen nymphs beneath the jacaranda trees. The intertwined lovers, who once graced the formal pond, had also vanished.

Rowland's mood darkened. This seemed a bit excessive. Wilfred was turning his house into a monastery. When he walked in, he saw that the housekeeper had also been busy inside the building. Every nude and abstract had been taken down from the walls, leaving only the austere family portraits that had hung in Woodlands House since before his time. The rooms seemed large and stark. Some of the heavy Victorian furniture Rowland had put into storage had re-emerged in the hallway, ready to reclutter the drawing room once he had removed his easels and paint. Mary Brown knew better than to touch those. Rowland Sinclair was not finicky about many things but he was particular about the tools of his trade.

"This is going to be a long month." Rowland gazed despondently at his studio.

"It's only a month, mate," Clyde said reassuringly. "How bad could it be?"

"I had beds for Mr. Isaacs and Mr. Jones put into your rooms, sir." Mary Brown oversaw the ongoing preparations with hands on hips.

"I guess we should move a couple of easels up there." Rowland turned to Clyde. "We'll need to paint somewhere. The rest of our gear can go into Edna's studio."

"The statues moved from the grounds have already been stored in Miss Higgins' studio, sir," the housekeeper warned. "It was rather a tight fit."

Clyde smiled. "Ed's going to love that."

"I suppose we'll have to take them up to the attic, then," Rowland sighed.

Since Mary Brown was clearly anxious to reorder the rooms, they removed their jackets, rolled up their sleeves, and began the task of moving the heavy easels to new locations. Rowland's bedroom was large. Even with the extra beds, there was enough room for two easels in front of the large arched window. More challenging was the bedroom's situation on the third floor.

Thus, when Edna and Milton arrived back at the house, they found Rowland heaving a cumbersome, oak H-frame easel precariously up the staircase.

"Rowly," Edna gasped as soon as she saw him. "I'm so glad you're back. Put that down and come and look at this." The sculptress waved *The Sydney Morning Herald* in her hand.

Of course, Rowland was unable to put the easel down halfway up the stairs, so he was compelled to carry it down again. He pulled out a handkerchief and wiped the back of his neck. "What?"

Edna handed him the paper. "It's horrible, Rowly. Poor Father Murphy."

Rowland looked at the front page. The headline splashed, "Boxing Day Tragedy." He read the subheading: "Deacon falls to his death from the belltower of St. Patrick's College." Father Murphy was dead.

Chapter Twenty-five

A Pleasant Dinner Party

It is one of the best things about English public life that political differences do not interfere with private friendships.

—*The Argus*

───────────────※───────────────

Rowland returned the phone's handpiece to its cradle, and turned towards his friends' expectant faces.

"Delaney doesn't seem to know a great deal," he said. "Murphy appears to have fallen from the belltower late on Boxing Day. Nobody knows what he was doing up there—his body wasn't found for a couple of hours."

"Did he jump?" Milton asked.

Rowland shrugged. "I gather that the police are being pressured to call it an accident."

"But Delaney doesn't think so?"

"Rather stretching the realms of coincidence, one would think." Rowland rubbed his brow. "Apparently the police are having a hard time getting any of the priests to talk to them. There was some kind of ecumenical dinner that night—place was teeming with clergy but no one saw anything. The archbishop's been on the phone to MacKay. Delaney's questioning all the seminarians and visiting clergy—trying to find out as much as he can about Murphy without getting excommunicated—apparently not easy."

Clyde made a face. "You're not suggesting the church has secrets?"

"Delaney would like us to speak to Bryan—see if he knows anything."

"He's deputising you?"

"Ed, actually. Bryan's always been drawn to her." Rowland spoke to the sculptress, unsure how she'd feel about trying to extract information from the deacon. "What do you think?"

Edna hesitated only briefly. "Why don't I invite him to dinner tomorrow—are they allowed out, do you think?" She looked to Clyde for an answer.

He looked back blankly. "I don't know. He's a grown man—surely he's not a prisoner."

"Just ask him," Rowland advised. "Presumably, he'll let us know if we need to break him out."

Edna made the call and, as it turned out, Father Bryan was both able and willing to join them for dinner the following evening.

She put down the phone. "He seemed quite keen to get out of the seminary."

"No bloody wonder if they're throwing priests from the belltower," Milton observed.

Clyde shrugged. "Bryan's a pretty regular sort of bloke, in any case."

Edna smiled prettily. "And so handsome." She frowned at the tragedy of it. "It's wasteful."

They spent the rest of the day reversing the impact that their residency had made on Woodlands House. The timing was probably fortunate. Rowland was unsure how a clergyman, however handsome, would view the more provocative pieces that usually adorned his walls. At the very least, it would make the poor man question his calling.

He went out to fetch Father Bryan from the ferry himself. Finally reunited with his beloved yellow Mercedes, he was enjoying being behind the wheel whenever possible, even if it was just a run to the Quay. Edna came with him.

They waited in the car as the ferry docked and its passengers disembarked. Bryan, distinctive in the black suit and collar of priesthood, walked off the ferry in the company of another man. They were in heated discussion.

Rowland climbed out of the Mercedes and squinted at the two men. "That's Hu."

"Really? What's he doing here? I didn't know he knew Matthew."

"Perhaps they met on the *Aquitania*," Rowland suggested, though it was not something he could recall. Aside from Van Hook's altercation with Bishop Hanrahan, the Theosophists had generally given the clergymen a wide berth. He waved and caught their attention. "Father Bryan, Hu!"

Hubert Van Hook seemed a little startled at first, but he accompanied Bryan over to the car. He shook Rowland's hand enthusiastically.

"Well, well, Sinclair…the people you meet standing on a dock." He winked at Edna. "Hello, doll. You been missing me?"

"Why, Hu," Edna said, jumping out of the car to greet the American and the priest, "how delightful to run into you. We're just about to take Matthew back for dinner—you must come, too."

"Yes, do." Rowland added.

"Well if it ain't my lucky day!" Van Hook replied. "First I run into the Father here and then you two…and now an invitation to dine."

"You'll come then?"

"Swell! I don't have my glad rags on, though." He glanced at Rowland's dinner suit. He moved on. "This your jalopy then, Sinclair?"

Rowland eyes flashed. Jalopy indeed. "Yes, she's mine."

Van Hook let out a low whistle. "You travel in style, Sinclair. I'll say that much for you."

And so they returned to Woodlands House with an extra guest.

"Humpty-doo, Sinclair! What gives? You didn't mention you were the ruddy president?" Van Hook exclaimed as they drove up the long winding drive with Woodlands looming majestically before them.

Rowland laughed. "We don't have a president, Hu."

"No kidding. Who runs the joint then?"

"It's hard to tell sometimes."

Clyde and Milton met them at the front door and they went into the now pristine drawing room where Milton poured drinks.

Matthew Bryan studied the portrait of Henry Sinclair which dominated the room with its stern image. The likeness had been painted in its subject's later years. Henry Sinclair's hair was grey; the years had lined his face with a kind of fierce severity, which silently and uncompromisingly declared power. Only his eyes, intensely blue, spoke of his youngest son.

"My late father." Rowland handed the clergyman a glass of sherry.

Bryan inspected the painting closely from just inches away. "He looks like a gentleman of stature, a man of conviction." His tone was approving, perhaps a little awed.

"Yes, I suppose he was."

"Aside from your eyes, there's little resemblance."

"Rowly hasn't any convictions," Milton assured the clergyman casually. "Hasn't even been arrested."

"I'm glad you don't look like him, Rowly," Edna raised her eyes to the portrait. "I always thought him a little frightening."

Rowland couldn't imagine the sculptress being frightened of anybody. Still, his father had been quite accurately depicted. Henry Sinclair had died whilst Rowland was still a boy, but the man in the portrait was the one he remembered.

Rowland noticed Mary Brown standing at the doorway, looking perceptibly put out. Perhaps she'd overheard. She still considered Henry Sinclair the master of Woodlands.

"Perhaps we should go in to dinner," he suggested.

Edna took Matthew Bryan's arm and led the way into the dining room. Despite the late addition of Hubert Van Hook, the table had been set elegantly and appropriately for a party of six; the polished silverware placed precisely around china monogrammed with the Sinclair crest. They took their seats as soup was served. The conversation was, for most of the meal, light and inconsequential.

When dinner was complete they returned to the drawing room, where Milton sat at the piano and Van Hook entertained with a repertoire from the music halls of America. Clyde was doing battle with his pipe, which it appeared was uncommonly difficult to light. Whilst they were thus engaged, Rowland and Edna spoke to Matthew Bryan of the death of his colleague.

"What was he doing in the belltower at that time of night?" Rowland asked.

Bryan shook his head. "It's hard to know. He was looking for Bishop Hanrahan, but he wouldn't have been in the belltower..."

"Bishop Hanrahan was there?"

"Just that evening," Bryan confirmed.

"How long had Murphy been working for the bishop?"

"We were both assigned to His Grace about six months ago."

"Poor Father Murphy," Edna murmured. "What could have been so wrong that he...?"

"Father Murphy was a man of God," Bryan corrected her sharply. "Only the Heavenly Father has dominion over life or death—he would not have committed such a sin."

"I'm sorry...I didn't mean..." Edna started hastily.

"Surely you don't think one of the other seminarians pushed him?" Rowland's voice held a note of challenge. Every now and then the righteousness of the deacon irritated him.

Bryan was unsettled. "Well no...an accident...he might have slipped..."

"We've been up there," Rowland reminded him. "It's hard to see how he could possibly have slipped over the balustrade."

Bryan struggled. Finally, he said quietly, "Michael Murphy joined the church after some kind of romantic disappointment."

"Did he confide in you, Matthew?" Edna asked.

"More poor Isobel than me. They were both from Dublin, you know."

"I didn't know," Rowland replied. "Not about Father Murphy, at least." He lowered his eyes. "Isobel, where was she…?"

"Rookwood," Bryan told him. "Isobel was laid to rest in Rookwood. It wasn't a big funeral."

"What do you think happened, Matthew?" Edna asked. "To Father Murphy and to Isobel?"

Matthew Bryan was visibly uncomfortable. For a while he said nothing, and then, he chose his words carefully. "It's difficult to say. I would not slander either of them. Neither would I wish to defame those around them. I think it was a sad and tragic episode. It's hard to know what evil lurks in friendly guise."

Rowland glanced at Edna.

"What on earth are you talking about, Matthew?" she demanded.

Matthew Bryan smiled. "It is not a conversation for such pleasant company." He turned towards the impromptu recital being rendered by Milton and Van Hook. "Particularly when we are being so well entertained."

"I think you're using the term 'well' rather loosely." Rowland grimaced.

Edna tried again to bring the clergyman back to Michael Murphy's sad end, but he would no longer be drawn on the subject.

"Leave it," Rowland whispered in her ear as he drew her away. He did not want Bryan to feel interrogated, and it was unlikely that a man in his position would say more.

They passed the remainder of the evening casually, talking mainly of cricket and films. The subjects of Isobel Hanrahan and Father Murphy were now both politely and conspicuously avoided.

Rowland stood to drive his guests home, whilst there was still time to make the last Manly ferry.

Bryan and Van Hook took their leave of Edna and Clyde whilst Rowland brought round the car. The Mercedes' Teutonic engine was loud in the stillness of the hour, disrupting the peace of leafy Woollahra with its attention-seeking roar. Milton climbed into the back with Van Hook, and Father Bryan took a seat beside Rowland.

The ferry had already docked when they reached Circular Quay. Bryan jumped out, waving them away as he boarded the craft.

Hubert Van Hook was staying at The Manor in Mosman, also on the other side of the harbour. It was a fair drive but Van Hook had missed the last ferry and as the Harbour Bridge had been opened only just before they had gone abroad, crossing it was yet a novelty.

"And so how are you getting on with Charles Leadbeater?" Rowland turned the Mercedes into The Manor's driveway. The large federation mansion, the Australian headquarters of the Theosophical movement, was outwardly traditional, overlooking the harbour from one of Sydney's most conservative addresses.

"I should have gone to India," Van Hook muttered unenthusiastically.

"What exactly are you doing here, Hu?" Milton prodded.

"I had to make old Charlie put his John Hancock to some papers before it was too late…legal stuff…the Society's financial arrangements can be complicated and Charlie always makes things difficult."

"So they sent you?" Milton's disbelief was audible.

"Absolutely. I'm an attorney."

"An attorney?…That's a lawyer, right?" Milton didn't try to hide his shock. "You're not a lawyer!"

"Really…on the level. It's what I do for a clam."

"You don't sound like a lawyer."

"Oh, I can wherefore and party-of-the-second-part like any other mouthpiece…but I'm on vacation sort of…so I speak like a regular person."

"Regular, my bloody hat!"

"Anyway," Van Hook went on, "Ma sends someone to check on old Charlie every now and then. Jiddu's decision to jump ship, you know—he didn't take it well."

"Annie's afraid of what he might do?"

"We're all afraid of what Charlie might do," Van Hook sighed. He stiffened. "Holy Mahatmas!"

Rowland slammed his foot on the brake as the figure stepped into the path of the Mercedes. He swerved hard, plunging the car into the low hedge which lined the drive.

Chapter Twenty-six

INTERVIEW WITH COLONEL OLCOTT

The Latest in the Theosophical World

"When Dr. Daly goes out he will probably meet Mr. C. W. Leadbeater, who was an English clergyman. Mr. Leadbeater worked in the Buddhist branch of the Theosophical Society, and subsequently renounced Christianity for Buddhism. Just like Mrs. Besant, Mr. Leadbeater was converted by our Theosophical literature."

—*The Brisbane Courier*

Rowland swore. He climbed out to inspect his car. To his great relief, he found her essentially unharmed. It was only then that he turned towards the figure whose sudden appearance had forced him to risk the pristine duco.

For a moment, Rowland wondered if he had struck his head in the collision. The man before him was tall. A long, grey beard reached his waist and seemed, by hiding the rest of his features, to accentuate the chilling glare of his eyes. He wore a cassock of some sort and a purple cape which fluttered in the gentle midsummer breeze.

Milton, who had joined Rowland outside the car, was predictably moved to poetry by the strange apparition, though he had the good manners to mutter his words.

"It is an ancient Mariner, and he stoppeth one of three. By thy long, grey beard and glittering eye, now wherefore stopp'st thou me?"

"Samuel Taylor Coleridge," Rowland replied, without taking his eyes from the alarming man. He speculated fleetingly on the presence of a medieval wizard in Mosman.

The figure raised a gnarled hand, pointed at him and roared, "Who, sir, are you?"

"Whoa Charlie—these bozos are my pals." Van Hook had emerged from the car. "Gentlemen, may I introduce the legendary Charles Leadbeater, master of mysticism and dubious dress sense."

Leadbeater disregarded the mockery in Van Hook's introduction with a wave of his hand. Rowland was unsure how to respond. Van Hook continued.

"This here is Rowland Sinclair and Milton Isaacs—first-rate fellas, the both of them."

Rowland offered his hand. Leadbeater put his palms together and bowed. "Namaste."

Rowland dropped his hand. "Yes, quite."

Leadbeater straightened. "Rowland Sinclair," he said. "The incomparable Annie Besant has written to me of your promise. I was told of your coming. I have been expecting you."

"Indeed." Inwardly Rowland groaned. He hadn't actually intended to use Annie Besant's letter of introduction.

"You must come in," Leadbeater ordered more than invited. "You should remove your motor from the hedge first."

He stood with his arms folded, clearly intending to remain until they complied with his command.

Rowland put the Mercedes into neutral and they pushed her back onto the drive.

"I could hold him if you fellas want to make a run for it," Van Hook whispered.

Rowland glanced at Leadbeater. He smiled, already looking forward to recounting the story. It was not every day one met a man in a cape. "She'll be right, Hu."

Once the Mercedes was out of the shrubbery, Leadbeater unfolded his arms.

"Very well." He waved towards the house. "We shall be away then—come along, boys." He flourished his cape and proceeded to skip, like some giant aging wood nymph, to The Manor.

Rowland looked at Milton. "I suspect even Coleridge would find this rather odd."

"Beat it, fellas. Fade. I'll alibi you. Jump the train 'cos the destination ain't pretty."

"What did he say?" Milton asked.

Rowland clapped Van Hook on the shoulder. "It would be rude to leave now, Hu."

"Rowly's always been excessively civil," Milton confirmed.

"Don't say I didn't warn you." Van Hook's mood was darkening.

They joined Charles Leadbeater in the main drawing room of The Manor. It had been decorated in the rich and colourful style of the colonial east. Fringes and tessellation finished cushions of opulent fabric strewn across intricately carved ebony couches. A triad of wooden elephants held aloft the inlaid top of a coffee table. The room was lit with candles, though an electric bulb hung unused from the ceiling. Amongst all this, Leadbeater lay stretched out on a divan, smoking a hookah.

"Good Lord—we've fallen through the looking glass," Milton said a little gleefully.

"So it seems." Rowland loosened his tie. "Let's just hope we can climb out again."

The hookah bubbled gently. "Annie spoke most highly of you and your friends, Mr. Sinclair." Leadbeater fixed Rowland with his rather disturbing gaze. "Please, sit, sit."

Milton stretched out on a divan in much the same manner as their host. Rowland sat tensely, his feet flat on the ground, his weight forward. Van Hook paced the room clearly agitated.

"I am pleased with your aura, Mr. Sinclair."

"For pity's sake don't start that nonsense," Van Hook snapped. "Rowly doesn't go in for that stuff!"

Leadbeater did not appear to notice the outburst.

"Annie thought you open to ideas of international brotherhood. She saw in you a longing for the sacred mysteries of the soul…"

"Demented old geezer!" Van Hook cursed under his breath, and continued with a muttering tirade that became progressively more profane.

Leadbeater turned to him quite calmly. "Now Hu, darling, I think that's enough. I fear you have been neglecting your meditations, since you left our care. You must forgive him, Mr. Sinclair. I'm afraid Annie has indulged his temper without correction. It is why she sends him to me from time to time…so that I can remind him of his past life amongst the children of God."

Van Hook responded furiously. "I know where you're heading, Charlie. Annie should have had you put in a nuthouse years ago…."

Rowland glanced uneasily at Milton. This was quite extraordinary not to mention uncomfortable.

"Of course it would grieve Annie greatly if I let Rowland Sinclair leave The Manor, without him agreeing to join me at a meeting of the Order of Co-Masons." Leadbeater returned to the original thread of his conversation as if Van Hook were not there.

Rowland would ordinarily have declined the invitation outright, but Van Hook was now engaged in a truly superlative oration of vitriol against the old man, who reacted only with well-aimed condescension. This was not how Rowland Sinclair was accustomed to people behaving. It unsettled him. He was, if truth be told, inclined to promise anything in order to leave.

"Yes, well, if Annie insists…"

"The next meeting is on the tenth of the month. Be here by five, and we shall go together."

Milton laughed.

"Of course, I meant the both of you gentlemen."

Milton stopped laughing.

Van Hook persisted in decrying Leadbeater.

The hookah continued to bubble.

Rowland stood. "Yes, well, we should be going. Thank you. Terribly sorry about the hedge…good-bye, Hu."

The American paused his invective for just a moment. "It's been swell, fellas."

They let themselves out and walked silently back to the Mercedes. When they were seated safely within it, Milton started laughing once again.

Rowland shook his head. "What the hell was that all about?"

Milton replied with a hint of admiration, "Leadbeater's mad as a cut snake."

"Hu didn't sound much saner," Rowland observed. "I gathered Hu didn't like him, but…maybe we should…" He looked back towards The Manor, a little concerned.

"Don't worry about Hu, Rowly. Americans just have an odd way of expressing themselves. He probably has a perfectly good reason to go on like that."

Rowland fired the engine. "Well, we've got till the tenth to come up with a plausible reason why we can't attend his Co-Masonic meeting."

Chapter Twenty-seven

Bradman's Duck

LONDON, Saturday

Headed "Rare Specimen" Tom Webster's *Daily Mail* cartoon depicts a colossal pigeon-toed, cross-eyed duck in an Australian cap, being led across the Melbourne Museum stage by a gloomily-attired undertaker.
—*Wagga Daily Advertiser*

Rowland groaned as he listened to the news report. A duck! A golden duck, no less. How could Bradman have been dismissed without scoring anything? Glad now he'd missed the actual broadcast of the Test match's first day, he turned down the Radiola's volume dial in disgust, glaring at the wireless as if it were responsible for the offending delivery.

Lenin sighed and slumped onto the rug, his single ear drooped despondently. It seemed, he too, was unhappy with this inauspicious start to the second Test.

Edna sat primly on the couch, struggling with needle and thread. "Oh, damn!" She watched a small floret of blood stain the fabric as she stabbed her finger yet again.

"What on earth are you doing?" Milton peered at her from over his glass.

Edna held up the blood-speckled sampler proudly. "Cross-stitch."

"Good Lord." Rowland's brow rose. "Why?"

"It's ladylike."

"It looks quite dangerous."

Edna sighed. "I'm not particularly good at it," she admitted.

Rowland picked up his notebook. "You have other talents."

Milton reached over and snatched the sampler for a closer look. "My grandfather was always doing these," he said. "I'm sure it's what killed him."

"Your grand*father*?"

Milton nodded; a smile twitched upon his lips. "Yes. Family secret—used to sit by the fire with his embroidery frame and his sewing basket. He was quite prolific."

"But your grandmother...?" Edna started, surprised.

"She just took the credit...lot less embarrassing for everyone that way," Milton replied solemnly. "Granny can't sew a stitch."

Clyde walked in, jacketless, shirtsleeves rolled up to the elbow. "Your car's ready to go, Rowly."

Whilst Johnston, the chauffeur, took care of the other Sinclair vehicles, Clyde insisted on servicing the Mercedes personally, just as he did odd jobs around the mansion despite Rowland's protestations that it was unnecessary. It seemed it made him more comfortable with the generosity of his friend's patronage.

Rowland closed his notebook and replaced it in the inside pocket of his jacket.

"Shall we go, then?"

Lenin whined, dropping his head dejectedly and grumbling.

Rowland bent down to pat the hound. "We won't be gone long, Lenin old mate." He lowered his voice. "You make sure that Mary doesn't throw you out with all my paintings."

Milton surveyed the walls, now devoid of anything but land-scapes and the odd family portrait. Mary Brown was unstoppable. "Maybe we should take him with us."

"It's a long way to Springwood with a greyhound in your lap."

"Ed won't mind." Milton slapped his thigh. "Come on, Lenin—do you want to go to a party?"

It seemed that Lenin did, and so it was decided. The hound would accompany them to the home and studio of the often controversial artist, Norman Lindsay, where they would see in the New Year at one of the parties for which he had gained notoriety.

They walked out and loaded their various carpet bags into the yellow tourer. Milton and Edna fought over the front seat. Edna prevailed by insisting the backseat gave her travel sickness and, consequently, it was the poet who shared the backseat with Clyde and the greyhound.

The drive into the Blue Mountains was one they had made often. Both Rowland and Clyde had spent weekends at Springwood studying the brilliance of Lindsay's pen draughtsmanship and etching techniques. Edna had posed for him—her face and figure appearing regularly in his etched illustrations of classical translation and poetry. Occasionally, her likeness would find its way into the political cartoons Lindsay produced for *The Bulletin*. She sometimes found this disturbing, but it was not for a model to dictate the forum through which the artist chose to exhibit.

The mountains in late December were clear and fresh. The drying winds of January had not yet turned the grasses yellow. The air was sharper, cleaner than in Sydney; it filled the lungs and made breathing a noticeable pleasure.

Lindsay's house was a sprawling country home, surrounded concentrically by wide verandahs, lush lawns and the gum and wattle of the Australian bush. Rowland pulled around the lecherous satyr who pursued a voluptuous nymph of naked cement—one of Lindsay's works.

A number of cars were already parked in the driveway. Lindsay's parties were by reputation, and in fact, elegantly raucous affairs. His guests were chosen from amongst the artistic and literary communities: painters, sculptors, poets, and novelists, and, of course, models. Nymphs of both flesh and cement had always run among the trees of the mountain property.

"It appears the festivities are in full swing," Milton murmured as he fiddled with his yellow silk cravat and pulled at the cuffs of his cream jacket. The lively strains of a jazz band and the distinct bubble of sparkling conversation drifted up from the bushland.

"They must all be at the pool," Rowland said, nodding towards the path which led into the trees. Lenin seemed content to lay in the shade of a mature elm, and so they left him to it.

Though the pool was only a short stroll from the main house, it was set in the natural woodlands in a way that seemed to separate it from civilisation and give the site an air of pagan abandon. It was probably why Lindsay chose it as the centre of celebrations.

An animated crowd gathered around the pool, some well-dressed, others undressed, very few in-between. Champagne had already loosened tongues and morals. Couples sat draped in each other by the water and uninhibited women posed naked and carefree for photographs with Lindsay's sculpted sirens.

Edna entwined her arm through Rowland's and waved to Lindsay and his wife.

The artist came forth, his arms outstretched. "Rowly. Wonderful to see you...how did you find the Continent? Not long returned myself. Appalling weather—people not much better. Edna, my darling. Did you see the new Siren by the herb garden...? you might recognise her. And Clyde—welcome, welcome..."

He stopped short suddenly as his eyes fell on Milton.

"You!" he roared. "Who invited you? You Bolshevik vermin of dubious breeding. You parasitic, uneducated fraud, purveying your vulgar utterances amongst learned men." Lindsay paused and poked Milton in the chest. "You unmitigated Jew!"

The partygoers fell into an uneasy hush broken only by the isolated nervous giggle.

Milton met the great artist's eye. "That's correct," he said dangerously. "Completely unmitigated, you pitiful has-been peddler of pornography. Masquerade as an artist all you want, Lindsay, we both know your only talent is titillating the repressed middle classes with your finely etched filth!"

Rose Lindsay rolled her eyes and moved next to her husband.

Norman Lindsay's wide, expressive mouth broke unexpectedly out of its angry line, and he laughed. He put his arm around Milton. "A drink?"

"Just one? You're becoming a bit *Ike*, Norman…"

The conversation returned to its merry boil as if it had never been interrupted. Rowland glanced at Clyde and shook his head. Milton and Lindsay had always maintained a peculiar relationship, from which had developed this rather alarming manner of greeting. It had become custom between them; good-natured, though Rowland suspected that neither spoke entirely in jest.

The jazz band resumed its music and soon their glasses were charged as they milled amongst the glittering personalities and creative minds about the pool. When the sun set for the last time in 1932, lanterns were lit and a picnic supper brought out. Milton lay indolently by the pool pouring champagne for the thirsty young things in the water, enjoying their attempts to entice him in. Regrettably, the poet could not swim. Edna had disappeared into the moonlight, in the arms of one of Lindsay's sons. Even Clyde was enjoying the amorous attentions of a young lady who was probably not Catholic. Rowland sat talking with Norman Lindsay, who reclined with his head in the soft lap of Mrs. Lindsay. The great artist gazed admiringly at the slightly inebriated woman who danced seductively by the pool dressed only in Rowland's jacket.

"We've missed you all in Sydney." Their host locked his hands contently over his chest. "How was your time in New York? I've always found Americans rather odd myself."

Rowland smiled as he remembered the séance. Wryly, he recounted the story to the couple.

Lindsay sat up, attentive. "Did you speak to him yourself—Houdini, I mean?"

Rowland regarded Lindsay uncertainly. "No." He did not add that he doubted that anyone had spoken to Houdini that night.

"I have conversed with Shakespeare and Apollo, and of course my brother Reginald—he died at the Somme, you know—but not Houdini. Tell me, did she use the ouija board?"

"No...I don't think so. She was channelling him I believe?"

Lindsay nodded knowingly. "It is a superb talent if one can master it. She was with the Theosophical movement, you say?"

Rowland shook his head. "Not anymore. She left over some scandal—just before the war, I think."

"Oh, Leadbeater."

"You're acquainted?"

"Yes. Eccentric chap."

"Quite mad, I'd say."

"Perhaps." Lindsay lay back into his wife's lap. "Might well send a fellow barmy, being disappointed by two World Prophets."

"Two?" Rowland's interest intensified. "I thought it was just Krishnamurti..."

"Before him," Lindsay said. "Leadbeater found a prophet in America of all places. He didn't last long."

"What happened to him—this first prophet?"

"Not really sure. They say he accused Leadbeater of all sorts of things—publicity nightmare for the Society. I suppose he couldn't really remain as the Theosophical messiah after that—so Leadbeater found a replacement in India." Lindsay's eyes narrowed shrewdly. "You're not thinking of joining the movement are you, Rowly?"

"No, not at all."

"Pity. Might help you shake that unfortunate respectability of yours."

Rowland laughed, noting the sheer number of uninhibited young women churning up the water like some kind of exhibitionist whirlpool. "There are much more pleasant ways of doing that, Norman."

He turned his eyes to the girl who still danced alone by the pool. It was about time he retrieved his jacket.

Chapter Twenty-eight

The Book of Constitutions
of the Ancient Grand Lodge of England

…if Secrecy and Silence be duly considered, they will be
found most necessary to qualify a Man for any Business
of Importance: If this be granted I am confident that no
Man will dare to dispute that Freemasons are superior
to all other Men in concealing their secrets from Times
immemorial: which the Power of Gold, that often has
betrayed Kings and Princes, and sometimes overturned
whole empires, nor the most cruel punishments could
ever extort the secret (even) from the weakest member
of the whole Fraternity.

—*(Ahiman Rezon)* 1756

The yellow Mercedes roared into the driveway of Woodlands
House. Its passengers were in good spirits; two days at Springwood had infused them with a kind of contagious bohemian
abandon. Norman Lindsay's genius, the creative force of his
personality, had inspired ideas for their own work. They talked
of art and literature, of technique and passion and of Lindsay's
mastery of the female form.

Rowland allowed the car to idle.

"Have you noticed that men are rarely painted as nudes?" Edna mused, thinking of the hundreds of naked women in Lindsay's work. She looked at Rowland who was guilty of the same bias. "Why is that?"

"Men look better in suits," Rowland replied simply, and quite honestly.

Clyde laughed. "I think you'll find, Ed, that it has more to do with the preferences of the man holding the brush."

"Small mercies." Milton opened the door and pushed Lenin out.

Rowland walked round to open the boot.

"Uncle Rowly!" Ernest Sinclair tore down the stairs and came to a stop before his uncle. "Good afternoon, Uncle Rowly. I trust you are well." The boy put out his hand.

Rowland shook the small hand. "Ernie…hello. I didn't think you were arriving till tomorrow."

"Can I sit in your motorcar, Uncle Rowly?"

"Of course." He lifted his nephew into the driver's seat and re-introduced his friends. Ernest had met them before, but the year that had passed since was a significant period in the boy's short life.

"Oh, Rowly, you're back." Kate Sinclair appeared at the doorway of Woodlands House.

Rowland ran up the steps to greet her. "Hello, Kate. I'm sorry we weren't here when you arrived…where's Wil?"

"He just popped out to check on Roburvale." She smiled warmly at Clyde who was climbing the stairs with Ernest on his shoulders. Perhaps it was a result of having so many younger siblings—Clyde had a way with children.

"Mrs. Sinclair," the artist said almost shyly, as he swung Ernest to the ground with a single brawny arm.

Milton dropped their bags onto the verandah.

"Oh, dear," he said. "Terribly remiss of us not to be here to welcome you, marm." He kissed Kate's hand, bowing as he did so. "I can only hope you allow us to redeem the transgression."

"It appears Milt has mistaken you for Queen Mary," Rowland muttered as Edna shoved the poet.

The sculptress kissed Rowland's bewildered sister-in-law. "Hello, Kate—you mustn't mind Milt, he's an idiot."

"Really…he is," Clyde nodded sincerely.

Kate smiled nervously. She had always found Rowland's friends charming though they frightened her a little.

"Shall we go in?" Rowland stood aside for the ladies. "I trust Mary's taken care of you."

"Yes, of course," Kate replied with a distinct note of uncertainty. "She and Mrs. Kendall are just getting reacquainted."

Rowland grinned. Both Mary Brown and Mrs. Kendall were accustomed to running things. Both had worked for the Sinclairs since before he was born; Mary at Woodlands and Mrs. Kendall at Oaklea. Neither was likely to concede.

They walked into the main drawing room, whilst Kate called for tea. Elisabeth Sinclair sat in the armchair with a book. She clasped rather than read it, looking about her uneasily, without any real recognition of the house that had once been hers.

Rowland bent down to kiss her cheek and her face softened with relief.

"Aubrey, darling, I'm so glad you're here. I've been feeling apprehensive since we came to this house. I was worried about you."

"No need, Mother," Rowland said calmly. "I'm perfectly well. How was your trip?"

"Oh, very comfortable. Your father took care of everything— you know how particular he is."

"You mean Wil, don't you, Mother?" Henry Sinclair had died more than a decade hence.

"Yes, of course, Wilfred." She laughed at her own mistake.

Rowland was relieved. To date it had been only he that Elisabeth Sinclair had forgotten, though her memory seemed to become a little more tenuous each time he saw her.

Milton eyed the sideboard with its various decanters regretfully, but he did not venture near it. Rowland reintroduced them all to his mother and they sat to partake of a civilised repast from awkwardly fine Royal Doulton.

Rowland noted that Kate purposely chose a seat facing away from the austere portrait of his father. Having no longer to compete with the work of his youngest son, the image of Henry Sinclair was once again the master of Woodlands House. Rowland smiled at his brother's gentle, timid wife. His father would probably have scared the wits out of her.

Edna sat down beside Kate, chatting easily as she sipped tea and passed sandwiches. Young Ernest demonstrated his proficiency with the yo-yo to Clyde and Milton. Rowland took out his notebook and drafted ideas inspired by Lindsay. It was into this agreeable gathering that Wilfred Sinclair eventually arrived. He seemed put out.

"Rowly, I'd like a word. Would you be so good as to come with me?"

"Certainly," Rowland stood and followed his brother out.

Wilfred took him out to the verandah. The Rolls-Royce was stopped in the driveway. Johnston polished the bonnet as he waited.

"I thought I told you to do something about your flaming paintings," Wilfred accused.

"I did. Woodlands looks like a nunnery."

"I'm talking about Roburvale."

Rowland grimaced. He'd forgotten. A large nude of Edna hung in the drawing room at Roburvale. He'd always considered it his best work, but it was undeniably naked. "Sorry."

"The Bairds are Presbyterian, Rowly."

Rowland stifled a laugh. "Sorry...I'll have it taken down."

"I've already seen to it," Wilfred replied. "It's in the car—just put it somewhere where no one will see it...bury it if you have to."

Rowland sighed. "You're dashed lucky I'm not easily offended, Wil."

On this, Wilfred conceded. "You do take offence a lot less than you give it." He checked his pocket watch. "You'd better get changed—Lodge is at seven. I'm assuming you have a clean dinner suit."

Rowland groaned.

"Don't be difficult, Rowly. There are a number of chaps to whom I wish to introduce you. They'll help you settle in at Dangar's." He returned the timepiece to his fob pocket. "I'm having an airstrip built at Oaklea," he said casually, skillfully quelling any rebellion.

Thus reminded of their bargain, Rowland left to have the offending painting taken up to his room and to change.

He showered and dressed, rummaging for cuff links and gloves. With Clyde and Milton now sharing his room, things were somewhat disordered. Rowland tied his bow tie with the ease and speed of a man who did it often. He found the small black case that held his Masonic regalia. Shoving the white gloves grudgingly into his pocket, he ran his fingers, rather than a comb, through his hair, and went back to the drawing room to wait for Wilfred.

"Are we dressing for dinner?" Clyde appeared distinctly panicked.

"No, you're fine," Rowland replied. "Wil's dragging me to Lodge."

"Why?"

"It appears I made a bargain with the devil." Rowland poured himself a glass of sherry.

"Oh, Rowly," Kate chided. "I'm sure you'll have a lovely time. I know Wil will enjoy having you with him. He's the District Grand Inspector of Workings now, you know."

"Good Lord...does he get a cape?" Milton asked

"Milt!" Edna glared reprovingly at the poet, but Kate smiled. "I'm not really sure—does he, Rowly?"

"I think he gets his own goat."

Wilfred cleared his throat. Rowland winced and turned to see his brother had entered the room, resplendent in white tie and tailcoat. The attire was symbolic of his office. Even within

Masonry, Wilfred Sinclair was an important man, and he was clearly not amused.

"I suppose we should be going," Rowland said with appropriate chagrin.

"Quite." Wilfred farewelled his wife and wished them all a terse good night. Rowland winked at Edna and fell into step beside him.

The ride into the city was short and, in that time, Wilfred apprised Rowland of the names of the Dangar, Gedye Board members he would meet that night. Rowland struck a pose of attention, whilst he searched his mind uneasily for recollection of the Masonic ritual he would need to get through the meeting. It had been well over a year since he had last attended. Standing at the back of the membership at his home Lodge in Yass, he could follow the man in front of him. Tonight he would be visiting Brother—they were seated in the front row. This could be awkward.

"North, South, East, West...," he recited mentally, trying to remember what came next.

All too soon, they were standing in the antechamber to the Inner Lodge. Visiting brethren were called to enter only after the ordinary business of the Lodge was done. Rowland placed his case beside Wilfred's and they donned their regalia.

Both the Sinclair brothers wore aprons that had been passed down through the generations. Freemasonry had long been a family tradition. They were from a great line of Worshipful Masters and Grand Lodge members. Of course, Rowland Sinclair was neither of these.

Rowland glanced at the door to the Inner Lodge room, intricately carved oak with a heavy brass knocker at its centre. Seated beside it, ready to test every man who sought entry, was the ceremonial Outer Guard. Rowland's spirits sunk further as he met the elderly man's piercing eye, the stony defensive set of his mouth. This was clearly a man who would die to protect the secrets of the Craft from the uninitiated—the test was not going to be easy.

It was possibly because of his preoccupation that he did not notice the other visitors who had entered the room.

Rowland decided he'd better prepare Wilfred for the fact that his Masonic ritual was exceedingly rusty. "I say, Wil, I'm afraid it's been a while since…"

At that point they heard a voice they both recognised. Wilfred put a steadying hand on Rowland's shoulder as they turned. Rowland's eyes were stormy before they were even laid on Colonel Eric Campbell.

The leader of the New Guard stood before them adjusting his regalia. He looked a great deal older than Rowland remembered, but then Campbell's fascist revolutionaries had fallen from grace in the time he had been abroad. Still, Rowland did not think the fall far enough.

Eric Campbell was obviously as surprised as they were by the chance encounter. His eyes narrowed and grew steely. He was not a man to retreat.

"Sinclair." He nodded curtly at Wilfred. To Rowland, "I'd heard you were back. What exactly are you calling yourself these days?"

Rowland felt the pressure of Wilfred's hand on his shoulder as he bristled. The room was beginning to fill with other visiting brethren arriving to don regalia.

"Remember where you are, Rowly," Wilfred cautioned calmly.

"I guess the regional Lodges are not so particular about their membership." Campbell's voice was cold, derisive.

"It's been a long time, Brother Campbell." Rowland virtually spat. "Have you seen Poynton lately? I always thought him a capital fellow…"

Wilfred pulled Rowland back before he could continue. "I believe we are being called."

He took Rowland aside as the brethren stepped forward, one by one, to be questioned by the Outer Guard and admitted to the Inner Lodge.

"Rowly, you don't need any more enemies."

Rowland regarded him incredulously. "You can't possibly expect me to greet Campbell with goodwill and brotherhood?"

Wilfred almost smiled. "No. Just don't give him a reason to declare war."

For a moment Rowland resisted, but in the end he nodded slowly. "Fine. I'll try to avoid him." He watched the door. There were now only a few visiting Masons left in the anteroom. He knew that as a member of the Grand Lodge, Wilfred would be called last.

"Brother Rowland Sinclair."

He stepped up for interrogation by the Outer Guard. The old man sized him up, deciding what test to put.

Rowland's face relaxed visibly as the first was asked. He remembered how to respond. The second question came as soon as the first was answered. Rowland recognised the ritual but, this time, he had no idea how to answer. He rubbed his forehead and looked frantically for his brother.

Wilfred exhaled. Then he spoke quietly to the Outer Guard. "I'm afraid Brother Rowland's been abroad for a while…I can vouch for him."

The watchful eyes of the Outer Guard moved from Wilfred's face to the jewels of office that hung from his collar. He nodded. "Happy to take your assurance, Right Worshipful Brother Sinclair," he said respectfully. The door to the Inner Lodge was opened and the younger brother of the District Grand Inspector of Workings announced.

Rowland followed the Master of Ceremonies across the rule and compass inlaid in the timber floor. The raised stage at the opposite end of the hall was burgeoning with Masonic official-dom. The Lodge's Worshipful Master sat on a wooden throne at centre-stage. Other office bearers were seated to either side. Immediately to the right of the Worshipful Master was an empty chair—presumably to be filled by Wilfred.

Rowland Sinclair was guided to a place on the front bench, just beside the chair of the Senior Deacon. Campbell was on the front bench opposite. Rowland took stock. He could vaguely remember the ritual of the third degree but he knew that either the first or second degree would see him undone. He could follow the Masons across the hall or on the stage, but he would have to remember to reverse the movements.

Wilfred was announced and welcomed. He walked to his seat on the stage.

The brethren remained upstanding as the charges were given and the ritual of the second degree begun. Rowland glanced at the letter G which hung from the ceiling, the symbol of the Supreme Architect. He was going to need whatever divine help he could get.

Chapter Twenty-nine

THE ROOKWOOD TRAGEDY
Burial of Martin Cusack

SYDNEY

The remains of Martin Cusack, the supposed Rookwood murderer, were interred at Rookwood Cemetery this morning. The cemetery authorities refused to allow the corpse to be buried in consecrated ground, consequently the burial took place in an allotment, the upper portion of which is set apart for the burial of paupers, and the lower portion of which is reserved for the burial of murderers and suicides.

There was no service, the coffin being simply taken from the hearse and lowered into the grave.

—*The Canberra Times*

"What the blazes were you doing out there?" Wilfred kept his voice down, but it was not happy.

The meeting had closed and the brethren were gathered in the South for supper, fellowship, and "moderate mirth."

"Was it that noticeable?" Rowland squirmed.

"Yes."

"Could we just go home now?"

"No." Wilfred steered Rowland towards the supper table. "There are some chaps I want you to meet—if only to prove you weren't drunk."

And so Rowland Sinclair was introduced to the esteemed men of the Dangar, Gedye Board. They imparted wisdom at length on matters of business, and the Craft. Brother Dooley suggested he practise his ritual to music, so that the rhythm could assist his memory. It seemed Dooley had memorised twenty-nine Masonic degrees to the songs of George Gershwin.

Fleetingly, Rowland imagined he saw Wilfred smile.

Other Brothers joined the conversation. They were not members of the Dangar, Gedye Board, but directors of the company's business partners. Very quickly, Rowland saw firsthand how business was done. He wondered what they did to pass the time at board meetings. No doubt he would find out.

Brother Campbell entered the commercial fray. It appeared his firm was engaged from time to time to advise Dangar, Gedye on matters of legal concern. On this occasion he remained cordial when he had cause to speak to Rowland. Neither was under any illusion, however. They would remain wary of each other, with good reason.

It was nearly eleven o'clock when they finally left the South. Johnston seemed to recognise his employers among the crowd of men in dinner suits, and pulled the Rolls-Royce to a stop smartly in front of them.

Wilfred frowned as Rowland walked around the car, flung open the door and climbed in. Johnston held the door open for the elder Sinclair who entered as a gentleman should.

They drove in silence for a while and then, unconsciously, Rowland began to hum Gershwin's "Embraceable You."

Wilfred took off his spectacles, looking hard at his brother. It was only then that that Rowland realised he was humming aloud. In his mind's eye the song was accompanied by Dooley and the machinations of the third degree. Wilfred began to laugh.

Rowland was more than a little surprised—Wilfred took Free-masonry very seriously and the Sinclair brothers did not often laugh together. But now they did. For that alone, the meeting had been worthwhile.

They returned to find Milton, Edna, and Clyde at cards. Kate had long since retired. A tray of Mrs. Kendall's shortbread sat on the sideboard.

"That's for you," Milton informed him. "Mrs. Kendall was very specific—apparently you're still growing."

Rowland took a biscuit and smiled. Suppers of shortbread and milk had been a feature of his childhood. Thankfully, Alice Kendall had realised that he no longer needed the milk. He was not averse to the biscuits.

Mary Brown was clearly disgruntled. She glanced at the plate of shortbread and sighed, sweeping the crumbs from around it with a cloth. Curtly, she told Rowland that Hubert Van Hook had telephoned for him twice, and seemed quite anxious to speak with him.

"I'll call him tomorrow, Mary," Rowland helped himself to more shortbread. "It's a bit late now."

"There was also a call from a newspaper journalist, sir."

"Are you sure it was for me, Mary?" Rowland remembered Edna had a suitor who was a journalist.

"Yes sir. They wished to ask you some questions."

"Could be to do with the *Aquitania*," Wilfred murmured, frowning. "Let me know if there are any further calls, Mary."

The housekeeper nodded. "Certainly, sir." Once more she wiped the crumbs from the sideboard.

Rowland considered the advisability of taking a third piece of shortbread. His hesitation was enough. Mary Brown took the tray of biscuits and holding it before her as if its contents had long ago spoiled, she left the room.

"I'll find out what paper this journalist is from and call his editor," Wilfred told his brother quietly. "The last thing we need is a scandal whilst the Bairds are here."

Wilfred said good night and left his brother to join the late game of poker.

Rowland divested himself of his dinner jacket and unfastened his tie as Milton dealt him in.

"Kate didn't want to play?"

"She joined us for a couple of hands of whist before she called it a night," Clyde replied. "She seems a bit nervous about her folks arriving."

"Oh," Rowland nodded. "The Bairds." His tone spoke volumes.

"What's wrong with them?"

"Nothing really—they've just never really left Scotland." Rowland wrinkled his nose. "Kate's father finds the Sinclairs a bit English for his taste...apparently we've forgotten our Gaelic origins."

"He disapproves of Wilfred?" said Edna, shocked.

"Not exactly...though I think he rather hoped his wee Kate would find a Scot."

"How did Wilfred meet Kate?" Edna was clearly intrigued. "She's from Glenn Innes, isn't she?"

"Wil knew her brother in the war."

"So he introduced them?"

"No—he didn't return. I think Wilfred went to see his family when he came back. I suppose he and Kate had the loss of a brother in common."

Edna reached over and rubbed his arm. "Don't worry, Rowly. We won't do anything to upset Kate's family."

Rowland smiled. "That's quite an ambition, Ed. They're Presbyterian."

Rowland rose early the next morning. He wanted to leave before Wilfred had a chance to ask where he was going. Clyde was already about, fixing a window sash in the drawing room, which he claimed was sticking.

"Where are you off to, Rowly?"

Rowland grabbed his hat. "Rookwood. I thought I should pay my respects."

"Isobel?"

Rowland nodded. "I feel badly that I didn't attend her funeral."

"You wouldn't have been welcome at the funeral, mate."

"I know. But still…"

"You're right." Clyde shut the window he'd just repaired. "We knew her, poor kid. I'll come with you. You'll never find the Roman Catholic section on your own anyway."

Afraid that the distinctive roar of the Mercedes' supercharged engine would alert Wilfred and lead to awkward questions, Rowland left the his car behind. Rookwood was in any case most easily accessed by rail. They took a train from Central out to the Rookwood Necropolis, where most of the departed citizens of Sydney lay at rest. The Necropolis sprawled across nearly eight hundred acres, divided into denominational sectors. They alighted at Cemetery Station No. 2, which some still referred to as the Roman Catholic Platform.

Rowland lingered for a while to study the sculpted majesty of the platform, and the ornate sandstone arches which stood over the line. The Cemetery Stations were the most elaborate railway buildings in Sydney. Adorned with angels and cherubs, detailed carvings of foliage—pears and pomegranates—the sheer beauty of this stop on the deceased's final journey may well have given comfort to those who accompanied the coffin. The peal of the station bell added to the hallowed air. Whilst Rowland had been to Rookwood before, he had never stopped here. Protestants were generally interred in the cemeteries closest to the first station. Milton's grandfather was buried in the new Jewish Cemetery which was serviced by the last station. Each of the buildings was constructed with a similar sombre magnificence, but the denominational details were distinct.

They walked towards the newer part of the Roman Catholic Cemetery, keeping a respectful distance from the graveside services being conducted. There was a hush to Rookwood, broken only by the background murmur of prayers, the chime of the station bells and the rattle of the mortuary trains.

Isobel Hanrahan's grave was barely marked, but she did lie in consecrated ground. A solitary figure stood before it, deep in personal reverie.

"Father Bryan."

"Oh, I say, hello." He looked down at the flowers they both held. "How thoughtful—there aren't many people over here to leave flowers for Isobel."

Rowland said nothing, glancing down at the new grave, lost and unadorned amongst the headstones and monuments. He thought fleetingly of Aubrey who lay unvisited in Ypres; but his brother was buried among comrades, those who had fallen with him. Isobel's final rest was in ground on which she had never set foot, among strangers.

"Good morning, Father." Clyde shook the clergyman's hand. "We didn't expect to see you here."

Bryan smiled. "Isobel was a wild one, but she was still one of God's children. It is for our heavenly father to judge her. We can but pray for her soul. I choose to do so here, where I can visit awhile with her."

Rowland wasn't really sure what Bryan meant. He placed his flowers at the base of the small wooden cross. The grave was devoid of the telltale wilted blooms that might have indicated someone cared about Isobel Hanrahan. "And His Grace?" Rowland challenged quietly. "Does he visit his niece?"

Bryan regarded him directly. "No, he does not. His Grace is a very busy man."

"Does he care who killed Isobel?" Rowland was aware that he was venting his ire unfairly.

"His Grace is convinced that certain unsavoury elements contributed to both the moral compromise and the death of his niece," Bryan replied carefully.

"Unsavoury elements? You mean me?" Rowland asked outraged.

Bryan shook his head. "No, not at all…well, maybe a little… His Grace believes that the occultists on board the *Aquitania* were involved in Isobel's disgrace, and in her death."

"Occultists?" Rowland was perplexed. "You don't mean the Theosophists?"

"They dabble in matters forbidden to God-fearing men. They commune with spirits and perhaps the devil himself. Surely it's not surprising that His Grace would be suspicious of them?"

Rowland's eyes flashed dangerously, but he stopped. He was not going to have this argument at Isobel's graveside. It was in any case Bishop Hanrahan, and not Bryan, with whom he should be taking issue.

Father Bryan seemed oblivious to the reception his revelations were receiving.

"His Grace has already spoken to your constabulary at length about his suspicions. I must say he is a little frustrated with the response."

"I daresay he is." Rowland was in truth pleased that Delaney was ignoring the bishop's nonsensical theories.

Bryan tapped the face of his watch. "I'm afraid I must be going. Can't tell you how much I enjoyed dinner the other evening, Rowly."

"Yes, we must do it again sometime," Rowland agreed absently, shaking the clergyman's proffered hand.

"And you must give my regards to Edna," Bryan continued warmly. "The cloth is a righteous life, but sometimes a lonely one. I do appreciate the friendship you have all shown me."

Rowland was again a little unsure of Bryan's intent. He felt a bit sorry for him—he seemed so eager for the company of others. He wondered how committed the deacon was to a life in the church.

They watched him walk away.

"You don't think he might have been in love with Isobel?" Clyde asked suddenly.

Rowland shrugged. "Perhaps…or perhaps he just feels sorry

for the poor wretch. I thought he spent more time with Ed than he did with Isobel."

"I guess he did."

Clyde put his flowers beside Rowland's. He regarded his friend carefully. Rowland was immersed in his own thoughts as he looked down at the mounded earth where the bishop's niece lay.

"What happened to Isobel is not your fault, mate. I know you feel guilty because of how it all came out—but she didn't leave you with many options."

Rowland shook his head. "Maybe. But it is somebody's fault. Some heartless bastard threw her into the harbour."

"Delaney's working on it. They'll figure it out."

Rowland eyes fell again on the wooden cross. It seemed to him, inadequate. "Do you think this is all…?" he started.

"They have to wait for the ground to settle before they lay a headstone," Clyde replied. "I'm sure this is just temporary… but we can come back and make sure."

Rowland hoped that was true. Not that he could do anything about it if it wasn't. How Isobel Hanrahan was commemorated was the prerogative of her uncle.

"My great-uncle Percy's in here somewhere." Clyde scanned the rows of headstones. "I might try and find him while I'm here—it'll make my mother happy—give me something to write to her about that doesn't break her heart."

Rowland smiled. "Break her heart? What on earth have you been doing?"

Clyde sighed. "I was the son for the Church, mate. The Joneses still owe God a clergyman and none of my brothers has stepped up."

"Oh—I guess you'd better go find Percy then."

"I'll meet you back at the platform in an hour?"

Rowland nodded as he checked his watch.

Clyde set off, walking briskly. Rowland spent a little more time at Isobel's graveside, and then wandered amongst the rows of trees lining the paths.

He found a seat in the formal gardens surrounding the chapel of St. Michael the Archangel. Mourners walked in the landscaped surroundings finding solace amongst the topiary and roses. Rowland reached inside his jacket for his notebook, and flicked through. He paused as he opened the sketches he'd made of Isobel—vibrant, mischievous, innocently displaying her swelling belly with no idea that it would give her away.

He turned to a clean page, and removed the artist's pencil he always stored in the spine. He sketched what he saw, finding his own form of comfort and seeing more in the process.

He drew the black-frocked matrons who came with sewing baskets to continue the ritual of years, the recent widows and widowers who carried their grief in barely composed countenances. He was unnoticed. The eyes of the bereaved were not focussed on a man sitting quietly with his notebook and pencil.

Rowland became engrossed in the study of a small girl in her best frock, who was conversing earnestly with a stone angel as she twirled and skipped about the statue. Her father sat watching from a nearby garden seat, cross and beads in his hands. Rowland drew the girl, simple gentle lines which caught her childlike glee in the angel. He sketched her father, the protective helplessness in his eyes, the way he gripped the beads wound around his hand.

"Sinclair!"

Rowland started toward the sound. The blow caught him as he turned. He staggered to his feet, disoriented, aware only of his inability to focus before he fell.

Chapter Thirty

THE ENGLISH MAIL NEWS
Killed At The Altar

DUBLIN

The Very Reverend Dr. Kavanagh, who has been the local parish priest for the last eight years, and was widely known, was standing at the altar engaged in the performance of his office when a statue of an angel ornamenting the front part of the structure fell without warning upon his head.

—*The Mercury*

If Rowland Sinclair had been a particularly religious man, he might have assumed he was dead. The first thing he saw once the blackness receded was saints. The flicker of candles gave their sculptured faces a kind of ethereal life.

He was lying on a pew. There was something cold and wet on the side of his head, and something hammering within it.

"Rowly, are you all right, mate?"

Clyde.

Rowland groaned and sat up.

The wet compress against his head fell away. Clyde put it back. "It's only just stopped bleeding, Rowly. Best hold it there for a while longer—it might need stitching."

Rowland suppressed a curse, aware enough to guess he was in a church. "What happened?"

"Not sure. I came looking for you when you didn't turn up at the station. Found you out in the gardens—Mr. Hartman here helped me bring you into the chapel."

Rowland noticed him then. The man with the little girl who talked to stone angels.

Painfully he proffered the hand that was not securing the compress. "Rowland Sinclair. I'm most grateful, Mr. Hartman."

"No problems—are you all right, Mr. Sinclair?"

"I think so—did you see what happened?"

"I'm afraid I was watching little Mary." He turned his head towards the young girl who knelt on the pew in front, looking intently at Rowland.

"I sawed it," she said. "God hit the man with an angel. He must be a sinner."

Hartman flushed red. "I'm sorry," he said. "Mary's ma, God rest her soul, passed away two weeks ago. Poor little poppet don't understand."

Rowland smiled ruefully. "Perfectly all right. My condolences for your loss."

"It might not have been God, Rowly, but someone did hit you with an angel—one of the small garden statues. It's a ruddy miracle he didn't kill you."

Rowland looked around him, taking in the opulent interior of the Catholic mortuary chapel. Wilfred would not be pleased if he was saved by a Catholic miracle.

"He shouted my name, and I turned," he said. "Probably deflected the blow a bit."

An elderly priest appeared then with a portly, red-faced man whom he introduced as Dr. London. Apparently the clergyman had found a physician among the mourners.

"We should call the police," Clyde said as the helpful doctor cleaned and dressed the wound on Rowland's right temple.

"I'll phone Delaney when we get back to Woodlands." Rowland flinched as some sort of liquid was applied to the lesion. The doctor had not had his bag—he wondered briefly if they were cleaning the wound with communion wine. For some reason the thought amused him. It seemed appropriate since he had been battered by an angel. "There's no point calling them out here…our only suspect is God." He smiled at Mary Hartman, whose wide-eyed stare had not strayed from him.

Clyde seemed dubious but he did not argue.

Rowland stood carefully. His head hurt like the blazes, but he was otherwise steady. "I'm fine am I not, Dr. London?"

"I suggest you consult your own physician as soon as convenient," advised the good doctor. "That might need stitching, but I don't think there'll be any lasting damage."

Rowland checked the time. It was getting towards eleven.

"The family's probably arrived already," he said regretfully. "We'd better get back and make sure no one looks too closely at Milt."

Hartman handed him his notebook. "You musta dropped this when you were clobbered. Mary picked it up."

"He's been drawing pictures in there," Mary chirped smugly.

Rowland was a little alarmed, wondering how thoroughly the little girl had been through his notebook. Mary giggled.

He flicked quickly through the pages, until he found his most recent drawings. He chose a picture of Mary, calling over her shoulder to the angel as she danced about in the statue's shadow. He tore it out and gave it to her father, before returning the notebook to his inside pocket.

Hartman looked long at the sketch, and for a while the grief Rowland had seen in the garden returned to the man's face. The widower said nothing but he shook the artist's hand.

As they made to leave, Rowland thanked Dr. London, and the priest who had found him, and discreetly left a generous donation in the offering plate. They departed for the short walk back to Cemetery Station No. 2.

"Are you sure you're all right, Rowly?" Clyde was still concerned.

Rowland squinted in the bright sunlight. "I have a rather tremendous headache, but I'm fine…though I…" He shook his head.

"What? Do you need to sit down?"

"Not at all…it's just that…I could almost swear it was Hu's voice I heard when I turned."

"Hu? Are you sure?"

"No, I'm not sure." Rowland frowned. "The blow might have confused my memory…but I thought…I'm probably imagining things."

"We'll have a word with him," Clyde said thoughtfully.

They jumped aboard a train, which took them back to Central Station. Clyde hailed a motorcab to take them to Woodlands House. It was now well after noon.

The wrought-iron gates of the Woollahra mansion were almost completely obscured by a throng of reporters. The motorcab stopped as they waited for the gates to be opened.

Rowland cursed as the flash of a camera assaulted his throbbing head.

"What the blazes is going on?" he said, bewildered and uneasy. What had happened in their absence to bring the media to Woodlands?

"Mr. Sinclair, do you have a statement?"

"Were you surprised by the announcement, sir?"

Rowland blanched as another camera flashed in his face.

The gates were opened and they drove through to the house. The circular drive was crowded with Rolls-Royces, and the occasional Armstrong Siddeley. The arrival of the extended Sinclair clan had begun. They paid the cab driver and walked hastily inside, anxious to find out why the press had gathered.

Wilfred Sinclair's furious voice was the first thing they heard. "He can't seem to go two days without doing something to embarrass the family! Where the hell is he?"

Rowland walked into the library from where the tirade ema-
nated. Kate was with her husband, trying in vain to soothe him.
Wilfred was bent over the large rosewood desk, with a copy of
the *Truth*. He rose as they entered.

Wilfred glared at his brother silently for a time. He picked
up the paper and tossed it angrily at Rowland. "What is the
meaning of this? What the hell have you been doing?"

Rowland glanced at the front page; Clyde read over his
shoulder.

The story ran under the headline: *Leadbeater discovers another
World Prophet*. A picture of Rowland Sinclair appeared with the
story—it had been taken at a gallery opening the previous year.

Clyde let out a low, incredulous whistle. Rowland ignored
the insistent ache of his head and read on in disbelief. It seemed
Leadbeater had decided that the young man sent to him by
Annie Besant was the World Prophet for whom the Theosophical
Society had been waiting, destined to take the place that Jiddu
Krishnamurti had abdicated. The story carried an alarming
amount of information about Rowland's background, his past
association with Colonel Eric Campbell of the New Guard and
his recent travels. There were quotes from the Bensons, describ-
ing the newly discovered prophet as a protégé of Annie Besant.
There was a statement from the leaders of the Co-Masonic
movement welcoming Rowland Sinclair to their ranks. The light
of greatness, the article reported, was apparent to Leadbeater in
the Australian's aura.

Rowland might have sworn if his sister-in-law were not in
the room.

He looked up at his brother. "Yes, I can see why you might
be upset."

"Upset! Rowly, have you lost your mind? When did you join
Leadbeater's band of blasphemous crackpots?"

"I haven't joined them. Leadbeater's obviously completely
daft."

"How does he even know you?"

"I dropped a friend out at The Manor a week ago."

Wilfred snorted. "Of course. Your friends."

Rowland frowned. He was quite used to Wilfred's lectures but he didn't appreciate being dressed-down publicly.

"Calm down, Wil. I'll ring the paper—set them straight."

"The damage has been done." Wilfred paced the room, implacable. "Half of Sydney will have seen this by now…"

Rowland scanned the article again and shook his head. "I really don't know what Leadbeater is talking about, Wil. I had no idea…"

"No, it never is your fault, is it, Rowly?" Wilfred was not ready to let go of his wrath. "Maybe if you didn't insist on living like some radical libertine with no respect for anything but your own pleasure…"

Rowland was beginning to flare. Clyde stood back awkwardly. Kate put a hand timidly on her husband's arm but Wilfred was not interested in being pacified.

"I suppose I should be grateful that you haven't invited Leadbeater to move into Woodlands!"

Rowland fought to respond peacefully. "I told you, I don't know Leadbeater—I've only met him the once."

Wilfred grabbed the paper from him.

"And the Besant woman? I suppose you didn't know her either."

"Annie is a lady. I'm sure she knows nothing about this."

Wilfred grunted and flung the paper into the fireplace in disgust.

"For God's sake, Wil," Rowland said angrily, "Do you think I aspire to being Leadbeater's latest messiah? The man's a lunatic—that's all there is to it!"

Milton and Edna burst into the library, clearly excited, a little jubilant. Edna had a paper in her hand.

"Rowly, have you seen…oh, you have…" Edna looked from Rowland to Wilfred and back again. "This must have been why Hu was trying to reach you."

Milton stood beside Edna, his lips twitching. Rowland gathered he was restraining himself with effort, waiting for Wilfred to be out of earshot before he laughed. Suddenly Rowland wanted to laugh too. The notion was, after all, plainly ridiculous.

"Rowly—what have you done?" Edna reached up to his face, noticing suddenly the damage to his temple.

Wilfred too, now saw the blood on his collar. "For the love of God, what now?"

"It's nothing."

"It's not nothing," Edna protested, turning his face so she could see the injury more clearly. "Gosh, does it hurt?"

Rowland moved her hand away firmly. "Shall we deal with Leadbeater first?"

"What am I supposed to tell everybody?" Wilfred exploded again. "Ewan's about to be christened in the Church of England and his godfather is leading some kind of insane cult!"

"Tell them it's a mistake." Rowland said wearily. He could hear voices in the hallway. Remembering that they had a house full of guests, he groaned and closed the door to the library.

"I'll go see Leadbeater and demand he retract all this nonsense."

Wilfred did not look appeased in any way.

Rowland pulled his brother aside. "Look, Wil, I know this is embarrassing. I'll understand completely if you and Kate want to choose another godfather for Ewan—honestly."

For a moment Wilfred hesitated, but in the end he shook his head irritably. "Just flaming well sort out this Leadbeater character!" He opened the library door.

Rowland nodded. "I'll go now."

"No." Wilfred regarded his brother coldly. "Katie, would you call Dr. Maguire? Have him come and take a look at Rowly." He held up his hand as Rowland objected. "I don't care why you've been brawling or with whom, but you're not going anywhere looking like some common street thug!"

Chapter Thirty-one

SHOOTING AFFRAY
Underworld Vendetta

SYDNEY

Phillip Jeffs, 32, known as "Phil the Jew" was shot in the chest and stomach at his home at South Kensington at six o'clock this morning. Only two hours previously he had been released on bail following a sensational trial at Darlinghurst, in which another man was shot in the leg. Jeffs was admitted to St. Vincent's Hospital in a critical condition, and it is doubtful whether he will recover.

The wounded man refused to give any information concerning the occurrence. He was conscious when admitted to hospital, and Jennings, the bail magistrate, attended to take his dying depositions, but beyond the statement that he knew the man who shot him, Jeffs refused to speak.

—*The Canberra Times*

Rowland fastened his tie over a fresh shirt. Maguire had inserted a couple of stitches to secure the wound above his temple—completely unnecessarily, he thought. Of course, the dour physician had been entirely indifferent to his opinion. Maguire had always appeared at Wilfred's beck and call, but he was never very happy about it.

Milton placed a glass of gin on the dresser before him. "This might help your headache, Rowly."

Rowland pulled on his jacket before he picked up the glass. "My head's fine, but thanks. This could help with the relatives."

Milton laughed. "Ed and I met a couple of them while you were out."

"How exactly did Wil introduce you?" Rowland was curious.

"I think he called us your business colleagues." Milton stopped for a moment before he added carefully, "There's a bloke here to see you…wants to wish you well in your new… appointment."

Rowland groaned. "Who?" He could tell by the uneasy tone of Milton's voice that he was not going to like the answer.

"Phil Jeffs…*the Jew*…apparently he likes the idea of knowing a World Prophet. Wants to shake your hand and tell you himself that you'll be welcome at any of his establishments."

Rowland swore. Phil the Jew was one of Sydney's most notorious criminals. He made a living from vice and violence. Rowland had encountered the gangster the previous year and he had no desire to continue the acquaintance.

"He's waiting in the conservatory."

"What! You let him in…if someone sees him…" Rowland made for the door.

"Steady on, Rowly. I'm not a fool. Your guests are all on the verandah…I sent Ed and Clyde in to make sure they stay away from the conservatory."

"I'd better go down and tell Jeffs to sod off then," Rowland muttered.

Milton replied quickly, seriously. "Don't be stupid, Rowly. You don't want to insult Jeffs. He'll slash you to pieces in front of your entire family and he'll still beat the rap."

Rowland cursed Leadbeater. The old fool had no idea of the trouble he'd caused. This was an absurd predicament. "Fine, I'll tell him to sod off politely."

Phil Jeffs was not alone in the conservatory. There was a young woman with him. Overtly beautiful, she, like Jeffs, was stylishly attired. Jeffs had made himself comfortable, seated in a wicker armchair with his feet upon another.

"Sinclair!" A grin spread slowly across his dark features. "Or should I say *Your Majesty?*"

"Sinclair will be just fine," Rowland replied.

Jeffs jumped to his feet and offered Rowland his hand. "Just came by to offer yer my congratulations. Don't want nobody saying that *The Jew* don't observe the proprieties."

Glancing at Milton, Rowland shook the man's hand. "Very considerate of you, Mr. Jeffs, but I'm afraid there's been some sort of mistake…"

Jeffs waved off his words. "I've brung you something to celebrate yer recent elevation." He beckoned to his companion. "Come over here, Nellie."

The young woman stood and taking a final drag on her cigarette, she walked over to them. The smoke curled softly from her scarlet lips. She moved elegantly, and regarded Rowland with large China blue eyes.

"May I present, Miss Nellie Cameron. Yer won't find a better-looking dame in Sydney."

Nellie Cameron smiled and put out a gloved hand. "So pleased to make your acquaintance, Mr. Sinclair." She was soft-spoken, her accent refined…her presence with Jeffs the only sign that she was anything but well bred.

"Likewise, Miss Cameron." Rowland gave no indication of his growing alarm. Nellie Cameron had a reputation almost equal to Jeffs'.

"I knew you'd take to her," Jeffs sprouted triumphantly. "Nell grew up posh, you know. Reckon she knows a few things about how to please a swank gentleman such as yer good self."

He pushed Nellie Cameron into Rowland. "With me compliments, Sinclair."

"I'm afraid…," Rowland started as Jeffs' gift stroked his shoulder.

"Don't be afraid, sweetheart," Nellie interrupted. "I can be gentle."

Milton choked.

"I'm afraid there's been a mistake," Rowland repeated, glaring at Milton.

"Yer'll need to keep this on the quiet, though, Sinclair," Jeffs warned. "Nell's old man don't like her making arrangements if he ain't getting his cut. Frank's gotta bit of a temper where Nell's concerned."

"Don't you worry, darling," Nellie crooned. "Frank's inside at the moment. We can keep this between ourselves."

"We're going to be late, Rowly," Milton said pointedly. "I believe His Honour is already in the drawing room…you know the judge doesn't like to be kept waiting."

Rowland accepted the lifeline. "I have a rather pressing engagement, I'm afraid," he said firmly. "As kind as it is, I'll have to decline your…invitation."

Nellie looked affronted. Despite his part in the offer, Jeffs was clearly delighted by her discomfit. "Been a while since yer were turned down, eh Nell? Losin' yer edge, I reckon…"

"Please don't be offended, Miss Cameron." Rowland tried to keep the encounter pleasant. "Regrettably, I do have a previous appointment…did you come by taxi? Why don't I have Johnston drive you home…?"

Phil Jeffs chuckled. "Fair enough, Sinclair." He tapped the side of his nose. "Just yer remember to call on The Jew if yer need any divine intervention on yer behalf."

"Yes, of course…thank you."

Later, Rowland would wonder how on earth he managed to get Phil the Jew and Nellie Cameron out of his house without a scene. It might have been that the idea of arriving back at Darlinghurst in a chauffeur-driven Rolls-Royce pleased her, or maybe she was simply uncomfortable with the magistrate "waiting" in the drawing room. Or perhaps the whole thing had been Jeffs' idea of a joke. At that particular moment, however, Rowland didn't especially care why they went, just that they did.

Milton ushered the pair out of the house by a side entrance so that they slipped anonymously into the black saloon before it passed the gathering of Sinclairs at the front of the house.

Rowland headed back upstairs to once again change his shirt, the collar of which, he fortuitously noticed, had somehow become smeared with red. Nellie's scarlet lipstick, no doubt. He was muttering and cursing when Milton checked in on him.

"It's all right, Rowly, they're gone."

Rowland shook his head. The day was just getting worse.

Milton tried to distract him. "Where were you this morning? What happened to you?"

Rowland told him the events at Rookwood.

"Bloody hell!" Milton sat down on the bed. "He hit you with an angel? Why would Hu want to kill you?"

"I don't know that he did. I could very well be wrong and in any case he might have been trying to warn me."

"If that were the case, why didn't he help you out, or at least check that you weren't dead?"

Rowland shrugged. "I don't know. Perhaps I'll catch up with Hu at Leadbeater's—I'll ask him."

"We'll do more than bloody ask him." Milton stood and, pushing Rowland away from the mirror, began fussing with his cravat. "I think Clyde and I had better go with you. Grab my green velvet jacket from the wardrobe, will you, Rowly?"

Rowland obliged, looking on dubiously as the poet fitted a feather to the front of his favourite black beret. Now that they were back in Sydney, Milton's attire had returned to its previous flamboyance. Rowland thought of Charles Leadbeater. At least the poet wasn't wearing a cape.

Clyde and Edna were still on the verandah taking tea with the Sinclairs' new houseguests, when he and Milton finally emerged. The sculptress seemed perfectly at home, chatting happily with rounded vowels, and pouring tea as Kate handed young Ewan among the ladies. To Rowland, Edna appeared to treat any inter-actions with the Sinclairs as an opportunity for theatre. Clyde sat uncomfortably, and quietly, with a dainty teacup in his large calloused hands. Ernest peered out from under the table, safe behind the crisp fall of white linen.

The conversation was being dominated by Roger Castle-maine, a cousin of Rowland's father. A man well in his seventies, he considered himself the family patriarch, and dispensed loud advice like a font of conservative wisdom. They entered at the end of a monologue. "…of course that was during the real war. It's not something you lads would understand."

Rowland glanced at Wilfred who maintained a stony-faced mask of stoic civility. Castlemaine's *real war* was the Boer War—the old man had always considered the Great War a skirmish of sorts, during which the Empire had given in to the more brutish warfare of lesser peoples. It was one of his favourite subjects.

Rowland suppressed a surge of ire—if Wilfred could endure the old fool, then he could do likewise. His head was throbbing again, however. Courtesy demanded that he spend some time greeting his guests despite his impatience to confront Leadbeater.

He welcomed them each politely, making vague enquiries and giving equally vague responses to theirs. Milton took a seat beside Wilfred, who studiously ignored him. The poet seemed to find that amusing.

Rowland sat beside his mother, casually deflecting any ques-tions about the *Truth* article as "nonsense." His Aunt Mildred, who had a nose for scandal, was persistent, but Rowland had become expert in evading the inquisitive probing of his relatives.

"And how precisely are you occupying yourself these days, Rowland? Your father had always thought you suited to the legal profession."

"Had he? He was mistaken, I'm afraid."

"Nonsense, Henry was never mistaken. He would be most disturbed that you have not yet settled down."

"Just weighing my options, Aunt Mildred."

"Young people these days have too many options." Mildred wagged a gnarled finger at her nephew. "It will be your undoing…that's just my opinion but I'm entitled to it."

"For goodness sake, Millie, leave the poor boy alone!" Elisabeth Sinclair patted Rowland's hand. "Aubrey's always made Henry very proud."

There was only a slight pause. Rowland barely blinked.

"I don't know how proud Henry would be right now," Mildred went on, ignoring the fact that she and Elisabeth were talking about different men. "It does not pay to be careless of one's reputation."

"Ernie, come out from there and show Aunt Mildred your yo-yo."

"Your reputation is very important, you know."

"He's really getting to be quite clever with it—show everybody that whirling thing you do."

Ernest obliged.

"A man's reputation is…oh my Lord!"

It was probably not the best place to be whirling a wooden object about one's head. The impact was inevitable: shattering the Royal Doulton teapot and sending the tepid brew in all directions. Mildred screamed and sat down, lamenting her nerves, as Mary Brown emerged to see that the mess was cleaned up and a fresh pot made with the minimum of fuss. The conversation moved from Rowland's reputation to china patterns.

Rowland pulled Ernest onto his lap. "Well done, mate," he whispered.

The boy nodded solemnly. "Uncle Rowly," he asked gravely, "what happened to your repustation?"

"Reputation, Ernie. Met the same fate as that teapot, I think."

"Can you paste it?"

"It will probably always leak."

He kept Ernest on his lap after that, in the hope that the boy's yo-yo would fend off his Aunt Mildred at least.

Eventually he stood, hoisting his nephew over the rail of the verandah and onto the lawn so that the boy too could escape.

"I'm afraid I have some business to attend to this afternoon, so you'll have to excuse me…," Rowland began.

Stanley Onslow, an uncle on his mother's side, laughed, a vibrating, jarring cackle that was hard to overlook. "I can only imagine what kind of business you young men are engaged in," he said in a whisper that was too loud and pointed for discretion. The genteel gathering tittered. Aunt Mildred seemed about to unleash another diatribe on reputation.

"Now Stanley, you mind your manners." His wife, a matron of extensive girth, spoke reflexively, as if it was an admonishment she made often.

In response, Onslow lowered his voice and hooked his thumbs in the pockets of his waistcoat as he leered at Edna. "I must say, old man, I like the look of the business you're doing here."

Now Rowland bristled immediately. "Just what do you mean?"

"I've asked Rowly to take care of some matters for me." Wilfred stood to place a warning hand on his brother's shoulder. "You best be on your way, Rowly."

Clyde put down his cup and stood hastily, in case they should attempt to leave without him.

Rowland felt a touch of guilt over abandoning Edna to contend alone with his family, but the sculptress seemed entirely unperturbed by the notion. The conversation had moved now to polo, and Edna was doing an admirable job of feigning interest.

"The reception commences at seven sharp," Wilfred informed him quietly. "Just make sure you're back in plenty of time…and let Leadbeater know that if he doesn't retract his nonsense he will be hearing from our lawyers."

They walked briskly outside, relieved to finally get away. Rowland told Clyde about Phil the Jew and Nellie Cameron. Clyde whistled in disbelief. "Good thing you got rid of them, Rowly. You would have been exuding a lot more than an aura if old Frank Green had got wind of this. He slashed the last bloke who messed around with Nellie."

"If I'd accepted Miss Cameron's offer, I have no doubt Wilfred would have beaten him to it."

Milton slipped eagerly into the driver's seat of the Mercedes. It was not a liberty he would normally have taken; Rowland rarely gave up the wheel of his beloved car. On this occasion, however, Rowland was still suffering the after-effects of the morning's assault.

The generous Teutonic engine roared to life—she was not a subtle machine. It was only as they were driving out in full view of the verandah that it occurred to Rowland that his brother would have preferred he use the Rolls-Royce, at least while the family was at Woodlands. The German origin of the S-class Mercedes-Benz had always been a cause of contention between the Sinclair brothers.

There were still a couple of persistent reporters outside the gate. Milton engaged the supercharger and gave them little chance to photograph Theosophy's latest World Prophet.

The mid-afternoon traffic was light in the city and they made good time across the Harbour Bridge and then to Mosman. To Rowland's dismay there were also several reporters outside the entrance to The Manor.

"Open up! It's His Holiness, come to see Mr. Leadbeater," Milton called to the man at the gate.

"For God's sake, Milt, shut up," Rowland muttered as he observed a reporter scribble the statement down.

The gates were opened immediately and the yellow Mercedes pulled up to the entrance of The Manor.

It seemed Rowland's new status had some benefits, for they were admitted without question and shown directly to Lead-beater's study. The Theosophist was not alone and appeared to be engaged in some form of heated exchange, audible through a slightly ajar door.

"Look, you bloody fool—if you don't listen to me you'll end up like Frannie."

"I really don't see what more I can do, Richard," Leadbeater's voice was calm in reply.

"Well, don't say you weren't warned, you mad bastard…"

The door was flung open and Richard Waterman stalked out. He stopped, momentarily startled by the presence of Rowland Sinclair and his friends. "I say…hello…didn't expect to see you here…terrible hurry I'm afraid…jolly nice to see you again." The newly widowed surgeon donned his hat and hurried out before any response was possible.

Charles Leadbeater emerged as Waterman departed. He was dressed in a pair of loose gathered trousers, over which he wore a type of smock, secured at the waist with a purple sash. The ends of his long grey beard were tucked into the wide band. He tinkled as he walked for his pointed slippers were sewn with small brass bells. On his head was a black fez complete with hanging tassel.

"Saints preserve us," Clyde murmured.

Leadbeater placed his palms together and bowed low. "Namaste. Welcome back, Rowland, my darling."

The unexpected endearment took Rowland's voice for a moment. He recollected his composure and spoke evenly. "Mr. Leadbeater, I wonder if I may have a word about your announcement?"

"Rowland, it would be my pleasure." Leadbeater beamed. He clapped his hands imperiously. "Shall we take some refreshment in the garden whilst we talk?" With a flourish of his arm, he opened the French doors and skipped outside calling, "Bring sustenance for the learned one."

Milton grinned. "After you, Learned One."

Rowland sighed. His headache was getting worse.

They found Leadbeater sitting cross-legged on a wicker chair on the lawn. Awkwardly, they took the adjacent seats. Maids rushed out with tea service, trays of cakes and a hookah.

Rowland began directly. "Mr. Leadbeater, your announcement yesterday was mistaken and ill-advised. I have come to ask that you retract it."

"It was not advised at all, darling," Leadbeater replied airily. "I saw your great destiny in your aura—clear, magnificent. I could not be mistaken."

"Regardless, sir," Rowland said tightly. "The announcement was made with neither my knowledge nor consent. I am not willing. I require you to retract it."

"Oh, I understand the mantle of World Prophet is heavy. You will become accustomed to the burden…in time you will embrace it."

"I have no intention of embracing it, Mr. Leadbeater. I must insist that you retract your announcement."

Leadbeater stood. He appeared not to hear. Raising his arms above his head he began to chant and skip amongst the chairs.

Rowland tried in vain to regain the Theosophist's attention. "Mr. Leadbeater…Leadbeater…for the love of God…"

Still the man skipped and twirled around them, chanting joyously in some unintelligible language.

Rowland was losing his temper. He stood. The chanting assailed his throbbing head.

"Dhamang, Saranang…"

Rowland's patience gave way. He reached out and seized Leadbeater by the beard, ready to pound sanity into the man.

A flash stayed him. More flashes exploded from through the hedge.

"Whoa, Rowly." Clyde grabbed him before he hit Leadbeater, who was still chanting in some kind of manic frenzy.

Rowland felt Milton's hand on his shoulder. "Let go of the beard, mate."

Rowland released Leadbeater, reluctantly.

More flashes.

"Rowly, we have to get out of here," Clyde nodded towards the hedge. "Photographers."

"Come on." Milton dragged him towards the driveway. "You'll be hearing from his lawyers," the poet shouted over his shoulder.

"Don't go, my darling," Leadbeater begged as he continued to skip. "I must prepare you. We have already lost so much time…I should have had you as a child…"

Rowland got into the car, a little stunned. The man was utterly mad. Milton gunned the engine and pulled out. They left Charles Leadbeater pleading on the lawn for his World Prophet to remain.

More flashes as the photographers captured their getaway.

Rowland pushed the hair back from his face, frustrated. No doubt his altercation with Leadbeater would feature in the next day's paper. Wilfred was not going to be happy. He was none too pleased himself.

Chapter Thirty-two

A Norman Lindsay Fantasy

A gift of fancy in writing as well as in drawing is shown by Mr. Norman Lindsay in *The Magic Pudding*. The story describes the adventures of Bunyip Bluegum (a native bear) and his friends Bill Barnacle (an ancient mariner) and Sam Sawnoff (a penguin bold). Bunyip decides to leave his little home in the gum tree because his uncle's whiskers blow about too much and get in the way. On his travels he meets Bill and Sam who are the owners of a magic pudding named Albert. There is a dark history attached to the way in which they acquired the delicacy. Albert varies his flavour to steak and kidney, apple or whatever the temporary owner wishes. Furthermore he rather likes being eaten.

—*The Argus*

It had been some years since the ballroom of Woodlands House had been used for an occasion so grand. The current master was not inclined to throw such formal receptions. This evening was to honour the newest Sinclair who had long since retired in the care of his nurse. Young Ernest had, however, been granted special permission to participate in at least the first hour of his little brother's party. He stood sombrely beside his father and uncle in the receiving line.

The Sinclair men were formal and dignified in white tie and tails. On that count Rowland had finally drawn the line.

It was not in fact the kilt that had set his resolve, but the stockings, garters, and other paraphernalia. It was just too much to ask. He had the Sinclair tartans Wilfred had ordered returned before Milton decided to borrow them.

Once it became clear that nothing would get his brother into a kilt, Wilfred abandoned the dress himself on the grounds that it was more important that the Sinclairs present a united front. Rowland had the uneasy feeling that they were preparing for a siege, but at least they were doing so in long pants.

The Bairds arrived in a blaze of Highland colour and pageantry. At their head was Fletcher Baird—Kate's paternal grandfather and, as far as Rowland could tell, some sort of clan leader. He was a generously built man whose girth burgeoned over the blue and green plaid of his kilt.

"Fletcher." Wilfred shook Baird's hand. "You remember my brother, Rowland."

"Cannot say that I do." Baird took Rowland in with shrewd cold eyes. "But I have read about him."

At a loss for response, Rowland waited for his brother's cue. He'd not yet had the opportunity to tell Wilfred of his latest encounter with Leadbeater.

Wilfred chose to ignore the challenge. "I trust Roburvale is comfortable, Fletcher."

"Excessively so, lad. We have no need for soft beds and feather pillows. In the Highlands a man oft lays his head on naught but hard stone and he is grateful to the good Lord for it. Still, your whisky cupboard is full and for that kindness, I thank ye."

Rowland bit the inside of his cheek. He was in enough trouble without laughing at this point. Fletcher Baird moved into the ballroom to greet his granddaughter, whilst the Sinclair men continued to welcome those that came behind him.

Rowland was, if truth be told, enjoying the spectacle that was the Bairds. Somehow they seemed to manage being the backbone of the Glen Innes Temperance League whilst maintaining a fondness for whisky. No one mentioned the inconsistency and all was well. Physically their kinship was declared by a preponderance of red hair. And, of course, the men were wearing kilts.

It seemed the *Truth* had been passed around amongst the Bairds and many had an opinion on Rowland Sinclair's new celebrity. Rowland stood by as Wilfred deftly diffused each pointed and indignant reference to the article.

"Don't complain, never explain," Wilfred directed him quietly when it became obvious that the curious, clearly disapproving prodding would continue.

Kate's Aunt Maggie beckoned Rowland aside—she smelled just faintly of lemon and whisky. Rowland smiled—he remembered Margaret. She'd always been partial to some appalling drink called a *toddie* which she consumed often for supposedly medicinal purposes. She had an interesting face, lively green eyes, and a beauty which the lines of age had faded only slightly.

"I read about you, Rowland," she said. "'Tis a bonny thing, a fine thing indeed."

This caught him by surprise.

"They always said I was a bit fey myself," she confided as she clasped his hand in both of hers. "Well done, my dear boy. How exciting...I have dreams, you see, when the moon is full—since I was a wee girl. The World Prophet! How very special...I had a dream before the last war—tin soldiers and black ink, and then another just recently when that poor racehorse died...it's a gift, a wonderful terrible gift...I understand, my boy." She rubbed his hand warmly once more. "You must let me show you the moon some night," she whispered before she went back to her husband's side.

Rowland stared after her for a while.

"Why, Mr. Sinclair, what a pleasure to see you again."

Rowland turned. She stood almost posed, wearing a rather unnecessary shade of pink, her platinum hair twisted high upon her head. Her gown, though painstakingly modest, was fashionably cut, and she met his eyes with an expectation of admiration.

Rowland shook the white-gloved hand. "Miss Bennett, I must say I didn't expect to see you here."

"Of course I'm here, silly," she said giggling. "We are to be godparents together."

Kate swooped in. "I'm sure I mentioned it, Rowly—we've asked Lucy to be Ewan's godmother…"

"I was frightfully honoured," Lucy chirped. "I adore children."

"Isn't it just perfect, Rowly?" Kate smiled at her friend, who laughed suddenly. Rowland remembered that Lucy Bennett had always laughed for no reason, and in a manner carefully contrived to look gay. He found it no less irritating now. "Why don't you show Lucy the rest of Woodlands before supper?" Kate continued. "I'm sure Wil can manage by himself."

Rowland nodded politely, wondering why Kate couldn't inflict her unmarried school chums upon her own relatives instead of tormenting her husband's only living brother. Surely there were eligible men among the Bairds—but for some reason they were allowed to drink their whisky unmolested.

"I'm sure Miss Bennett doesn't…"

"I would be delighted to tour your gracious home, Mr. Sinclair." She smiled prettily and took his arm, glancing up at him with obvious warmth, a poised flirtation.

Rowland stopped. Good Lord. It appeared Lucy Bennett was the only person in the room who had not read the *Truth* that morning.

A gentleman to the last, he conceded and took Lucy through Woodlands as quickly as he could, only half listening to her empty gushing.

"This is an impressive house, Mr. Sinclair, quite exquisite. Of course it needs a woman's touch." She laughed inexplicably again. "My cousin, Mr. Thomas Beckett—you might know him as Bingo—has a twenty-roomed house in Potts Point…but it was never a home whilst he remained a bachelor…he's married now and his wife, Martha—we call her Muffy—formerly a Miss

Cameron of the Bowral Camerons, has made it entirely elegant. Soft furnishings: they make all the difference. Nothing speaks of taste and good breeding like a well-chosen chintz."

"Indeed," was all Rowland could manage in response. He suspected that Lucy's pointless monologue was more than a little related to the nervous need to fill what would otherwise be an awkward silence. She'd probably stop babbling if he simply made conversation.

"Oh my word, this is magnificent!" Lucy moved enthusiastically towards a large painting of irises. "What smashing colours." She turned back to him. "Oh, of course," she said with sudden epiphany, "it brings out the blue of your eyes."

Rowland blinked. Lucy Bennett thought he chose paintings to match his eyes. What could he possibly say to her?

And so he stood by as she continued to extol the uncontroversial landscapes and still life paintings, which now adorned his walls, picking out the blue in each piece as if it was some kind of artistic theme. It was unfortunate. His own work, if it had been allowed to remain on his walls, might have scandalised Lucy into retreat. As it was he was defenceless.

Rowland turned back towards the ballroom. The music had stopped. "I believe they must be sitting down for supper," he said relieved. "Perhaps we should be getting back."

Lucy Bennett's eyes fell, disappointed. "Certainly, it would not do to be missed."

Kate Sinclair had directed the seating arrangements and so the return to the ballroom gave him little reprieve. Still, he was saved from an explanation of how the right chintz could change his life.

The first course of salmon and roe was served, and then the toasts began. As far as Rowland knew, such formalities had not been planned for the evening. The Bairds just liked to make speeches as they drank. Initially they drank to the health of Ewan, then to his parents and his elder brother. Fletcher Baird led a toast to the Sinclairs with a speech that included an extended history of their apparently forgotten Scottish roots. Wilfred responded, as a gentleman should, with a toast to the Bairds. By then the evening was getting quite celebratory. Having saluted all the relevant family, various kilted men stood to quote Burns in what appeared to be an homage to food.

Rowland was now struggling to understand the Bairds at his table. Individually they had been quite coherent, but the conversation of their kinsmen seemed to thicken their hybrid brogues, until the exchange seemed like an extended growl with the word "lad" thrown in occasionally. Even those who had started the evening without accents of note seemed to absorb them.

Wilfred was deep in conversation with Kate's father. Douglas Baird was a champion of the New State movement which sought to secede the New England region from New South Wales. Wilfred Sinclair was politically sympathetic and so the discussion absorbed them both earnestly, despite the geniality around them. It appeared Wilfred had no trouble understanding his father-in-law.

Lucy sat between him and Kate, and the two women talked as old friends through the evening. It seemed to Rowland that Lucy was a great deal less vacuous when she was not talking to him.

Rowland turned towards the tap on his shoulder. Edna whispered in his ear. "Isn't this fun? I have no idea what they're saying, but it's like being in Aberdeen again."

"Quite," he replied, noting how enchanting the sculptress looked in green. She had been seated on a table with Milton and Clyde and several of Kate's cousins. He introduced her to Lucy Bennett. Edna spoke to her cordially, for she had neither cause nor predisposition to be possessive of Rowland. Lucy was less warm. Edna seemed to find that somewhat entertaining.

The final lines of an ode by Robbie Burns were rendered by Archibald McRae, a cousin of Kate's.

"…Auld Scotland wants nae skinking ware
That jaups in luggies:
But, if ye wish her grateful prayer,
Gie her a Haggis!"

"Gie her a Haggis!" came the enthusiastic reply from the hall.

Edna giggled. "My goodness, what on earth is a Haggis?"

Rowland did not respond, his attention caught by the rise of Milton Isaacs from his chair. Milton had taken to combing his hair down over his forehead. The result gave him a somewhat untidy, dissolute air, but fortunately the word "Red" was no longer visible on his brow. Clearly the opportunity to recite was too much for the poet and he could be silent no longer.

"O, who would be a puddin',
A puddin' in a pot,
A puddin' which is stood on
A fire which is hot?
O sad indeed the lot
Of puddin's in a pot."

Edna nearly squealed with delight. "The Magic Pudding!"

Rowland could feel Wilfred's glare as Milton launched into the next verse. The ballroom had fallen into a kind of confused silence as the long-haired poet answered Scotland's greatest bard with Norman Lindsay's bad-tempered, talking pudding.

In Rowland's experience, the Scottish sense of humour was somewhat elusive, and they were a little sensitive about Burns. Most of the Baird men carried some sort of ceremonial dagger in their garters. Rowland's knowledge of Scottish history was a little hazy, but he did recall that the medieval clans were fond of stabbing each other to death at dinner parties.

"I'd better get back, in case they try to hit him," Edna said, laughing. She returned to take her seat beside Milton who was still on his feet.

"Rowly!" Wilfred was livid.

Rowland looked at him innocently. There was really nothing he could do now. Milton continued reciting:

"...I hope you get a stomachache
For eatin' me a lot.
I hope you get it hot,
You puddin'-eatin' lot!"

For a moment there was silence, whilst the Bairds considered whether they were being mocked, and the Sinclairs were unsure.

Into this uncomfortable lull, someone began to clap. Margaret Baird had decided first and, in doing so, ensured Milton's recitation was at least neutrally received. The poet bowed and as usual failed to attribute the verse.

Supper continued and at its conclusion, Wilfred took Kate onto the dance floor. Rowland smiled. He was always touched by how much Wilfred obviously adored his young wife. Such romantic notions were not something one would expect from the elder Sinclair. If it wasn't for the way Wilfred regarded Kate, Rowland might have worried that his brother was always unhappy. Instead it seemed that melancholia was just the natural set of his face

The Bairds watched on unimpressed. They were Presbyterian. They didn't dance.

Because he really couldn't avoid it, Rowland asked Lucy Bennett to dance and they joined the couples on the floor under the disapproving gaze of the Glen Innes Temperance League.

Eventually the censorious scrutiny extinguished any enthusiasm for dancing and the floor became empty. The piano was opened and one of Kate's aunts worked the keys. The Bairds gathered about to sing Scottish ballads which were apparently not as morally perilous as a quickstep.

And so it was over the background of "I Belong to Glasgow" that the serving maid attempted to make herself heard. She tried to speak discreetly over the noise. She seemed a trifle flustered.

"Excuse me, Mr. Sinclair, there's a man of cloth…a Catholic priest…at the door wishing to see you. He's most insistent."

Rowland stood. What was Bryan doing at Woodlands? "Thank you, I'll…"

Wilfred grabbed his elbow.

"Let the gentleman know that Mr. Sinclair is otherwise engaged," Wilfred directed the young woman.

"Wil…"

"Go ahead," Wilfred prompted the servant.

"I beg your pardon, sir," the woman said anxiously, "But Mrs. Kendall has already told the gentleman that it is not convenient. He refuses to leave—insists that he must see Mr. Sinclair now. It is, he says, a matter of urgency."

Wilfred's face hardened. "Call the police—have him removed."

Rowland shook his head. "Don't be ridiculous, Wil. I'll just go determine what the problem is. Father Bryan's not a bad chap—it must be important."

"I don't want a scene," Wilfred warned. "This morning's exhibition was bad enough without the Papists descending upon us as well."

"There'll be more of a scene if you call the police." Rowland didn't wait for him to reply, walking quickly out of the ballroom. He was still in the hallway when he heard the furious, intemperate bellow.

"Sinclair!"

Chapter Thirty-three

LEGACY FOR LEADBEATER

The estate of the late Mr. W.B. Rounsevell, of Glenelg (South Australia), has been valued for probate purposes at £34,000. The Adelaide Theosophical Society is the chief beneficiary. A legacy of £100 is left to the Rev. Charles W. Leadbeater of Sydney, and also to the editor and publisher of the Theosophical paper in Melbourne.

—*The Argus*

Rowland realised his mistake the moment he heard the voice. Perhaps he should have let Wilfred call the police after all.

Bishop Hanrahan stood, flushed and bellicose, in the large tiled vestibule of Woodlands House. Dressed in the black robes of his office, he nevertheless looked more like the fighter he once was, than a man of the cloth. He'd been drinking.

They were not entirely alone. The haze of blue smoke wafting from the adjoining drawing room gave away the guests who had retreated there to smoke and drink scotch. In the corner of the vestibule, almost cowering, was one of the lower-ranked clergyman who seemed to shadow the bishop. It was not Bryan, and Murphy was now dead, so the deacon remained nameless.

"You!" Hanrahan pointed at Rowland, waving a copy of the *Truth* in his other hand. "Viperous predator. It's all come out now. You were always one of them—not even a Christian man!"

Rowland sighed. Wilfred didn't want a scene.

"Your Grace, would you like to talk in the library?"

"I would not. Is it not bad enough that you destroy a young girl's life, but then you stand over the poor child's grave and gloat as your evil master claims her mortal soul."

Rowland was startled. How did Hanrahan know he'd been out to Rookwood?

The doors to the drawing room were opened. Rowland groaned. Fletcher Baird stood in the doorway with his pipe.

"She was not a bad girl, Isobel. Spirited, but not wicked. Not till she took up with you!"

A few more kilted men came to the doorway with their pipes to watch the confrontation. Hanrahan did not seem to notice them at all.

"I'll not be letting you get away with this, you know," the bishop shouted, his voice discernibly slurred. "Your money and your fine position will not be enough to save you from God's justice."

Rowland was wary. He wondered if Madding had returned Hanrahan's gun.

"What exactly can I do for you, Your Grace?"

"You can do nothing for me, Sinclair!" Hanrahan spat. "'Tis your own soul you'd be helping by confessing your sins, by admitting that you have taken a dark path out of the sight of God."

Rowland heard the footfall behind him but he didn't turn, unwilling to take his eyes off the bishop. Wilfred Sinclair stopped behind his brother. He was to the point.

"I have organised a motorcab for you, sir. I think it is time you left."

"I'll not be leaving before I've said my piece. A man should declare the devil as he sees him!"

"Oh, for God's sake!" Rowland muttered, exasperated. The devil? This was really too much. It was preposterous.

The Bairds remained at the doorway watching intently.

"Rowly," Wilfred cautioned as the flare of Rowland's anger became apparent. He walked past the remonstrating cleric and opened the front door.

"You are trespassing on private property, sir. I'll thank you to leave my house forthwith."

Bishop Hanrahan glared at him.

Rowland watched the man's hands in case he reached for a gun.

"Very well." He glowered at Rowland and spoke to Wilfred. "I shall leave you and your murdering brother to the judgement of God!"

"Murdering!" Rowland started after the clergyman, outraged.

"Leave it, Rowly." Wilfred stepped between them. "The bishop is going." To Hanrahan he said, "You'll be hearing from our lawyers, sir."

Hanrahan grunted contemptuously and stalked out to wait for the motorcab. The clergyman who had accompanied him, had long since made a run for it. Wilfred closed the door.

The silence was awkward.

"Wilfred," Fletcher Baird said finally, "could I have a word?"

Edna carried a laden tray into the conservatory. Rowland sat on the wicker settee with Lenin's one-eared head in his lap. He was drawing Ernest who was lying on the floor sorting his marbles by colour and size.

Edna poured a cup of tea and shoved him gently as she came round to put it in his hand.

"Stop looking so glum, Rowly. This will blow over."

"Have you seen the paper?"

Edna picked up the latest edition of the *Truth,* which lay discarded on the coffee table. A half-page picture of Rowland Sinclair clutching Leadbeater by the beard whilst Clyde held him back appeared under the headline, "Unholy Row."

"Oh no!" Edna looked at him sympathetically. "Has Wilfred seen…?"

"Oh yes."

"Daddy's a bit cross," Ernest didn't look up from his marbles. "Can I have a biscuit?"

"Of course, darling." Edna put a plate of shortbread on the floor next to him. Lenin jumped down from the settee to partake.

It had been a long night. Whilst he had not been party to the conversations, Rowland gathered that the Bairds no longer considered him an appropriate godfather for Ewan. He couldn't really blame them and he would have stepped down willingly if Wilfred had allowed it.

It appeared that whilst Wilfred Sinclair thought his brother a disgrace, he would not tolerate that opinion from anyone else. Rowland would be Ewan's godfather even if he had summoned the devil and murdered half of Sydney. Wilfred would have it no other way. Kate supported her husband without question but the situation was distressing for her. Rowland did not see how it could have been any worse.

"How's your head?" Edna pushed his hair away from the injury to inspect it. "Does it still hurt?"

"I'm fine, Ed—just feeling a bit sorry for myself."

"You have been a little unlucky lately," She sat on the arm of his chair and rubbed his shoulder.

"Wil doesn't seem to think luck has a lot to do with it."

"Of course. He wouldn't." Edna smiled. "Where is Wilfred?"

"Making phone calls. Eric Campbell is moving to have me expelled from Lodge, and Dangars is not so keen to have me on the board anymore." He paused. "No wonder Wil thinks I engineered this."

"He doesn't—?"

"No, not really…but he's not happy."

Milton and Clyde came into the conservatory.

The former was singing some ditty he'd picked up the night before, complete with Scottish inflection.

"…Will you stop your tickling Jock!

Dinna mak' me laugh saw hairty,
Or you'll mak' me choke.
Och, I wish you'd stop your nonsense,
Ye'll mebbe tear ma frock…"

"Rather an odd song for a man to sing, Milt," Rowland interrupted him, testily.

"My Lord, you're conventional when you're out of sorts," Milton replied blithely. But he did stop, looking intently at Rowland. "Cheer up, mate—are they preparing the gallows for you?"

"Don't give them any ideas."

Milton sat down. "So, the bishop came a-calling?"

Rowland glanced uneasily at Ernest. The boy rolled his eyes and sighed. "Very well, Uncle Rowly, I'm going."

"Thanks Ernie, you're a gentleman."

"That's all right, Uncle Rowly," Ernest replied solemnly. "I know you'd do the same for me…we are nothing, if not in the street."

Rowland was momentarily perplexed and then he recognised Wilfred's dogma in his nephew's words. He smiled. "I think you mean discreet, Ernie, nothing, if not discreet. You can take Lenin if you like, but don't go near the street."

They waited as Ernest took the misshapen greyhound out onto the lawn.

"His Grace seems to think I murdered Isobel," Rowland said finally.

"His Grace is unhinged," Clyde replied. "I wouldn't worry about it."

Rowland frowned. "He knew that I went out to Rookwood."

"He might have talked to someone at St. Michael's," Clyde suggested. "He is a bishop."

"Or he could have seen you just before he tried to kill you with the garden ornament." Milton was less keen to clear Hanrahan.

The thought had crossed Rowland's mind.

"Rowly, have you spoken to Detective Delaney yet?" Edna asked.

Rowland flinched. "Damn—I forgot. With all this Leadbeater nonsense, I've been a mite distracted."

"Right," Clyde said firmly. "You'd better get in touch with him."

Mary Brown came into the conservatory.

"A Mr. Van Hook called for you, sir, while you were in with Mr. Sinclair. I didn't want to disturb you."

"Oh, Hu—I've been meaning to call him." Rowland put down his tea. Wilfred had spent at least an hour ranting at him that morning. Rowland did not blame the housekeeper for not wanting to disturb them.

"He would like you to meet him at The Manor at noon, sir. He believes that he may be able to help you sort out the matter with Mr. Leadbeater."

"Thank you, Mary." Fleetingly, Rowland wondered what Mary Brown and the staff thought of recent events. He checked his watch. It was half past eleven. "I had better get moving...I'll call Delaney when I get back."

Clyde and Milton stood. The poet picked up the paper, pointedly. "We'd better come, don't you think Rowly?"

"We're still not sure if Hu was involved with what happened to you at Rookwood," Clyde added.

"We'll all go," Edna decided. "We'll be back after lunch with good news."

Rowland wasn't sure that turning up at The Manor en masse was the best idea, but Edna had already donned her hat and gloves and was heading out the door. "Hurry up, Rowly, we'll be late."

"Mary, would you let Mr. Sinclair know we won't be in for lunch?" he asked, as he collected his own hat and retrieved his jacket from where he had last discarded it. He had no doubt that the housekeeper would inform Wilfred where they were going. Outside Woodlands, Mary Brown was the soul of discretion, but her loyalty lay with Wilfred. He didn't really mind but he was aware of it.

The pack of reporters and photographers outside the gates of The Manor had grown if anything. Rowland and his friends were admitted without question once again. The servant who answered the door was apologetic.

"Mr. Leadbeater is meditating in the gazebo, sir. He does not like to be disturbed."

"Is Mr. Van Hook here yet?"

"I don't believe so, sir."

"Perhaps we should wake Leadbeater up," Milton suggested.

"I can assure you, sir, Mr. Leadbeater is not asleep," the woman protested sharply. "He is meditating. He may not even be in his body."

"Well, surely he'll return for the World Prophet?" Milton persisted. "Rowly's got a golden aura, you know."

Being the only person present not accustomed to ignoring the poet, the servant seemed confused. "Well…I…"

"What say we wander up to the gazebo to see if Mr. Leadbeater has finished?" Rowland offered.

"Mr. Leadbeater does not like to be disturbed." The woman remained adamant.

"We'll ensure he's back in his body before we talk to him." Rowland was resolute. He didn't have time for this nonsense.

The grounds at the back of The Manor were lined with trees and hedges, and so the gazebo was not immediately visible from the house. Rowland walked a little ahead of his friends who allowed him to take the lead. He was, after all, Leadbeater's beloved prophet.

The gazebo was a large structure fashioned in the style of an Eastern pagoda, painted in the bright colours of the subcontinent, rather than the whitewash of traditional British garden houses. It was surrounded by a tall hedge of camellias, which created an appropriate feeling of solitude. Rowland ran up the steps, feeling a slight twinge in his leg for the first time in days.

Leadbeater was sitting cross-legged on the wooden floor. He was slumped forward. Rowland stopped. Perhaps the old man had projected out of his body. The others clattered noisily up the stairs behind him but Leadbeater did not stir. Odd, but then everything about Leadbeater was odd.

Rowland approached cautiously and then he noticed the red in the folds of the man's voluminous smock. Blood.

He reacted quickly, moving to Leadbeater's side. "He's bleeding…Clyde call for…"

The shot was muffled, and it was only because the post in front of him splintered with the bullet's impact that he realised they were under fire.

"Get down!"

Chapter Thirty-four

Theosophical Society

Blavatsky Lodge of the Theosophical Society entertained the delegates who gathered from all parts of Australia for the annual convention. Greetings from overseas sections were brought by Miss Mary K. Neff (India) and Miss Clara Codd (USA). After the reception several scenes from *As You Like It* were performed by a group of talented pupils from the Garden School, Mosman directed by Mr. Norman F. Clarke. In the afternoon Bishop Leadbeater received members of the Society at The Manor. Bishop Leadbeater also broadcast from The Manor, through Station 2GB, a contribution to the Symposium on Theosophy as a bridge-builder between the seen and the unseen.

—*The Sydney Morning Herald*

———————————⚬⚬———————————

The second shot would have killed him if he'd still been standing.

Edna screamed. Rowland pulled her under him as another bullet hit the pagoda and splints of wood flew in all directions.

Milton swore.

Clyde tried to look for the source of the bullets. A fourth shot and then a fifth. He got back down. A sixth shot hit the trellised doorway, and then, nothing.

They did not move for several minutes.

"I think he's gone," Rowland said finally.

"Or he's reloading."

Rowland looked towards Leadbeater. "We've got to get help."

"Is he dead?" Clyde asked.

"I didn't have time to find out before the shooting started. If he isn't he'll bleed to death soon." Rowland raised his head cautiously. "I'll go—you lot stay down just in case."

Clyde shook his head. "No, I'll go. It's more likely you he was shooting at, mate."

"How do you figure that?"

"This is the second time you've been shot at, Rowly. Not to mention what happened at Rookwood."

"Don't go, Rowly," Edna whispered still under the protection of his arm.

She was trembling. He could feel it. He didn't argue and he held her tighter.

"Be careful," Milton warned as Clyde made ready to go. "If you hear anything at all, get down. He's probably somewhere behind the hedges."

Keeping his head and shoulders down Clyde crawled out of the gazebo and ran for the house. They watched him go, breath held, waiting for the shooting to start again. It didn't.

When it was clear that Clyde had reached the house, Rowland focussed on Edna.

"Ed, are you all right? You're not hurt, are you?"

She let go of him. "I'm sorry. I panicked. I don't like guns."

He smiled. "It's the bullets I have a problem with. I'm going to go check on Leadbeater now, all right?"

She nodded. "I'm fine."

He moved guardedly towards the Theosophist's body. He found the man's mouth buried in the hairy grey mass of his beard and put his ear to Leadbeater's lips. He couldn't hear anything.

"Is he dead?"

"I can't tell."

Edna dug into her handbag and produced a compact. She tossed it to Rowland. "Hold the mirror up against his mouth," she said.

Rowland did so. A very faint mist fogged the glass. Rowland closed the compact and handed it back. "He's alive."

He and Milton worked to move Leadbeater into a more comfortable position, without standing themselves. By the time they had laid the man prone and applied pressure to the bleeding wound in his back, the sirens were audible.

Soon the grounds of The Manor were teeming with police. Charles Leadbeater was stretchered into an ambulance whilst officers forced reporters and photographers back. Clyde dragged them into the house out of reach of the cameras. Rowland and Milton were now splattered with Leadbeater's blood. It would not make a good picture.

Edna found the kitchen and made tea whilst they answered a barrage of questions from junior officers. And then Delaney arrived.

He sent the other constables to search the grounds for evidence and sat down. He shook his head. "You're determined to get yourself killed then, Rowly."

"One doesn't normally expect a gunfight in Mosman," Rowland muttered.

"I was talking about what your brother's going to do." Delaney grinned. "…oh, that bad already?" he asked, when Rowland failed to smile.

"Poor Rowly's had a rather trying week," Edna confided. "He's a little grumpy."

"I see." Colin Delaney loosened his tie. "How about you tell me what's been happening since we spoke last…other than being named a messiah, of course."

Rowland remained unamused. He started with Rookwood and what had happened in the gardens of the Chapel of St. Michael the Archangel.

"So this kid," Delaney wrote furiously in his notebook, "she saw someone hit you with an angel?"

"I believe she said God hit me with an angel."

"I think the Good Lord may have an alibi, so let's just assume she was mistaken about that bit," Delaney frowned. "Who could she have mistaken for God?"

"I don't know," Rowland shrugged. "What does he look like?"

"Protestants!" Clyde shook his head. "Don't you people ever go to church? He's a big old bloke with a long, grey beard... isn't he Colin?"

Delaney nodded. "That's what I've heard."

"Bloody hell...Leadbeater...had to be!" Milton made the improbable leap.

By now, even Rowland was smiling.

"All right, let's forget about the description," Delaney decided. "You said the perpetrator shouted at you before he slugged you with this statue?"

"Someone shouted at me."

"What did they shout?"

"Just 'Sinclair'."

"And you thought you recognised the voice? From just one word?" Delaney was dubious.

"It was the accent. I thought it was Van Hook...but I may be remembering incorrectly...it was just before someone tried to crack my skull."

"Fair enough." Delaney stopped to think. "Tell me about today. What were you doing here?"

"Hubert Van Hook phoned—wanted me to meet him here."

"And you were willing to meet him, despite what happened at Rookwood?"

"I'm not sure what happened at Rookwood, and he said he would help me talk to Leadbeater."

"You spoke to him?"

"No—he rang while I was being lambasted by Wil. My housekeeper took the message."

"What exactly did he say?"

"That he would meet me at The Manor at noon and we would deal with Mr. Leadbeater together."

"And what is Mr. Van Hook's relationship with Mr. Leadbeater?"

Rowland thought uneasily of Van Hook's open hostility to Charles Leadbeater. "Hu grew up in the Theosophical movement. I think Annie Besant sent him to check on the old man—Hu didn't seem to like him particularly."

"Rowly," Clyde reminded him. "What about Waterman? He was here."

Rowland had forgotten. He told Delaney of the conversation they'd overheard the day before between Richard Waterman and Charles Leadbeater.

"Well, that is interesting," Delaney tapped his fingers on the table.

"The first murder," he said suddenly, flicking back through his notebook to find the name. "Orville Urquhart. Tell me what you know about him again."

"Raised in the movement, like Hu," Rowland replied.

"How did Van Hook get on with him?"

"I gathered they were not friends."

"Urquhart was involved with Isobel Hanrahan," Milton volunteered, apparently unsure of whether Rowland's good manners would keep him from mentioning this.

"Was he the father of…?"

"I guess only Isobel really knew." Edna answered as the men beside her were clearly uncomfortable with the subject. "But I don't think she'd known him for long enough. My guess is that she was in trouble before she ever boarded the *Aquitania*."

"This is where Father Murphy may be our man," nodded Delaney. Rowland had called him previously with what they had discovered of Murphy's past connection with Isobel Hanrahan. "The coroner estimates that Isobel Hanrahan was at least three-and-a-half months pregnant when she died. It can't have been anyone she met on the boat." Delaney looked directly at Rowland here.

Rowland did not respond. To his mind the matter had been concluded beyond any sort of public speculation with Isobel's confession that he could not have been the father.

"Have you determined what happened to Father Murphy, Detective Delaney?" Edna asked.

Delaney shrugged. "Well, he didn't slip." He rubbed his nose. "Van Hook and the girl—did they know each other?"

"I don't think so." Rowland was intrigued by the question. "Why?"

"It's the only thing that doesn't fit with Van Hook...but I suppose we could be looking at two different murderers."

"You think Hu killed the Theosophists?"

Delaney pulled a folder from the briefcase at his feet. "We've been checking backgrounds since I spoke to you prior to Christmas...we had to send abroad which held things up—but we found some interesting facts about your Mr. Van Hook." He opened the folder and pulled out a photograph. "This was taken before the war."

Rowland studied the picture closely. A younger Charles Leadbeater stood at its centre with a number of boys about him. If it hadn't been for the fact that Rowland spent so much time studying and painting faces, he might not have recognised the youthful visages. As it was, he thought he could pick Orville Urquhart. Even as a child there was something arrogant about his face, the way he posed in front of the bespectacled boy beside him. A couple of the other faces seemed familiar too, but most of all he recognised the young Hubert Van Hook, standing with Leadbeater's hands on his shoulders.

"That boy there," Delaney pointed at Van Hook, "is the child Leadbeater first declared as the World Prophet."

"But that's Hu." Clyde took the photo from Rowland and examined it.

"It seems that Leadbeater's identification of her son as prophet convinced Mrs. Van Hook to leave Mr. Van Hook and take the boy to India for training," Delaney said shaking his head. "And then of course, Leadbeater changed his mind."

"So it was Hu, not Krishnamurti, who accused Leadbeater of indecency?"

"It seems." Delaney pulled out various reports on the matter. "Said Leadbeater misused him. Leadbeater was cleared—apparently young Orville Urquhart spoke in his defence. Essentially, he called Van Hook a liar."

"That explains why Hu hated Urquhart, I guess." Rowland was reluctant. Despite everything, he liked Hubert Van Hook.

"Why would Hu want to kill Rowly?" Edna asked.

"Dunno." Delaney looked at Rowland. "Did he have a problem with you?"

"I don't think so. I can't see him…"

"Perhaps he wanted to be World Prophet again," Clyde suggested. "Maybe that's his gripe with you, mate."

Rowland shook his head. "I still can't believe…"

"Well, where is he?" Milton demanded. "He arranged for you to be here, Rowly."

"We're looking for him," Delaney assured them. "My guess is he's on the run—but we'll flush him out."

"And till then?"

"You should be careful, Sinclair. Don't agree to any more meetings."

Rowland leant back in his chair casually. "If it was Hu, he's a bloody awful shot. In at least ten shots he's only managed to get Leadbeater."

Delaney checked his watch. "I'd better get back to headquarters."

"What about Leadbeater?" Milton asked. "Is he going to pull through?"

"I'll keep you posted." Delaney stood. "You folks go home and keep a low profile. I'll increase the patrols near your house."

Detective Constable Delaney walked them out to the Mercedes. "I'll have the boys clear out the reporters so you can get out without being front page again."

Rowland shook his hand. "Thank you, Colin—you know where to reach me."

"Of course." Delaney smiled faintly. "Technically speaking, you're still a suspect."

Chapter Thirty-five

EXPENSIVE CARS

The most expensive chassis on the British market is the 45-50 h.p. Rolls-Royce and the 50 h.p. double-six Daimler, the prices of both of which range from £1850. Complete cars, of course, vary in price according to the coachwork fitted, but one of the standard models of the 50 h.p. Daimler is an enclosed drive model with a fixed head, listed at prices ranging from £2500. Special coachwork jobs cost as much as £1200 to £1300 on other chassis, bringing the total price up to £3000 or more. There are also, of course, Continental chassis which sell at the same price, but the Import duty partly accounts for their high prices. These include the 45 h.p. Hispano-Suiza chassis (£1950), and Isotta Frasbin sports (£1850); super sports, (£1950). Another expensive English chassis is the 40 h.p. Lancaster (£1800).

—The Argus

"God, Rowly!" Wilfred slammed his fist on the desk in frustration. "How can a grown man stumble from one compromising situation to another?"

"I'm not particularly happy about it either, Wil."

"You're not happy about it! You don't intend it! And yet you carry on moving around in the midst of your own personal crime wave!"

Rowland rubbed his forehead. His head throbbed again. He really just wanted to shower and change. His waistcoat was still spattered with Leadbeater's blood.

"Kate's upset, the Bairds are about to declare war, I've spent the entire morning trying to keep you from being blackballed from every respectable establishment in the state; and now, it looks like it's just going to get worse!"

"I'm sorry," Rowland said quietly. He was sorry. He felt bad for Kate.

Wilfred leant back in his chair. "Damn it, Rowly, if Father were alive, he would have had you committed by now!"

Despite himself, Rowland smiled. Wilfred was right. Their father would not have been nearly so understanding. Henry Sinclair might well have sought a clinical solution for the behaviour of his youngest son.

"What would you have me do, Wil?"

"Nothing! I don't want you to do anything at all!" Wilfred sat forward. He spoke slowly, uncompromisingly. "Until we've got through this christening, I don't want you to leave the house. If you can't step out of the door without getting into some sort of trouble, well then you can bloody well stay here!"

Under normal circumstances Rowland would not have tolerated such directives from Wilfred or anyone else—but Delaney had already advised him to keep a low profile and Ewan's christening was the next day. Still, he did not agree graciously.

He stormed out of the library gladly, and took the stairs two at a time to his own rooms. The prattle of relatives gathered in conversation on the landing, faded as he approached. Rowland nodded but otherwise ignored them. His house had become a hotel of sorts and he had no doubt that the guests found the warring Sinclair brothers entertaining, if nothing else.

He had showered and changed, and was in the process of searching for a suitable tie, when Clyde came in.

"If you're looking for your navy tie, Milt borrowed it," he said, as he closed the door.

"Oh…" Rowland pulled a green one from the rack instead, and slung it around his neck.

Clyde cleared a space before one of the easels placed in front of the bay window, and began rummaging through his paintbox for colours.

"How did it go?" he asked, as he set out a basic palette. Wilfred had summoned Rowland as soon as they had walked in the door.

"It appears I'm under house arrest."

"Delaney?" Clyde was surprised. "He doesn't seriously suspect…?"

"No, it's Wil."

"Well at least Woodlands is a bit more comfortable than the central lock-up."

"There is that…where are Milt and Ed?"

"Milt's taking some girl out to the pictures—he just left. Ed is showing your Aunt Mildred the photos from our trip abroad."

"Aunt Mildred?" Was there no one the sculptress could not charm? "I'd better go down, in case she needs rescuing," he murmured.

Clyde laughed. "Mate, you can't rescue Ed."

"Nevertheless," he adjusted the knot of his tie, "a man's obliged to try."

Edna was in the drawing room that had been his studio, with Mildred and Kate. Boxes of photographs sat on the coffee table and the three women were on the couch chatting over a selection that Edna had taken in London. Mildred was expounding on how aspects of the city had changed since she had last been home to England.

"Rowly, hello." Edna greeted him brightly. "You're all cleaned up then?"

"Cleaned up?" Mildred's ears were sharp. "What have you been doing that you need cleaning up in the middle of the day?"

"Artists!" Edna didn't miss a beat. "They're always covered in paint."

Mildred sniffed. Clearly, artists did not warrant her good opinion. Rowland smiled. His aunt might have preferred to know he was covered in blood.

"I didn't realise you'd taken so many pictures, Ed."

"Oh, there were more…these are just the ones that came out properly…I was just sorting them into boxes…I'm thinking of having an exhibition."

"Of photographs? Surely not?"

"Oh, Rowly, don't be so territorial. I'm sure there'll always be some sort of place for you painters."

"How comforting."

"I'm sure your brother could find you an appropriate position, Rowland," Mildred Sinclair intoned from the couch. "Something with prospects."

Rowland chose to ignore her. He sat down and shuffled through a pile of photos from the *Aquitania* as he listened to a surprisingly amiable conversation between his Aunt Mildred and the younger women. He'd always found her an old dragon. Clyde was right. Edna didn't need rescuing.

He browsed through photos of their staterooms, the decks, various members of the crew. Milton, Clyde, and himself posing in front of lifeboats, playing shuffleboard, and at the swimming bath. Annie Besant with Krishnamurti and Urquhart. He studied a photo of Isobel with Fathers Bryan and Murphy. There was something about that photo that caught his particular attention, but exactly what, he wasn't sure.

"Katie…oh, Aunt Mildred, Miss Higgins. What are you ladies doing?"

Rowland looked up as Wilfred came in.

"Edna's just showing us the pictures from abroad," Kate replied. "Come and have a look, Wil." Her eyes flitted anxiously from her husband to his brother. It was in her nature to make peace where she could.

Wilfred took the armchair beside Rowland's. There was a small box of photos on the floor near Edna's feet. He took those.

Edna started. "Mr. Sinclair, those are…"

She left it. Wilfred was already looking through them—the pictures she'd taken in France. Rowland hadn't seen them yet.

Wilfred worked through the sheaf engrossed—Ypres. The Menin Gate. The grave of Aubrey Sinclair.

"My God, Ypres," he said quietly. "You didn't tell me you…"

"Of course I did," Rowland glanced at the photograph his brother held. He hadn't been aware that Edna had taken it.

Wilfred stared at a picture of Rowland standing by the white cross that bore the name of Lieutenant Sinclair. "I'm glad you did." He smiled faintly. "Aubrey would have got a shock—you were just a lad when we sailed." Wilfred shook his head as if he had only just realised. "You do look like Aubrey, you know. It's uncanny."

Rowland said nothing. He wasn't entirely sure how he felt about being his brother's physical twin.

They talked for a while of the war cemetery at Ypres, the town and the people. Rowland wondered what Wilfred was really thinking. His brother never spoke of the war, what he had seen, what he had done. He never spoke of Aubrey as a soldier— though, for time at least, the Sinclairs had served together.

Eventually Wilfred stood. "Come on, Rowly, Ernie's waiting."

"For what?"

"We're going to William Street. Ernie's so taken with that Fritz monstrosity of yours that I thought it's about time we updated."

"And you want me to come? It'll mean leaving the house, you know."

"Don't be smart, Rowly," Wilfred said, irritably. "You seem to know a bit about motors—you may as well make yourself useful."

Rowland stood. He recognised the olive branch. "Of course."

Wilfred still held the photograph of Rowland at Aubrey's grave in Ypres. "Miss Higgins, would you mind if I kept this?"

"Not at all, Mr. Sinclair."

"What picture is that, Wilfred?" Mildred asked. Her hearing

was not the best and, distracted by Kate and Edna, she had not caught the conversation of her nephews. "Why do you want it?"

Wilfred slid the photograph into his jacket. "It's just a photograph of Rowly, Aunt Mildred."

"I should think we've seen quite enough pictures of Rowland in the papers," Mildred said haughtily. "It's altogether unseemly—your father would certainly have had something to say about it."

"But Rowly takes such a lovely picture." Edna smiled impishly at Rowland, who had become resigned to this kind of open censure. "He's really rather photogenic."

"The Sinclairs once knew what it was to be respectable. It's a shame poor Henry didn't live long enough to show you a firmer hand, Rowland—our good name has suffered for it!" Mildred continued regardless. "Of course, that's just my opinion, but we are all entitled to an opinion."

"You were telling us about your time in Italy, Aunt Mildred," Kate intervened.

"We should be off," Wilfred decided. "Let's go, Rowly."

And so the Sinclair brothers spent the afternoon in the luxury motor showrooms of William Street. Rowland tried valiantly to interest Wilfred in the latest Buicks and Cadillacs, even the celebrated Hispano-Suiza, but the elder Sinclair remained determined that only the British could build cars. There was a moment of tension when Rowland informed his brother that the Armstrong Siddeley did not amount to "updating." Wilfred dismissed the supercharged "Blower" Bentley as a race car designed for "young louts," and inevitably they found themselves back in the more staid Rolls-Royce dealership, in which the Sinclairs were well known.

In the end, Wilfred Sinclair purchased a Rolls-Royce Phantom II Continental. As a somewhat reluctant concession to the modern tastes of his brother and son, he did take the unprecedented step of buying the floor model, which was British Racing Green. The car was a bargain of sorts, having been originally ordered and commissioned by a Sydney surgeon called Waterman, who had since fallen on hard times.

Chapter Thirty-six

OLD MAN PLATYPUS

Far from the trouble and toil of town,
Where the reed-beds sweep and shiver,
Look at a fragment of velvet brown—
Old Man Platypus drifting down,
Drifting along the river.
            —A.B. Paterson, *The Animals Noah Forgot*

———————————— ✺ ————————————

Ernest Sinclair giggled. The child was normally so solemn that
Rowland was almost startled. They were reading Paterson's *The
Animals Noah Forgot*. The book would not be published for a
few months, but Rowland had procured a signed, advance copy
from Norman Lindsay who had illustrated the volume. It was to
be a christening gift for his youngest nephew but, as was often
the way with such things, it was Ewan's elder brother who was
getting the benefit of the book.

"Read another one, Uncle Rowly. The one about the
Pladipus."

"Platypus. I think we'll be going soon, mate."

"Oh." Ernest frowned. "Will it take long?"

"I'm afraid so, Ernie, but it's got to be done."

"Why?"

Kate saved him from what was getting dangerously close to a theological question by arriving with Ewan in her arms. The child was dressed in the long, linen christening gown that had now been worn by three generations of Sinclairs. A piece of shortbread was pinned by a ribbon to the heavily smocked bodice—apparently a Scottish tradition.

Lucy Bennett flounced in behind them, wearing a pink dress printed with some kind of large swirling floral. Rowland wondered if it was chintz.

"Good morning, Mr. Sinclair. Doesn't Ewan look just delectable?"

Rowland glanced at Ewan who was drooling on his frills. "Quite."

Kate smiled. "All the Sinclair men are frightfully handsome—don't you think so, Lucy?"

Lucy blushed and laughed. Rowland cringed. Why was Lucy Bennett the only person in Sydney who didn't read the *Truth*?

In her way, Kate Sinclair organised for her eligible brother-in-law and the marriageable Lucy to travel to the church together. Consequently Rowland arrived at St. Mark's, Darling Point, in a state of amused irritation. For the first time in his life, the church was a refuge. Once inside the gothic chapel they could go about the business of getting Ewan christened and he would no longer have to listen to the tedious adventures of Lucy Bennett.

The church was already full of Sinclairs, Bairds, and their related families. Kate's people had chosen a more conventional attire for this occasion, but they had compensated by installing a lone piper near the font. They clutched their Presbyterian bibles in front of them like some sort of shield against the corrupting extravagances of the Church of England.

Rowland shifted uncomfortably under disapproving austere gazes from pews of Bairds. It was as if he had sprouted horns. He looked up at the triptych of arched, stained-glass windows at the head of the church and thanked the Lord that they weren't his in-laws.

Despite the dubious reputation of his uncle and godfather, young Ewan Dougal Baird Sinclair was quite adequately christened into the Church of England, without incident.

The families both returned to Woodlands House for a celebratory luncheon. By two in the afternoon, Ewan, and the more elderly members of the Sinclair family, were having afternoon naps. The remainder gathered in various parlours and sunrooms, playing cards, drinking tea, and reminiscing. The garden became a sanctuary, free of relatives.

"The Bairds left rather early." Edna lined up the wooden ball with her mallet. "Is it because of you?"

Rowland shook his head. "No—they're going to church."

Edna took her shot, knocking Rowland's ball into the roses. "Wasn't that where you were all morning?"

Rowland smiled. "They don't feel like they've been to church, apparently—they've gone to the Presbyterian chapel in Edgecliff."

"Oh, they're very pious."

"More belligerent than pious, I think." Rowland retrieved his ball. "It's rather a team sport, this religion thing."

"Colin Delaney called." Edna changed the subject. "Mr. Leadbeater is still unconscious but he's alive."

"Have they found Hu?"

"No—they think that the Theosophists may be hiding him. He wants you to be careful until they arrest him."

Rowland frowned. He still couldn't believe Hubert Van Hook wished him dead—it didn't make sense.

Edna laughed, poking him playfully with the handle of her mallet. "You look a bit like Wilfred when you scowl."

It was midnight. Woodlands was quiet. Even the servants were asleep. Rowland closed the door of his bedroom quietly behind him. He had dressed hurriedly and in the dark after tossing sleeplessly for the few hours since he retired. It had been just a thought, but it plagued him. He had not wished to wake Milton and Clyde on what might be a fruitless fancy.

Under normal circumstances, he may have wandered down in his robe—it was his house after all. He was, however, unsure of the nocturnal habits of his houseguests. The sight of a man in pyjamas and a robe could well shock his Aunt Mildred into a heart attack, or at least a scene.

He knocked gently on Edna's door. There was no answer. Turning the handle carefully, he went in. The bed was still made and the sculptress was not there. Rowland did not stop to wonder who she was with. Edna did not belong to him, and she would walk away if he ever let her suspect how deeply he loved her. He'd learned to shut his mind to her lovers. Somehow he'd accepted that Edna was not his, though not that she might never be.

He found her boxes of photographs. Stacking them atop one another, he carried them downstairs.

Rowland went through the boxes, quickly finding the collection he was after. There was something there—he was sure. The pictures from the *Aquitania*—the photograph of Isobel and the deacons, and the other of Annie and Urquhart which had caught his attention earlier, before he had been distracted by Wilfred.

He stared at them under the light and laughed. It seemed obvious now.

Lenin whined and nudged his leg insistently.

"Len, go away…What? Do you need to go outside, mate?"

He put the photographs into his pocket and moved into the hallway. "Come on then, I'll open the back door—just don't start barking or Wil will have us both."

He let the dog out through the conservatory. Insistently eager to get away, Lenin bolted into the grounds as soon as the door was opened.

Rowland cursed. He would have to go out and find Lenin now, or the dog would start barking as soon as he lost interest in the rabbit or whatever it was that he was currently chasing.

He ducked back into the kitchen to find a torch and shortly thereafter emerged into the grounds in search of his hound.

Faintly, he could hear the high-pitched squealing sound Lenin made when he was particularly excited and happy. Rowland was surprised. He didn't think his ungainly, track-rejected dog would actually ever catch a rabbit.

He headed off towards the sound.

"Len, Lenin—here boy," he called softly. Just more joyous squeals in response.

He was coming towards the old tack shed that Edna used as a studio. It was a fair way from the main building and, at the moment, crammed with the sculptures that had been removed from the garden and the paintings banished as unsuitable, during the transformation of Woodlands back into a house of repute.

The beam which lit his way had not yet revealed the dog, or the source of Lenin's happiness. He reached the tack shed—where the hell was…?

Someone grabbed him from behind. A thick wad of material pressed against his face. Rowland reacted fiercely, twisting to get himself free. The assailant had the advantage, pulling him backwards till he fell heavily onto the cobblestone path. Still the material was clamped against his face. He couldn't shout, he couldn't breathe. Lenin was growling but the dog was obviously restrained. Rowland's lungs felt ready to burst. His attacker was saying something but now there was a roaring in his ears as he struggled for breath…and then the sounds grew faint and he knew nothing more.

Chapter Thirty-seven

SUSPECT AT LARGE
Women and Children Warned

SYDNEY

The primary suspect in the shooting of Mr. Charles
Leadbeater, at Mosman, remains at large. Women and
children have been warned not to go out unaccompa-
nied. The man, an American, is believed to be in hiding
and may try to escape by fleeing the country. A police
cordon now surrounds the district in which the fugitive
is hiding. It is hoped that he will be forced to surrender
through hunger.

—*The Sydney Morning Herald*

"Rowly, Rowly…come on, pal, wake up."

Rowland groaned. Someone was slapping his face. He opened
his eyes.

"Stop hitting me, you idiot!"

Hubert Van Hook sat back, relieved.

"Whew…I was beginning to sweat."

"What happened?"

"I was trying to make sure you didn't holler when you saw me, and then you fainted, I think."

Rowland sat up. "I couldn't breathe," he said curtly. "That happens when some blasted fool covers your nose and your mouth."

"Shoot, sorry, pal—I got carried away. I thought you'd panic if you saw me and scream bloody murder."

Rowland rubbed his face. "No—I'm pretty sure you didn't try to kill anybody…though you might have smothered me by mistake."

He looked around. Van Hook had dragged him into the tack shed—it appeared like the American may have been holed up there for at least a couple of days. "What have you done with my dog, Hu?"

Hubert flicked Rowland's torch into a corner where Lenin was tied to a trough. The dog seemed to have settled to sleep. "He's been keeping me company on and off…goes goofy when you scratch his belly…ugly mutt but he's got a great smile."

"What are you doing here, Hu?" Rowland stretched gingerly.

"Hiding."

"From the police."

"Them too…they think I killed Charlie."

"He's not dead…not quite. Why'd you set me up with that meeting at The Manor?"

"I didn't."

"My housekeeper took…you didn't call…" Rowland groaned in realisation.

"No—it wasn't me, pal." Van Hook sat down on an upturned urn. "Look Rowly, I recognised someone the other day…I didn't say anything 'cause I thought every man's got a right to move on and it could have been just a coincidence."

"Coincidence?"

"That he should turn up now when Theosophists are being popped off. I knew him a long time ago."

Rowland nodded. "I know—Arthur Urquhart—Father Matthew Bryan is Arthur Urquhart."

Van Hook was visibly shocked. "When did you figure that out?"

"Just now, actually," Rowland replied. "It was something Ed said about me looking like my brother…I started looking carefully at the photos she took on the ship…there's a resemblance when you're looking for it. I suppose I can't blame him for not wanting people to know…particularly now he's with the Church."

"There's more to it than that, pal."

Rowland nodded. "I was afraid of that. What do you know, Hu?"

"The dirtbag tried to kill me."

"You don't say? When?"

"The day he belted you with that statue—I tried to warn you. Art asked me to meet him at the church there that morning, but I was late. He heard me shout out to you…I saw his eyes, Rowly, old buddy. He meant to kill you and meant to kill me…I punked out—got the hell outta there."

"Why on earth didn't you go to the police?"

"I tried to call you—I wanted to talk to you before I went to the police with some crazy story about a homicidal priest."

Rowland nodded, remembering the messages from Van Hook. He hadn't returned the phone calls. "I'm sorry, old man—I thought you were just calling to warn me that Leadbeater planned to name me his flaming messiah."

"You couldn't have called me back anyway, pal, I was on the lam…calling you from wherever I could."

"I don't understand, Hu…you're a lawyer…surely…?"

Van Hook took a deep breath. "I'll level with you, Rowly. I knew you had contacts, and I was hoping you could help me sort this out real quiet like. My clients back home ain't the type of fellas you bring home to meet mother, and they ain't going to be happy that their mouthpiece is mixed up with some crazy spiritual movement…Geez, my wife doesn't even know that I do work for the Theosophists."

"Your wife…you're married?"

"Left Lucy and the girls in London for a few months."

"The girls?"

"I've got two…real little sweethearts." Van Hook took a photograph from his pocket.

Rowland looked at the picture and shook his head.

"What…? What's wrong with them?" Van Hook challenged.

"Nothing at all," Rowland said quickly. "They're perfectly charming. I just can't believe you've never mentioned you had a family before."

"It's like this, Rowly…" Van Hook scratched his head trying to find the words to explain. "I've moved on from the movement in a lot of ways…but you know I love Annie and Jiddu's like a brother to me, so every now and then I sort some things for them, catch up, meditate…that sort of thing…call it penance for past misdeeds…but I keep it separate. Lucy—my wife, she's not a member…in fact she thinks the Theosophists are "dangerous heathens." She'd probably leave me if she knew I was involved with them again."

"So you live a double life?"

"Don't we all, pal…to some extent at least?"

"This is a bit extreme, Hu."

"Not really. When Lucy decided she'd take the girls to London for the season, I figured it'd be a good chance to sort out the Society's affairs. I'd be back in Chicago before they got home and no one would be the wiser."

"So now you're hiding in a shed." Rowland dusted himself off. "Look, Hu, the police have been looking into your background…they found some stuff about you and Leadbeater."

"Oh, that." Van Hook's voice was flat.

"It's true, then?" Rowland asked uncomfortably.

Van Hook studied him, and then sighed. "I was Charlie's prophet for a while and, yes, I made the allegations of indecency."

Rowland shook his head. "Bloody hell, Hu, I would have wanted to kill him."

"Well, I didn't," Van Hook replied. "The allegations weren't mine."

290 *Sulari Gentill*

"I don't follow."

Van Hook rubbed his face. "You gotta understand, Rowly, we were just kids. Art was my best friend—never took to Orville—but Art was good people back then. And Charlie was always a bit queer…you've met him."

"But he didn't…"

"Not me…but Art…maybe…probably. Art couldn't say anything. His parents believed completely in Charlie."

"So you made the allegations for him?"

"Art convinced me that it didn't matter who made the allegations…we just had to do something about Leadbeater." Van Hook shrugged. "We were kids."

"What happened?" Rowland asked.

"Orville Urquhart spoke up for Charlie, called me a liar." Van Hook laughed ruefully. "I guess I was."

"Christ, what a dashed mess."

"Art went to live with his grandmother soon after that. He's changed a bit…I only just recognised him the other day on the ferry…he used to wear peepers—couldn't see much without them."

"Peepers?…Oh you mean spectacles." Rowland recalled the boy in Delaney's photo whom Orville Urquhart was jostling aside. Spectacles—of course. That's why Bryan was such a hopeless shot.

"Good grief, Hu, why didn't you take all this to the police?"

"When I finally worked up the guts to go to the cops without you, they were looking for me. My word against a priest," Van Hook's voice became bitter. "And considering my past…I'm an attorney, remember…I know how the cops work…it'll be much easier to close the case on me than to start messing with the Church."

"So you came here?"

"Thought your joint was so big I could hide out till I figured out my next move…the cops wouldn't look for me here—nor would Art."

"Why does he want to kill you?"

"He's got it into his head that I'm helping the Society to steal his inheritance."

Rowland chewed his lower lip, digesting Van Hook's revelations.

"I suppose it's no great surprise that he shot Leadbeater."

"Lots of reasons to kill Charlie," Van Hook agreed, "and the money as well…Charlie was one of the Urquhart trustees."

"And me?"

"Beats me, pal. I thought you fellas were buddies."

"Do you think he killed the others?"

"Frannie, maybe."

"Mrs. Waterman? Why?"

"She might have recognised him—they were tight back then."

Rowland stood up. The string of murders, improbable accidents and misfortunes upon the *Aquitania* were all falling into place. With his brother dead, Arthur Urquhart was the sole heir to the Urquhart fortune—provided the trustees were out of the way. Charles Leadbeater and Annie Besant. Edna had mentioned the deacon would go to India soon. But Isobel—she would not have known who he was, she was no threat to him…unless… Isobel's child…could it have been the deacon's?

"Come on then." He moved towards the door.

"Where are we going?"

"Back to the house." Rowland checked his watch. It was one o'clock. "I'll call Delaney at the first decent hour. It'll be rather more than just your word—in the meantime you can stop living like a stray cat."

Van Hook grabbed Rowland's hand, shaking it gratefully. "Thanks, pal. I'm in a tight spot."

Rowland smiled. "Don't mention it, Hu…we prophets should stick together."

"Rowly?" Clyde turned on the lamp when he heard the door open. "What the…? Hu!" Clyde sat up, still too sleepy to respond appropriately to the fact that a wanted murderer had walked into the room.

"Shhh," Rowland warned as he came in after Van Hook. "You'll wake everybody."

Milton now sat up too, gaping dumbly at the two of them.

"Why don't you take my bed, Hu?" Rowland sat down in the armchair and loosened his tie.

"Are you going to tell us why you're giving your bed to a criminal?" Milton asked groggily.

Van Hook didn't seem offended, his attention caught instead by the nude of Edna which now leant against the far wall after being expelled from Roburvale.

"Shoot Rowly, how do you expect me to sleep with that in here? …Cripes!" Van Hook stared at the painting. "So this is what you do?…No wonder you're not short of a clam."

Rowland shook his head, affronted by the reduction of his art in such a way. "Philistine."

He brought Clyde and Milton up to date, quickly and briefly. It was the poet who reacted violently.

"Is Ed back yet?" he demanded, suddenly bolt upright.

Rowland shook his head, not sure why Milton thought Edna needed to know about this now.

Milton jumped out bed, swearing furiously as he dragged on his trousers.

"Milt…what?"

Milton cursed again. "Ed's with him, Rowly…Bryan, Urquhart…whoever the hell he is. He was supposed to be talking to her about some kind of religious sculpture for the church. She went to meet him."

Rowland paled. He stood. "Where were they going?"

"No bloody idea…a church of some sort…I don't know." Milton was starting to panic.

Clyde was now also fumbling for clothes.

Rowland checked the time. One-thirty. He opened the door, no longer concerned about his sleeping guests and ran down the stairs. He called Delaney at home.

It took a little time to make the detective understand. Admittedly, Rowland was becoming progressively more desperate.

Milton, Clyde, and Van Hook had followed him down.

"Look, Rowly—just stay put," Delaney said finally. "I'll brief the superintendent and get some men out straight away and then I'll be over. Don't go anywhere."

Rowland hung up.

"What the blazes!" Wilfred had been woken by the noise and had come down to investigate. He gathered almost immediately that this was not some late-night bohemian revelry. There was a sense of genuine dread in the room.

Rowland paced, agitated.

"Rowly," Wilfred said, "what's happened?"

"Ed's with some bastard who's murdered at least three people, and we have no bloody idea where they are." Rowland shook his head. He was scared cold.

"You've called the police?"

"Yes."

"Right," Wilfred said evenly. "So we wait. Rowly—sit down." He turned to Milton, who was swearing continuously. "Mr. Isaacs, I understand that you are distressed. Nevertheless, there are women and children in the house."

Rowland ignored his brother, pacing distractedly. His mind was working furiously—where could they have gone? Edna would stand out at St. Patrick's—he wouldn't take her there. The sculptress was meeting him to talk about a commission—a religious statue. For what? A church—is that where she'd met him? He turned to the poet. "Milt, think! What was the name of the church?"

Milton sat with his face in his hands. "I don't know, Rowly. She didn't say—it was just some church that needed a statue."

"Did she say anything about the statue?"

"An angel—she was excited about it—some kind of avenging angel."

"An archangel?"

"Yes, that was it."

Rowland's eyes were bright, the blue seemed to intensify. Rookwood...where the clergyman had tried to kill him. The chapel. It had to be. "St. Michael the Archangel," he said slowly.

"Yes—that's him."

Clyde moved towards the door. "All right, let's go."

"Go? Where the blazes are you going?" Wilfred was startled.

"Rookwood." Rowland was already at the front door. "Wil, wait here for Delaney, will you? Hu, you too. You can tell Delaney exactly where to go."

"What in the King's name is going on here?" Roger Castlemaine blundered down the steps in his robe and nightcap. "Have we been burgled? Are they still here...where do you keep your guns, boy?"

Suddenly, the entire related gaggle of Sinclairs was descending the staircase all shouting at once.

Wilfred stood between them and his brother, abandoning all thoughts of convincing Rowland to wait. Any such endeavours would be fruitless anyway.

"Right, then—we'll manage things here. Be careful, Rowly—don't do anything stupid."

Chapter Thirty-eight

THE CONFESSION

Tonight will be the last of the William Anderson dramatic season at the Tivoli Theatre, the production being James Hilleck Keid's powerful drama, *The Confession*. The chief theme of the play is the secrecy of the confessional, and the agony of mind endured by a priest, who, having heard a confession of a murderer, has to stand aside.

—*The Advertiser*

Edna attempted to breathe evenly, trying to control the shaking. Her joints screamed and cramped. She'd been bound for hours now, incapacitated as much by terror as by the ropes knotted tightly into her flesh. The small confessional was airless. It was black—she could see nothing but she was aware of the knife. He pressed it against her cheek occasionally to remind her, swearing he'd cut her face first if she made a sound.

The mourners had saved her. For a while, at least. What made them seek solace in the chapel so late, Edna did not know. She suspected they were a little drunk, on some post-wake pilgrimage to a graveside. But it forced him to retreat into the confessional, until they had gone. One of them had even come into the cubicle, completely unaware that on the other side of the partition, the kindly priest confessor held a blade at the throat of a young woman.

Edna lay on the ground at his feet, her tears silenced by an icy consuming fear. He was calm, patient, coldly ruthless.

He placed the point of the knife at her temple as the voices of the inebriated mourners faded. They were going. The sobs came now, convulsing, hacking gasps.

Bryan kicked her in the back and called her a whore. But she couldn't stop. She cried.

He used the knife, cutting the bonds at her ankles, running his hand lewdly along the length of her leg. She choked and begged him to leave her alone.

"Matthew... please."

Bryan slapped her.

"Shut up—I know what you are."

He dragged her to her feet. She stumbled—her legs were numb after being bound for so long.

Bryan seized a handful of hair, dragging back her head. He stopped as a silver glint caught his eye. He snatched the locket, enraged. The chain snapped.

"This is Isobel's locket, you thieving harlot!" He flung it away and forced her up. "Come on, Miss Higgins, it's time you apologised."

Edna was confused, dazed. Bryan pushed her onto her knees before a pew and placed paper and a pencil onto the bench in front of her. The chapel was lit only by the candles the mourners had struck in remembrance. The soft light cast Bryan's shadow long, a dark giant on the wooden floor. His layman's clothes only added to her bewilderment, her disorientation. He cut the bonds on her wrists and shoved the pencil into her swollen fingers.

"Now write!" he barked taking the knife back to her temple. He brought his face close to hers. "You can write, can't you? You're an educated whore, aren't you? Surely, Sinclair wouldn't take on some illiterate piece. He's a man of means and breeding, I'm told."

Edna didn't know how to respond. How could she not have known he despised her so?

"Darling Rowly," Bryan said, "Go on—write—Darling Rowly!"

Edna wrote. She didn't understand. Was this a ransom note? Was she writing her own ransom note?

"I was jealous," Bryan dictated. "I'm sorry—write! I must pay for what I did to Isobel Hanrahan…Now, sign it…sign it!

He folded the finished note and placed it into his pocket. The knife, he put at her spine. "Now, Miss Higgins, we're going for a walk. We're not likely to see anyone, but if we do, you will remember that any move that displeases me will be your last." Bryan pushed the point of the blade against her skin.

The prick of steel seemed to calm her, bring her back from pure terror. Her only chance was to keep her wits.

They walked out of the chapel, his arm around her as if they were lovers. Bryan was right. The cemetery was deserted. The midsummer moon was only just waning but the way was barely visible away from the chapel.

Edna gathered herself, collecting the remains of her shredded will. There would be a time to fight. She would wait for it.

Bryan took her to the newer section of the cemetery, the point of the knife constant at the base of her neck. They stopped at the simple cross that marked a fresh grave. The flowers that lay there had been recently placed, the petals wilted but not brittle. This was where Isobel Hanrahan lay.

Edna thought quickly. Did the deacon think she killed the bishop's niece? Was he taking revenge for her death?

"Matthew…" Her voice was hoarse and forced. "I didn't hurt Isobel, I promise you…"

Bryan laughed. "I know full well you didn't," he said quietly, scornfully. "But someone has to take responsibility. You can blame your precious Rowly for this. If he'd let it be, if he hadn't started nosing around with his connections and his lackey policemen, Isobel could have been quietly forgotten, and you wouldn't have to account for her death."

"You...it was you...you killed Isobel," Her horror for that moment overcome fear. "My God, she was pregnant."

"She couldn't stick to the story, could she?" Bryan replied angrily. "She declared Rowland Sinclair's innocence to the world...it was only a matter of time before the bishop became suspicious...started looking at who else might have sampled his precious Isobel. Stupid girl couldn't stick to the story!"

He pushed the sculptress down, so she knelt on the soil. He kept the knife at her neck, reaching into his pocket with his other hand.

Edna felt the panic rise again in her throat—it choked her.

He pulled out a small flask and removed the stopper with his teeth. Bryan smiled as if something had suddenly amused him. He spoke solemnly but his voice was cut with derision. "Corpus Christi, sanguis Christi."

He pushed the flask against her lips, forcing them open, and tipped the contents into her mouth. Instinctively Edna pulled away and spat and gagged. Now she would fight. She clawed at him.

Bryan let the knife drop and grabbed her hair determined that she should drink. He jerked back her head and as she opened her mouth to scream, he poured the poison into her throat.

Chapter Thirty-nine

POISONING SPARROWS

Vinegar and Strychnine

Mr. E. Watters, of Tallygaroopna, has been very successful in poisoning sparrows by a simple, but novel method. Sparrows are notoriously shy of taking wheat that has been poisoned. Mr. Watters mixes one ounce of strychnine in a 2 lb jam tin of vinegar. This is sufficient to poison a bushel of wheat. Two or three "free feeds" of unpoisoned wheat are given to the birds and then wheat flavoured with vinegar is given. This is followed two or three evenings later by the poisoned wheat. Mr. Watters poisoned over 1000 sparrows at his first attempt using only 10lb of wheat.

—The Argus

Anyone watching may have assumed that the three men who burst into the chapel of St. Michael the Archangel were in an almighty hurry to repent. But the only person who saw was the chapel's rector. He had been woken by the roar of the German automobile and watched in his robe and slippers from the window of the presbytery. They did not seem like the faithful—he suspected they were up to no good. There had been far too many dubious visitors to his church this night. A cautious man, he turned to call the police.

Rowland sat down in the front pew, disappointed, terrified. He'd been wrong. There was no one here.

Milton sat next to him, his panic was now silent.

Rowland felt himself unravelling. "Where could he have taken her?" He slammed his fist against the back of the pew. "I was so sure..." He stopped. Something glinted near the altar, in the light of the last candles. He walked over and picked it up.

"Ed's locket," he said as Clyde came over to him. "The chain's been snapped—they were here."

"So what's the bastard done with her?" Milton demanded. "Where would they go from here?"

Rowland stared at the locket, willing it to tell him where the deacon had taken Edna.

"Can I help you, gentlemen?" The rector stood at the door of the chapel, still in his robe.

The rector. Of course. Rowland felt a late surge of hope.

"Father...we're looking for someone...she was here with a man..."

Clyde intervened.

Rowland let him do so, aware that he was sounding a little incoherent in his desperation to find Edna.

Clyde explained quickly that they were looking for a young woman who had been taken forcibly by the man she was with, that the couple had come here that night.

The old priest sighed, nodding sympathetically. "I'm afraid this is not the first time I have been called to aid the protectors of a young woman's virtue." He sat on a pew, settling to dispense his wisdom. "It does distress me that my church, God's house, would be used to lure a woman of such purposes, but morality is not what it once was..."

Rowland grabbed the priest's shoulder. "Father!"

Clyde held him back. "Rowly, take it easy…did you see them, Father?"

"I saw them," the rector replied, startled. "Wrapped up in each other, they were…quite inappropriate. They left just a few minutes ago—towards the new graves…"

Suddenly Rowland knew. Isobel Hanrahan's grave.

"Thank you, Father," Clyde called as they ran past him.

They left the Mercedes where it was—it would be faster to cut straight through. They stopped only to grab torches.

The new graves were only half a mile from the chapel as the crow flew. They covered the ground quickly, weaving through headstones at a sprint. The more recent gravesites were obvious by the lack of headstones and monuments, sad mounds marked only by wooden crosses and temporary tributes. It made Bryan and his victim all the more visible in the muted light of the moon.

Rowland saw them struggling before he raised his torch. Edna was gasping—the crazed clergyman had her by the throat. Rowland exploded, throwing himself at Bryan.

Bryan turned immediately, surprised. He hit back, a pewter flask in his hand impacting on the wound he'd inflicted to Rowland's head a couple of days before.

Rowland reeled back, momentarily stunned by the blow. The gash had reopened. He wiped the blood out of his eyes, oblivious to everything but relief and fury.

Clyde was with Edna, holding her as she gagged and retched.

Milton threw his fist at Bryan. He made contact but not directly. The deacon reefed out the wooden cross from the ground and swung at the poet's head. Milton ducked the first but the second sent him to the ground. Now Rowland had regrouped. He hit Bryan in the face, sending him flying back against a headstone. He grabbed the deacon by the collar and hit him again. Bits of shattered tooth flew from the man's jaw. Rowland could hear Edna choking and vomiting behind him.

Clyde shouted. "The bastard's poisoned her, Rowly."

Rowland pulled up Bryan's head. "What did you give her? What was it?"

Bryan spat blood at him.

Rowland punched him. "What did you give her? Tell me or so help me I'll kill you here."

For a moment the deacon looked like he would laugh. "Strychnine."

Matthew Bryan didn't see the next blow, as Rowland sent him into darkness. Milton pulled Rowland away from the unconscious man.

"Leave him, Rowly—he'll swing anyway. We need to get Ed to a hospital…"

Rowland nodded. "Get the car…I don't think we have much time."

Rowland dropped to his knees beside Edna. He took her from Clyde's arms. Her head and neck were beginning to spasm, her face bruised by the beating that Bryan had given her. She didn't seem aware of what was happening.

"Ed, listen to me…you'll be fine…just don't…" He held her tightly trying to still the convulsions.

Clyde watched in horror. He'd got Edna to vomit up as much of the poison as he could—but she was in a bad way. It would be too late by the time they got her to a hospital.

The Mercedes screamed towards them, its headlamps casting the scene into stark brightness. Milton drove straight over garden beds and small shrubs in his haste. At this point Rowland couldn't have cared if the poet had driven his beloved roadster over a cliff. Edna writhed and sobbed in agony in his arms.

"Rowly, is your paintbox in the back?" Clyde asked.

"Yes," Rowland replied too distraught to wonder at the question.

Clyde ran to the car and threw open the luggage compartment. He unlatched Rowland's paintbox and rummaged through the trays.

"Thank God," he muttered as he found some sticks of charcoal. He returned to Edna, crushing the sticks in his hand as he went.

"Rowly, I've got to get her to swallow this," he said holding up a handful of roughly crushed charcoal. "I'm not certain, but I think it might absorb some of the strychnine."

Rowland was ready to try anything. They pushed some of the black pieces into Edna's mouth. "Come on, Ed, just a bit more."

Edna coughed, choking on the dry substance.

"She can't swallow it like that," Rowland said, despairing. "There's water in the car." He turned to Milton. "With the drinks." The Mercedes' beverage compartment held soda water, a mixer for the spirits.

Milton moved quickly and returned with the bottle.

Gradually they fed Edna the charcoal and washed it down with soda water. The spasms and convulsions continued.

Rowland carried her into the car and they tried to make her comfortable. He had just started the engine when they heard the sirens: Colin Delaney and his officers had arrived. With them, Van Hook and Wilfred, in the latter's new green Continental.

"Rowly, wait!" Wilfred stayed his brother. "I've brought Maguire with me."

Rowland nodded. Of course Wilfred would think to bring a doctor. God, he hoped it wasn't too late—it couldn't be too late. Wilfred Sinclair stood quietly by his brother, as Maguire did his work.

Maguire was typically dour, but he was gentle with Edna. Clyde told him about the strychnine and what they had done with the charcoal.

"When I was droving, we saved a working dog who had taken rabbit bait that way," he explained nervously.

The physician accepted the information, giving no indication as to whether they had helped or harmed her with their attempt at remedy. He checked Edna quickly, treated her with something from his bag, and had her moved into a police car which he immediately dispatched for the hospital. Maguire spoke only to Wilfred before he left…Rowland saw him shake his head. He walked to his own car. Clyde and Milton followed.

"Sinclair, where do you think you're going? We'll need to speak to you." Delaney left Bryan in cuffs in the custody of his officers as he came after Rowland.

"I'm going to the hospital Col, unless you plan to arrest me."

The detective started to say something but then he looked up at Rowland Sinclair and changed his mind. "Go—I'll see you there."

Chapter Forty

Young Woman's Suicide

Statements at Inquiry

SYDNEY

Evidence that the deceased had stated her intention of taking her life was given by several witnesses yesterday during an inquiry by the City Coroner. Reginald Ernest Prior, a nephew, of the deceased, said the deceased was despondent and on one occasion referred to the death of a girl from strychnine poisoning, adding, "How long did it take to kill her?" On several occasions the deceased indicated to the witness that she wished to take her life. He afterwards heard that the deceased had died from strychnine.

—The Age

Rowland rubbed his face. The pressure of his palms on his eyes seemed to appease the ache behind them. It was mid-afternoon. The reception room at St. Andrew's Hospital was crowded with men awaiting news of Miss Edna Higgins. Only her father had been allowed into the private room in which she lay stricken.

"Rowly." Wilfred Sinclair handed Rowland the jacket which he had discarded sometime before dawn. "Come along, old boy—Detective Delaney wants to talk to you."

Rowland shook his head. He was not leaving the hospital. Not till he knew Edna was safe.

"He's just in the next room." Wilfred motioned towards the matron's office in which Delaney waited as he gripped his brother's shoulder. "There won't be any news for a while."

Twenty-four hours. Edna needed to survive the first twenty-four hours before they could be confident that the strychnine would not kill her.

Rowland got up.

Wilfred pushed the jacket at him once again. "Get dressed." Even under the circumstances, Wilfred did not consider shirt-sleeves "dressed."

Rowland pulled on his jacket. Clyde and Milton played cards listlessly behind him. Hubert Van Hook was in custody. Perhaps it was time to sort matters.

The hospital office was small, cluttered but neat in an over-stocked way. Colin Delaney rose to shake his hand.

"Hell of a thing, Rowly," he said sympathetically.

Rowland nodded. He took the seat to which the detective directed him.

"We've spoken to your friend Van Hook," Delaney started. "But we have a problem with Bryan."

"What kind of problem?"

Delaney sighed. "I gotta tell you Rowly, a lot of villains are really bloody stupid—they'll brag about what they've done to anyone who'll listen. Matthew Bryan—he's not stupid."

"What's he saying?"

"He claims that he was trying to prevent Miss Higgins ingesting the strychnine, when you and your compatriots attacked him."

"That's bloody preposterous! Why would Ed voluntarily drink strychnine?"

"Bryan says she killed Isobel Hanrahan in a fit of jealousy over you. Overcome with remorse she confessed to him. Apparently he gave her a penance of fifty-two Hail Marys but, unsatisfied with the absolution he provided, she decided to take her own life."

Rowland laughed bitterly. "The idiot still thinks Ed's Catholic. She wouldn't know the first thing about making a confession, even if she had cause to do so. I doubt she knows what a Hail Mary is." He pushed the hair back from his face. "Ed was never jealous of Isobel in any case—she had no reason to be."

Delaney hesitated. "Look Rowly, why don't you come back to the station with me? Sit in on the interview. I think having you there may be exactly what I need to get Bryan to snap. I've noticed he flares up whenever you're mentioned. If you were to talk to him…"

Rowland shook his head. "I'm not leaving this hospital."

"What if I have Bryan brought here?"

Rowland shrugged. He needed something to distract him. Edna had been heavily sedated as they waited, hoped, for the tremors and spasms to pass.

And so, an hour later, Rowland Sinclair sat down opposite the man who called himself Matthew Bryan. The latter was in shackles, but otherwise calm. His face was bruised, his front teeth broken. A rosary was wrapped around his hand. Rowland held Edna's locket in his.

Bryan's face broke into a smile.

"I say, Rowly, it's a jolly relief to see you…how are you holding up? You look wretched…"

Rowland stared at him silently.

Bryan sat forward, earnestly. "This has all been a rather appalling misunderstanding. How is Edna?…I wasn't too late, was I?"

Rowland regarded the man with such loathing that it seemed to chill the unventilated room.

Delaney took a seat beside Rowland.

"You can give it up, Mr. Urquhart," he said quietly. "We know who you are."

"We're all entitled to find God and start a new life, Detective," the prisoner replied smoothly. He looked beseechingly at

Rowland. "Dear God, Rowly, you don't believe I would try to hurt Edna?"

Rowland glanced carefully at Delaney. He spoke slowly, with control.

"Don't worry, Father, Ed will be awake in an hour or so. I expect she'll be able to clear this up."

"Edna's all right then..." Bryan was only slightly unnerved. "That's splendid news. I do hope she remembers clearly..."

"Ed confessed, you say? I must say that surprises me." Rowland kept his eyes on his hands lest they give him away.

"Confession is both a duty and a solace for members of the Catholic faith, Rowly. It's not surprising that in her darkest moment, Edna would seek absolution as she has done since her first holy communion."

"Ed's a Protestant, Father, and not a very good one at that."

Bryan's eyes flickered but he recovered quickly. "I do believe, in her heart, Edna had converted, Rowly...you know yourself she attended Mass on the *Aquitania*. Perhaps she imagined that she had...she was very distraught, hysterical, I'm afraid."

"I suppose she would be if she killed Isobel."

"Don't be too hard on her, Rowly. She was consumed with love and jealousy...it is for the Heavenly Father to judge Edna, not us. Remember *thy will be done on earth as it is in Heaven...*"

Rowland interrupted. "Oh, I don't judge Ed. I don't know why she thinks she killed Isobel but it's not possible...perhaps she was, as you say, hysterical."

"I didn't want to believe she could have murdered Isobel either, Rowly, but..."

"Ed was on deck when Isobel was thrown into the harbour—with Milton and Clyde and hundreds of other people. You weren't on deck, of course, so you wouldn't have known."

Bryan said nothing; his eyes narrowed.

"Perhaps Isobel did jump to her death ..." Rowland played with the locket in his hand. "I don't think she ever got over the death of Orville Urquhart...I suppose you understand. He was your brother."

Bryan flinched, just slightly. "I don't think Isobel loved Orville."

"Oh…that wasn't my impression…Mr. Urquhart seemed to have a way with the ladies."

Rowland watched as Bryan's nostrils flared.

"Did Mr. Urquhart recognise you, Father? I suppose he would not have expected to see you in the cloth, without your spectacles?"

Bryan's voice was brittle. "Orville rarely recognised anyone but himself."

"So he didn't know you?"

The rosary strained as Bryan clenched his hand. "No, he didn't know me."

"I thought that given his relationship with Isobel you might have had cause to cross paths."

Silence.

Delaney broke it.

"It's a shame Father Murphy can't give us an insight into Isobel Hanrahan's life in Dublin since they were such friends." Delaney now took Bryan's gaze. "It's interesting, though… Bishop Hanrahan seems to have no knowledge of any particular intimacy between Murphy and his niece…he thought instead that it was you, Father Bryan, who she sought when troubled."

Rowland laughed. "His Grace always did jump to rather ridiculous conclusions, didn't he, Father?" He turned towards Delaney and waved his hand dismissively. "Ignore the old fool, Colin—Isobel had no interest in the Father here…I doubt she looked upon him as a man."

Bryan's eyes were fixed on the silver pendant in Rowland's hand. His brow was damp with sweat and his breath ragged. He was decomposing. His words were hoarse. "Do you think she loved you, Sinclair?"

A smile played on Rowland's lips. "Why, of course."

Bryan shook his head. "He was just like you—my dear little brother. Arrogant—it was always all about him."

Rowland pushed further. "I guess Isobel loved him, too."

"Isobel didn't care a toss for him, or you, Sinclair!" Bryan's accent was suddenly different—its edge harder, more common—he lisped slightly through the jagged chip of his teeth. "You were a mark, that's all. Another rich fool."

"You killed Isobel, didn't you Father?" Rowland said coldly, unable to hold back any longer. "Didn't you? And the child she carried. Your child, I suppose, not Murphy's. Is that what you were afraid he'd tell me?"

Bryan snorted furiously.

Rowland smiled. His voice remained icy. "God, what am I saying? Isobel would not have taken you as a lover."

Bryan reacted. Rowland Sinclair had found the soft underbelly of his resentment.

"She played you, Sinclair, and she did it because I asked her to."

"Then why kill her, you cold-hearted bastard?"

"Because she failed, because she couldn't stick to the story, because she started having fantasies about home and hearth." Bryan practically spat the last.

Rowland said nothing. He waited.

Slowly the deacon realised the effect of his words. For a moment there was panic, a desperate search for explanation and then, a chilling resignation, almost a relief. Matthew Bryan had accepted the noose.

"Isobel couldn't betray me in the end though, could she?" Rowland said evenly. He felt the need to mount some sort of defence for the murdered girl, to redeem her somehow.

Bryan chuckled, careless now. "In the end she would have watched me kill you, as she did my beloved brother. They're women, Sinclair. Original sin. Weak, pathetic whores—all of them. You'll see eventually…if she survives." He smiled cruelly, as if amused by the memory of what he had done to Edna. "If she doesn't, you'll thank me…"

Delaney grabbed Rowland's shoulder as he launched forward, incensed. The detective held him back, and Bryan laughed.

Rowland composed himself, just barely. There were things he wanted to know now.

"You tried to shoot me on board. How were you going to blackmail a dead man, you bloody fool?"

"You have a family," Bryan replied glibly. "People had seen you with Isobel—you wouldn't have been around to deny it. How much is a Sinclair bastard worth, do you think?" He leant across the table until his face was close to Rowland's. He whispered. "Of course, I wouldn't have needed to do it if you'd just agreed to marry poor Isobel…she'd still be alive."

"Murphy and Francesca Waterman," Delaney intervened because Rowland was beyond words. "You killed them simply because they knew you?"

"I have been rather busy, haven't I? Frannie would have told Jiddu eventually—was always besotted with the Holy Sambo."

"But why now?" Delaney continued. "And why on earth would someone like you join the Church?"

Bryan shrugged. It seemed he had given up trying to protest any form of innocence. "I was a pious man once—had no need for my inheritance or my parents—just wanted to get as far away from them and their blasphemous causes as possible."

"So you entered the priesthood?" Delaney was leading him now.

Bryan nodded. "I was assigned to the bishop. I met Isobel… she opened my eyes to the pleasures of the flesh." He rubbed his chin, thoughtful. "It's hard to go back once you've realised what women are for. It was only then I started to think about what Annie and Leadbeater had been doing with my money… what they were stealing from me. Of course it wasn't till later that I figured out that Van Hook was involved." He chuckled. "Maybe I'll hire the back-stabbing rat to defend me."

"And finding Annie and Krishnamurti on the *Aquitania*? Was that just luck?" Delaney asked.

"No. The World President of the Theosophical Society does not travel quietly," Bryan replied, rolling his eyes. "It was public knowledge that she'd be travelling on the *Aquitania*. The bishop hadn't actually planned to embark for a month after the *Aquitania* had left, but I was in charge of making his travel bookings.

Once the bookings were made Isobel convinced him not to break them…told him it was a sign from God that the colonies needed him or some such thing." Bryan's eyes sparkled as he spoke of Isobel. "She was quite good at that sort of thing…a natural liar, really."

"Did Isobel know you planned to kill your brother?" Rowland was sickened by the thought. Could the enchanting, lively girl he had almost loved, have been so callous?

Bryan turned to him, his face set with pity and contempt. "Yes…she cried and carried on afterwards…but she knew. She lured him to the lifeboat…she had a way about her." The deacon smiled. "But you'd know all about her ways, wouldn't you Sinclair?…of course you weren't man enough to go through with it."

Rowland's face became stony. "Go to hell!"

Bryan laughed, strangely gleeful. "Yes, it looks like I might."

For a moment there was nothing as Rowland considered whether it would be fair to strike a man in shackles. In the end he resisted.

Edna's locket pressed into Rowland's palm, as his grip tightened about it. He spoke dispassionately to Delaney. "Do you have what you need?"

The detective nodded.

Rowland Sinclair stood up. He walked out of the room without another glance at the man who called himself Matthew Bryan. It was finished, and Milton was right. Bryan would swing.

Chapter Forty-one

RESOURCEFUL MOTHER

ROCKHAMPTON

Gladys Hinchcliffe, aged three, drank a quantity of strychnine. Her life was saved by the resourcefulness of her mother who administered a simple salt and water emetic and later gave the child some charcoal followed by a drink of milk.

—*Northern Territory Times*

Edna Higgins opened her eyes slowly, burrowing back into the cushions of the chaise lounge. She could hear Rowland and Clyde discussing colour palettes somewhere nearby. It was past noon; the morning sun no longer cast its shaft through the glass panels of the French doors. Rowland had carried her down that morning so that she would not have to spend another day confined to her bed. It had been five days since she had come out of sedation to find the men she lived with gathered about her hospital bed. They'd acted as if she'd just woken from the dead. She had told them to go home and shower.

As she grew stronger, she had spoken to them and the dashing Detective Delaney of what Bryan had done to her. Now they seemed reluctant to leave her alone. Edna could see that becoming a problem, but for the time being, she was glad of it.

Milton was the first to notice she was not asleep. He looked up from his book. "That we are well awake? It seems to me that yet we sleep, we dream."

"Shakespeare." Rowland smiled at Edna.

Milton was not finished. He raised a finger. "Why then, we are awake; let's follow him; And by the way let us recount our dreams."

Rowland sighed. "He also wrote 'Man is but an ass'."

The poet was unrepentant. "How are you feeling, Ed?"

"A little tired."

Rowland frowned. "Shall I carry you upstairs?"

"Oh, no—not yet."

"Ed's afraid of that nurse your brother hired to look after her." Milton checked over his shoulder lest the subject of his revelation appear.

Rowland glanced at Edna sympathetically. Wilfred had a talent for finding the most grim-faced staff. He'd surpassed himself with Nurse Harrington—the woman was altogether terrifying.

Lenin clattered across and licked Edna's face before he tried to climb onto the chaise with her. Clyde grabbed the dog's collar and pulled him off. "Are you hungry, Ed? Mary left a plate for you…there was some shortbread too…"

"Mary took that away I think," Milton informed them. "She seems to have an issue with the crumbs."

Edna shook her head. Her appetite hadn't returned. All she could taste was charcoal.

"You should eat something." Clyde's broad honest face bore out his concern. "Nobody wants a thin model, Ed…you'll lose work."

Rowland's eyes lingered on the sculptress. For the first time Edna felt a twinge of self-consciousness under his gaze. She knew she had become angular. Gone were the gentle curves and rounded lines of her figure, the feminine shape that seemed to so suit the sweep of the brush. Still, when she did raise her eyes to Rowland's, she could see no difference in the way he regarded her.

"There's a Depression," he murmured as he pulled the notebook from his inside pocket. "She'll be cheaper to paint like this."

Edna laughed. "Has Hu sailed yet?" She nestled comfortably into the pillows which surrounded her. Hubert Van Hook had called a couple of days before to say goodbye in his own colourful and entirely incomprehensible manner. Having been cleared, he was joining Annie Besant and Jiddu Krishnamurti in India.

Clyde nodded. "Yesterday. He'll have an interesting story to tell Annie."

"Provided they can figure out what the hell he's saying," Milton added.

Clyde flicked open the *Truth*, scanning the pages for mention of Rowland Sinclair. "You seem to have fallen out of the headlines, Rowly. How did Wilfred manage that?"

"He bought the paper."

"You're joking!"

"Of course I am…Wil wouldn't buy the *Truth*—*The Sydney Morning Herald* maybe…*The Age* in a pinch…but not the jolly *Truth*!" Rowland regarded at the paper in Clyde's grasp disdainfully. "Standards, old boy, standards."

Clyde grinned. "Where are the illustrious Sinclairs? The house seems rather quiet."

Aside from the servants, they were alone at Woodlands.

"Half of them went to the races, and the rest went to church to pray for the half at the races." Rowland began to draw Edna. "Oh, Ed—before I forget. More flowers arrived whilst you were asleep."

There had been a steady stream of bouquets delivered for the sculptress.

"That's lovely," Edna said without lifting her head. "Who sent them?"

"Bishop Hanrahan."

Clyde looked up surprised. "My God!"

"No—just the bishop, I'm afraid." Rowland winked at the sculptress. "It wasn't even addressed to Jezebel."

"He's obviously feeling guilty." Milton snapped his book closed.

"Why would he feel guilty?"

"Between his niece and his deacon, a lot of people died." Rowland's eyes lost their humour. Isobel.

Edna watched him. A couple of days ago, he had sat at her bedside and told her of Bryan's claims. She knew he was still haunted by the deacon's words, that he had wanted the bishop's niece to be innocent. Rowland seemed to accept that Isobel Hanrahan had reasons for wanting to seduce him, but he had not thought it quite so calculated.

She curled up her legs to make space on the chaise. "Rowly darling, come here."

Rowland did as she asked.

The sculptress shifted to face him and reached out for his hand. What did it matter what really happened? Rowland had cared for Isobel. "You only have Matthew's word that Isobel was involved," she said softly. "She can't defend herself."

"You think she didn't know?"

Edna held his gaze, steadily. "Only Matthew says otherwise and he's...he's a cruel man, Rowly—you shouldn't doubt how you saw Isobel."

Rowland shook his head. "I just feel such a fool."

"Do you still have those drawings you made of Isobel?" Clyde asked suddenly.

"Yes." Rowland closed his notebook and handed it over.

Clyde flicked to the sketches of the bishop's niece. "I don't see a cold-blooded murderer's accomplice here, mate—just a bit of a girl with appalling bloody taste in men."

Rowland took back the notebook and studied his own sketch. He smiled faintly.

Edna squeezed his hand. "You leave your memories of Isobel be."

"So what's going to happen with Arthur Urquhart?" Milton asked.

Rowland shrugged. "There'll be a trial, I suppose. Delaney's convinced he'll hang."

Milton returned to his book. "Good."

"What are you reading, Milt?" Edna changed the subject. She wasn't yet ready to think about the fate of Arthur Urquhart.

"Rowly's book—*Isis Unveiled*." Milton held up what many considered the founding thesis of the Theosophical movement. "There's some interesting stuff in here…I don't know if I'm reading this right, but apparently we are all gods." The poet straightened to suit the title. He waved a finger at Clyde. "Of course some of us look the part more than others."

Clyde snorted. "You'd fit right in with Leadbeater and his band of bleeding nutters!" He turned to Rowland. "What happened to him, anyway?"

"He's recovered—he's going back to Perth in a couple of days. I believe Wil has sent lawyers to the hospital to make sure he doesn't say anything more before he goes."

"Wise man, your brother."

Milton's head lifted, a familiar poetic inspiration once again lit his eye. "For he knoweth vain men: he seeth wickedness also; will he not then consider it? For vain man would wise, though man be born like a wild ass' colt."

There was silence as they all waited for Rowland to make the attribution. With his traditional British education, he was best equipped to defend the works of poets past from the shameless appropriation of Milton Isaacs.

Rowland's face was blank as he struggled to place the line. He could find nothing. Finally, he conceded. "You know, that was so incomprehensible that you might actually have written it."

Edna gasped. "Surely not…" They had never known the poet to actually write anything.

"Of course I did." Milton was triumphant, smug.

"The Bible," Clyde said tersely. "The Book of Job, to be exact."

"Oh, really?"

"You just let him steal the word of God, Rowly."

"Book of Job, you say…I might have to look at that again," Rowland replied with no intention of ever doing so. He turned thoughtfully to Clyde, his smile just slight. "Do you have any idea what it means?"

Clyde shook his head in disbelief. "Protestants!" he muttered in disgust.

Epilogue

NOT A THEOSOPHIST

AMSTERDAM

The seventh annual camp of the Order of the Star of the East was opened last week by Krishnamurti, who a few years ago was hailed by Mrs. Annie Besant as "the New Messiah," and it closed today in drenching rain. In his closing address, Krishnamurti repeated that truth was only attainable through realisation. No spiritual organisations were needed. Asked if he was still a member of the Theosophical Society, he returned an emphatic negative. He urged the complete cleavage with the past, and said it was futile to try to reconcile the new with the old.

—The Argus

Arthur Urquhart was hanged on 7th September 1933, for the murder of Isobel Hanrahan, and the attempted murders of Edna Higgins and Charles Leadbeater. Jurisdictional issues prevented him being tried for the murders of Orville Urquhart and Francesca Waterman. The death of Patrick Murphy was ruled an accident.

◇◇◇

Hubert Van Hook eventually returned to Chicago where his family and his legal practice were waiting.

◇◇◇

Annie Besant died on 20th September 1933, in Adyar, India. Until the very end of her life she campaigned for social and political reform. After a brief ceremony in the Co-Masonic Temple at the headquarters of the Theosophical Society, Dr. Besant's bier was carried by admirers to a pyre for cremation. She was movingly eulogised by the Rt. Reverend Charles Leadbeater, and mourned around the world. Rowland Sinclair hung her portrait at Woodlands House amongst his more scandalous works and a painting by Picasso.

◇◇◇

Charles Webster Leadbeater died in Perth on 1st March 1934.

◇◇◇

The Theosophical Society continued despite the loss of World Prophets and the death of both Annie Besant and Charles Leadbeater. It still welcomes seekers belonging to any religion, or to none, who are in sympathy with its Three Objects:

- To form a nucleus of the Universal Brotherhood of Humanity, without distinction of race, creed, sex, caste, or colour

- To encourage the study of comparative religion, philosophy, and science

- To investigate unexplained laws of nature and the powers latent in the human being.

◇◇◇

Jiddu Krishnamurti continued his work as a philosopher though he never rejoined the Theosophical movement. He visited

Australia on a number of occasions, where he spread his word and caught up with old friends.

◇◇◇

The reward offered by Mrs. Harry Houdini for any person who could successfully communicate with her late husband was never collected. She herself stopped attempting such contact on the tenth anniversary of his death.

◇◇◇

On 30th January 1933, Adolf Hitler was sworn in as Chancellor of Germany.

◇◇◇

Archibald Leach went on to achieve some success as an actor, appearing in several motion pictures. He changed his name to Cary Grant.

◇◇◇

Colin Delaney was promoted to Detective Sergeant in recognition of his sterling work in the apprehension of the "Cruise Ship Killer."

◇◇◇

Satisfied that Woodlands House was no longer a haven of satanic activity, Bishop Hanrahan stopped calling unexpectedly on Rowland Sinclair. He remained in Sydney doing God's work with conviction and volume.

◇◇◇

Rowland Sinclair assumed his directorship of Dangar Gedye and Company, and although his Masonic ritual remained hesitant, he did acquire the collected works of George Gershwin.

◇◇◇

Wilfred Sinclair used his considerable influence to secure a place for his brother in the flying school of Charles Kingsford Smith. An airstrip was built at Oaklea and a hangar purchased at Mascot. It seemed Wilfred Sinclair had plans that involved both Rowland and the Gipsy Moth.

◇◇◇

The citizens of Sydney went about their business, coping as best they could in the difficult economic times with its massive unemployment, barely noticing the vacancy that remained for the position of World Prophet.

Acknowledgments

It has been said that there is no person more excruciatingly grateful than the debut author, who, consequently, should be forgiven for feeling the need to formally acknowledge every person she has ever met. I am no longer a debut author, but I am no less grateful than I was when *A Few Right Thinking Men* was published. Indeed, if anything, I'm more appreciative of the time, energy, and good will it takes to support those of us who refuse to do anything but tell stories. So I beg your indulgence as I make this public acknowledgement of a sincere and personal gratitude to:

My husband, Michael, who is so familiar and comfortable with the 1930s that one suspects he's a lot older than he's willing to admit, who is my partner in this and all things…except crime…he draws the line at crime.

My boys, Edmund and Atticus, who are still convinced I could improve this series with a few werewolves and the odd vampire. I have agreed to think about it.

My father, who not only encouraged me to follow my dreams but demanded that I do so.

My sisters, Devini and Nilukshi, who have never rolled their eyes in my presence…about my books anyway.

My childhood co-conspirator, Leith Henry (nee Baird) who lent me her support, her advice, and her family name, and without whom I might long ago have collapsed in a heap of self-doubt.

The indomitable J.C. Henry, whose name I also appropriated for the purposes of this novel, and who is now demanding his own series.

Deonie Fiford who edited this book with insight, wisdom, and warmth, who left encouraging notes in the margin that made the task of re-writing a joy.

The Marshalls, the Wainwrights, the Kynastons, the O'Briens, Wallace Fernandes, Alastair Blanshard, Laurie Keenan, Stanley Sparkes, Cheryl Bousfield, Lesley Bouquet, and Rebecca Crandell—all of whom I have prevailed upon, from time to time, to provide me and the characters of this book, with opinions, inspiration, and personal idiosyncrasies. In the last case, I didn't always ask.

The people of Batlow, Tumbarumba, Adelong, and Tumut, whose extraordinary support for a local writer is deeply valued.

The greater community of reviewers, bloggers, booksellers, and readers who have read, spotlighted, and promoted the Rowland Sinclair series. I am in awe of your power and truly, truly grateful.

Harper Collins Publishers Australia, who are the publishers of Norman Lindsay's iconic work, *The Magic Pudding*, and who kindly gave their permission for extracts of that text to be reproduced in *A Decline in Prophets*. Thank you for your generosity.

And finally, to be safe…everybody I've ever met.

About Sulari Gentill

A reformed lawyer, Sulari Gentill is the author of the *Rowland Sinclair Mysteries,* eight historical crime novels (thus far) chronicling the life and adventures of her 1930s Australian gentleman artist, and the *Hero Trilogy*, based on the myths and epics of the ancient world. She lives with her husband, Michael, and their boys, Edmund and Atticus, on a small farm in the foothills of the Snowy Mountains in Australia, where she grows French Black Truffles and refers to her writing as "work" so that no one will suggest she get a real job. So far, it's worked.

Sulari has been shortlisted for the Commonwealth Writers' Prize—Best First Book, won the 2012 Davitt Award for Crime Fiction, been shortlisted in 2013 and the 2015 Davitt Award, the 2015 Ned Kelly Award, the 2015 and 2016 Australian Book Industry Award for Best Adult Book, the NSW Genre Fiction Award, commended in the FAW Jim Hamilton Award and offered a Varuna Fellowship. She was the inaugural Eminent Writer in Residence at the Museum of Australian Democracy.

She remains in love with art of writing.

To receive a free catalog of Poisoned Pen Press titles, please provide your name, address, and e-mail address in one of the following ways:

Phone: 1-800-421-3976
Facsimile: 1-480-949-1707
Email: info@poisonedpenpress.com
Website: www.poisonedpenpress.com

Poisoned Pen Press
6962 E. First Ave. Ste 103
Scottsdale, AZ 85251

CPSIA information can be obtained
at www.ICGtesting.com
Printed in the USA
BVOW03s1453081116

467233BV00003B/66/P

9 781464 206832